# *Aaron*
# *Brock*
# *Cole*

## Hathaway House, Books 1–3

# Dale Mayer

HATHAWAY HOUSE, BOOKS 1–3
Beverly Dale Mayer
Valley Publishing Ltd.



ISBN-13: 978-1-773364-27-8
Print Edition

# Books in This Series:

Aaron, Book 1

Brock, Book 2

Cole, Book 3

Denton, Book 4

Elliot, Book 5

Finn, Book 6

Gregory, Book 7

Heath, Book 8

Iain, Book 9

Jaden, Book 10

Keith, Book 11

Lance, Book 12

Melissa, Book 13

Nash, Book 14

Owen, Book 15

Percy, Book 16

Quinton, Book 17

Ryatt, Book 18

Spencer, Book 19

Hathaway House, Books 1–3

Hathaway House, Books 4–6

Hathaway House, Books 7–9

# About This Bundle

*Welcome to Hathaway House, a heartwarming military romance series from USA TODAY best-selling author Dale Mayer. Here you'll meet a whole new group of friends, along with a few favorite characters from Heroes for Hire. Instead of action, you'll find emotion. Instead of suspense, you'll find healing. Instead of romance, … oh, wait. … There is romance—of course!*

**Welcome to Hathaway House. Rehab Center. Safe Haven. Second chance at life and love.**

### Aaron

Former Navy SEAL Aaron Hammond has no idea how he wound up at Hathaway House, Texas. Nor does he particularly care. All he can see is his anger. Anger at the betrayal that destroyed his physical body and at the loss of the future he wanted but that he'll never have now. He's a cripple, less than half a man, and all he can look forward to is a half life, alone with himself and his pain.

Dani Hathaway runs Hathaway House with her father, an ex-military man nicknamed the Major, and she knew Aaron and his brother SEAL Levi in another life. Levi was a good friend to her through her difficult teen years, but it was Aaron who caught her eye more than a decade ago. When she heard what happened to him, she moved heaven and earth to get him to Hathaway House, where she could help him regain his health and return him to the man he used to be.

Old feelings resurface as Dani continues to push Aaron to acknowledge that his life is not over, and that, if he chooses, he can find both love and a future at Hathaway House.

## Brock

Former Navy SEAL Brock Gorman has been at Hathaway House for more than a month with minimal improvement to either his physical or mental health. An vehicle accident on base two months ago caused major hip, back, and shoulder injuries that took away any chance he had of ever going on a mission again. Making it through BUD/S training and into the SEALs teams was the crowning glory of Brock's life. Now it's gone. Why try to get better when he has nothing left to live for?

Physiotherapist Sidney Morning has been away from Hathaway House for nine months of specialized training. When she returns, there's Brock. And, while she loves the tough cases, he might be more than she can handle. He's big. He's strong. He's stubborn. He's gorgeous. And he's not making the efforts needed to get better. But, if Sidney can get under his skin and force him to jumping hurdles he's not interested in jumping, she can help him see that there are things which still make life worth living.

Sparks fly as Sidney and Brock fight their own emotions and each other, pushing Brock where he needs to go. … If they are lucky, he might find both healing and love at Hathaway House.

## Cole

When Navy SEAL Cole Muster entered Hathaway House weeks ago, he was doing well. His meds were under control; his recovery was progressing at a safe rate, and he was getting better every day. But, left to his own devices, Cole pushed himself too hard and took himself off his medication—and ended up causing himself harm and earned himself time in a hospital. Now he's returned, hoping that Hathaway House can get him back on track one more time.

RN Sandra Denver feels responsible for what happened to Cole. She was his nurse and should have realized that he wasn't ready to leave Hathaway House. His setback was her fault, or at least she could have prevented it, if she'd made sure he was taking those meds she gave him daily. Now that he's back, she's finding it hard to trust not just him but herself. And she understands, when Cole has a hard time trusting himself too, it won't make his recovery any easier.

For Cole's sake, Sandra must help him overcome his stumbling blocks as well as her own. With any luck, they'll find a second chance at recovery, for both of them, at Hathaway House.

**Sign up to be notified of all Dale's releases here!**
https://geni.us/DaleNews

# *Aaron*

## Hathaway House, Book 1

# Dale Mayer

*Chapter 1*

WHERE THE HELL *am I?* Aaron Hammond understood this was Texas. But he'd never seen this corner of it before. A place he couldn't have imagined. If he'd been asked to guess his location, he'd have said Kentucky, with the rolling green hills, white-fenced fields and … horses.

Aaron reached out his hand to stop the orderly's progress. It already choked him that he couldn't manage this short distance on his own. Accepting help was one thing—charity was the worst though.

They had come from the parking lot—which was just dust and gravel, nothing even close to resembling the clean medical facility he'd left this morning. He took several deep gulps of the fresh country air and wondered what life had done to him. He'd gone from a spotless naval hospital, with daily visits to a top physical therapy department, to this. Sure, he'd been screaming and hollering to get the hell out of there. That will happen when you take an active, top-of-the-top, best-of-the-best SEAL and knock him flat—removing what was left of his leg and ripping the shit out of his back. He wasn't paralyzed, but it would be a long time before he was whole again. He could live without the leg. He didn't have much choice—he had to live without a leg—but he wanted to make sure his back was strong enough to carry the extra burden.

Unnerved by this 180 jolt to his system that had him feeling unbalanced and off-center, he went on the defensive.

"What the hell is this place?" he asked. He'd arrived by ambulance—the paperwork had been exchanged, and now he was in the care of this man who, according to the tag on his colored shirt, was named George. Aaron had ignored the earlier introductions.

"Hathaway House," George replied calmly.

What kind of name was that anyway? It sounded like a last patch of ground for aging horses. Which just might be appropriate, considering the ones he could see in the distance. "How the hell did I get here?"

"This was chosen to be the next-best step in your healing and recovery. You signed the transfer papers."

"See? I hear those words, but they don't compute." If there was one thing he liked, it was all his boxes checked—his *T*s crossed and his *I*s dotted. Not to mention he was a bit of a computer geek. None of this made any sense. He understood code, but he could decipher nothing here—just a blank slate of confusion. Sure, he'd signed transfer papers, but he'd had no idea he was coming to a place like this.

"I believe you requested a change of scenery." George pushed him up the ramp. "This is a great place."

The new deck opened out into a much better view. If this was a ranch, it was like none he'd ever seen before. It looked like a converted old school, with some kind of a Western theme. It wasn't terribly pretty, and yet it wasn't terribly institutionalized either. It had … character. He gave a half snort under his breath and settled back into the wheelchair. Instead of going through the double entry doors, George pushed Aaron around to the back of the deck and stopped, letting him take a look.

Beautiful green fields to the left, more fields to the right—a mix of horses thrown in. He wasn't exactly sure, but he thought he also saw a donkey and maybe a mule. The animals grazed happily. A picture-postcard moment. They looked happy and to be enjoying life as best they could.

His heart went out to one of the horses, an animal meant to race and run for miles, with some kind of artificial leg. How the hell did they get the horse to accept that? As he watched, a three-legged dog came running toward them, its tail wagging. Another dog came running, a set of wheels attached to its back, and barking like a crazy man.

Then Aaron understood.

This wasn't a place just for injured people, this was for injured animals too.

A heavy breath escaped his chest. As much as he hated to think he didn't belong here, a part of him said he belonged more than most. He looked down to where his leg should've been, then back at the dog with wheels. The animal didn't seem to give a damn, even missing both hind legs. That old phrase, *life is a bitch, and then you die,* ran through his head.

He'd been saying that over and over again for most of his life. But now, for the first time, he wondered what it would take to change that attitude, to be more like the dog's? He reached out a hand, wincing as this odd angle pulled on his back. The dog reached up and shoved his nose into Aaron's palm, as if he knew Aaron's range of movement was limited.

Aaron gently stroked the top of the dog's head and scratched behind his ears.

"Lots of animals are out here," George said. "The little guy with the wheels is called Racer. The three legged one is

Tipler."

George pushed the wheelchair forward until they came around to the back where the deck widened again into an area that ran almost the full length and width of the house. Multiple chairs were set about, and wheelchair ramps ran up and down. At the back of the deck, parked close to a heavy wooden railing, was a very large black man, missing both legs, cuddling with the smallest dog ever.

The realization came to him that, although he was here, in a brand-new environment, nothing had changed. He was still surrounded by people as broken and defeated as he was. He made an effort to glance away from the big man and the tiny dog but not before he had caught the man's gaze.

The man studied Aaron for a moment and then gave a slow smile. "Welcome. Right now you hate it. You want to be anywhere else but here. However, in a couple weeks, you'll never want to be anywhere else."

Aaron was pretty damned sure that would never happen. He gave a curt nod before George pushed him through the open-wall space into a massive living room or community area. George pushed the chair all the way through the room, back to the front doors they'd avoided in the first place.

Once there, George stopped at the reception desk. "Dani, this is Aaron."

Aaron studied the woman who had changed the tone of George's voice. She was young but not too young. She was pretty but not too pretty. In fact, a whole lot about her was just right. Yet something was also familiar about her.

Well, that was just too damned bad. The chances of him ever having a sexual relationship again were zero. He might still have his genitals, but he hadn't seen one sign that the damned thing worked anymore. No way in hell would he start a relationship as half a man. Better if he bowed out forever. Friendships without benefits would be his new normal.

He looked up at the woman, her huge chocolate-brown eyes and the soft look in them. He'd never seen that look before, at least never turned in his direction. He gave her a curt nod. "Morning."

"Good morning, Aaron. I've been looking forward to your arrival."

Inasmuch as he wanted to say a lot about that—how he didn't want to be here, and actually why *was* he here?—the only thought in his mind currently was about losing himself in those eyes swelling with compassion. A gaze that said she knew and understood his thoughts, his turmoil, but was happy to see him anyway. A gaze that made him want to believe in a better life. That such a thing was possible—even though he already knew differently.

How sad was that?

DANI HATHAWAY HAD awaited his arrival for days, and she'd fully expected him to not recognize her. She'd hoped he would, but ... well, it had been a long time. What she hadn't expected—and should have, all things considered— was his anger.

Dani returned her attention to the paperwork in front of her before facing the computer screen to check Aaron in.

Another angry soldier. Angry at the world. Angry at himself. Feeling guilty, feeling hurt, and—more than anything—feeling confused by it all.

She understood. No, she'd never been to war. No, she

hadn't been injured in some horrific event. No, she hadn't spent a lifetime dealing with catastrophic circumstances, but she'd been dealing with men like Aaron for a long enough time. In fact, her father had been one just like him. But the major, as everyone called him, was somebody else now, thankfully.

Having taken over the active business management of this place a long time ago, she'd helped build it to what it was now. The center was her father's pet project, and it had a full team of doctors, physical therapists and counselors. He'd started this massive undertaking, and she'd been more than willing to step in and help carry on. The major was more or less only here for support now … and to help keep spirits up on both sides of the equation.

In the beginning, Hathaway House had been a saving grace for her father. It'd been just the two of them and Gram for so long. Dani's mother had died when she was just a little girl, and she had been raised by her father and her grandmother. Then they had lost Gram too.

She worked here to do everything she could to help these men turn their lives around. The center's work was a gift that kept on giving. As these men healed, the families living in turmoil around them also healed. That part she knew all too well.

When her father had come back from the war, he'd been angry-quiet at times, then explosive and volatile toward others. Broken in body, he had also fractured something in his spirit. He'd been a good man, but he had been through so much that some of that goodness fell through the cracks of this new persona. It had taken a lot of work, and many years, for him to pull it together and become the man he was today.

She knew that love was the answer, but it was more than love—or rather more than that marshmallow kind of love that people understood when they thought of the word. Sometimes love meant you had to take the hard line and had to force people to do things they didn't want to do. Not necessarily a role she enjoyed, but she had to do it, so she did. And, from the looks of things, Aaron would need a little bit more of the tough love than most of the men who came here.

George would get him settled into his new room. Dani glanced down the empty hallway. Soon she'd go in and officially welcome him, make sure he didn't need anything, and then she'd turn him over to the team who would rally behind him.

Except there were a few secrets in Aaron's case. His medical files should have come with the folder she'd received. She searched her email, and, sure enough, they had been sent along with his other records. Her desk was piled high, so it had to be here somewhere. She spied the large envelope leaning up against the edge of the desk. She pulled back the flap to ensure the file was complete, with X-rays and notes, and ... yes, it was. Perfect.

Dani grabbed her clipboard and clamped in a New Resident's Questionnaire, then slipped a couple pens into her pocket and walked down the corridor toward Aaron's new room. He'd been given a spot on the left, facing the horses. All the rooms in Hathaway House were lovely, but, of course, a few were better than others. He had been given one of the nicer rooms as a special request from the donor paying for his stay.

That someone had paid for him was a key issue here. It was expensive to treat the men and women properly. She wished she could open the doors to everybody in need, but the reality was she had not been able to find any state or governmental grant money, so private funding had to cover the bulk of Aaron's costs and fees. Of course insurance covered a lot, but often there was a shortfall. The center ran at a slight loss most times. It took a lot of money to get the specialists and therapists they needed here and to build the equipment prototypes. Only the best would do for these people.

At the doorway to Aaron's room she knocked. She wanted to make sure George was done and Aaron was settled in. When no answer came, she knocked again. When she heard a disgruntled sound inside, she slowly opened the door and peered around the edge. He was lying on his back on top of the bed.

"Good morning."

Aaron rolled to the side and stared at her. He gave a disinterested shrug but said quietly, "Morning."

She walked in with a bright smile and handed him the clipboard and a pen. "I need you to fill out this New Resident form. It shouldn't take too long, and once the paperwork is done, I will let the team know you're ready to see them."

He brought his brows together and stared at her. "What kind of team?"

She knew it wouldn't be the kind he wanted. He would never again be part of the elite military teams who took on some of the most dangerous assignments in the world. Even if they could put him back together again, the military wouldn't take him back. Just the facts of life.

In a gentle voice, she said, "Your medical team." She walked over and hit the buttons on the bed to raise him higher so he could write.

"Oh." His shoulders shook slightly, but he picked up the pen and looked at the paperwork. He went to the first page. She waited—she'd learned long ago that the best way to get the paperwork completed was to not give anybody the option of avoiding doing it.

When he was done, he reached out, returning the clipboard to her. She motioned toward it. "Turn it over. There's a second page."

"Of course there is." With a frown, he slowly made his way through the second set of questions. At the end, he signed his name and held it out again. She took the clipboard, noticing he didn't offer the pen.

"Do you want a notebook and a pen to keep here?"

He shook his head. "A couple should have arrived with my bags."

"Good," she said cheerfully. "But, if you happen to need more, let me know, and I can grab one for you." As she headed toward the door, she said, "Lunch will be in two hours, but coffee is being served in the communal room that George showed you earlier. The wheelchair is yours to use while you're here, or crutches are in the closet, if you'd prefer." At the doorway, she turned to look at him. She motioned with her arm. "Take a left from here for the communal room. Feel free to explore, but please do not leave the main floor. As soon as I get all the paperwork together, I will let the team know you're ready."

Then she left him to his own space and his grim dark thoughts. He had no idea how lucky he was. Hathaway House operated at full capacity at all times with a long waiting list ahead. The donation hadn't been an outright secret, but a note said that the donor preferred to keep his identity under wraps for the moment. She'd do her best to keep it that way.

The same donor had helped several other people, but dozens more were in need. The center did do some pro bono work, but they still had to pay the bills, so only four patients were cared for free of charge and in rotation. As soon as one healed and went home, they went through their files and invited the next candidate to join them. So far the system had worked well.

The last thing she wanted was for Aaron to feel like he was accepting charity. According to his file, his pride was only second in size to his stubbornness. He was a warrior, but warriors also made the worst patients.

Hopefully she was up for the challenge.

# Chapter 2

A SHORT WHILE later, Dani returned to Aaron's room. "The paperwork's out of the way." She flashed her brightest, most cheerful smile. "How do you feel now?"

Aaron gave her a shuttered look but answered politely, "I'm fine. Just a little tired after the trip."

She nodded in understanding. "Traveling is stressful. The position you have to sit in often strains your type of injury. Still, you're here now, and once you've had a chance to rest, we can get started on your medical treatment."

Dani pulled up a chair and sat down beside him. "I have a list of your medical team, each of whom you'll meet this afternoon. Everybody will make a point of stopping by to talk to you about the treatments and evaluations that might need to be done." She handed him the sheet from her clipboard. "In preparation for your arrival, the team met to discuss your case."

He took the sheet without a word.

"This is the team who's been pulled together for you— specialists who know and understand what you are going through. You see the name at the top of the first page? Dr. Herzog will be acting as your MD. Below that is your physical therapist, Shane. He's great," she added warmly.

"We have assigned Dr. Klein for counseling." She studied his face for a reaction but still found nothing. "When they arrive, each will go over the treatment you will receive and who else you might need as part of your team. We are team-based here, so, when it comes to getting your prosthesis built and adapted, it'll be all within the same team. We have an engineer on staff who will handle that work."

She glanced at the sheet in his hand again, noting the fine tremor in the paper. "However, everyone needs to work together to get you through the different stages, so you'll have the health and strength and coordination to get used to the prosthesis." Dani looked up and glanced his way to see if he understood.

Only he wasn't looking at her. He studied the sheet of paper she'd given him. "Understand?" she queried gently.

He nodded. "Nothing to understand yet. Except why do I need a counselor?"

She smiled at him. "That's a mandatory part of the treatment. You'll find it fairly noninvasive, and Dr. Klein's a great guy. It's important that we heal not just your physical body but also your emotional body."

"What about my spiritual body? I don't suppose you have an altar here to pray to?" he snapped, sarcasm dripping from his voice.

"No, there's no chapel. However, if you wish something brought into your room or want to speak to a clergy member, we can certainly see to that. We're nondenominational, but we accept all." She smiled at him again and said, "Even you."

He narrowed his gaze at her, as if not sure how to take her teasing.

She laughed and stood, waving her arm around the room in a sweeping motion. She said, "This is your room for the duration of your stay. Most people are here for anywhere from two to ten months, longer if needed. Obviously we do our best to get you self-sufficient fast, so you can continue living the life you want at your own chosen location. However, it's not always possible to get people moving about as much as they would like to be.

"You have your own private bath," she continued, indicating the closed door on the opposite wall. "Some of your work will be done in here. Otherwise, you will be expected to show up at therapy rooms on time and under your own power. If you're not ambulatory enough to do that at any time, then we'll arrange for somebody to come get you. You will need to discuss that with your doctor and your therapist." She spun around to look at him. "You're welcome to dress in your own clothes. However, the therapist will give you a set of comfortable clothes to wear for the physiotherapy sessions to avoid any strain or limits on your ability to do the work.

"Laundry is done once a week. Three meals are provided, at approximately six to nine, eleven to one and dinner runs from five to seven, all in the common area, as well as snacks anytime throughout the day if you're hungry. The schedule is on one of the sheets. We'll start with the basics and move on from there. If the doctor has any dietary requirements for you, or if you have any special food allergies or requests, then tell the doctor," she said. "We have dieticians on staff as well, if you have any concerns."

She continued to run through her spiel, covering all the high points, but she could see his eyes glazing over. She brought her speech to a quick close and walked toward the door. "And remember, this is not prison. However, you are required to stay on the premises all the time. We have day trips into town, and you are always welcome to visit the horses or see the other animals and to wander the gardens whenever you like. Do, please show up for your appointments as required. If you need to go into town, then make the arrangements with me or one of the other staff. We have buses going in on a regular basis." She reached the door. "If you're not up to the day trips and have special requests, staff does shop for residents as well."

"How do I get a hold of you?" His voice was deep, serious, and dark.

"Good question. I'm glad you asked, because I forgot." Upping the wattage of her smile, she fished the cell phone from her pocket and handed it to him. "Everybody at the center gets a basic preprogrammed cell phone to contact every one of your team. My number is right there. We haven't had to take away any phones yet, so please don't abuse it and become the first person where we have to do so."

His lips twitched.

*Good.* Aaron needed to lighten up. Anything that helped him to feel better was good with her. "Other than that," she said, "I will be around. As I run the center, I'm often at the front desk or in my office. Otherwise, you can find me out with the horses," she added cheerfully. "Over 100 patients are here, and, together with all the support staff, you'll have plenty of people to talk to. It's important that you get out and spend time with others. Everyone is quite friendly, and most are in similar situations to yours."

"And if I don't want to?" He turned and moved his head to look at her. Again, a flat stare.

Her smile hardened just a fraction. "It is your choice of course, but if nothing else, there are beautiful gardens to see and animals who could use a bit of attention. The vet clinic is on the ground floor, and the animals there definitely need to know we aren't here to hurt them."

His gaze narrowed thoughtfully. "You do animal surgeries here?"

"Some. We have a full medical facility for animals and people." She was proud of all they did here. "The local hospital is also an important part of our treatment programs, and the two surgeons who work with us work out of there."

At that, his eyebrows popped up, making her laugh.

"We're a very unusual center, and trying to categorize us will fail."

He gave a clipped nod. "Good. The traditional centers haven't worked out so well for me."

"So give us a chance," she suggested. "You might be pleasantly surprised."

Her phone rang as she stood there. She glanced down at the number and smiled. "That's my call to visit with Helga."

Silence. Then, as she had hoped, he asked, "Helga?"

She raised her smiling gaze to him. "Yes, she's a Newfoundland dog that was hit by a truck. She's getting fitted for a new leg. She's had muscle transplants, and she's doing well. The engineers built a limb that would work, and the vets built a stump that could work with it. She had a few other injuries, but she's a real sweetheart," Dani said warmly. "You'd like her."

"Where is she?"

"Downstairs."

More silence. He contemplated the wheelchair in front of them and then turned to stare out the window. "Maybe another time."

"No problem." She did her best not to show the tiny pang of disappointment she felt inside. It would take time for him to adapt, but she found the animals were the biggest icebreakers of all. People often related to their losses in a way that allowed them to disconnect from their own pain and troubles. They would root for an animal where they'd often given up on themselves.

"Helga will be downstairs for several more days," she said. "After that, we might bring her up to visit."

"Does she have a home?"

Dani shook her head. "Nobody who would claim her. That often happens when an animal is severely injured. Nobody wants to be responsible for the vet's bills."

He nodded. "That might get expensive for you."

She shrugged. "We try not to be too selective. An animal in need is an animal in need." On those words she turned and walked out of the room.

SHE DIDN'T REMEMBER him. Aaron didn't know what to think about that. Except both disappointed and relieved. He wouldn't have to answer difficult questions but then neither did he get a chance to reconnect.

He looked down at the list of team members and, despite his doubts, was impressed that the facility was this organized. He didn't recognize anybody on this list, but at least he had the names to start with. He would research to see if these guys were any good or not. He hoped so, but he didn't expect a miracle anymore. So far the only attempts to get him upright again had been via crutches. While that had worked for a while, his armpits had eventually swollen up badly because they were taking too much of his weight with his bad back. He needed a prosthesis that would work. And he needed his back fixed.

Normally he'd be sent home, entailing multiple trips back and forth for prosthetic limb fittings, but somehow it wasn't working. His stump refused to heal. His back injury, his mental state—he didn't know what else—was hindering his expected progress. So he'd ended up here. Who the hell knew this place even existed?

He certainly hadn't, not before it was brought up as an option. Thank God for his VA benefits because his savings surely wouldn't cover all this. Seemed only fair since he had lost a leg for his country.

He didn't know if the problem was his leg or his back. There'd been talk of more surgery because the stump was so raw. Also talk about surgery on his back. He didn't know if the doctors here were specialists or even if they were likely to be any better than those he'd already seen. All that just because he'd wanted a change of scenery ... That didn't mean he'd needed to transfer here.

Surely Walter Reed should've been enough. Or had someone else had a hand in this move?

Of course he was no longer in the military. Hadn't been for the last six months. Somehow that also meant he was no longer fit for any other job in the military either. SEALs didn't retire and neither did they take on desk jobs in the navy. They weren't geared for it. After being the best of the best, finding out you were now like all the rest was—or worse—disheartening.

He'd heard of many moving on quite happily, and indeed, some of them excelled in their second careers. From another place and time his brother, Levi and Ice, his partner, had set up a new company; and they were hiring ex-military, even if disabled. Maybe down the road ... when he could handle a job. Sure, he was on disability now, but that wasn't the same thing as getting mobile again. Still, he had little to no relationship with his brother. So begging for work was hardly the way he wanted to open the door again.

He wanted off disability as soon as humanly possible. He didn't like charity—from anyone.

So who had helped bring him here—and why?

And what cruel joke did fate play that put Dani in his sights again—the one woman he'd always wanted and couldn't have. Even if he wasn't a SEAL anymore, the honor code among military brothers never ended. Best friends' little sisters—or even brothers' former girlfriends—were always off-limits.

Always.

Yet here she was, taunting him. And, at this stage of his life, he couldn't do anything about it.

# Chapter 3

HATHAWAY HOUSE WAS always busy. Today was more so than most. Dani barely had a chance to even consider Aaron's progress weeks in. He was always in the back of her mind. Something was just so sad and defeated about him. She'd read his chart, and she understood the doctors' confusion. Something had stopped him from healing. They figured it was mental and suggested he go to the psychologist. He'd refused. A part of her didn't blame him, but also another part argued, if you continue to do the same thing over and over again, you get the same results. And so far that hadn't worked out for Aaron.

If he wanted to heal he'd have to open up to what was bothering him.

Her father had gone through the same process, when his healing progress had come to a complete halt. Even wanting—or hoping—for improvement was different than this. Like a delicately balanced point in Aaron's medical treatment, and in his life, he could either rush forward and beat it, or he would slide backward in a descent difficult to stop.

She remembered sitting on her father's bed, crying for him to fight, when he'd reached out a hand and asked, "Why?"

It'd stunned her then, hurt her terribly, but she'd come to understand that moment when he gave up. Thankfully her father had turned his mental state around and was now living a completely different life. However, at the time, she'd felt so betrayed. Because, in her mind, she hadn't been enough for him to care about or to fight for, even though in her heart she knew it wasn't true.

She understood that anybody, in the same condition her father had been in, couldn't or didn't want to care about anybody else. They were so focused on how lousy they felt physically, plus how sad and depressed they were emotionally about their supposed nonexistent future, that it was almost impossible for them to relate to how any other person felt. Then, once on that negative pathway, they believed they were a burden to everyone around them and everyone would be better off if they were dead.

Added to that was a lot of them believed everybody else would be better off with them dead. She'd heard more than a few patients at the center bring that up. Depression was a fine-edged sword. It clicked like a light switch, flipping on and off so fast sometimes. That was also why they worked in teams here. If anybody had an inkling that something was going wrong with a patient, they could talk to the rest of the team.

She answered the main landline phone once again while checking her watch. Melissa, her new front office girl, should be coming in any time.

It couldn't happen fast enough. Dani hadn't been in her own office for most of the day because she'd been busy dealing with the front desk and a lot of the other admin responsibilities. Jessica had shown up and then had left early with a family emergency. Of course Dani had stepped in, which meant her work was pushed back again. She had a lot of charts and files to organize, and a never-ending stream of bills to pay. Just as Melissa walked in the door, Dani's other phone rang. She glanced down to see who was calling and smiled. "Hey," she said, delighted to hear the voice on the other end. Levi had been her best friend growing up, and the bond was still strong today.

"How is he?"

"Confused and disturbed. Not understanding how or why he's here. Not depressed but not overjoyed."

"Words like *apathetic, depressed* and *giving up* were what the doctors talked about when I spoke with them," Levi said. "He's my brother, whether he wants to acknowledge the relationship or not."

"We'll do what we can for him," she promised. "At least he's here. That's the hardest part of the battle. And we won't let him out of here until he's strong enough to handle life on his own."

"Good, glad to hear that. Keep my name out of everything, will you?"

"Of course. That shouldn't be a problem as he doesn't remember me. By the way, how is the new company going?"

"So far, so good. I'll do my best not to create any more patients for you."

She laughed at that, then hung up the phone. With a wave and a smile at Tammy, one of the front counter receptionists, she headed back to her office. Levi was a good guy, and he'd helped out with a lot of other cases here. She didn't know what the problem was between him and Aaron, but Levi talked about Aaron, and from what she understood, Aaron did not talk about Levi.

They'd both been injured in military operations. Both SEALs but in completely different locations.

Family was important at times like this. That she well

knew. But if Aaron wasn't willing to open up and let Levi into his life, she could do little to help.

She stopped at her office doorway and shuddered. Her desk was stacked high. George came down the hall toward her, pushing an empty wheelchair back to the front desk. He took one look at her face and said, "You work too hard. Time to shut down and go home for the night."

She waved at her desk overflowing with piles of documents and said, "Really?" She was torn. Part of her wanted to dive in and clear off that pile, and the other part of her wanted to walk away.

George reached over, grabbing the doorknob and pulled the door closed in front of her. "See? Just like that." He gently put an arm around her shoulder and turned her toward the front desk. "You were here at 6:00 a.m., and now it's five o'clock, and you're still here. Go get a meal. Take a break. If you feel like you have to come back, then do so, but you need to rest sometime, Dani."

The trouble was, she knew he was right.

"I hoped to go see Helga again," she murmured as she walked to the front door, wrapping her arms around her chest. Once he'd made the suggestion, exhaustion hit her. "She needed support today."

George laughed. "That dog has barely had one second alone. She's probably wishing all these humans would give her some peace and quiet. We've all been down there multiple times today—you included. Now leave. Go take care of yourself for once."

With a grateful smile, she walked out the front door and stood on the porch, taking several deep breaths. She closed her eyes and let the sunshine and the cool breeze wash over her. A sound from the right made her smile. "Hello, Midnight," she called out.

The answering neigh made her heart light, and her shoulders straightened. No matter how much work was needed to run this place, it was all worth it. Her own home was just on the other side of the tree line—still on the property but separate. She spent every day at the center as it was, so it was important for her to have a bit of space to call her own.

She walked down the steps and over to the fence. Midnight immediately raced toward her. He shoved his big long nose into her hair and neck and blew gently. She stroked the soft felt muzzle and kissed his nose, murmuring sweet nothings to the old horse she'd had since she was just a little girl. She'd done her damnedest to make sure he had a home till the end of his days. He was one of the few fully able-bodied horses on the place. He was hers, and he always had been. Sticking close to the fence, she walked up the line, talking to Midnight as he walked beside her. "It's been a long time since we went riding, hasn't it, buddy?"

He nickered sorrowfully at her side.

At the point where the path turned and headed toward her house, she gave him one last gentle pet and then walked to the house.

"Dad, you home?"

Silence. The inside of the house felt cool, as though nobody had been home all day. Chances were, he hadn't been home at all. He was worse than she was. He'd eat anywhere anytime but only if put in front of him. He no longer cared about meals—he just cared about people and animals.

There were worse things in life. She opened the fridge, spotting the container of leftover stew from several days ago. She brought out a pot and warmed it up. If nothing else, she would eat a hot meal at home tonight. It was beautiful outside, but the last few days had been very stressful. The work was just too much. She needed to hire an extra person but wasn't sure they could afford that.

She reached for her cell phone and called her father. When he answered, she said, "There's a hot bowl of stew here, if you're ready to eat."

He mumbled something about staying and playing cards with somebody downstairs, and he'd eat later. Typical. She dished up some for herself and then went to the table and sat down. The food was delicious, and she was ravenous, but she still couldn't relax. Aaron kept invading her mind. She'd seen a lot of patients come and go at the center. Some stayed a long time, some quickly dealt with what they needed to.

They'd only ever had two cases where they couldn't help. One had ended up with cancer that had metastasized so quickly there'd been nothing they, or anybody, could do for him. The other had refused all help. Dani was bound by the law, and if the patient refused to receive care, Dani could do nothing.

It had broken her heart, but her hands were tied, and she couldn't change the situation. They'd brought in extra specialists and his family members, but nobody could dent the barricade he had around his soul. He'd asked to be shipped home, and that's what they'd done. He'd taken his own life less than three months later.

She hated to think of Aaron heading in either of those directions, but his was a case that defied logic. Sometimes the soul just needed more than what anybody could do for the physical body. Regardless, she was determined Aaron wouldn't become another statistic. Besides, she owed Levi that much. He was counting on her to turn the tide for his brother's sake.

After she finished eating, she stood and washed her bowl. She wished she had brought Aaron's file home with her. It often helped her deal with the residents if she went through their medical histories carefully enough to understand who they were and what made them tick. Sometimes it made for very disturbing bedtime reading, given the injuries that many of them had sustained.

She considered returning to her office and dealing with all that paperwork and then reconsidered. She was just too tired. On the other hand, going to the veterinary section and spending some time with the animals could well brighten her soul instead. Making a quick decision, she grabbed her sweater and almost ran down the hill. Several people were in the common area, and George had been right. Helga was having a hell of a time in the middle of the room. Everybody had a hand or a toy or something for her.

When Helga saw Dani, she barked. Dani walked over, bent down and gave her a big hug. As always, the animals helped restore her good humor. That great big face didn't hurt either. Laughing, she backed away and walked to the other cages where she systematically spent a few minutes with every animal. It was so important for everybody to know somebody cared.

It was the least she could do. So many people had said she couldn't combine humans and animals in the same center, but in her mind, they were a natural pairing. People healed better when they had animals around, and animals healed better when they had people around. To her, that was what a marriage should be all about—a natural pairing. When she finished her tour of the room and was in front of Helga again, she bent down to scratch the big dog and then turned and walked out.

Maybe she would go grab Aaron's file. Take it home with her. She walked upstairs and down the hall, suddenly aware that she would pass Aaron's bedroom. Of course she needed to check in, make sure he was okay. He was the brother of her friend. He had been an old friend of hers too. She wouldn't ignore him.

If her heart whispered that she was caring a little too much, she was well-known for that. She put her heart and soul into this place, and that also meant into every person who walked through the door. His door was open, which she was glad to see, but he was alone, lying in his bed in the dark. She checked her watch. Only seven forty-five. She gave a short knock on the open door, but he didn't move.

"Aaron, it's Dani."

He shuffled and rolled to his back.

She took a hesitant step forward, always aware of people's privacy. "How are you doing?"

"I'm fine."

His voice was riddled with pain. She walked over to the bed. "Did you see the doctors today?"

He nodded. "Yes. And, yes, I had food. And, yes, everybody's been to see me. And, yes, I'm okay."

"Yet you're not," she said bluntly. "I can hear the pain in your voice. I can see it in your body language. Do you need a doctor to see you?"

"No." His voice was cold, hard, with no give in it. She'd seen this before, time and time again. She perched herself on the edge of his bed without asking. Then she reached over and picked up his hand, feeling the scars on his fingers. She didn't remember seeing anything about scar tissue on his fingertips. She'd have to talk to the doctor about it. Maybe they could do something to better heal his fingers.

"Pain comes and goes," she said. "Whether you like drugs or not, there's no healing if you're so twisted up with pain that your body can't function and take care of its own needs."

Even in the shadows of the night, she could see the stiffness of his body, as if he were willing the pain away. She gently stroked his fingers, his palm and the back of his hand. "Even a little bit of pain relief helps the muscles to relax. You've been in a lot of different positions today, and your body wasn't accustomed to all that movement. A muscle relaxant is not a painkiller, but it will have a huge effect on the tension riddling your body right now."

He didn't say anything, and she watched his face until he finally gave a short nod. She patted his hand and stood. "I'll be right back."

Dani went down to the medical room, pulled out her keys and let herself in. She walked to the far wall, where they kept the medications, and she dumped two muscle relaxants into a small cup for Aaron. She walked back to his room, refilled his water flask and then helped him take the two pills. She'd have to remember to add the medication to his file chart and see that he was offered more through the night.

"Thank you," he said, his voice easier.

"No problem. You have a Call button here if you ever need it. You know that, right?"

He nodded.

Of course he knew that, but it would take a hell of a lot more for him to let go of that hard shell of his and ask for help. She walked toward the bedroom door, then said, "Remember, we can all be strong sometimes, but we can't all be strong all the time. I'm glad you accepted this little bit of help because it'll make your healing that much faster."

At the doorway, she paused to say, "Have a good evening."

"How's the dog?"

She dismissed the interruption and stepped back into the room, a warm smile on her face. She kept her tone light and bubbly. "Helga is just lovely. She's getting thoroughly spoiled downstairs."

"Good, and so she should. Every dog should have somebody to love them."

"The same goes for every human being."

"Maybe not those who don't deserve it."

"I don't believe that. Just because you might not think someone deserves it doesn't mean that's true. So often people come here, and they hate themselves for something they either have or haven't done. Or that they're alive, and all their friends are dead. This isn't a case of being deserving. It's a case of you're here, and you need to grow, and you need to heal. If there's anything we can do to help you make that happen, then we'll do it."

He turned his head to face her. "Anything?"

She nodded, a little hesitant, because she'd heard a lot of sexual innuendos in her time, but, willing to give it a shot and see what he was asking, she said, "Within reason of course."

He struggled, grunting, as if asking would be hard.

"What is it you think we can help with?" she asked gently.

"Any chance I can see the dog?"

Her smile bloomed. "Absolutely. How about now?" He stared at her for a moment, his gaze on the wheelchair. He bit down hard on his jaw, but he nodded. He sat up slowly, as if his body would still cry in pain from the day's travels, but then he seemed to relax, as if it wasn't as bad as he'd expected. She brought the wheelchair to him and said, "Do you know how to get into this on your own?"

He looked at her and said, "I think so."

"Well, give it a try."

She stayed at his side, just in case, but knew, if he could succeed at this, it would give him some self-confidence and would help him save face, which mattered to him. His upper torso was strong, even if his back was still showing some damage. His injury limited his range of movement as he struggled into the wheelchair on his own. When he did, he turned to her, his face flushed with success.

"Excellent," she said. "Now let's head in this direction."

She led the way, not offering to push him, but knowing it would be a fine line between him doing this on his own and overdoing it, considering he had had to take a muscle relaxant. When the double doors to the elevator opened wide, they waited for several people to get off, and then she stepped in first, letting him maneuver his way in afterward. She hit the button for the vet clinic downstairs and studied him. He looked better already. Still something was so wrong about seeing reasonably healthy adult males confined to bed. They always looked so much more vibrant when they were up and moving around. She knew, for herself, that it felt that way too.

HELGA *WAS* SPECIAL. He was glad he'd made the effort to see her. The relationship between a man and a dog was something unique. Especially when they were both in need.

However, he didn't want to be in this position. This dog could break his heart. He should leave well enough alone and ignore her. In fact, maybe he shouldn't have come here in the first place. He'd been showing off.

Dani still didn't recognize him. It bothered him, and at the same time, it pissed him off. Sure, it had taken him a few hours but then *bam*. He knew her, but she didn't know him.

How the hell had that happened? To someone like him? Here he was, an invalid, and here she was, running a center, and a massive center at that. Their lives had crossed and changed and parted, apparently to be forgotten forever. He would never have thought such a thing was possible. Back then she consumed his thoughts all the time. The high school, hormonal, teenage-rage years. Tough days. He also had a love-hate relationship with his brother. In truth, he hadn't thought about her since those high school days. Not really. Not often. Not like an obsession or anything. Back then she'd always been Levi's friend. Not one who Levi went to bed with. *Supposedly* ... No, those were his party girls. Back then, Dani had been in a category all her own—his special friend. Somebody who Levi had always confided in and talked with for hours over coffee. He was always at the end of the phone if she called. He'd go running whenever she needed him.

It had never mattered that Aaron had always been in the wings, watching and hurting, because he was not welcome to join in that *special* relationship. In fact, he'd have done anything back then to take his brother's place. Who knew how time would switch their positions and put them in this spot? True, he hadn't recognized her at the beginning. That was most likely from being inundated by so much else. Then, as he'd been lying here this morning, it hit him. It was *her.*

Fate was a bitch. He was finally in a place where she might see him separate from his brother, but he wasn't whole anymore. He'd cut out everything in his life that had to do with Levi, and in a way, she was a big part of that too. Except that, by the time Aaron had cut Levi out of his life, Levi hadn't had anything to do with her for years either. He'd moved on.

At least Aaron thought Levi had. Aaron had a sense of doors opening since coming to her center. How that could be, he wasn't sure. If Levi was opening doors to her, was Levi also opening doors to his brother? To the things Aaron had walked away from?

Aaron wasn't sure he was ready for that. Besides, he hadn't asked to come here. Sure, he'd signed papers to authorize the move. It wasn't like he'd been kidnapped, but … he'd had no idea *she* was here. He hadn't known what this place was. How could he? He left all that up to his insurance and his VA benefits. That just brought him back to why the hell he was here. How had someone known to put his name on the list? Because Aaron had heard about the long waiting list from the medical team. Maybe he'd been bumped up the line because of someone. He'd be pissed if that was because of Levi and all the people he knew. That was the one connection between Levi, Aaron and Dani aka the Hathaway House. Or it would be the one connection between the three of them, except that she didn't seem to know who the hell Aaron was.

Why the hell was it that the one woman in the world he'd always been interested in would now see him as he truly was—broken?

## *Chapter 4*

D OWNSTAIRS WAS ONLY a shade less noisy than it had been a few minutes ago. The upstairs was wheelchair-friendly, but the downstairs was slightly less so. She opened several doors and waited for him to pass through, making a mental note that they must get powered openers put on these core doors. Once they reached the common room, she could see still a good dozen people sitting with Helga. Dani stood beside Aaron in his wheelchair and said, "Helga, somebody else is here to see you." The Newfoundland lolled on her back, twisting to look at her. She gave a small snuffling bark, seeming to say, "Good. You come here then."

Dani laughed. She'd seen the same behavior in animals and humans alike. They could do whatever the hell they wanted to when nobody was looking, but the minute somebody was there, it was all about getting more attention. She crouched down and clapped her hands lightly. "Come on, Helga. Not everybody has to come to you. You need to get up and work that leg a little bit."

Helga woofed quietly, her big bushy tail wagging in a full sweep across the floor. But Dani refused to move. Instead she sat cross-legged on the cement floor and called Helga again. Then, in a surprise move, Aaron snapped his fingers beside her and said, "Helga, come."

Helga looked over at him and gave a deep woof. She got

slowly to her feet. She was quite able to walk, but now, without the prosthetic leg on, her gait was rather awkward as she made her way to him.

"Nice touch," Dani murmured to Aaron. "Why did you think that would work?"

"Big dogs are usually well-trained. They have to be, otherwise they'd hurt somebody," he said. "But often, when the animal gets injured like that …" He shrugged. "They get lazy."

*Exactly the same for people*, Dani thought to herself. But, by then, Helga had already laid her great big head in Aaron's lap, accepting his strokes of attention.

Dani let the two of them enjoy meeting each other, and before long, it was a full-blown cuddle session. Helga crawled into the wheelchair alongside Aaron. He laughed as Helga's big head snuggled up against his face. In another move that half-surprised Dani—she'd seen so many miracles between animals and humans before—she watched as Aaron wrapped his arms around Helga's great big chest and hugged her tight.

Helga didn't mind in the least. She didn't make any move to get away, and indeed, she looked like she was just cuddling closer. She was a big weight to support though. Dani gave them a few minutes, and then she worried it would be too much for Aaron, and he wouldn't know when to stop. She stood and went to grab Helga's collar to pull her back, but Aaron said, "Don't."

At the choked emotion in Aaron's voice, she let her hand drop. If he needed a few minutes longer, then she would give him a few minutes longer. She let her gaze drift to the others in the room, but nobody was interested in what was happening with Helga. In fact, several card games were going on at the far side of the room. She laughed. So this was where her father was. Judging by the stack of busted toothpicks used as betting chips in front of him, he was taking his friends to the cleaners again. "Hey, Dad, how you doing?"

He glanced over at her and smiled. "Doing well. King of the toothpicks."

Her grin widened as the others grumbled. She wasn't sure if they were having a friendly game or if somebody was cheating, but with the particular men involved, she wouldn't be at all surprised either way. At one point, they'd deliberately played games where they would cheat to see how far they could go before the others noticed. All in good fun.

She dropped her gaze to the big man and the big dog next to her. Amazing how Helga wasn't even moving. She was tucked right up against Aaron's chest, all settled in. Dani stroked her silky ears. Finally Aaron straightened and released his hold on the large animal. Helga slipped back slightly, at least enough so she could wash his face with a great big lick. With a chuckle, Dani walked over to the sink and grabbed some paper towels. She dampened them and brought them back for him. "Here. This will help clean up some of that slobber."

"It doesn't matter. She's a beautiful dog."

In fact, she was more than a beautiful dog. She'd make an awesome therapy dog. But Dani'd have to think that concept over. A dog like Helga required a lot of space. Here she would certainly have room for Helga, but Dani couldn't keep taking on every injured animal out there. There were months when she couldn't cover the bills as it were. Still, it was something to consider if Helga had the same effect on patients as she just had on Aaron. With a gentle woof, Helga got down and then sprawled to the floor, stretching out at their feet.

"Do you want to stay down here for a bit longer, or do you want to go back upstairs?" she asked Aaron.

He turned the wheelchair around with a last look at Helga and said, "Let's go back upstairs."

As he maneuvered to the doors leading to the elevator, she said, "You're welcome to return and visit anytime. Just be aware that, on certain days, the place can be frenzied, depending on what surgeries are scheduled."

"I'd like to come back down."

"Have you worked with animals before?"

"I wanted to be a veterinarian, before I went into the military."

"Oh, wow." She felt a jolt at that news but couldn't exactly say why. Levi hadn't mentioned it. Then again he might not know. "I think the animals missed out on something then, during all the years you were in the military."

He shrugged. "Only so many things one person can do with his life."

"Only so many things one person can do with his life *at one time*," she corrected. "You have a whole new future ahead of you. You get to choose what to do now."

She hadn't meant the last line to come out sounding a bit too blunt, but running a place like this made it hard for her to not interfere.

Still her words had an effect, and he was silent all the way back to his room. Once inside, he wheeled himself straight to his bed as she stood hesitantly in his doorway. She knew she should ask if he needed help but had a feeling he would be okay. From the stiff look of his back and the blank look on his face, she figured she was in the way now.

"Okay, I'll leave you for the evening then," she said, backing out. "If you have any trouble getting in and out of bed, or need anything else for the rest of the evening, make sure you call somebody, please." She turned and walked out. No response came from him. No goodbye, no thank you, nothing. Just silence.

She shrugged. Well, she'd take every little bit of progress that she got. The rest would take time.

HOW MANY TIMES would people imply that they knew what was good for him, when they obviously didn't?

He'd been through every damned medical test known to man, so why was he still sitting here in the same place three months later? And all for what? To sit here for another three months and have nothing happen? The doctors didn't know why he wasn't progressing.

But he'd seen Helga down there. She'd progressed faster than he had. Why the hell was that? Even though she'd been beaten and hurt and abused, she still allowed herself to trust people. Maybe she'd learned to trust again while she was here. Maybe being here, in this place, had helped her to heal emotionally. And, as a result, had that emotional healing allowed her to heal physically? Or maybe she'd never lost her sense of trust at all.

He'd certainly done a lot of reading on the subject, and he knew that psychological healing didn't just happen on one level. It had to happen on multiple levels for maximum progress. Well, he'd certainly stalled, and he knew a lot of that had to do with his feelings of betrayal and his lack of trust.

He hadn't gotten his injuries in an enemy skirmish. It would have been bad enough if he had, but this was way worse. No, it was an act of betrayal. He was pretty damn sure Cain had done the unthinkable and gone over to the other side. For money. Only Aaron couldn't prove it.

That made it even worse. He'd loved being in the military, loved being a SEAL, loved being part of something bigger, making a difference in the world. To be one of the best. An honorable profession. Honor was supposed to be in this world. Among his unit. Everyone should follow an honor code, but especially those who fought for their country—particularly a SEAL.

Instead his friend—his best friend—Cain, had gone rogue on a mission. He'd been offered a ton of money to turn his back on his friends, and he'd taken it. He'd blown up the camp himself. Two men dead. Two escaped major physical injury. Cain had disappeared, and then there was Aaron—who couldn't help, who just lay there, fighting the grief for his friends as they'd died in front of him. He had rejoiced for his other friends who, although scarred emotionally by what had happened, could live full healthy physical lives. In fact, they remained in the unit, still fighting the good fight.

But not him. He was caught in between. In no-man's land. He couldn't return to the military. At this point, he couldn't see himself living an aggressively physical life in any way. Yet neither was he dead like his other friends. Unless dead inside counted.

Of course no one understood what bothered him so badly. That anger that consumed him. An anger that never went away. He'd killed several people, all enemies, but the betrayal of his best friend still ate at him. How could Cain have done this to his unit? They were all good men. How did one turn his back on people and say, "Screw it?" And blow them all up?

He stared down at his hands as they slowly fisted once again. He worked on his breathing, trying to regulate it before rage overwhelmed him. An anger-management issue, the doctors had called it. A refusal to accept his current circumstances. He'd seen shrinks, but he hadn't opened up. How could he?

No one believed him.

He'd seen Cain's laughing face as he had pushed the remote on the detonator. A detonator that Aaron hadn't realized was in his buddy's hand until it was too late. Even then, he wouldn't have believed it was rigged to blow. Who would? They were at war—but not with each other.

Then it was too late. As the ground around him exploded, he'd realized the truth. Only Cain had disappeared. Forever. As far as the military was concerned, he was classified as missing in action. Aaron had tried to tell the brass what had happened until he was blue in the face. Nobody listened. Maybe they were listening on the sly, but publicly there would never be that acknowledgment. It didn't happen. SEALs didn't go rogue. There was no such thing as a mole inside a SEAL unit.

Aaron didn't give a damn what they called it. He just wanted somebody to say he'd spoken the truth. Then he wanted somebody to hunt down and kill that asshole Cain. David and Mark did not deserve to die. Both damned good men. That Cain could've done that to his SEAL brothers defied logic. It made Aaron look twice at everybody he thought he knew, as if they were all strangers. Maybe many of them were—maybe they were ready to turn around and stab him in the back.

So, although he'd spoken to several shrinks, he hadn't given them all of his festering anger because they were all military too. After he had been branded a liar, it was hard to go backward. Every time they didn't believe him was like being called a liar all over again. That ate at him too. He'd written several letters to the commander, hoping somebody would listen to him, but the responses he'd received were lukewarm, and they just wished him a speedy recovery.

Basically they figured he was just dealing with sour grapes. Maybe he was. But it was more than just his inability to get off this bed and hunt down that asshole who put him here. For David and Mark's sake, and for his own. Stephen and Charlie had moved on with their lives. They'd survived, and Aaron wasn't involved with them anymore. They hadn't seen what had happened—they hadn't seen Cain's face.

In fact, it was worse because they'd figured Aaron had caused the bomb to blow. They said that he'd been careless and that he'd caused an accident by not looking after the equipment properly. That Cain had gotten away with this and that Aaron should be branded as the responsible party was just too much to let go of.

That brought his mind back to Helga. Maybe if he was a dumb dog, then he could forget, but he wasn't. He was a man caught twisting in a web of lies and a grief that ate at him. He leaned back on his bed and slowly breathed out. In a low voice, he muttered, "Goddammit. I will avenge those deaths."

"Will avenging those deaths make you any happier?"

He froze. Damn. He forgot he was almost never alone anymore. Ever since the accident, orderlies, nurses, or doctors were around. Those well-meaning folks who had good intentions for his health. He rolled his head sideways and glared at Dani. "You can leave now," he said pointedly.

She smiled. "Of course I can. So can you." She turned and walked out.

Instantly he felt like a heel. He wasn't angry at her. In fact she was one of the nicest people he'd seen in a long time—and sexy as hell. Of course now he looked like an angry, vengeful asshole. That wasn't what he meant either, but, as he lay here, he'd realized he couldn't let it go. He sat up and wondered about going after her. It was evening. It was late. Surely she didn't live in the center by herself, did she? He glanced down at the phone she'd left beside him, picked it up, and pressed her contact name, not allowing himself to second-guess his actions.

As soon as she answered, he blurted out, "I'm sorry. I didn't mean to take out my anger on you."

Her light laughter warmed his heart. "That's fine, but you do need to work on forgiveness and letting go. I'm sure I'm not the first person to tell you how it hinders your healing."

"No, you aren't." He sighed, still very irate at himself and at the world in general. "The trouble is, just because people say I should forgive, doesn't mean they give any solid instructions about how to make that happen. When you're angry, when you're full of rage, not even at the circumstances but at somebody specifically that you can't even talk to, to clear things up ..." He closed his eyes and rubbed his forehead. "Anyway, I'm sorry." He quickly hung up the phone. He was a fool to call. A fool to even apologize. He was here to deal with his shit. She had to be used to it. He just hadn't wanted to be yet another asshole in her day.

Chapter 5

---

THE TWO SIBLINGS, Levi and Aaron, possessed more testosterone than a whole naval ship full of men. Dani had never understood how that was possible. She had no siblings, but her father wasn't full of conflict, although he was a big gruff, strong male presence. He wasn't aggressive or looking for confrontation. So she'd grown up not expecting that. Yet, whenever she'd seen the two brothers together, they'd almost frightened her with their intensity.

Levi had always been quick to reassure her that she was never in any danger. That this went on all the time. Well, that might be, but it wasn't comfortable for her. Now that she saw Aaron in his present shape, she wondered if she should mention something about knowing him. But it had been a long time ago, and she didn't want to bring up any possible connection to Levi. Because he didn't want Aaron to know who was paying for his treatment. She smiled. It was an interesting and heartwarming development in their relationship, but, at the same time, it was complicated. She sighed. There were always complications.

Still, it was nighttime, and a whole new day awaited tomorrow. Back home, she undressed and got ready for bed. She needed a good night's sleep. They'd had the odd break-in over the last few years but nothing major. They had installed a new security system, but she was still getting used to it. Every once in a while the alarms went off and woke her up. A few days ago, the alarm had gone off several times. She woke up to the slightest sounds now, waiting to see what had bothered her.

Hopefully tonight she'd sleep all the way through.

When her alarm woke her at six, Dani yawned and stretched, feeling pleased. A whole night's sleep for herself, where she hadn't woken up once. So a good night at the center too. She checked her phone just in case, but Aaron's was the last call.

It was early enough that she could get out for an hour on her own. She grinned. She would slip out for a horseback ride. She dressed quickly and headed to the stables. She'd take out Sable, a younger mare, who had been with her for years. The horse had been abused and, as a result, was often afraid of men and of being closed in. Her stall was always open to the field behind. That way she could come and go as she wanted.

Dani threw a western saddle on her and cinched it up. Instead of a bit in the horse's mouth, she placed a bosal over her nose and draped the reins across her neck. She led Sable out to the sunshine, where Dani hopped on with the ease of long years of practice. Calling out to Midnight to join them, she led the way to the back fields. They had several hundred acres here, and the ranch backed up to thousands more of open range.

If she did nothing more than ride the fence line, looking for potential problems, it would make her happy. The sun was up, the heat was down, and fresh air blew gently across the fields. It was hard not to think of a more perfect day. With Midnight keeping pace at her side, they followed the fence line. Dani was thankful it was in good shape.

However, she realized it had been a while since she'd had the farrier in to trim hooves. All the animals needed regular maintenance too. A good one was just down the road who often did the work pro bono. An added blessing. She'd have to remember to give him a call when she got back.

Only, by the time she'd finished her ride, her phone rang, and when she finally made it to the center, she discovered that chaos reigned. One patient was set to leave, and his ride hadn't arrived. Another patient was transferring in, and he'd come in several hours early. His room wasn't ready because the other patient hadn't left. She smiled at everyone and did her best to ease the situation. She called for help.

"We'll get this sorted out immediately," she said in her best calm administrator's voice. "In the meantime, let's get everybody settled as best as we can."

She took charge and led the new arrival to the deck and had a fresh cup of coffee brought to him. Her father was handy, so she grabbed him and told him to visit. By the time she'd gotten the room cleaned out, the departing patient was settled on a different part of the deck, waiting until his ride showed up. Another quick sort out done, and the new patient was settled in his room too. With a beaming smile, she walked through the place into her office, closed the door and exhaled loudly. "Oh, thank God."

These mornings when unexpected things happened were challenging, but they were usual occurrences in centers like this. They had over seventy part-time and full-time staff members, and sometimes life just happened. Sometimes in a good way. Sometimes in a bad way.

She sat down at her desk and stared at the flashing light on her telephone. With a sigh, she picked up a pen and notepad, and ran through her voicemail messages. After that, she checked her email and discovered dozens of new messages requiring immediate responses. Rubbing her temple, she realized it would be one of those days.

She got up, poured some coffee and then did a quick walk around to see how Aaron was doing—a better way to start her day than all the pressing emails and phone calls. She stopped at his room. The door was shut, so she gave a quick knock. "Aaron, it's Dani. How are you doing this morning?"

No answer. She frowned. Given the security and privacy rules they had established, along with common courtesy, she could hardly walk in on him. Instead, she continued on. She quickly did the rounds, stopping in and visiting with several people in need of a boost. Impulsively she slipped downstairs and found Helga in the middle of the room in front of her adoring audience, with Aaron on the floor with her. She stopped in the open doorway and smiled. This was better than she could've hoped for. They were fitting Helga with a new cup for her stump, but she wasn't interested. She kept kicking it free. The stump had healed enough on one side, but she'd had an accident and had bruised up the other side pretty good. Dani walked over and reached down to cuddle Helga's head, helping to calm her while the men fitted her new back leg.

"Good timing." Stan, the vet, turned to look at her with a big smile.

She glanced over at Aaron and smiled. He reached up and stroked the big dog across the belly. "She's a beautiful dog."

Stan laughed. "She's got the best personality, but she's awfully big to push around when she doesn't want to do something."

"So we make sure the right thing to do is easy, and the

wrong thing is difficult," Dani said with a grin. That was a familiar phrase of her father's, one that an old cowboy had taught him.

"Isn't that the truth?" They finally buckled on the leg, and then they helped Helga onto her feet. They watched as she walked awkwardly around the room, adapting to the new prosthesis. Stan looked over at Dani. "We don't usually see you around here in the morning."

"You shouldn't be seeing me now either," she said with a laugh. "My email inbox is full. My voicemail is overloaded, and my to-do list is out the door." Her grin widened. "Hence I'm hiding."

The two men grinned at her. She loved that smile of Aaron's, with just a hint of likeness to his big brother's. She had never really seen it before. "You look so much like your brother right now." The words slipped out before she could stop them.

His smile fell away, and he stared at her. In a quiet voice, he said, "I didn't think you remembered me."

Her eyebrows shot up, and she scrambled to cover up her slip. "Not remember you? How is that possible?" She forced a wicked grin. "The two of you are very memorable."

She watched the flush of pink staining his neck and smiled.

To give him a moment, she turned her gaze at Stan, who had been watching the exchange with interest. "I knew Aaron when he and his brother were still living together, years ago. We were all a whole lot younger then."

"We were," Stan said. He reached up to pat the salt-and-pepper hair on his head and added, "Still not longing to go back there for anything. I'm quite happy with this stage of life right now."

He returned his attention to Helga and said, "I'll take her out back to one of the runs and see how she does on her own, when we're not all around to give her this much attention."

"Good idea. I'd better make my way upstairs again." She turned to Aaron and added, "Did you come down here in your wheel—?" He was standing, having gotten his crutches under him.

She nodded approvingly. "Crutches are hell on the armpits," she said, "but there's just something nice about being on your feet."

He inclined his head and slowly hobbled past her. She studied his movements, realizing that, even with lots of experience and knowing how to use them correctly, the crutches still pained him.

She followed Aaron to the elevators and stepped inside with him. As the double doors opened onto the main floor, she asked, "Are you interested in having a coffee?"

"Are you asking Levi's younger brother, or are you asking me, as I stand before you now?"

That jolted her into turning and staring at him in surprise. "Well, I have no problems with having coffee with Levi's little brother, because I quite liked him way back then, the same as I liked Levi. However, I would like to have coffee with Aaron, as he stands in front of me now."

Boy, had that opened up a whole different set of attitudes she hadn't expected. Maybe something deeper and darker rooted was involved in their sibling rivalry that she didn't know about. She would have to talk to Levi and get the details. Maybe that's what was holding Aaron back. That little bit of resentment could cause wounds to fester inside and out. He didn't need to completely bare his soul in order to heal, but it did need to be cleaned out.

They walked onto the deck, and she was overjoyed to see the sun still shining. They passed George, and he grinned at them. "You guys going to relax for a little bit?"

She laughed at him. "It does happen. Maybe not enough but it does happen."

"I'm heading to the kitchen. Can I get you some coffee?"

She beamed up at him. "Two coffees would be lovely. Thanks, George."

He waved over at the far side and said, "Go grab a comfy chair. I'll be back in a few minutes."

She collapsed onto one of the deep cushions along the far corner as Aaron sat down at the table beside her. "Today would be a perfect day to play hooky. Except I have so much work to do."

"If you need a day off, then take it," he said. "Life is way too short, as I'm finding out."

"Well, playing hooky when you're all alone isn't much fun. If I had a boyfriend, then maybe. Or a best friend to go for a long bike ride …" She shrugged. "As it is, I have a ton of work to do. So I should just focus and get that all done."

"How is it that you don't have a boyfriend?" he asked, astonishment written across his face. "I'm sure lots of the guys are falling all over you. You're gorgeous and look at the work you're doing here."

She smirked. "If you remember way back when, guys weren't falling all over me then either. I was falling all over *them*. I had more crushes than any girl my age. But I was also a klutz. I fell every time I tried to wear high heels, and every time I put on makeup, I looked like a clown." She waved at the vast area behind them. "This is finally me. Natural. Jeans and a T-shirt. What you see is what you get."

"Still one thousand guys should be lining up to see what you've got," he said calmly. "I don't remember any of the rest of that, because I had a crush on you so bad back then."

Her laughter fell away, and she leaned forward to stare at him. "Honestly?"

He nodded, and that grin she'd only seen once or twice, but remembered from way back when, peeked out. It was a heart-stopper. With a little bit of a hook on the side, meant to reach out and grab the heart and yank. She felt herself yanked right now. "No way."

"Oh, yes way."

"Why didn't you say something?"

"Because you were my brother's girl. How could I say anything to you?"

She fell back against the seat cushion and stared at him. "I was never Levi's girl. Levi was my best friend. I was one of his best friends, but we were never boyfriend and girlfriend—and definitely not lovers for that matter."

Aaron settled back to stare at her, his gaze intense, as if deciphering whether she told the truth or not.

She opened her arms and held out her hands. "Honestly."

He turned his head to stare off into the distance, and she wasn't sure just how this discussion had changed something, but it had. As if something fell off his shoulders, and he could sit easier. Taller.

His revelation affected her too. She wasn't even sure how, but it did. She'd always liked him, but in her head, he was Levi's little brother. Just as off-limits as he apparently felt she was.

Sad. But very interesting, given where they were now.

GEORGE DROPPED OFF their coffees and left them to themselves again.

Aaron stared across the long green and grassy fields ahead of them. His mind churned. She hadn't been Levi's girlfriend? There hadn't been anything between them? He tried to cast his mind back and remember exactly what Levi had said, but too many years had gone by. Too many arguments between them. Too many heated words exchanged in anger to remember anything for sure.

He'd certainly had the impression that not only were they boyfriend and girlfriend but that they were lovers. Had it been Levi who had put that idea into Aaron's head, or had Aaron just assumed that fact, and Levi had let it ride? That would've been Levi too. If Aaron had jumped to a conclusion without asking, Levi would just ignore his brother and let the assumptions go on. He'd always been like that.

What possible reason would there have been for him to lie to Aaron? Unless Levi didn't want Aaron to know that they weren't lovers. Maybe Levi wanted to be closer to Dani back then. It would look like a failure in his eyes if Aaron had assumed that they had that level of a relationship and they hadn't. Aaron almost smiled at the thought. He also hadn't exactly been a prize himself back them. There'd still been a ton of anger, and he had been on the wild side.

If Levi was a good friend of Dani's, he might not have wanted Aaron anywhere around her. Levi always was protective. He'd always been a champion of the underdog, standing up for the little guy. For a long time, Aaron had resented that. As the younger brother, he felt his older brother should have stepped back earlier. Only Levi didn't seem to know how.

Then they were two brothers with a different mother, and that made a difference too. After his own mother had died, he'd gotten wild. Levi had already lost his mother and had a more distant relationship to Aaron's mother. Although cordial, they weren't close. Their father had insisted on good relationships on the surface—for the public to see. Yet, as Aaron thought about it, he realized Levi had been the spitting image of their father—who was an abusive bastard when out of the public eye—not taking after those tendencies though, just carrying on his father's looks. So Levi'd been closer to their father while Aaron had been closer to his mother. He'd bugged Levi about it a lot growing up.

By the time Aaron became an adult, after a tumultuous few years, just enough distance was between the two of them to separate them. After his mother's death when he was fourteen, he'd gone a little crazy. He was angry at life and everyone in it who wasn't hurting the same as he was. That included Levi. As he grew up, he'd made no attempt to cross the growing divide between them. Only three years were between the brothers, but it might as well have been sixteen.

He hadn't even thought about if his brother was distressed by the loss of his second mother. Mostly because he'd been so sure Levi wasn't. Yet how could he not have been? He'd spent fourteen years with her. There had to be some connection.

Of course he'd never asked Levi. She just arrived one day, and for a while, she was there all the time. Of course, if Aaron were Levi, he'd have taken her to bed. The two brothers were both healthy young males, and that had been the drive back then. He stared down at his hands and frowned. Not so much anymore.

"Thoughts?" Dani's gentle voice broke into his trip down memory lane.

He gave a hard shake of his head but managed a gentle smile for her. "Levi and I have been at loggerheads for a long time. I thought something was a given back then but wasn't."

Her smile bloomed. "I never lost track of him," she admitted. "We'd talk every now and then. When he went into the military, he took a different path, and he became so immersed in it I think a lot of us just felt left out."

"Levi is like that. Very focused." Aaron wasn't exactly sure how to feel right now. He'd been seriously crazy over Dani back then. Had he known she wasn't with his brother, would that have changed the outcome years ago? Or what potential lay before them right now? If he had ever hated what he'd become, it was now. He wasn't a whole man. He wasn't sure what he would do for a job or career. It wasn't like he would be the solid provider he'd always expected to be.

"Levi's turned his life around. His injuries were bad, but he's recovering," she said with a smile. "Even better is that he's not in the military, and now he has a whole new company and a whole new life." She spread her hands on the table, and with her gaze directly on Aaron's, she said, "I'm proud of him."

Aaron swallowed hard. He wanted to be proud of his brother. He wanted to think such feelings existed. But he wasn't sure they'd ever get past all the other garbage they'd had growing up. As he looked back, even he could see that a lot of it was caused by his own anger problems. "I haven't talked to him in years," he said. "I'd heard he'd been injured, but by the time I got the whole story, he was back on his feet and doing fine again."

"Well, it certainly wasn't that fast, but he is definitely back on his feet. He's running a private security company here in Texas right now." She picked up her coffee and took a sip. "I don't know what happened between the two of you, but he's certainly hiring a lot of former military men for his company."

"Ex-military doesn't mean damaged and disabled," he said, his voice hard. The last thing he wanted was charity.

"Well, he's got Stone, Merk, and Rhodes with them. They were injured as well in the blast that caught them all up—although not as badly, I believe."

"Right, the men in Levi's unit. Levi's secret unit. The best of the best." That must've been very hard for his brother. "Maybe he started the company so his unit would have employment." He almost laughed at that. It took a hell of a lot of effort and time, not to mention money, to set up a company. Most people wouldn't do that just to give a few friends a paycheck.

"Oh, I don't think so. Maybe it started out as something like that, but he's gotten pretty big. I think a good dozen-plus men work for him now. They are looking at opening a second office on the West Coast too."

Tempting. But he was a long way away from doing something like that. Interesting that Levi took on disabled men. Giving them a new life. Aaron knew a lot of vets who had less than a full life. In fact, they were living on the streets, surviving day-to-day, while trying to find new purpose in their world gone crazy. So many vets just stayed at home and watched TV.

Not the life for a warrior. Even after the war was over.

Again it didn't matter, because he wasn't whole. Yet, he

couldn't keep that thought from rolling around in the back of his mind.

"So back to when you had a crush on me," she said in a teasing voice. "I never knew. I'm surprised."

He snorted. "I'm not. Back then I was a very angry teenager. I'd lost my mom a few years earlier and pretty much hated the world. I wouldn't have let you know anything back then. My father drilled a few things into us both that Levi and I agreed upon. *Integrity and honesty.* A combination of traits that's very hard to come by in this world. But Dad forgot all that when he had a bottle in his hand." He picked up his coffee cup and stared at the thick black brew. "Because somebody else didn't follow those simple rules of ethics is why I'm here."

She leaned forward to stare at him. "What do you mean?"

He wrestled with himself. Should he tell her? Would it just put her off? Come across as sour grapes? On the other hand, she'd read his file and likely some notes were in there about him fielding the blame, accusing a fellow officer.

He settled back, looking for a way to change the conversation.

"No," she snapped at him. "You can't say something like that and then walk away. Obviously this is very important to you. I need you to tell me what's going on."

Woodenly he placed his cup back on the table and brushed away nonexistent crumbs. "You won't believe me," he muttered.

"That's not true. I can't make a decision as to whether I believe you or not if I don't know exactly what your story is."

He glared at her. "The military doesn't believe me, so why would anybody else?"

"I'm not anybody else."

She had said it so simply, he realized the truth. She wasn't coming from a background of protecting the military. She was somebody looking from the perspective of healing.

He took a deep breath and slowly explained about being in Afghanistan and how they'd been expected to face enemy fire and deal with the dangers of landmines on a daily basis. It wasn't that they didn't expect to be injured—they always knew it was a possibility—but because they were doing what was right and protecting their country, they just always shrugged it off.

He stopped talking for a long moment. She reached across and cupped his fist in her hands. His white-knuckled fist. He made himself continue.

"I'm an EOD specialist," he said with a humorless smile. "At the camp, we were sorting through our supplies. We were making explosives for a run to be done the next day. I had four men with me. Two were working off to the side, but two were right beside me. I looked up to see my best friend, Cain, standing there in front of me, with an odd look on his face. Then he said something weird. He said, 'Have a nice life,' and then he turned and walked away. I studied him for a long moment, confused, and then I called out, 'What are you talking about?' He turned and held up a device in his hand. A detonator. He said, 'I'm sorry, but this is what I mean,' and he pushed the button.

"I was already running toward him, hoping to stop him. The blast lifted me up and threw me a good twenty feet away. I woke up in the hospital to find out my two other buddies had taken the blast full-on. The two off to the side survived with just a few scrapes. Of course I lost my leg and damaged my back." He forced his fingers to open wide and spread them across the table as she continued to cover his hands with hers. He stared down at her long slim fingers resting against his big thick muscled ones. He shook his head.

"It wouldn't be so bad if it wasn't such a betrayal." He gave an ugly laugh. "No, it still would be as bad. Because nobody in the military believed me."

She leaned forward. "What do you mean, they didn't believe you?"

"They didn't believe Cain deliberately blew us up."

She sat back, a look of shock and disbelief on her face. "Did Cain die in the blast?"

"Cain is listed as MIA," he said calmly. "But he was running damned fast in the opposite direction of the blast when I was after him. So …" His anger spiked. "Missing in action might be the truth, but if that's the case, he's missing because he wants to be."

"That's horrible," she cried.

He realized he had to get the last of it out. "It's worse than that. Because they didn't acknowledge Cain had done this deliberately, and they needed to look for reasons, they put the blame on me, saying I had been careless. That it was my fault everything blew up. Essentially saying I killed my friends."

Then he sat back, feeling the same damned wall of defeat crushing in on him.

# Chapter 6

BACK IN HER office, Dani sat in her chair and stared out the window for a long moment. Betrayal, as root causes go, was a big one for Aaron. She didn't blame him one bit, and she could also see how that betrayal was compounded by those who he had trusted, respected and looked up to. Not believing in him was creating this massive pit of anger. No wonder he wasn't healing. She wasn't sure what she could do to help, but he had to do something to move past it.

The only person she knew with those kinds of connections was Levi, but she wasn't sure he even understood what his brother had been through. It would be a betrayal again, from her, if she were to talk his brother about this without Aaron's permission. If he had wanted Levi to know, then Aaron would've called and told his brother himself. Yet a part of her mind understood that thanks to the estrangement, Aaron wouldn't say anything to Levi.

Her fingers itched to grab the phone and call Levi. But she held back. It was very much a tangled web right now. She had a history with both of them but not enough of a history, according to Aaron. She still couldn't get over the fact that he had had a crush on her. Because she'd had a crush on him back then too. Levi had told her that Aaron was a bad deal. He was messed up and needed to get his head straight before anybody could spend time with him. She had believed Levi because she trusted him. Maybe he had been right back then. When she listened to Aaron talking about the loss of his mom and the anger about his brother, when she remembered the bits and pieces that Levi had said to her, she could see how all that would gel.

The thing was, Aaron was still a bit of a messed-up guy right now. One vague idea of how to help came to her, but she figured he might get very angry about how it came to be. So, if she had any feelings forming, or if she wanted any relationship with him, she would have to kiss all that goodbye because he would never forgive her for crossing the line.

Not that any relationship interested her at the moment. Not after Jim. And a lot of the residents here were either clingy or straightaway asking her to marry them—she'd had something like seventeen proposals over her time at Hathaway House. Then others were standoffish and didn't want anything to do with single women. That usually stemmed from a belief they were no longer whole men. They were incapable of being who they used to be, and therefore, who they were now was less than satisfactory. So, an already attached woman was less threatening to them.

Of course that wasn't true. So often they were much better men now because of what they'd been through. Then again it was also unprofessional to have a relationship with a patient—unethical, if not downright illegal between a doctor and a patient. So, even though she was not a doctor, she'd avoided even the smallest hint from any of the patients like the plague. Which was why Aaron's presence was suddenly very confusing. The rules had always been black-and-white for her, until he arrived and brought his own set of problems with him.

Aaron was also the only patient she'd known in the past, before they came here. Maybe that made the difference.

She picked up the phone once again and immediately put it down. She needed his permission to bring this to somebody else's attention. She ran her hands over her face.

"What do I do?" she whispered to the empty room. "I didn't tell him our conversation would be confidential." But she also knew it would be a betrayal, no matter how she looked at it. As she sat here, wrestling with the dilemma, her phone rang in her hand. She turned to look at the number and froze. As if Levi had read her mind. She answered the call, her voice tentative.

"How is Aaron doing?" Levi asked.

She was stumped. She didn't know what to say.

"What's the matter?" This time Levi's voice had a hard edge. "Has he had a relapse?"

"No," she said slowly. "In fact, maybe it's a breakthrough, but I don't feel I can discuss it with you because it's confidential. But …"

"But what?"

"Something's holding him back from healing. I just don't know how to help him get through this."

"Shrink?"

"No. Maybe justice?" She winced. That was the can opener for ten more questions. Questions she didn't have answers to. She brightened. Maybe if Aaron would tell Levi … "I guess there's no chance you can come in and talk to him, is there?"

"I don't think so. He doesn't want to see me," Levi said calmly. "I haven't seen him in a long time now."

"You might be able to help him with something. Something that your specialized skills and connections could possibly get him answers to." Then she took a big breath and continued. "Maybe not. He says the case is closed, and he's been blamed. There's probably nothing anybody can do."

"Case closed? Blamed? What the hell happened?"

"Shit. I didn't mean to say that blame part, honest," she cried out. "I'm no good at keeping secrets. But ethically I can't say anything. Something is wrong. Something is stopping him from moving forward."

"His accident?"

She didn't answer. How could she?

"I'm on it. I heard about what happened, but I didn't believe it at the time. Still, shit happens to all of us sometimes. Let me look into it." He hung up.

She placed her phone on her desk and stared at it. Then the tremors started. Oh, dear God, what had she done? If Aaron ever found out that she had talked to Levi about this, Aaron wouldn't ever speak to her again. Any potential friendship, let alone a relationship with this man, drifted right out of the window. He'd already been betrayed twice, by Cain, then the navy—a third betrayal would be too much. "I didn't betray you," she whispered into the quiet room. "I didn't mean for it to slip out. But Levi is the best person to resolve this."

She shook her head. It didn't matter. There was no redeeming this. She wasn't one to take half measures, and she'd certainly blown it wide open this time. The only thing she could hope for was that Levi did find something to fix this problem and potentially to provide the avenue for Aaron to move on with his life. Sure, he also had a bit more reconstructive surgery to go through and more therapy to deal with, but he wasn't far from being a fully able male again. However, he had to get his mind focused on his healing, off his revenge on Cain and clearing Aaron's name with the navy.

She studied all the paperwork on her desk needing her attention and realized that, if nothing else, she had a perfect diversion to keep her mind off of what she had just done.

Her trick worked for several days. She stopped in to say hi to Aaron on a regular basis. She was nearly successful in convincing herself the whole thing would wash away, and it wouldn't have any effect on their renewing friendship. Then, at odd times, she'd remember how she'd let the cat out of the bag, and she'd wince and realize just how delicate balancing her relationship with Aaron truly was.

"This is bad news, any way I look at it," she muttered to herself once she was back in her office again.

She loved the long glances between them, the bright smile when he saw her, her uncontrollable urge to see him, her daily detours so she could catch a glimpse of him. Obviously something was developing between them, but it was bittersweet. She just felt like she was in quicksand, and if she said the wrong thing, it would all slip away. Whenever she felt like that, she'd sit down and say, "If I have to sacrifice my relationship with him in order to have him healed, then so be it."

But she wanted both.

She dove back into work to bury the fear and panic of losing him once again. All those years she'd been out of touch, it had been easy to believe he'd moved on with his life and was probably happily married with the prerequisite two-and-a-half kids.

Then the tears rose, and she realized she would lose him forever this time if he found out.

She shook her head and snapped at herself. "Stop being a

fool."

She got another file and opened it, determined to whittle down some of this never-ending paperwork in front of her. When her phone rang, she didn't think about it. She just grabbed it and answered it.

"Dani, I want to see Aaron."

*Levi.* She sucked in her breath. "Do you think that's a good idea?"

"I think I have to. I've found some information, but I need to confirm the details with him."

"The thing is, I didn't tell him that I told you any-thing—"

"And you didn't tell me anything. Nothing that I hadn't already heard anyway. But I do have some questions. If I am to find a solution to this, I need to talk to him."

"By phone?" she asked hopefully.

"No. I think this is better done in person." An awkward silence followed, where she tried to figure out how bad this would be for her, when he added, "Is something going on between the two of you?"

*Maybe?* "No," she answered in a shaky voice. "I just feel like I did something wrong by telling you that little bit I did."

"If it's meant to be ..."

"Easy for you to say. I know he already feels like he's been betrayed by everybody. I just can't be one more in the long line of people who he can't trust."

"If you believe this is holding back his healing, then this is what he needs to do to get better. Isn't it worth it for his sake?"

She pinched the bridge of her nose, and even though hot tears burned the corners of her eyes, she nodded. "Absolutely. It's worth it for his sake. I'll just be collateral damage," she said bitterly. "But who cares, right?"

"Don't look at it that way," he said, his voice softening. "My brother's not a fool. It might be a little bit rocky for a while, but he'll understand why you did it."

"Will he?" she said willfully. "Well, I guess it's better now, before we get any farther into what might or might not have been."

"Good. I'm flying in tomorrow morning."

And he hung up. Again.

WHEN AARON WOKE this morning, he was still cussing himself out for having spoken like he had with Dani. It had been days, but it still ate at him. He was a private man and didn't want pity from anyone—especially her. Like he'd gone back in time to be that teenager, so in love with the classy girl in front of him, that he'd been awkward as hell. He hadn't been trying to woo her, but he'd certainly been honest, and she'd listened. He was grateful for that, but he hadn't wanted to dirty what was between them. Of course assuming something *was* between them.

He got up and worked his way to the shower. He hoped the stream of hot water would improve his mood. He had been fiercely independent from the beginning, but some things were just impossible to do. He had his crutches, but that was also damned hard on his back. The doctors had some special surgery they'd wanted to do, but he'd been resisting. Now he was wondering why he was so against it.

He figured he should have a working prosthesis, so that if his back wasn't strong enough, at least he could still walk.

Unfortunately he hadn't improved to the point of getting the prosthetic limb he wanted.

Moving carefully, he headed to the bed where he slowly dried off, then dressed. No way would he wear hospital clothes again. They'd given him one set for all the tests, but he'd been quick to change back into his everyday clothes. The thing was, he didn't have very many of those either, and he wasn't taking the damn Hathaway House bus to buy more, but as soon as he got the damned address of this place, he planned to order some online.

That thought stopped him outright. He let out a short, sharp laugh. Since when had shopping therapy been a solution to his problems? Still, if it would help, then he'd take it. He looked around for his schedule, trying to remember what was on tap this morning.

So far, everybody had treated him fairly delicately, but he knew the kid gloves were coming off on the physio pretty damned soon. Shane was already notorious for hard work and pushing Aaron past the point of exhaustion. Yesterday had been more about seeing how far he could work and how much strength he could apply. He figured today he would get his ass kicked. The one good thing about this place was that, after they'd done their tests, they'd quickly brought in support bars that helped him get in and out of bed. In fact, just enough extras were attached to his bed that he could do a lot more for himself. He realized that having independence went a long way to improving his mood as well.

Of course these extra mobility aids could very quickly become torture instruments too. He didn't doubt it. Some of the bars had pulleys and weights attached to the sides, so who knew?

He sat on the bed, beads of sweat still rising on his forehead, even after he was finally dressed. He wondered if he should use his crutches or the wheelchair to get to the breakfast buffet. He checked his watch. He was running a bit late, but using the wheelchair seemed like giving in. If nothing else, he was damned stubborn. He grabbed his crutches, took a deep breath and moved quickly and efficiently to his door. He didn't expect to see Dani anytime soon, but that didn't stop him from looking around the corners to see if she was close by. He made his way onto the deck and took a seat in the morning sunshine. On the far side, a long buffet was set up, but he wasn't sure he was up to carrying a tray and using only one of his crutches. He'd seen lots of guys do it, but he hated the thought of being the one who fell flat on his face—or rather, fell flat on his eggs. Maybe he should've brought the wheelchair after all.

George appeared at his side. "Aaron, go get in line and pick out what you want, and I'll carry the tray for you."

"I was watching the other guys and how they manage to carry it with the crutches," he said with a dry laugh. "But I figured I'd be the first one to fall and end up wearing breakfast instead."

"The thing to remember around here is, you're not likely to be the first to do anything," George said with a big grin on his face. "Takes time to learn some of these tricks. Let's head over. First you eat. Then we can do a couple runs with empty trays, and then try it with a cup of coffee and a treat, before attempting the full shebang."

That was a hell of a good idea.

Slowly the two of them made their way across the space to the buffet where George picked up a tray and a plate, then poured a cup of coffee. Together they walked along, Aaron making his choices. George never cheated him once on portions. "How can the center afford to feed all these people an unlimited amount of food three times a day?"

"Eating right is a huge part of healing," George said firmly.

As they arrived close to the end of the line, he was surprised to see somebody making smoothies behind the counter. "What are in those?"

"Very healthy stuff. How do you feel about kale, whey powder, and fresh fruit with a whole pile of other stuff in there?"

"Not as bad as I expected," he said with a smile. With George carrying the laden tray, they made their way back to the table in the sunshine. Aaron kept his gaze on the deck, working carefully around the gaps between the planks. They reached the table, and George placed the tray on its surface. Aaron glanced up to grab the back of his chair.

He froze. "Holy shit."

Levi, Aaron's older brother, and the only family he had, laughed. "Now that's a hell of a greeting, kiddo."

Aaron winced. "Please don't call me kiddo." He turned his gaze to the man beside his brother and let out a gasp of delight. "Stone?" Instantly he reached out his hand to shake Stone's. Stone and Levi had been buddies since forever, but then so had Aaron and Stone. Aaron turned to look around the common room and the deck and said, "Are you the only two here?"

"Merk and Rhodes are off on a job right now, so I dragged Stone out with us."

Just then one of the most striking blondes Aaron had ever seen arrived at his table, carrying a tray. She placed it down, reached over and kissed his cheek in the softest, gentlest way he could ever have imagined. In a voice that matched her kiss, she said, "Hi, I'm Ice."

She sat down between Levi and Stone. Both men reached over and helped themselves to items on the tray she'd brought while Aaron sat in stunned amazement. He'd heard about Ice. Hell, her reputation was well-known in military circles. Had heard the rumors about her and Levi, but Aaron had never thought he'd meet her. It wasn't like they had any kind of real familial relationship. When he regained his voice, he said quietly, "Nice to meet you, Ice."

She sent him a beautiful smile. She patted Levi's hand and said, "See? I told you we'd be welcome."

A subtle shift occurred in the table's energy. He stared down at his breakfast, his mind in turmoil, but he wouldn't waste the food. He set about eating. After a moment and several bites, he said, "Of course you're welcome. Levi's the only family I have left."

She gave Aaron a nod of approval. Damn if he didn't feel like that was something he needed. He glanced over at Levi and added, "I have no idea why you're here." Then a thought occurred. "Did Dani call you?" he asked, narrowing his eyes.

Levi gave him a blank look and said, "No, she didn't. I called her."

Aaron sat back, his stomach churning. *What had she said?* "Why would you call her?" Aaron hated the suspicions rolling through his mind, but they were there, and he was damned if he would hide them any longer. His life had been blown to shit in more ways than one. He wanted things on the table, straightforward and honest.

"Because she told me you had arrived here at her place."

"Is that why you came running here to see me? Or was it to see her?" Aaron shot his brother a quick look. He shook his head. "Part of that rings true, but the other part does not." He continued to eat while he thought about it.

"Part of it is true, yes," Levi replied quietly, "but I'd also heard rumors. Rumors I didn't like the sound of."

Aaron laid down his fork very carefully and leaned back to study his brother. "Rumors?" he asked, his voice low and hard. "What rumors?" Aaron let his gaze drift from his brother to Ice and then to Stone—both of whom were quietly eating—before zinging back to his brother.

"Rumors I never believed. That I don't like hearing. That I came to clear up."

If Aaron thought his own voice had come out hard, he'd forgotten how icy-cold his big brother could be when he was displeased. And this went well past displeased. In fact, Levi was seriously pissed.

Aaron narrowed his gaze at his brother. In a low voice, he asked, "Why are you so upset?"

"Because of the implication that you messed up."

Aaron dropped his gaze to his food and worked to control his breathing. Either that or throw a fit and send all the food on the table flying in the red haze of rage that threatened to wash over him again. When he could breathe, he realized Ice had reached across the table to lay her hand on his fists. Fists that even now were forcing the tips of his nails into the palms of his hands. Slowly he released his fingers and stretched them out.

"I did not mess up." When he could, he raised his gaze and stared at his brother, willing him to believe him. "I didn't do this."

Levi studied him for a long moment, then gave a clipped nod. "So who the hell did?"

Aaron blinked. His brother believed him. Feeling as

though a huge weight had been lifted off his shoulders, he quietly launched into an explanation of what had happened. When he finished, he studied the three faces across from him, feeling lighter than he had in months. No love was lost between him and Levi. Yet the old adage was true—blood was thicker than water. And these three were even angrier than he was.

Shocked, he realized that made him feel a whole lot better. And suddenly his appetite spiked again.

With a small smile, he picked up his fork and said, "Seeing as I can't do anything about it, what are you going to do?"

*Chapter 7*

HOW WERE THEY making out? The question burned inside her, but Dani deliberately avoided the deck and the breakfast buffet in order *not* to see Levi with Aaron. Would he know that the meeting was her doing? Would he hold it against her?

She bolstered herself with the thought that at least what she had done was the right thing. Even if it damaged the slow-budding relationship between the two of them. Besides, they were adults now. If he couldn't deal with this, then they had no basis for a relationship anyway. With her mind still going around and around in circles, she tried to focus on work.

Until she heard a cough in the doorway. She glanced up and blinked at the man whose broad form filled the frame.

"Levi!" She bounded off her chair, raced to the doorway and flung herself into his arms. The force of her actions sent him backward into the hallway. He laughed, picked her up, and swung her around in a huge hug. When he put her back down, she realized two other people were watching them. She flushed, but with her arm still looped around her best friend from so long ago, she grinned at the stunning Nordic-looking woman in front of her and said, "And you must be Ice."

The beautiful woman laughed and opened her arms.

"Hello, Dani. Nice to finally meet you." The two women hugged, and Dani instantly felt the connection of a potential new friend. Then her gaze landed on the big man standing behind Ice. Taller and broader than Levi.

She grinned. "Stone." She opened her arms. "Why the hell didn't you come here to recuperate? We would have had a blast together."

The big man gave a shout of laughter and picked her up in a gentle hug. She'd always been amazed that somebody so strong could be so delicate. She leaned her head back and studied his face in surprise. "You look really good." When the flush rose on his cheeks, she reached out and stroked his neck, saying, "I guess that means you have someone in your life, huh?" Stone put her down, and she stepped back slightly. "I thought you were waiting for me," she teased.

His grin widened. "No chance to duck. It hit me, and I fell bad."

"The bigger they are, the harder they fall …" Dani looked over at Ice and grinned. "Isn't that right, Ice?"

Ice chuckled. "Certainly has been my experience."

Dani glanced around to see any sign of Aaron, but he wasn't with them. She motioned the three to follow her back into her office. "How was your reception?"

With the four of them in the room and the door closed, it was definitely crowded. She took a seat behind her desk. "I'm sorry there isn't a third chair in here."

"We're not staying anyway," Levi said.

"Oh?" She studied his face. "Did he tell you?" She sure hoped so, because she didn't want to be in the position of betraying him yet again. Some details he needed to share on his own.

"I asked around and got a lot of the details before I

showed up. Then got him to confirm them, so we have something to go on."

She nodded. "Can you do something about this?"

"We're on it."

"Good." Relief flooded her, and she smiled. "Getting to the bottom of this would be a huge comfort to him. The rumors and accusations have been eating away at him."

"It doesn't mean that the answers will make him happy. We can look into it, but there's no guarantee we can change anything," Ice warned her. "This is a sucky situation, but we'll do our best."

"I understand that." She knew all too well. "Even just that you believed him will mean a lot to him."

Levi stood. "Let's hope this has a positive effect on his mental outlook so he can heal."

Dani turned to look at Stone. "Does he know about your leg?"

Stone shrugged. "No idea."

"Do you mind if I tell him?" she asked.

"Tell him whatever you want. The sooner he comes to terms with it, the better." Stone's grin brightened his face. "It's not so bad. We're having a lot of fun with various prototypes."

"Prototypes?" she asked, fascinated. "I'm scared to ask."

Ice laughed and also rose, standing beside Levi. "It's probably a good thing if you don't. Think blue-steel, weaponized, fancy carving. One leg for Sunday outings, one for grunt work around the place, one for missions ..." She shook her head and patted Stone's arm. "I like his racer-leg the best."

"Hey, my mission leg is the coolest ever—"

"No, it's nice all right, but given the carving on the blue-steel one … particularly with the design that Lissa etched—how cool is that, to find a woman who could do such things?"

"She had no idea she could either," he admitted with a shy grin.

"What's this?" Dani asked. "Your partner does metal etching?"

"Never has before, but she's got a definite gift." He beamed. "There's also not likely to be any end of raw material for her to work on."

They had a laugh over that.

"We need to go," Levi said. "It was wonderful to see you, Dani … and thank you."

"It's lovely to see you guys," she said mistily. "I hope he doesn't hold it against me."

"I didn't tell him anything that would implicate you," Levi said. "He won't know from us."

"No, but like you, he's very intuitive, and I'm a terrible liar."

"No lying required." Ice smiled at her. "Besides, if we can help him, he should be thanking you."

"As if …" Dani's lips turned downward. "I just can't stop feeling guilty."

The other two walked out into the hallway. Levi stepped forward and lowered his voice. "You don't still have that same crush on him, do you?" he asked incredulously.

She winced. "Not really. More a case of what attracted me back then is still something that attracts me now. He's a good man. I guess I like him …" She hated how her face was warm. She could only hope Levi would ignore it.

He lifted his gaze to stare behind them and then focused it on her. "Back then he was wild. He was hurting and lashing out at everyone else. It's one of the reasons why I tried to keep you away from him."

She thought about that. "Your reasons were valid. I wasn't in the best of shape myself."

"I don't know who he is now," Levi said in a low voice. "But what I saw this morning … well, that's a man I'm proud to call my brother."

She beamed. "Thank you. That was my impression too."

She stood in the doorway and watched as they left. She was sad to see them go. They'd been great friends once, but their lives had split and gone in different directions. Nice to know they still liked each other as adults. She was so happy Levi had found Ice. They were perfect. They looked like an all-powerful Viking couple from days gone by.

She turned in the direction of Aaron's room. Should she find him or wait? Knowing it was cowardly, she stepped back into her office. She would see him eventually. Now, with a happy heart, she finally dove into the work awaiting her.

HAD HIS BROTHER only left two hours ago? His physio had been absolutely bone-chilling, as if he'd been worked to exhaustion and then tossed into the river to fend for himself. Every muscle ached—his body was soaked in sweat, and he was so damned hot he didn't know what to do. Shane, his physiotherapist, said, "Pool, then a massage."

"Pool?" Good Lord, he hadn't seen anything close to that here. He brightened at the thought. He was so damned hot he wanted to fall in right now.

Shane laughed. "Absolutely. Let's go." He motioned at the wheelchair, and Aaron collapsed into it gratefully. Shane grabbed towels from a nearby shelf, dumping them in Aaron's lap, and then wheeled Aaron into the hall and then the elevator.

"Is the pool inside or outside?"

"Both."

Aaron raised an eyebrow at that, but he was delighted to hear it. He'd been a huge swimmer years ago. In the military, he'd always excelled at all water activities. That was one of the reasons he'd become a SEAL. It was just his thing.

They traveled down to the level below the veterinarian clinic. Shane opened the double doors to a massive walkout basement, where a large portion of the pool was inside and huge doors opened up to the outside.

"Jesus, this is incredible."

"A lot of money has been spent in making this the best place it can be," Shane said quietly. "This pool alone was a huge chunk of change." He wheeled Aaron to the men's changing room and opened the door, calling out as he went in, but it was empty. He pushed him in farther and dumped the towels to the side. He walked over to another rack, picked up a couple pairs of swim trunks and brought them over to Aaron.

"Put on the one that suits you the best, and that'll be yours to wear while here, so it goes back to your room with you. Get changed and come out on your own." Then he walked out, but just before he closed the door behind him, he said, "I'll be waiting here for you."

Still hot, but knowing that the cool, refreshing water was waiting for him, Aaron struggled into the pair he hoped would fit. He tied up the decorative front laces and then wheeled himself to the door. The double doors opened automatically, making it that much easier for him.

He found Shane already in the water. He swam over to the side and said, "Can you get in on your own?" After the morning he'd run him through, Aaron wasn't sure he could do anything. His leg felt more like butter than a body part. It was a challenge, but he was damned if he would give in that easy.

"As long as I don't have to do anything with style, I can get in." He locked the wheels of the wheelchair right beside the railing, put down his good leg and stood. Two hops and he was in the pool. As the cool water closed over his head, he almost moaned with joy. No matter what they had put him through this morning, this was worth it. Maybe this wouldn't be such a bad place to stay after all.

# Chapter 8

WHEN SHE COULDN'T stand it any longer, Dani finally forced herself from her office and made her way to Aaron's bedroom, only to stare at the empty space. She shook her head. After spending the whole morning avoiding rushing to see how he was, now that she finally got up the courage, he wasn't even here. She'd consulted his timetable, but someone had made a change. As was their right, depending on what they were working on. Sometimes the patients just needed to get out of their rooms for a change of scenery.

She headed to the cafeteria. It was a bit early, but there was a chance he'd gone to eat.

Appetites ran the length of the spectrum with their patients. Sometimes they couldn't get full, and sometimes they couldn't even eat.

No sign of him. She made her way to the big deck but again nothing. The pool was on the other side. She didn't think he'd be ready for that yet, but she heard voices coming from that direction.

She snagged a coffee and then carried it to the far side of the deck where it overlooked the pool and the patio below. There he was in the water, kicking out strongly, with a bit of rock 'n' roll movement to his body. He was having a little trouble staying in a straight line, but he was doing fine. She walked down the stairs and sat down on the patio. She might as well enjoy being outside. She hadn't been in the pool herself for weeks, and that was sad.

She watched as he did several laps. When he finally stopped, he stood and brushed the water back from his head, and she could tell how happy he was. He turned his face to the sun, letting the rays beat down on his dripping features. Now *that* was the Aaron she used to know. Fun-loving, happy-go-lucky, flirty. Even with his eyes closed, he was a hell of a man. Then he opened them and gazed straight at her. She jumped. When she got ahold of herself again, she said, "How's the water feel?"

"Gorgeous. You should come in."

Not a hint of anger or annoyance in his tone. So he wasn't angry with her? That was a good sign. "Can't today—too much work for me to do."

He scoffed. "You can come in anytime you want to."

In truth, she could, but she rarely did. It wasn't that she didn't like the water, but it wasn't her first instinct when shaking loose the stress and turmoil of her day. She'd head to the horses every time.

He swam to the side of the pool near where she sat and folded his arms atop the tiled deck.

She picked up her cup and said, "If I'd known you were down here, I would have brought coffee."

"I would've enjoyed it," he said with a smile. A companionable silence hung around for a moment, until he said, "Did you phone Levi?"

She started. "Levi called me." That, at least, was the truth.

Aaron stared at the tiles and brooded.

"How did the visit go?" she asked quietly.

He shrugged. "Levi's different."

"It's been ten years. We're all different," she said drily.

He looked up at her and nodded. "I definitely am."

"Maybe that's a good thing. Maybe everybody can get along now."

He raised an eyebrow at that but didn't say anything. "It's just that the timing is odd."

Her heart sank. She wouldn't be able to get away from this. "Odd, how?" she asked in a cool voice. She picked up her cup of coffee and took a sip, staring out at the fields of green grass and white fences. This area was particularly lush-looking, and she appreciated the beauty of it.

"I tell you about my problems, and the next thing I know, big brother's racing in to help."

She froze. Then she swiveled her gaze to stare right at him. "Levi came to help?" She placed her cup down and leaned forward eagerly. "Is there anything he can do?"

"I don't know. He's making some inquiries for me." Just then Shane called from behind Aaron.

Feeling like she'd been given a reprieve, Dani picked up her now-empty cup and said, "Well, coffee break's over. I'm heading back up. It looks like you have more work to do." At his groan, she forced a light laugh and said, "You know you love this."

"Certainly more here than I did before." He dove under the water and headed toward Shane.

She watched his powerful muscles bunching naturally in the water. He had an affinity for swimming—she could tell. The rest of his body was lean, and that was what counted. Scars covered his back, and she could see where some of the muscles had atrophied. She knew swimming would help strengthen his whole body. As she watched from the stairs,

Shane went over some stroke techniques to work Aaron's back. She almost felt sorry for him. He would be sore tonight. Then again, if what he said was true, he would welcome it. Most of the injured military guys who came here, needing help, were grateful at the end of a workout. If nothing else, it gave them an outlet for all the stress and frustration they had gone through. A whole lot of things were worse than that.

Happier now that he didn't appear to hold a grudge against her, she headed back to work. He wasn't the only one needing help.

She had several other patients coming in for various issues over the next couple of months. Of course she was expecting dozens all the time. But she had no set schedule months out. Too much depended on the patients' conditions.

She was looking forward to having these three men as they could be great cheerleaders for each other. Three men—good friends—had been injured in Afghanistan—Brock Gorman, Cole Muster and Denton Hamilton and Elliot Carver was a part of the same group but wouldn't be ready to come to her center for months. They'd all known each other, but they'd been over there at different times. One had coverage but would need a boost, one had zero coverage, and she was trying to find some grant money for him. And for the third, she'd been approached by somebody else to pay for his stay. She still had a lot of work to do before it was possible to bring in the men. She idly wondered if Aaron knew any of the three. It might make him feel better to know he had friends here, all struggling to get back to their former physical selves.

Sometimes friends helped each other, but there were also

times when a patient wanted to suffer alone so no one would see them—so they wouldn't appear weak. At times though, there was just no hiding it. For some, it was important to keep that strong-man image. Sometimes having friends around bolstered that desire to stay strong while the injured man tried to hide from his friends how much he was suffering.

She pulled out their files and took a closer look. She had a couple people she could call on to see if anybody wanted to make a charitable donation. Brock looked to be the closest fit, as he already had some coverage. She picked up the phone and called Morgan Hennessy. In his eighties, Morgan had always helped out in the past. That didn't mean he would this time, but he'd been injured himself in the military, and nobody had helped him back then. He was now a wealthy philanthropist, and he was a godsend when she was in need. She smiled as he answered the phone and said in a warm voice, "Hi, Morgan. It's Dani ..."

INSTEAD OF TIRING him out, the swimming invigorated him. Aaron's back muscles were responding even better than expected. It had taken a lot to press them into service, but now, even though he was shaky at the edge of the pool, he felt damned good.

Staring down at his stump as it hung over the edge, he realized he had so much to be grateful for. For some reason, that deadly cycle of his big ball of anger and self-pity over the last few months was easing.

He was glad those two emotions were not who he was. He wasn't sure what was different now, but something had shifted. Then he realized it wasn't about who he wanted to be but was about his brother—seeing his brother and realizing Levi had believed his story. That Levi would make some inquiries on Aaron's behalf made all the difference. As if Aaron could stand taller, stand straighter, as if finally his words were deemed the truth by somebody whose voice counted.

He stared across the beautiful pool, wondering when he'd realized Levi meant that much to him. Aaron should have reached out himself. Typical though, Levi had connected instead. Aaron idly wondered again if Dani had something to do with bringing Levi to the center today. As Aaron stared at his surroundings, feeling a sense of hope inside for the first time, well, he felt so damned good right now it would be hard to be upset.

Maybe he didn't need to pressure Dani about Levi. She'd seemed fairly natural in her responses. At times he was still surprised to see that she lived, worked and spent her spare hours here. Amazing how time had moved on, and she'd found what appeared to be her calling. Aaron had also seen her father running around at various times, now a beaming benevolent man. Aaron remembered hearing from others at the center about her father's history and how he'd started this place, so Aaron could imagine Dani had been involved from the ground up.

Funny, he didn't know much about Dani's father when they were younger. Although he remembered something about him being hurt and Dani struggling. He thought she'd planned to go to college but couldn't remember for what. You'd think he would remember, as everything else about her was stuck in his head. Then again school hadn't been important to him back then. In any way, shape or form. All he wanted to do was get through it the best he could and as fast as possible.

When he'd been accepted into the military, his life had started. Of course the military had also brought his life to a grinding halt a decade later. He stared down at his hands. Maybe trauma was like that—he'd hit a wall, and everything stopped. Once he realized he was being blamed and that nobody believed him, all his defenses went up, and he had locked himself inside.

"Hey, what are you doing? Sleeping here?" Shane asked, standing beside him. "Shower time. Then it's off to lunch and I promised you a massage."

"Both sound great." Using the railing he hopped up on one foot, then he turned and looked around, but his wheelchair was pulled back a few feet, out of the way of people walking around the pool. He had no crutches, not to mention the tiles were now wet from where he'd been sitting, all the way to where Shane now stood. Aaron motioned at the crutches and asked, "Shane, can you pass me those?"

Instead, with a big grin on his face, Shane said, "Here, use my arm and step." He reached out a thick forearm for Aaron to use as balance as he took two hops to the wheelchair before moving smoothly into the showers.

By the time he was done and dressed and heading back out the door, he could feel the fatigue setting in. Not that it mattered because his appetite was even bigger, raging to be fed now. So food first, then a massage in bed. He'd be asleep in no time. With a sense of satisfaction at his morning, he headed off to do just that.

B Y THE TIME the dinner buffet was setting up, Dani felt good about her day. She'd made great inroads into her paperwork. She'd contacted several benefactors and had already received enough to cover the three men at the top of her list.

Tossing down her pen, she decided that was enough for the day. She got up and exited her office, closing and locking the door behind her. In the hallway, she stood and studied the activity around her. There'd been no major upsets for a couple of weeks now, and a general air of peace and contentment filled the center. It was all good.

"Dani, got time for dinner with your old man?" Her father ambled toward her, with a big lazy grin on his face.

She beamed. "Best offer I've had all day."

He hooked his arm through hers and gently led her toward the dining hall. She didn't always eat here. Many times she preferred to go home, but she knew her dad wanted to be here. Dinner was likely to be a catch-up session on shoptalk, but that was their relationship these days, and she hadn't had a good discussion with him for a long time.

The dining area was busy, but the two of them could always find a place in the far corner if they wanted it. She sometimes felt guilty about keeping a table just for them when she only used it maybe half the time, but it was important for her to know she and her father always had a spot to meet and eat. He seemed to be perfectly content to live most of his life down here. He was well-known to the staff and had lots of friends among the patients. Those he didn't know he made friends with very quickly.

But instead of serving themselves right away, he wanted to sit and talk over coffee first. While she was happy to visit with her dad, she wondered if something else was going on.

"So how are the newest arrivals doing?" he asked with a smile.

She narrowed her gaze at him. "As far as I know, everyone's settling in nicely," she said smoothly. "Anyone in particular you're asking about?" But she knew. Of course she knew.

"I understand that Aaron, Levi's younger brother, is doing better."

She felt his aging blue gaze pierce her. "Yes, he is." She laughed quietly. "I'm surprised you didn't bring it up earlier."

"I was waiting for you to say something about it," he said, leaning back with a twinkle in his eye. "So how is he? You had quite the thing for him way back when."

"I did not," she protested. "I might have had a *little* thing for him back then, but it wasn't that bad. He was just so … larger than life."

He snickered. "This is somebody who watched you go through years of that sideways look, flushes and giggles, and moody staring into the middle of nowhere," he said. "Allow me to now hold a different opinion on that."

She rolled her eyes. "Whatever. Your memory is obviously a little bit lacking."

He chuckled. "I thought I saw Levi come through this

place this morning, but I can't be sure because, boy, that man is a far cry from the kid who used to hang around the house all the time."

"It was Levi. You didn't see much of him toward the end, when he headed into the military, but he's definitely the same person. He came to visit his brother."

"Good. Family should stick together."

After that, things returned to more mundane business about finances, and she told him about Morgan donating money to help a couple more people get the treatment they needed.

He beamed. "We need more people like him," he said. "Many people are in need."

"Even if we had all the money in the world, we wouldn't be able to help them all," she said. "We have to be realistic. We'll help those who we can."

"Who's coming next then?" he asked. He picked up his cup of coffee and sipped it, staring at her over the rim. "You know how I like to know who's coming in."

She shook her head. "You're just seeing how many more friends you can make out of the new patients. Soon, but no idea how soon will be Brock Gorman, Cole Muster and Denton Hamilton and hopefully Elliot Carver. The first three need financial assistance."

He frowned. "What's happened to the insurance companies these days?"

"The military is handling Denton, but he's not quite ready to travel, and Brock has a lot of medical insurance but not quite enough to cover our place," she admitted. "But with Morgan covering the balance for Brock and all of Cole's fees, we should have all three men in soon. They were in the same arm of the military, and they know each other. I was hoping that being here with friends would help them push each other into better circumstances.”

“I agree, in theory, but we don’t have three empty beds, do we?”

She shook her head. “No. I have one. I’m working on getting Brock’s travel arrangements completed first, since he can essentially move in at any time. We also have someone releasing next week, so in theory, we could take Cole too. But as far as Denton is concerned, we could be looking sometime weeks away.”

“Have you considered bringing in more staff?”

“I don’t have much choice, seeing as Susie and Dennis handed in their notices.” She propped her chin on her palm and rested her elbow on the table. “Susie’s returning to school.”

“Why is Dennis leaving?” her dad grumbled. “I really like that man.”

She chuckled at her father’s indignation. “Because he and Susie are an item, and she’s attending school in California. They aren’t willing to be apart.”

“Damn.” He stared off in the distance. “Is she picking up skills we can use later?”

“Absolutely. Physiotherapy.”

“Before they leave, make sure they know they are welcome back.”

“Yes, Dad,” she replied drily. He meant well, but he said the same damned thing every time they had a similar situation. “I doubt it will happen, knowing Susie’s family is back west, so …” She glanced at the buffet line and noticed it had shortened. “Are we planning on talking the whole night or getting something to eat too?” she asked, teasing.

He bounced to his feet. For somebody who’d been

through all the health issues he had, he moved very quickly. They were soon standing at the buffet and serving themselves some delicious-looking grilled salmon. By the time Dani had filled a plate and headed to their table, the smell reminded her just how absolutely empty her stomach was. As she sat down, she said, "I don't think I've eaten all day."

Her father raised his gaze. "What? You have to start looking after yourself." He lifted his fork and shook it at her. "Don't make me sic the staff on you and have them remind you all the time that you can't neglect your own health."

She shuddered. "Please don't."

As they sat there, talking and enjoying dinner together, she glanced around the dining room, feeling a sense of pride in all they'd accomplished. Sure, there'd been a lot of hiccups along the way, and more hiccups could certainly appear in the future, but for the moment, things were doing rather well.

"You have a look of satisfaction on your face." Her dad's voice interrupted her musings. "What's up?"

She put down her fork, and reaching across the table, laid her hand on his. "Just thinking about this special project you started way back when and how fantastic it's all turned out," she said warmly.

He laced his fingers through hers and squeezed them. "I couldn't have done it without you, girl."

"Well, it's been a team effort getting it this far."

At that they both quieted and ate their meals. It wasn't long before she stood up to head home and turned to her father. "You coming home tonight?"

"Of course I am. Just as I do every night, but in the meantime, I'll go downstairs and take a look at our four-legged patients."

She stopped gathering their dishes. "I'm out of touch today. Did we get somebody new in?"

"Well, a rosy boa who's got a way-too-long slice on its back," he said. "And we have a Maine Coon cat that looks like he's been through more than his fair share of troubles. The team'll have to work on taming him in order to change his ways, although that crippled back leg will halt his hunting days. Treatment will be difficult because he can't be touched easily." Then he gave her another bit of news. "We got a little filly in today. Less than a year old."

She raised her eyebrows at that. "Normally I know when horses are coming in. Why wasn't I told about this one?" she asked in surprise. Then shook her head. "Listen to me. Like everyone isn't run off their feet already."

"I think everybody considers this one theirs," he said with a laugh. "She's small, beautiful and loves people."

"Where is she?"

"In the back stall all by herself, but old Maggie is in the stall next door to keep her company."

"Can't she be in the same stall as Maggie?"

"She likes people, but she's not sure about other horses," her father said. "It looks like the owners kept her in the house, and so all she knows is people."

"Well, come on. Let's go see her." She hated to think of a horse being kept as a pet. They were meant to run free and to be wild. Or at least pastured where they had lots of room to move and run with other horses.

She quickly walked over to the elevators. She admitted to being a little miffed at not hearing about the horse earlier. Normally Stan would have done that right off.

When she reached the vet's office, with her dad only a step behind her, Stan was looking stressed and harried and had his hands full with a monster-size cat. Her father raced forward and grabbed a second towel to help wrap up the critter's legs.

Stan stepped back with a relieved laugh. "Good timing. This guy just about got the better of me." As it was, his arms showed signs of the cat's displeasure.

Dani walked over and gently held out a hand to the cat. With his arms and legs bundled up in the towel, he couldn't scratch her, but she wasn't sure if he wanted to be petted or if he just wanted to take off her hide. However, he accepted her caress and a quick scratch behind his ears. His eyes were still wild-looking, but he was calming down.

"What's wrong with him?" she asked.

"Broken back leg that healed crooked. It's causing all kinds of damage on the joints."

"I heard that another horse was on the premises." She glanced over at Stan. "Is that true?"

He lifted his head, a confused look in his eyes. Then his gaze cleared, and he said, "Yes. I meant to let you know earlier, but my day's been like this since I first arrived."

She nodded. "I suspected as much. What's wrong with her?"

"Nothing and everything." He shook his head. "She was treated as a pet until they realized they couldn't keep it up. Her hooves are in rough shape. They are still so soft, and unfortunately one of them is cracked, so we'll work on that. She's also very skittish about other horses, having never been around them."

Dani couldn't imagine. "I'd like to see her when we're done here."

He waved her off and said, "You don't need to stay. Go down and visit her. Her name is Molly."

With a glance at her father, she smiled and left them to it. That tomcat wasn't interested in having anybody look after him, whereas Molly appeared to be very much a people-person. Dani walked to the attached stables where Maggie had her permanent home. The older horse would be close enough that Molly could see, hear and touch her on the nose, if need be, at least until they saw how Molly handled being with another horse. Dani came around the corner to look into Molly's stall and spotted a pair of crutches leaning against the barn door.

Her heart raced. She had deliberately avoided him all afternoon and evening, but was it possible …? She leaned over the half-door to look in at one of the prettiest little fillies she'd ever seen. Even more heartbreaking was the sight of the big man sitting at her side, gently brushing her, with a look of absolute adoration on his face.

"Hi, Aaron. I wasn't expecting to see you here."

HEARING THE FAMILIAR voice, Aaron turned to study Dani, her gaze locked on the little horse in front of them. He remembered her being one of those horse-crazy girls back then. He could just imagine how this little heartbreaker would affect her. "I heard about her earlier," he confessed. "I couldn't *not* come down and see her."

"You get to spend as much time with the animals as you can manage without avoiding any treatments," she said with a laugh, not moving any farther.

"You coming in?"

"Maybe I should just leave the two of you together," she admitted. "Sometimes the animals are the best healing force we have."

"That doesn't mean there isn't enough to go around." He motioned toward the door. "Come on in and say hi. This little girl's Molly."

"How's she getting along with Maggie?"

On cue, Maggie's head popped over the side. Then she gave Molly a nicker. Molly nickered back.

Now *that* was a good sign.

He watched with joy as old Maggie gently dropped her head over the stall to make sure the little one was doing okay. Molly hobbled over to the side and leaned against the wood so Maggie could get as close as possible.

Instead of walking to Molly first, Dani headed to Maggie and gave her a good scratch and a cuddle. "You just love new ones, don't you, Maggie? The eternal mother, that's what you are."

"That's a good thing because Molly could sure use some guidance." Aaron looked at the small animal, a flash of pain crossing his face. "Whatever possesses people to treat animals as if they're humans? This horse lived in the house, going up and down stairs and had a bed."

Dani shook her head. "I can see people doing things like that when the animals are small and adorable, but very quickly it becomes impractical, and it's not healthy for the animal, never for a horse. What do you do when she reaches Maggie's age?"

"It's ridiculous."

He sat back and watched as Maggie gently cuddled with the filly. One of Molly's hooves was bandaged, and she'd need some rehab work, but she appeared to be in good health otherwise. "At least she didn't stay there very long."

"Exactly." He reached over and grabbed a crutch, and

using it as a lever, he rose. With his other crutch, he hobbled to the gate. He went to open it but found Dani there ahead of him. She opened it up for him and then followed him out, closing the door on the two animals.

"They're beautiful," she said. "Both of them."

"Especially right now. That connection. That bond. They don't care about the garbage that came with each other. They don't care about likes, dislikes, pain or fears. It's just all in the moment for them."

He felt her gaze searching his face and realized he had revealed a little too much of his personal thoughts.

"Too bad we didn't know that," she said, injecting some humor into the conversation. "All those years ago, when we knew each other. And yet, we *didn't* know each other or how much things would change since then."

"But none of it's baggage we have to bring forward."

"We're not the same people we were back then."

"True enough," he said with a note of bitterness in his voice. "No matter how much I try not to dwell on it, it's hard not to."

"Molly's lost a lot too. Just like you."

He waved an arm. "You think I don't feel guilty because I'm bitching and whining, and yet I'm so much better off than so many people? The thing is, it doesn't make it any easier. I'm still missing a leg."

"Did you know Stone's missing a leg too?"

He turned to stare at her. "What?"

She nodded. "You didn't notice it because his prosthetic limb fits so well that he moves easily. He's gotten so used to it that it almost doesn't matter to him anymore." She shrugged. "I'm sure he went through hell in the beginning. I'm sure there were long days and dark nights when he wished things were different, but he's back in action, doing exactly what he's always loved doing."

Aaron set his crutches to the side and rested his arms on the stall door. "I remember hearing something about that," he admitted. "But when I saw him, he looked so natural, so normal, that it never occurred to me. Most of the time I'm fine. It was just a leg. I can replace that if I need to. Once I get these back muscles fixed and the last couple surgeries done, I'll be good to go." He paused for a moment. "Honestly I feel more positive than I did before. A lot of that is thanks to this place, but at times, I feel the loss so much more, like I'll explode from the fallout."

"Of course you do," she said in a quiet voice. "It's important to honor that loss. But then it's just as important to pick up and move on."

"You must think I'm a fool."

She walked away, her hand reaching out to pat him on the shoulder as she went past. "No, I think you're just at a point in your life when you have to decide if you want to move on or if you want to stay stuck and wallow."

Maybe it was her words, maybe it was the note of rebuke he heard in her tone, or maybe it was the pat on the shoulder that reminded him of the last pat she'd given Maggie as she walked away, but he snapped, "I'm not a pet."

She turned and bunched her hands on her hips, glaring at him. "You certainly aren't. You're more like a caged grizzly."

He reached out and grabbed her hand, jerking her toward him, but she shook herself free from his grip and snapped, "Don't you dare!" Images of Jim flooded her brain.

"Don't I dare what?" He glared at her, then saw something in her expression. He frowned now, considering her reaction. Although, to her, right now, she probably didn't note the difference between his earlier glare and his thoughtful frown.

"Don't treat me like that." She shoved her face into his, her gaze hard. "You don't have the right to push me around."

His eyebrows rose. He hadn't done it roughly. But what he intended to do probably wasn't a good idea either. Still, her rage didn't stop him from trying. Like with any abused animal, he slowly reached out to Dani and tenderly placed a hand at the back of her neck and pulled her inexorably toward him. "I wasn't pushing you," he said softly. "I was pulling you."

When her face was right next to his, their noses almost touching and his warm breath against hers, he whispered, "I would never hurt you. I just want to kiss you." And he gently covered her mouth with his.

# Chapter 10

JUST BECAUSE, DEEP inside, she had been hoping they'd get to this point didn't mean she was ready when it happened. Of course, it took a heightened event—a fight—for them to cross the line and to show their true feelings. Still, she wanted this, and she'd always been an all-or-nothing kind of girl. She threw her arms around his neck and returned his kiss.

Instantly his arms closed around her like a vise. His fingers widened on the back of her head to shift her position so he could take better possession of her mouth. Dani felt like she was drowning in joy when the sound of a cough interrupted them.

"Sorry, you two," Stan said brightly.

Instantly they broke apart.

"I should check on Molly before I hopefully go home, sometime soon."

Flushed and overheated, Dani pulled her hair back in a nervous motion. "Sorry for blocking your way. I have to get home too." She quickly brushed past the two men. Belatedly she glanced around and realized, with great relief, that her father wasn't here. If he'd come with Stan, she'd never have heard the end of it.

She kept to the less-traveled routes to the center and let herself out the back door. Well past time to go home. Her cheeks were hot and flushed from the kiss, and emotions raced through her. What had she done? Although she was blasting herself for overstepping the line, she couldn't regret the moment. Now she knew Aaron cared. Now she knew he was interested. She could work with that. She was patient. She could wait until he was ready for so much more.

She ran toward home. The sound of Midnight moving in the side paddock caught her ear. She walked over to the horse as he neared the fence, and she threw her arms around him in a big hug. This was what she needed. Her old friend. She had spent hours sharing her lost and broken loves with Midnight. Now look at her. For so long, she had been afraid she'd never find true love. Afraid it had just passed her by. She'd watched all her friends get engaged, get married and have children while Dani had had a few relationships but never found *the one*. She admitted to herself she'd worried it was too late, and she'd missed out. Maybe now she could finally have that relationship she wanted.

Instantly her critical side stepped in. *Whoa, Dani. You've been here before. You thought you had that relationship a time or two already. Take it easy. Go slow. If you're lucky, this will be your second chance with Aaron. But don't count on it. He walked out of your life ten years ago, and you didn't see him again until now. What's to stop him from walking away once he's back on his feet and healthy again? Are you prepared to give your all, only to turn around and not see him again for another ten years? If ever?*

The trouble was, she was prepared to do exactly that. But was he?

Two good legs would've given Aaron the same fast exit it had given Dani. Instead, he struggled to get his crutches under his arms while Stan stood nearby, grinning at him like a fool.

"Don't make too much of that," Aaron warned.

But his words went unheeded as Stan's grin widened. "How would you expect me to take it?"

Hobbling away as quickly as possible—without looking like he was escaping—Aaron threw back, "Just a kiss between old friends."

"I don't know why you'd want to fool yourself," Stan said, "but there's no way in hell *that* was between old friends. That was between new lovers. And congrats, by the way."

Aaron stopped and slowly turned to look at Stan. The man was still grinning at him. "What do you mean, congrats?"

"Dani hasn't had a relationship in over a year. Her last breakup was pretty ugly," Stan admitted. "We've all been keeping a close eye on her, but she hasn't let anybody else get close." He pointed at Aaron and said, "You're the first one. So you can bet we'll be watching."

"So then, what's with that congrats?" Aaron said drily. "It sounds more like a warning to me than a wish of good fortune."

"It's only a warning to treat her right," Stan said quietly. "Her heart is solid gold, and she's helped a ton of people here."

Aaron studied the older man's face and nodded.

He'd turned to leave again when Stan called back, "Did I hear something about you'd planned on being a vet?"

Aaron snorted. "I see the rumor mills are just as bad here as they are elsewhere."

"Worse," Stan said cheerfully. "But, if that's true, do you want to help down here sometimes? I could really use it."

Aaron laughed wryly. "So it's not about whether I was interested at one time in being a vet but more of whether I would volunteer now."

"Both work for me if I get some extra help." Stan shrugged. "These animals need love and attention. I only have so many hours in a day."

"Don't patients upstairs come down to help out?"

"Patients and staff," Stan said. "Of course it's a mutually beneficial arrangement."

"So you still need more people, or are you just offering me something to do with my time while I'm here?"

Maybe his tone had come out a little too harsh because Stan leaned against Molly's stall door and crossed his arms over his chest. "So don't come." He shrugged. "No real skin off my nose. But anybody who's watched you with the animals can see how much they affect you. So I guess it's not an olive branch but an invitation. If you'd like to spend time with them, then do. If you don't want to, then don't." Stan gave him curt nod of dismissal and walked into the stall to check on Molly.

Aaron hesitated. He'd let his irritation get the better of him. And felt like a heel. Just because he had his issues didn't mean he could snap at everybody. He thought about apologizing to Stan and then wondered if not better just to let things lie. Depressed again and hating that sensation of having done wrong, he started to leave. Something he'd been trying to do for the last ten minutes. But then his conscience prodded him, and he couldn't let things end on this note.

He turned and hobbled toward the stall door. Quietly he watched as Stan checked over the little filly and then put his arms around her to hold and to pat her. The filly buried her face into him and nudged him with her big nose.

It was a special moment. One Aaron was glad to see. Because Stan was right. Aaron did love animals. Abruptly he blurted out, "I'm sorry."

A look of surprise on his face, Stan turned toward him. "No need to apologize. I understand. If it will make you feel any better, this place is full of other people who have been wounded in more ways than one. The animals help. If you already have an affinity for our furry friends in the first place, it's not a bad way to train for a new career."

Aaron winced. "That's a lot of years."

"Were you planning on doing anything else during that time?"

He'd heard similar lines before from various people but this time it struck home. "I do have a Bachelor of Science degree," he said quietly. "I've never applied to vet school."

"When, and if, you're ever ready to take that step, we'll write a reference letter for you," Stan said with a smile. "God knows we could use another vet around here." He straightened and faced Aaron. "When you're more mobile, I could use an assistant too."

"That's a very generous offer."

"I can train somebody to do the work I need done. I can't train anybody to have the same affinity with horses and other animals that you do. That's a natural gift you have. Something you should be proud of."

"It would be nice to be proud of something," Aaron replied drily. "When life kicks the shit out of you, it's good to find something to help hold you up."

Stan grinned. "I don't know your story, and you don't have to tell me, but I do understand the man who stands in front of me. So, whatever the hell is bothering you, you either need to fix it or move past it. A whole life out there is waiting for you."

On that note, Stan exited the stall, secured the door and headed toward the outdoor exit. He gave Aaron a brief wave. "See you tomorrow."

Aaron made his way upstairs with Stan's words ringing in his ears. Was it even possible to consider his suggestion? It would be a long commitment, but would that matter when it was something Aaron had always loved and had hoped to do? He'd turned his back on that dream to go into the military. To follow Levi's steps and to prove he was as good as his brother. Aaron had taken to the career well. But life was different now, and it was time to bring out the other dreams and to see if they still held the same magic.

He stared down at where his leg used to be and realized that many of his issues were more mental blocks than anything else. Nothing was stopping him from leading a more fulfilling life. It was all about his mindset, his attitude. If he could deal with those, going back to school would be an option … or rather it might be a necessity, given the fact he had to create a second career for himself now.

So why not become a vet? Why not make one of his biggest dreams come true? Of course his mind immediately jumped to another dream he'd had for years.

Was it possible that after all this time a relationship with Dani could come true too?

# Chapter 11

T HE NEXT SEVERAL days and the following weeks settled into a routine. Dani stopped by to see Aaron in the mornings when she first arrived, spending a few minutes laughing and joking with him, before heading to her office. Out of habit, she would check to see where he was and what he was up to at lunchtime. Sometimes they connected to sit together and eat, and sometimes it didn't work out. But, as the days slipped by, she realized just how much their moments together meant. She'd catch herself staring into space with a silly smile, thinking about him, completely ignoring the work in front of her. Like now. She gave her head a shake and laughed. "It's like you're a damned teenager again, girl."

Her father popped his head into her office and studied her face. "Glad to see you looking so happy today. Can you share the joy?"

She grinned. "No way. I get enough teasing around here as it is."

"So does this have something to do with Aaron?" he asked with a chuckle. "All the wagging tongues say so."

"So I hear," she said. "Maybe it's just nice to spend time with an old friend."

Dad walked in and sat down in the spare chair. "Hardly an old friend, my dear. An old flame maybe."

"No, a crush. He never got to the flame part, remember?"

"That's because you were hanging around Levi so much. I bet Aaron hated that. Probably figured you were his brother's girl. Nothing like jealousy to come between siblings."

"He barely knew I existed," she said, shaking her head. "Besides, that was a long time ago." Truthfully she knew he had liked her a little back then. Over the last few weeks, they had talked every day, and she had to admit to loving the blossoming relationship.

The only dark spot was the lack of any follow-up on Levi's part. Her hand itched to pick up the phone and call him, but she held back. He'd call her when he knew something and was ready to share.

In the meantime, Aaron had made tremendous progress. She'd originally booked him for six months at Hathaway, but she didn't think he would need all that time. At that thought, the corners of her mouth turned down. She had no idea what she would do when he left. It was a good thing—he would be able to move on, but what would that life entail? And maybe more importantly to her, who would he move on with?

"Have you discussed his future with him?" her father asked curiously. His head tilted slightly, as if he'd get a better view of her reaction that way.

She cast her gaze to her cluttered desktop and shook her head. "No. It's too soon."

"No, it's not," he said with a smile. He stood and added, "It's never too early for something like that."

Walking toward the door, Dad turned and said in a quiet voice, "Loving Aaron will never be easy. He's a complex, difficult man, who has a lot of issues from his military years and who now sees himself as less than complete. Even when he gets his prosthesis and is fully functioning, even with his back fixed, he'll never feel like he's whole. It'll take a lot of effort on your part to make him feel that way." He hesitated. "Just make sure you're ready to take that step. It could take him years to get over what he's been through. He might never overcome his wartime experiences."

She understood where Dad was coming from. He had been there himself. And he cared. She smiled warmly at him. "It *will* take years for him," she said. "That's okay because I have years of experience here and a lot more years of personal experience with you."

A chagrined look came over his face. He scuffed his shoes on the floor as he shoved his hands into his pockets and said, "I guess I was quite a trial, wasn't I? I'm sorry about that."

Dani rose and rushed to him, almost knocking her chair down in the process. "Don't think that. Never. It was a difficult time for you. The worst part for me was feeling so helpless. All I could do was lend emotional support or hopeful words, encouragement."

He reached out and hugged her gently. "You did a damned good job. I hope Aaron won't need as much for as long. He's a young man, and he's healing beautifully. I'm sure he'd heal that much faster with a lovely young woman at his side. I just don't want you to get hurt again."

She looked up into his eyes and said, "I don't want that either. But I think it's too late. I already love him." Quiet for a long moment, she added wistfully, "Maybe I always have."

ONCE AGAIN, THE days fell into a simple pattern—therapy, lunch with Dani, exercise, more therapy, and then, if Aaron was lucky, he caught a glance of her at the end of her day. If he was even luckier, he got to spend the evening down with Stan in the vet clinic and with Dani herself.

They fell into an easy camaraderie. Something was developing that was precious. Something beyond his expectations. Something that was beyond what he'd hoped for. What he thought couldn't happen in his life anymore. His world had been so black. He'd been so full of loss and anger and grief that he hadn't seen there was light. That there were people who didn't care about his leg, or his disability, or the fact that he wasn't as strong and big and healthy as he used to be. She had known him back then. She knew him now. Apparently, she still liked him. How lucky was he?

He still had lots of questions about being with her. There was also fear. What if he didn't like those answers? He didn't want to push it. An idyllic bubble was surrounding them right now, and for once, he didn't want to blow that. Fantasies were only possible as long as one could still believe. Reality was going be a bitch, if it turned out to be something different.

He could feel himself getting stronger, day-by-day. A little more adept—a little more comfortable with the reality of crutches and wheelchairs. At that thought, he laughed.

Dani was walking at his side as they headed toward the pool, and she smiled and said, "It's nice to hear your laughter, but what was that all about?"

He explained. "The new leg alone was interesting. I can see unlimited potential for design creativity, to make these legs a work of art. I used to do metalwork way back when in high school." He remembered that he'd loved it.

She cast a look at him and said, "I remember you brought home a candleholder or something one time, and it broke."

He stopped and stared at her as the memory slammed into his mind. He laughed again. "Okay, so maybe I wasn't so good at metal art, but I enjoyed it."

After his swim, they headed outside to where the horses were. Molly was in the pasture with Stan. Her hoof was healing, but she was confused by fences and by the different bushes in the paddocks. Aaron still couldn't believe somebody had kept a horse in a house. What was wrong with people?

"She is beautiful," Dani said happily. "I'm so glad that when we first converted this place just for Dad's recuperation, we kept the space for the animals intact."

He turned to look at her. "How did that come about?" He waved an arm and said, "It's a great pairing, but at the same time, not exactly what most people would think to do."

"It was a former veterinary school, which offered very specialized training. The doctors and residents were housed upstairs, and a full veterinarian clinic, including a surgery ward, was on the main floor." She turned to look at the buildings and fields around them. "When it closed and fell into disrepair, the property dropped in value. At the time, my father was desperately in need of something to help him through his pain, his loss and he bought it. Because the upstairs was easier for him to navigate, he set up in one room and brought in physiotherapy on a regular basis. A local vet asked about using the existing facilities for his practice, which started the animal side of things. The vet worked downstairs, and the animals came and went on a regular basis. Then two of dad's cronies moved in, and the physio-therapy part increased, and it just evolved from there."

"It's nice to see what you started with grew into a business with your own two hands."

"Actually it snowballed," she confessed. "Luckily Gram was here for him at the time as I was studying business. Each week when I came to see how Dad was doing, I realized this place had changed him, given him a whole new lease on life. Plus, he was getting stronger physically. I decided to stay and commit myself to the project with him. Now look at the place," she said with a big smile.

"It's pretty amazing," Aaron said. "I'd love to have been a part of this. Of the development and construction."

"There were days, weeks, where I didn't think we'd make it."

"It's not just a business—you're helping people, and you're helping animals." He turned, leaning his back against the rails, and stared up at the massive two-storied facility. "You even have room to expand, if you need to."

She laughed wryly. "I'm not sure I could handle much more."

A waft of warm air hit the back of Aaron's neck. He turned to look at Maggie behind him. He reached up a hand and gently caressed the older mare. "The animals need help just as much as people. Your place here is massive."

"Yes, it is." She studied the building. "Dad's responsible for bringing in some of the modern facilities, like the pool, and the handicap ramps and rails. Everybody deserves a chance to heal in whatever way they require."

He nodded and gave her a small smile. "Well, I do appreciate it."

She smiled back, slipping her arm through his, and said,

"Good. How about we get a cup coffee before I head to my place?"

"How about we take that coffee and go to your place?" he said with a laugh, knowing it wasn't possible, might never be.

She grinned. "Wishful thinking on your part, mister. No undercover activities for you for quite a while." She gave him a comic leer.

He chuckled, relieved to see he could joke about the subject. "Undercover? I don't think I've ever heard it referred to in that way before." He rolled it around on his lips and said, "But I do like it."

"What, the activities or the word?" she teased.

He leaned in and kissed her gently on the cheek. "Both."

She smiled and kissed him directly.

With the sun going down and his heart hammering against his chest, this was as poignant as it was beautiful. He reached up to cup her face. He turned her slightly and kissed her properly. Deeply. Passionately.

When she responded with a fiery heat of her own, he spun just enough to pin her against the fence, his body holding her captive in his arms. He shared a little of his passion. If she had any idea how much he wanted her, she'd run for the hills. As she met him kiss for kiss, as her arms reached up and around his neck to hold him close while her hips pressed tight against his, he realized she was a perfect match for him in every way.

Then he felt something else. Something he hadn't felt in a very long time. He withdrew his lips and crushed her against his chest. He'd been afraid for so long his body had forgotten how to make love. Maybe he was injured to a point where the doctors hadn't even been aware. Like something was wrong with him mentally or physically or emotionally, and therefore, he'd never make love to someone again. But the proof was in his arms as his body responded in the most satisfying way.

Overwhelmed, he buried his face against her neck and just held her close.

## *Chapter 12*

*WAS HE CRYING?* She wasn't sure what was going on, but something major was breaking for him. He held her so tight, as if he would never let her go. She reached up to stroke his cheek, and sure enough, she felt wetness at the corners of his eyes. That made her heart ache all the more for him. She wrapped her arms around him and hugged him close. Finally he regained some control and released her. He stepped back slightly, a bit of a cocky smile on his lips, and leaned on the fence. "Sorry. That went a little further than I intended."

She smiled up at him. "Nice to know that much passion is on the inside." She reached out and stroked his bottom lip.

"Hey, that's my line," he said with a smile. "If I ever get out of that hospital bed permanently, you know what's coming."

"When you leave that hospital bed," she teased, "you know exactly where I live." She patted his cheek. "It will be months yet as nothing should distract you or slow down your healing process. And on that note," she added, "I'll head to my cabin." She reached up and brushed a gentle kiss across his lips, then turned and left him staring after her.

It was a beautiful evening, but she had shivers racing up and down her arms, which she tucked against her chest to hide. She just needed a few minutes alone. The passion they had shared took her by surprise and frankly shook her to her core. She'd always thought they'd be explosive if they ever got together. Yet, she'd never expected them to be a couple, so she hadn't had any real hope of that evolving. Now it was all she could think about.

She was sure she wouldn't get any sleep tonight. That man was lethal. And she couldn't be happier. She'd also felt his response to her and had wondered if that had been part of his overwhelming emotion. One day he might tell her. In the meantime, she'd do what she'd always done and just accept every step of progress he made with gratefulness.

She wasn't a prude, and she'd been through enough herself. She also knew she couldn't just go to bed with somebody without caring, without that emotional connection. She'd been there, done that and regretted every last minute. But she'd also been to bed with men who she had thought were forever, and that hadn't worked out so well either.

As a young girl, a teenager on the brink of womanhood, she'd attended all the parties and get-togethers where everyone went for the easy sex. That was the reason she'd ended up with Levi. He'd been interested, but she hadn't been, not in that way, and somehow they'd still remained friends—a friendship that had lasted as he went through several girlfriends over time. He'd watched her go through half as many boyfriends.

She'd been a good girl—the sweet, simple innocent girl on the block. Growing up, Gram had been the strict moral influence in her life with black-and-white views of what was right and what was wrong. Dani had been terrified of having sex because of Gram. It took Dani a long time to take that step. She figured Gram was watching over her and would poke her in the ribs—like she used to all the time—and say, "Stop that!"

On the other hand, Aaron had been a party animal. That had never appealed to her. She had been raised differently. But coming of age with two very sexual males, Aaron and Levi, had been an alluring temptation to change her way of life. Still, she knew better. The only way to protect herself was to back off and shut down that part of her. It had worked well.

She went to college and found someone she cared for, and she thought that was it. They had a year-long relationship, and, just when she thought he would ask her to marry him, he broke it off instead.

She'd been devastated. It was a hard lesson, but one she'd learned from, and she went on to several other relationships. Another one almost ready for that wedding ring. Her father had hated that man—Jim. Dad had tried so hard to stop her from marrying the wrong man.

She wondered if she was just getting too old for relationships. "On the shelf," as her grandmother would've said. Maybe she needed to just accept her life as it was. She shook her head. Like hell she did.

Aaron had always been the one who made her pulse jump. When he walked into a room, she lost the ability to speak coherently. Levi had laughed at her. The last thing he'd wanted was her hooking up with his playboy brother. So he'd done his best to keep them apart. Maybe that had been a good thing. Back then, it wouldn't have been so sweet. But now she wasn't that same foolish girl, and Aaron was no longer the playboy, and she really liked what she had discovered about him.

She was glad they'd had these months together, getting

reacquainted. They would have been more perfect if Levi had found something about Cain. Dani believed it was a necessary step for Aaron's healing. She just didn't know how Aaron would react if there was no happy ending. Would it keep him down for the rest of his life, or would he finally put the past behind him and move on?

Heavy questions. She knew from her own experience that men dissatisfied with life became very difficult over time. That was why Jim had gotten more and more abusive. It had started out small, with just insults and comments about not looking after herself, or not wearing makeup and not caring enough to pretty herself up for her man.

She shook her head at the hard memories. Now she knew he'd simply been grooming her to accept even worse treatment down the road—because, of course, it had gotten worse. Much worse. At that time, she was working at the center full-time, and Jim was a mainstay here. Everybody else wasn't happy about their relationship, but very few said anything to her about it. When some did, she didn't welcome their criticism. Of course she didn't—she was in a relationship, looking forward to getting married and maybe starting that family she wanted.

The abuse had worsened. A couple people told him off, and Jim got belligerent and ugly. He had his revenge in private. He'd been living with her, in her house, for six months. She hadn't realized just how much the stress had affected her until her father took her to one side and said she had to stop.

"Don't you see what's happening to you? You've lost weight. You're jumpy and timid. You're easily startled. A door slams, and you're ready to break apart." Dad shook his head and wrapped his arms around her. "Dani, I love you. I can't stand to see you tortured this way. Get rid of him."

"It's not that bad," Dani whined.

"How bad does it have to get?" her father snapped. "He beats you, and the next time he could kill you." He shook his head. "I've already lost your mother. I couldn't lose you too—and never that way."

At that point she could see the fissures in Jim's personality. Then they quickly became major cracks. She just didn't know how to heal them. She had tried to explain this to her father, but he'd been adamant.

"There is no healing this. It will just get worse."

She looked back over that long year and had finally become aware of the slow and insidious increase in abuse, which she'd learned to accept. Then came the final straw for her. They'd had a fight. A huge fight. He'd beaten her thoroughly this time. When he stormed out of the house that night, he had tossed all kinds of insults at her. She picked up the phone and called 9-1-1, asking for both an ambulance and the sheriff, and finally called her father.

Jim remained in jail, somewhere in the middle of the country. She hoped he never came back. She'd done everything she could to make sure he stayed where he was for as long as possible.

Thankfully he hadn't broken her body physically that night, though God knows she had plenty of bruises and sprains and dislocated fingers and even one shoulder. All that was truly damaged was her trust and her heart and, of course, her soul. She'd come to understand the healing effect of the animals because she'd spent more time downstairs with them than she had upstairs in her own medical bed. She had needed that. Later she'd emerged feeling a whole lot more balanced. Capable of smiling again, even though she still didn't talk about it. Her father had brought it up once or twice but only as a sign that she was handling life better now.

How interesting that he hadn't said anything about Aaron. Because, yes, Aaron was dealing with some difficult stuff, but she didn't see the same issues of abuse inherent in him—despite his own father being abusive. After all, Levi wasn't like that. Maybe she should ask her father, just for added confirmation. If she had listened to his advice about Jim in the first place, things wouldn't have gotten so bad.

As she walked into the house, she found her father sitting in front of the big picture window overlooking the complex, holding a cup of tea. She walked over and sat down, slipping her hand into his free one.

He looked at her for a long moment and then said, "You've been looking very happy these last few days. What's bothering you now?"

"Earlier you said Aaron would have a hard time adapting." She searched his eyes. "Did you mean he would end up like Jim?"

He placed his cup of tea down, his eyebrows shooting upward. "Oh, my dear, no. No, not at all. I don't see the same abuse or violence in Aaron. Believe me, if you were falling down that rabbit hole again, I would have said so immediately. No. That's not it. What I do see is self-incrimination. He blames himself for something terrible. Like he's a prisoner to this issue. He has to let it go, or he'll never be happy. And, by extension, you won't be either."

She reached her arms around her dad and hugged him tight. "I thought about Gram today," Dani said as she settled in her chair next to Dad. "I miss her."

Her father smiled. "She was a force, that's for sure."

"I'm grateful she helped raise me," Dani said. "I'm even

more grateful she was there when you were sick. Because I didn't know who else to turn to. Without her, I would have been lost."

"You and me both," he admitted. "In my darkest days, she swung the light so I could find the way back. I knew, deep down, that I needed to be there for you, but she had to point that out to me." He shook his head. "She never let me forget it was my duty to make the best of every day and to not just walk away because it was easy." He laughed. "Sometimes nothing was easy about my life, but you? Well, you are truly a blessing."

He grabbed her hand again. "This is the happiest time of my life now. You have put so much life and energy into this place," he said. "To see all of it coming together, and to have all these new friends coming to this place, then going on to have full and satisfied lives … Well, you should be happy with what you've accomplished."

She smiled and shook her head. "This isn't what *I* accomplished, Dad. It's what *we* accomplished."

They sat in companionable silence for a while, looking out the window as the sun slowly settled over top of the complex. Just when she thought she might get up and make herself a cup of tea, he asked in a low voice, "What will you do when it's time for him to leave?"

She settled back into place. "What do you mean?"

He turned to look at her directly. His gaze was clear and honest but also searching as he studied her. "His life isn't here. He'll leave and pick up the pieces of wherever his life was. Will you stay, or will you leave?"

She stared at him in astonishment. "I'm not leaving. I'm not going anywhere."

"Aren't you?" he asked quietly, sadly. "What if it's the

only way you can keep Aaron?"

She stared at him in stunned amazement. It had never even occurred to her, but it was possible Aaron would need to leave. If that happened, what would she do? Her voice low, she gave her dad the truth. "I have no idea."

AARON LEANED AGAINST the fence, watching her as she walked toward her house, her trim figure moving smartly. She stopped to caress one of the horses, who nickered at her across the fence. He smiled. She did love animals.

The center was an ideal place for her. This was where she belonged.

As soon as that thought crossed his mind, he shuffled around so he could stare out across the fence and horses. If this was where she belonged, it followed that she wouldn't be happy if she had to leave. Could she leave? This was her place. Not like she could just sell her shares and move on. Although she could hire a new manager fairly easily. But she and her father had fashioned this place into what it was today.

So what about him then? Was he thinking about a permanent relationship with her?

No doubt that he wanted more, but he was hardly a good bet. He didn't have a job. He was settling into his physio and scheduled for a minor surgery here. Martha, one of the team, had intimated that after a couple tweaks on the stump, he could have a different—better—prosthesis made. In other words, he was healing. He looked forward to a future that wouldn't require him to stay here. But if he wasn't here, then how would he carry on a relationship with

Dani? If he wanted to further that relationship, how did he stay here?

He stared out across at the pasture, tormented by the unending thoughts. His surroundings were truly stunning, but what did he have to contribute? He was a soldier. A fighting machine. Or, at least, that was what he had been. He didn't have very many skills that he could convert to a civilian life. He understood he was at a crossroads and capable of making his own choices right now.

Stan had said he could use the help, but that didn't mean the center could afford to hire somebody. It was one thing for Aaron to stay here and help out while he was a patient, but it was an entirely different matter to help out afterward but not get paid. That obviously wouldn't work either. How could he live with himself if his wife supported him? He was all for women's rights, sure, but that "kept man" scenario wouldn't work for him either. He needed to at least help financially in a relationship and be a fully independent, contributing member of society. He didn't care about who was the so-called breadwinner of the family, but he needed to know that, should anything happen and the center be forced to close down, he was fully capable of supporting her.

Just thinking about the word "wife" made him feel warm inside. Was it even possible? With a final glance at the fields, he realized no answers were out there, so he grabbed his crutches and slowly made his way back to his room.

He hoped his brother would call soon. He opened his wallet and pulled out the only picture he had of Levi. After a decade of hoping to never hear his brother's voice again, all he could do now was wait and stare at the phone, wishing that something would finally break for him.

He sat down on the bed, only mildly tired. He was getting stronger. All because he was here.

The center had a hell of a system. How he'd gotten in, he didn't know. With his upcoming surgery and the cost of the prosthesis … The military had covered him for months, but then he'd been informed he was now down to his disability pension. Just what did that mean? Seemed to him the permanent loss of his leg—not to mention the end of his military career—entitled him to some permanent benefits. He would make the needed phone calls tomorrow to see where he stood. After that, he could plan. Maybe he would go back to school. He'd saved for years, but would it be enough?

Then again, maybe there was no money for such dreams. He didn't know if any navy benefits would allow him to rehabilitate himself into a new career—or if grant money was available for him. But it was certainly worth asking, and for the first time, he realized he would ask. He'd let life run its own course for a long time. Now he would pick up the reins and direct the way he wanted to go.

Soon he was in bed, pleased and happy to see that his body was not totally exhausted this time. When his phone rang, he checked the caller ID. *His brother.* Excited, yet nervous at the same time, he pushed himself into a sitting position and answered.

"Aaron, it's Levi."

Levi's tone was grim, and Aaron's heart sank. "I gather there's no news?"

"There is news," Levi said cautiously. "Your MIA buddy might not be MIA. We've got word he's in Afghanistan, operating as a mercenary."

Aaron straightened. "You ran him down?"

"Not yet," Levi cautioned. "But the intel seems good. We've spoken to a friend in Africa who has contacts there. With any luck, we can talk to him."

"Even if you do, no way he'll tell you the truth. It's not his style." Aaron knew that fact, to his own detriment.

"Yeah, but we're hoping somebody will talk to him and gain his trust."

Aaron was silent, thinking about Levi's suggestion.

Then Levi added, "This issue could take a little bit longer to resolve than we'd hoped."

"And therefore costly," Aaron said flatly. "I don't have any money to help pay for this."

"I didn't ask for any money," Levi snapped. "Just pulling in a few favors. No money's exchanging hands here at all."

Aaron took a deep breath. "Good to know," he said in a more neutral tone. "I'm a little sensitive on that whole charity thing."

An odd silence hovered on the other end, but then his brother didn't know him anymore either. Had they ever known each other?

Levi remained silent, so Aaron continued. "Thanks for the update. Let me know if you track him down in person. Even proving he's alive would be a big help. The navy didn't believe me when I said Cain had walked away. If they catch him, that proves one of my statements, and maybe that will give credence to the others as well."

"Will do."

Aaron stared down at the phone in his hand, excitement surging through his system. It would be hard to sleep now because not just excitement bothered him—there was anger too. To think that asshole had created a whole new life for himself, with no repercussions for his actions, was untenable.

No way could Aaron let that continue, but without proof, he couldn't move forward.

*No money had changed hands.* Good. He didn't want to be beholden to Levi in any way. He didn't want to owe anybody and definitely not his brother. It just went back to that whole sibling rivalry thing, having an older brother looking after him. At this point, he wanted to be his own man. Hell, he already was his own man. He didn't need his brother's charity.

He didn't need charity from anyone.

Except that small voice in the back of his head told him he *was* already accepting his brother's help. That finding Cain was charity on Levi's part. But Aaron had damned-well accepted it as his only option. Yet, he also recognized how it was very good of Levi to even consider this.

Then he understood. If somebody had treated Levi that way, Aaron would have stepped up too.

Reminding him, blood *was* thicker than water.

T HE NEXT MORNING, Dani stood in the doorway of Aaron's bedroom. She found it empty, even though it was earlier than normal. Frowning, she went to the reception area and on through to the dining room, built around a big circular layout. No matter which direction she took, she would end up in the big open space where breakfast was being served. She studied everybody seated at the tables but still saw no sign of him. Trying to appear casual, she poured herself a cup of coffee and wandered onto the deck, searching. Maybe he'd gone out with the animals. She'd done that a few times, particularly after a bad night. The animals offered comfort that few humans could because along with that comfort, they didn't add judgment. What a glorious feeling to know they accepted you and didn't care about the other issues in your life.

She took the stairs down to the lower level and heard a splash in the pool. Then she knew. He'd gone for an early morning swim. With a bright smile on her face, she walked to the edge of the pool and studied him. He'd either had a hell of a bad night or had woken up to a hell of a bad morning because he wasn't just swimming, he was driving his body forward, forcing it to be stronger. She'd never seen him swim this hard or this fast. A relentless determination was in his strokes, as if he could outswim something bothering him.

When he flipped and turned at the far end and came back and then repeated it again and again and again, she knew something was seriously wrong. With her heart sinking, she sat down casually to wait. When he finally broke off and stopped, his lungs were heaving, and he gasped for air. She waited for him to turn and look around, only he didn't. He rolled onto his back and did a lazy backstroke to the shallow end. There he pulled himself up and sat on the side of the pool.

"Good morning," she said in a low voice.

He turned to look at her, but no smile was on his face. From the fatigue in his muscles, it looked like he'd overdone the swimming too.

"That was quite a swim you just had," she said in a neutral tone.

He shook his head. "I don't know about a swim, but it felt like the devil was chasing me." He grabbed his towel and quickly ran it over his face and his upper body. He maneuvered to the bench and pulled himself up. There, he strapped on one of the early prosthetic prototypes, with extra padding around his stump, and grabbed his crutches, just in case. He slowly made his way to her.

As he grew closer, she saw his hands trembling. She quickly got up and pulled out a chair for him. "Sit down," she scolded. "You've overdone it again."

He shook his head. "Did I?" He gave her a lopsided grin and said, "It's probably a good thing. Tough night. I needed to work off some frustration."

She slowly retook her chair. "What brought it on?"

"Levi called me." He studied the coffee cup in her hand and then looked at the stairs, as if contemplating whether he had the energy to make the trip.

She kept her gaze on his, her heart tingling in worry at the thought of what Levi might've said. "And?"

Aaron shrugged. "Some intel came back saying the asshole who did this to me may be working as a mercenary in Afghanistan."

Her mouth dropped open, and she stared at him. "Oh, my God, that's wonderful news!"

He stared at her moodily. "Is it? So he has gone on to live the life he wanted, with no repercussions for his actions, and yet look at the end result for me ..." He pointed to where his leg should be.

She reached across and covered his fingers with hers. "It also means that, if anybody can catch him, they can prove he isn't MIA and that you didn't lie."

"That's what I told Levi. But it still doesn't mean Cain will admit to what he did. Because, of course, why would he? He killed two US soldiers."

She gently stroked his hand, trying to find the right words to help him deal with this. She now understood the drive behind the swimming. Maybe it'd been the best thing for him after all, but he'd obviously overdone it because he was shaky and exhausted. "Do you want a cup of coffee?" she asked.

He shook his head. "No more making it easy on me. If I want coffee, I'll get up the damned stairs and get coffee. Bad enough Levi's doing this instead of me handling it."

"You have a real problem with charity, don't you?" she asked quietly, her heart sinking. If he had any idea what she and Levi had concocted between them to get Aaron here ... She finally understood just how big a problem that would be for him.

He stared at her, silent.

"Maybe you should change your perspective on that and see it as a helping hand," she pressed on. "If people don't know you're in need, they can't help. Sometimes they have to be told."

"I don't want to accept a helping hand."

"Nobody wants to be in a position where they have to accept a helping hand," she retorted. "But you, my father and even I have all done it when necessary. So you accept it. You get back on your feet, and then you move forward. If you can pay it back, you do, and if not, you accept that you will turn around and help somebody else when the time is right." By now her voice had turned hard and snappy.

She liked a lot of things about Aaron but not his "poor me" attitude. He would have to get over that damned fast because she wouldn't take much more of it. She also knew fear was driving her because once Aaron found out about Levi paying for his brother's stay here, the shit would hit the fan. And she'd be part of the fallout. If that was the case, she would do all she could to push this guy, mentally, physically and emotionally. Then he could move on to have a good life. Even if that meant without her.

But instead of her words spurring him into action, he studied her, his brows knit together on his forehead. She realized she'd opened a can of worms she hadn't meant to.

"You never mentioned you were here in a hospital bed."

She sat back and gave him a cool stare. "Why should I?"

At that he had the grace to blush. "I'm sorry. That's your private matter. And I'm being a bit of a bear, aren't I?"

She gave a serious and decisive nod. "Yes. Lots of people are here to help you, but they can only help you if you're willing to accept it. There's not always a price tag for help in this world."

She picked up her cup, finished it and said, "I'm getting a second cup of coffee." With that she turned and walked up the stairs. She didn't look to see if he was following her. If he didn't want any more help, that was fine with her. She wouldn't deliver any more cups of tea or coffee, even though she had no problem with that. Because to her, that wasn't charity. It was being kind. Being nice. She understood he hadn't had a whole lot of that in his life. But that was no excuse. It was time he learned.

"SHIT." HE STARED at Dani's retreating back as she took the stairs. He'd certainly pissed her off and only now realized how he had offended her about helping people. That was what she did at the center. Here he had this opportunity, and instead of appreciating what he had, he was getting his back up at the thought of the least bit of charity. Like when she'd bring him a cup of coffee. Which was often. Since when had that become a charity thing? He felt like a heel. At the same time, some residual anger about Cain still ran through him. He'd also overdone it in the pool, and he knew therapy would be a bitch today.

But it wasn't—it was much worse.

As if understanding how emotionally messed up he was today, the physiotherapist focused those negative energies of Aaron's into working on his back with some weight-lifting exercises. There'd been such strong promise lately as Aaron could feel his strength building up, slowly but surely. The pain had even eased, but right now, Shane was all about getting down to the meat and working those muscles hard.

Then the physiotherapist said something magical.

"If you keep up progress like this, you may not need that surgery at all."

Aaron turned to stare at Shane. "It's a possibility?" He would do anything to avoid that surgery.

"We weren't sure you'd need the fifth surgery when you got here, and now that your muscles are strengthening and building up, there's a good chance we can fix this without more invasive cutting and stitching," he said.

Aaron bowed his head for a moment, giving silent thanks for this.

Then he went at it hard again.

If he had any hope of getting back to where he was before—strong, agile and fit for duty—even though, with the missing leg, the military would never accept him now, he would still do his damnedest.

He wouldn't fail because of a lack of effort.

When the session was done, he stood, wavering on his foot, sweat dripping off his face, goose bumps popping up all over from the supreme sense of power rippling through him.

"Massage time. You need a heavy, deep one today."

"I do. I can feel the muscles trying to knot."

"Well, we're not letting them. Let's go."

They moved over to the table where Aaron took off his shirt and wiped the sweat from his body. The window was open, letting in a cool breeze. The therapist had left, and Aaron knew Chuck would be in soon. He was a hell of a masseur, and he and Shane took turns at the different shifts.

Stripping down to his boxers, he rolled over and let his body flop on the long bench. Even that hurt like shit. He had overdone it.

But if it got him back to health—without more surgeries—then it was all worth it.

Chuck came in a few minutes later and worked Aaron's muscles deeply, kneading to release the tension and knots. The worst massage session ever. By the time Chuck was done, Aaron wanted to cry with relief.

"Sauna, then shower. Let those muscles rest. We'll skip this afternoon's physio."

Chuck walked to the door and then turned back. "Next time you need to work off some frustration, ease up before you trash yourself. We can't have you slowing your progress with an injury."

*Injury.* Odd, Aaron hadn't even considered that. If a pulled muscle could easily sideline him, or much worse, if that muscle was in his back …

For the first time he understood how stupid his frantic swimming session this morning had been. He'd wanted to release that building rage, but he hadn't thought it out.

As someone … maybe Dani … had said, it was all about balance.

# Chapter 14

G OOD THING SHE had a ton of work to keep the niggle of fear and resentment at bay. She knew how detrimental negative thinking was. The rules were no different for herself than anyone else here.

"Dani?"

She looked up to see Stan in the doorway, a hesitant smile on his face.

"What's up?"

"I wondered … if you have a moment, could we talk?"

"Sure." She waved at the chair opposite her desk.

He closed the door. "I know there are programs for those who don't have enough money to come here, and you tap into those all the time, but do you know of any for retraining some of the men?"

She frowned, her mind running across the various programs. "A lot of grant money is available, but each has a set of criteria to be met in order to apply. If they are veterans, some money is there, but they'd have to go through their own channels for that."

"Right." He looked out the window. "I was thinking about Aaron."

"Oh," she said in surprise. "Is this something he's been talking to you about?"

"He always planned to go to vet school, but after his

mother died, he ended up in the military. Vet school would be four more years."

"He is a veteran, so money could very well be there for him to achieve those goals," she said. "But it's not that easy to get into the program, is it?"

"He does need references and preferably some work experience, but no reason he can't do it." Stan shrugged. "He's a young man, and this would give him a wonderful future, particularly as it was his original passion."

"What is it you want me to do?"

Stan stared at her. "I can see this relationship developing between you two. Has he mentioned anything about his future?"

"Not really." She shook her head again. "I don't think he can see that far ahead yet. He's waiting on a bigger issue to be resolved first. In a way he's completely blocked until it is."

"Oh."

"And again why?"

"Well, I offered him some hands-on experience helping me here. And, since I'm on the board, I wondered about writing a recommendation for him."

She raised her eyebrows. "It would be a nice thing for you to do, but maybe you should ask him about it first. Because if it's something he's only considering but isn't serious about, then there's no point putting in the effort."

Stan stood and said, "I was hoping you'd bring it up with him and see what he says. Because what he tells me might be something different than what he tells you."

She considered that. People often did just as Stan had described. Sometimes they were just making conversation and didn't understand how somebody else perceived their words. She nodded. "Okay, I can do that."

Stan's expression became one of relief. "Thanks. Of course I can't guarantee he'll get in. But if you would agree to let him do volunteer work here, then it would help his chances. Like you said, there are ways to make it happen, but I don't want to be pushing myself in where I am not wanted."

She agreed with that part. The only person who could answer these questions was Aaron himself. It wasn't a light undertaking to go to veterinary school, involving years of dedicated hard work and effort. So it had to be something he hadn't just casually tossed up in haste. He needed to commit himself to a major undertaking. She agreed with Stan in the sense that, if Aaron wanted this, there were ways and means to make it happen.

Of course she also had to pick the right time to discuss it with him. She wasn't sure that was right now. She knew today was a positive step forward after hearing Levi's news, but she could understand how it would bring up a ton of negative emotions for Aaron. She stared down at her coffee cup and wondered if she should check in on him. It was almost four o'clock.

He'd had a long hard day already. She picked up her coffee cup. His room was in one of the short side hallways, so she couldn't casually walk past. She headed straight there but found the door shut. She frowned and checked the schedule on the door, but he didn't have anything noted for right now. It also didn't mean he was inside. She knocked once, then twice. No answer. She turned and headed back to her office. He might be sleeping, or he could be visiting with others. No way to know. However, if she wanted to track him down, she knew of one very likely place to find him.

She caught sight of Shane at the front desk, talking to

one of the new girls.

A lot of the staff members were single, and bringing in just one new person always caused a shift in the energy of the place. So far Melissa seemed to be working out fine. She'd been to hell and back herself because of a car accident, so she certainly understood what rehab entailed and could empathize with everybody in the center. To date her sympathy had seemed genuine, as well as her interest in everyone's well-being. As long as she was capable of doing the job, Dani couldn't ask much more of anyone.

Shane noticed Dani and headed in her direction. "Hey, Dani. How's it going?"

She leaned against the doorjamb of her office and smiled at the man who'd worked for them for five years now. He was very popular with the patients, considered a hard taskmaster but fair, which was a great balance for the residents. "Not too bad. Aaron really knocked himself out in the pool."

"He sure did. Physio was pretty rough on him afterward too. I believe he's sleeping right now." He shook his head. "I suggested speaking with his counselors before next week, so he could work through some issues. Obviously something prompted the hard swim this morning."

"That was a good suggestion. Hopefully he'll take you up on it." She doubted it, but she was willing to give Aaron a chance to prove her wrong. He couldn't stay stubborn all his life.

Just most of it.

Considering his day, and not having touched base with him earlier, she hung around the office a little later than normal, then walked through the common room to see if he'd shown up yet. When she saw no sign of him, she headed for the dinner buffet and studied the patrons. It was early yet, so not too many were eating, but the ones who were appeared to be enjoying it. She walked along the buffet, just to see just what was on offer. She found it hard to resist the fragrant baked ham and roast beef right at the end. Maybe she'd eat here after all. She smiled up at the chef. "This looks awesome, Gabriel."

He smiled back. "Grab a plate and sit down and enjoy. You work too hard."

She laughed and shook her head. "Why do you keep telling me that?"

"You know it's true." He didn't give her much choice. He lifted a plate from the stack and served her a slice of ham and a slice of roast beef. He nudged her down the aisle. "The broccoli in cheese sauce just came out of the oven. It's good."

It was hard to refuse at that point, so she helped herself to a serving of the vegetables and sat down on the deck. She was hungry, having foregone lunch. She had to get out of the habit of missing meals. No food, just work wasn't how it was supposed to be. As she enjoyed her meal, a shadow fell across the table. She looked up to see Aaron.

"Do you mind if I sit?" His voice was gruff.

Before she had a chance to answer, he sat down—heavily. She looked at him in concern. "Are you sure you shouldn't go back to bed?"

He raised his head and glanced her way. "I'll be fine," he muttered. "I need to eat so my muscles can heal."

Definitely a day where he had done too much. Even his voice was heavy and tired. His face had no color, and his lips looked bloodless. Alarmed, she said, "Part of me wants to get the doctor."

She was already out of her chair when he stopped her.

"No doctor. I'm fine. Just tired. I wouldn't object to a cup of coffee though, if you don't mind."

She poured him a cup, at the same time snagging a small plate and picking up two cream puffs. Depending on where his blood sugar was, these would help him. She brought his snack and drink to him, relieved to see he looked a little better now that he was resting. Obviously the trip from his room to her had been enough to wear him down. That wasn't good. She'd hoped he'd made better progress than that by now.

She placed the cup and plate in front of him and sat down to finish her food. "I guess you won't be going for another crazy swim again anytime soon."

"No," he said. "This'll set me back a few days."

"Only a few days? Good," she said with a bright smile. "Nothing you can't recover from, and now you better know your limits."

He looked at her for a long moment and then smiled. "You're always optimistic. You see sunshine and roses instead of the reality."

"It's only your reality if you let it be," she replied calmly. "I prefer—no, I choose to—see the bright side. There is enough negativity in my world. I don't need any more."

He devoured the two cream puffs and then slowly sipped his coffee as he watched her eat. "Dinner looks good."

She nodded, her mouth stuffed with broccoli. He glanced over at the buffet table. She could see him contemplating getting there on his own. She swallowed and said, "Give me a minute, and I'll get a plate for you." She watched his mouth open to protest. In a low, hard voice, she said, "Remember, there is a time to accept help."

He stared at her and then slumped in his chair, resting.

"Thank you. I think I will accept your kind offer."

She laughed. "That was hard for you, wasn't it?"

"Damned right it was." But he had a big grin on his face.

HE WATCHED HER leave. She was just so damned nice, he felt like he had no business being beside her. She was so clean and fresh and honest, and he felt dirty. This stain on his soul—would it ever get clean? Levi and his people were doing their best to track down the man responsible. As a last resort, they might end up forcefully capturing Cain. As far as Aaron was concerned, they could kill the bastard, but Aaron wanted Cain to come clean first, and Aaron wanted the proof to go to the brass upstairs.

For all he knew, the brass had changed. Very likely the people who thought Aaron had lied weren't even around anymore. He stared down at his clenched fists. So close and yet so far away. It was all out of his hands. That was what got to him. He could do nothing to make this any better. He couldn't grab his old buddy and pound the truth out of him. As far as Aaron knew, his brother was probably the best person for the job, but what if even he failed?

How helpless would Aaron feel then?

Yet, he couldn't have asked more of his brother. Still, the waiting, sitting and more waiting were killing Aaron, even though he had a wonderful place to do it in—a supportive and strong place, helping him get better day by day. However, in his anger, he had set back his progress. His ire was to be expected, after getting the news he had. Even now, the tension still ran through his muscles, even after swimming too hard, lifting weights too heavy. Aaron knew better—

now—to push his body further.

His brother was doing what he could. All Aaron could do was sit back and wait.

No, he needed to do what he could do – and that was heal. The truth, while it would set part of him free, getting healthy, strong and fit again, well, that would offer him a whole new future.

# Chapter 15

DANI WOKE UP to birds singing and sunshine floating into her bedroom. She bounced out of bed, had a quick shower and dressed, then raced to the center. She was eager to see Aaron, but then this had been her routine for weeks.

She hurried through the center, waving happily and calling out morning greetings to everyone in her path. She stopped at her office to confirm she had no emergency messages, and then she carried on to Aaron's room. It was empty, but then that was no surprise. He'd been steadily gaining in strength and doing a lot more every day. She grabbed a cup of coffee and walked onto the deck. "Good morning, George. Have you seen Aaron?"

George smiled at her and said, "Last I saw him, he was with your father, and things were looking pretty serious." He shrugged his shoulders and said, "Aaron didn't look upset or anything. Just looked like he wanted answers."

"Answers?" she repeated back.

But George had no further information. She looked around but found no sign of either man. Feeling slightly worried, she wandered down to the pool level, searching for them. No sign. She walked through the doors and found the two of them sitting at one of the poker tables where her dad played a lot.

The conversation did not look good.

With a sinking heart, she probably understood exactly what was going on. She walked straight over and placed her cup down and sat. "Good morning," she said with a forced cheerfulness. "I've been looking all over for you."

Silence reigned.

She studied her father's face, but he wouldn't look her in the eye. She turned her gaze toward Aaron and found him glaring at her. She raised her eyebrows. "What's the matter, Aaron?" She kept her tone pleasant but cool.

"Why didn't you tell me?"

"Tell you what?" She frowned, not willing to confirm anything—yet.

"That I'm a charity case here?"

"No one is a charity case here," she replied, adding a bite to her tone. "That just insults everyone."

Aaron's glare deepened. "Who is paying for my care here?"

"A donor, who asked to remain anonymous." She crossed her arms over her chest and glared back at him. "You might want to consider that you're one of the lucky ones."

"Or you might want to consider I won't like what's going on here," he shot back. "If not, why didn't you say something about it at the beginning?"

"*Because* the donor asked to remain anonymous," she repeated. "*Because* we didn't want anything to slow down your healing." She leaned forward, into his personal space. "*And* you might want to consider that you've come a hell of a long way very quickly. Where else have you had such success?" She paused, giving him ample time to reply.

He settled back against his chair, looking like he wanted to say something.

She sat and waited. Inside, her heart was breaking, but she was resolute. Donors were an important part of this project, and she couldn't have him getting on his high horse just because somebody had offered to help before he was ready to accept it. "We ensured that *nothing* slowed your progress down."

"You lied to me."

She gasped. "I did not."

"Yes, you did. If not in actual fact, then in concept." He sneered. "Is that the only way you can get a man? Pick one who's not quite whole and have him see you as a savior? Well, I don't need a helping hand from anyone. Especially not you." He stood up and hobbled shakily out of the room.

Dani sat there, her breath shaky, as she watched him exit.

Her father reached across the table and grabbed her hand. "Give him a chance to get over it," he said in a soothing voice.

She shook her head. In her mind, he was an idiot not to see the great advantage he'd been given. If there was one thing she hated, it was a lack of appreciation for receiving donor money. She could deal with not being appreciated herself, but she sure as hell thought Aaron should appreciate the rare gift he'd been given. "There shouldn't be anything to get over. It's his damned pride and ego. He needs to take a step back and let that go."

"Whoa there, Nellie," her father said in a reasonable tone. "I know you can understand when a man is down as low as Aaron was, the only thing he has is his pride. His ego keeps him propped up. Inflate that ego a little more, and he can face the world with a big smirk and an 'I don't give a shit' attitude. But if you take that away ..." He patted her hand and nodded to himself. "Just give him some time. Wait for this to all blow over, and he'll be fine."

She doubted it, but even if he did get over it, would she? It didn't matter. Nothing else could be said at the moment. She deliberately turned the conversation to different things until she finished her coffee. Then she stood, dropping a kiss on his forehead. "Thanks for always being here, Dad."

"I didn't want to be here this morning, to tell you the truth. But he cornered me."

She gave him a big hug. "He had no right to do that, but as we know, he's not been thinking things through lately."

She picked up both of their empty cups and returned to the dining area. She placed the cups on one of the trays for dirty dishes and headed to her office. Her relationship with Aaron had shifted and would never revert back. *He'll leave now.* She stood at the window and stared out at the horses. *This is where I need to be regardless.* No way would she tell Aaron who his benefactor was because it would just make him angrier.

In her continued desire to help him, she had found herself caught between a rock and a hard place. The principles of the center were very clear. When a donor asked to remain anonymous, she did just that. She wouldn't violate such a request. Since the funds came from a friend of hers, she was doubly invested to keep his secret. Which would make it just that much worse from Aaron's viewpoint.

Levi had called her, thinking her place could help Aaron. She had agreed. She wanted to help. Levi had offered to pay outright, even though she had explained their four-patient policy for pro bono treatment. She'd transferred Aaron here to offer him the best of the center's abilities, and yes, she'd been curious. Once upon a time, Aaron had been such a driving force in her life that she'd wanted to see him again. But that was not how business decisions were made here. So, at Levi's request, she'd put his brother's file before the team for approval. They had all gone over Aaron's history and each had given the go-ahead. The team had said yes, and they had the needed funds. All Aaron had to do was get better.

He had done that in spades. She just didn't know what he would do now.

How stupid she was to get involved with anybody at the center. She buried herself in work for a few hours, until a knock came at the door, and she looked up to see Dr. Herzog. She smiled at him, but he didn't smile back. She leaned back and crossed her arms. "What's the problem?"

He took a hesitant step inside the door and said, "Aaron Hammond requested a transfer out."

Dani stilled the knots in her stomach, even though she had expected this. It came as a shock regardless.

"Did he give a reason?" She hoped he'd kept their relationship out of it because she still had to work with everybody in a professional capacity, and it would be damned hard to do if they thought she was the reason behind a patient's transfer.

"Something about not being anybody's charity case ..." Dr. Herzog's voice trailed off. "I asked him to explain, but he went silent." He came farther into the room and sat in the guest chair. "He's done really well. We've been thoroughly impressed with his dedication to his own healing. Whatever's going on right now, it's not good. It's better if he stays here for at least another month, but if he wants to go, we can't stop him."

She nodded. "Do you think it'd do any good if I talked

to him?"

"He asked specifically that nobody talk him out of it."

She pulled a pad of paper toward her. "Where does he want to go?"

The doctor stood up, relief evident in his voice. "I don't think he has any idea. Maybe you can make a few phone calls and find a place for him?"

She nodded. "I can give him the general contact information for the VA office. Once he's settled where he wants to be, they can tell him which VA hospital would be nearest to him."

Dr. Herzog nodded back. "I guess that's the only option he has."

"His problem is somebody generously donated for his care. Yet, he got his back up when he found out." She shrugged. "It's his option to return to the VA hospital. His choice."

After the doctor left, she sat there, frozen for a moment, figuring out what her own options were. She still couldn't tell Aaron about Levi being the donor. And it no longer mattered because Aaron was leaving anyway. However, she could do one last thing. She reached for the phone. When a woman's voice answered, she said, "Ice, is Levi there? I need to talk to him about his brother."

Levi came on the phone. "Dani? What's up?"

She tried to explain, but when grief overtook her, she began to sob.

"I'll be there in the morning," was all Levi said.

She hung up the phone and wiped away the tears. She needed to get out of here. She needed to go someplace where her love and affection would be accepted and not rejected. The animals. She stopped in little Molly's stall, delighted to see her now snuggling up against Maggie. The two enjoyed seeing her. She spent several minutes cuddling them both and then walked out and did the rounds. Enough animals were here that any time she needed to mend her broken heart, they came willingly. How sad that she was likely to be here every day for a while now.

Still, she'd been in this position before. This was nothing new. She would overcome it like she had everything else. Feeling a tiny bit better, she walked home. Tonight she just wanted to be alone.

ANGER STILL BURNED through Aaron. He pushed himself harder and felt heavier than he ever had before. Every one of his team told him to ease back and take it easy, but he just couldn't. It burned him to think he wasn't here just because his VA benefits covered it. The knowledge that he was here because some unnamed person had paid his bill churned in his gut. A charity case! He was damn sure nobody's charity case. He had money. Maybe not enough money for this, but he had money to go to a decent center. Sure, he'd received great care here, and he'd enjoyed his time, but that didn't mean he couldn't get the same care somewhere else. That was what his VA benefits were for, right?

Nobody needed to pay for him. He'd always been capable of looking after himself. Even when he got to his room last night, he hadn't been able to resist doing sit-ups and push-ups. Now it was morning, and he had essentially had no rest. His stomach churned, his head was heavy, and he kept feeding it with more anger. Because the only thing he had left was anger. Betrayal was something he'd lived with for so long that, sure, maybe he was looking for it in other people, but ... he hadn't expected to find it anymore. Not really.

He'd thought she was different.

But just like his best friend who had blown him to shit over in Afghanistan, she'd blown him to shit here on home soil. He couldn't accept that.

A hard knock came at the door. He considered ignoring it, when it came again. The forceful knock made him realize he couldn't evade the upcoming confrontation. That was just fine with him as he was spoiling for a fight. If anybody from the center tried to stop him, well, they could get the hell out of his way as he was leaving as soon as he could. Today if possible.

"Come in," he snapped, ready to stand up to whatever was coming.

The door slammed open, and Levi stepped inside—a very cold and angry Levi.

The surprise at seeing his brother pushed Aaron back to the bed. Suddenly, he was afraid this had something to do with the favor Levi was doing for him. "What's the matter?"

Levi turned and slammed the door shut, before confronting his brother. "You're the problem."

"What?" Aaron frowned at him, anger churning in his gut again. The temper that hadn't been very far under the surface since yesterday was firing already. "What are you talking about?"

In typical Levi fashion, he didn't hold back. "How dare you target Dani for your little pricked ego. I'm the one who hooked you up with her center after the grapevine told me about your tirade at Walter Reed, needing 'a change of scenery.'" He took a breath. "I knew how much progress the patients here were making. So I'm the one who paid for your care here. I'm the one who asked Dani to not tell you. You have a problem with that, then you tell me." He took three steps closer to his brother and glared at him. "I'm right here. You want to take a swing at me? Do it. Get it out of your system. But it'll be a long, cold day in hell before I let you blame Dani for something you should be thanking her for, and on your knees while doing it. So stop acting like a pissed-off child, throwing a temper tantrum."

Aaron's jaw dropped. He shook his head. "Why? Why tell Dani not to tell me?"

"If you'd known I had paid for it, would you still have come?"

"No. Hell, no."

"Which is exactly why I told Dani not to tell you."

He stared at his brother. Five minutes ago, he thought nothing could have taken the temper right out of him, but Levi had shoved a fist down Aaron's throat, grabbing that fiery red ball of emotion and tossing it right out the window. Aaron sagged on the bed. He instantly realized what he had done to Dani. He'd blamed her for something she had no choice in. Because, just like Levi, when she made a promise, she kept it.

"I didn't want to be a charity case," Aaron muttered. "All I could think about was that I was no longer a man, no longer capable of standing on my own two feet, doing what needed to be done. Here people had to pitch in to treat me, bolster me so I could do what needed to be done."

"Don't be stupid. We all need help sometimes." Levi glared at his brother. "You think I liked staying in the hospital for so long? Do you think I'd have stayed if I wasn't forced to?" Levi shook his head and paced back and forth.

"Do you think Dani didn't have other people lined up to come here? Even now she has dozens of people to take your place." He leaned forward and shoved his face into Aaron's. "She did this as a favor to me. So you owe her a goddamned apology. If you don't want to be here one more day, that's fine with all of us. You pick where you want to live and transfer to whatever VA hospital you can get into. Then you can get the hell out of here." Levi waved his hand dismissively at him. "You're damned near well anyway. You could go home and look after yourself from here on out."

He turned around, slammed the door open one last time, and walked out, not even bothering to slam it closed.

Aaron was left with the shambles of the mess he'd brought on.

He stared at the empty doorway, realizing Levi would likely have gone straight to Dani. Just where Aaron should've gone first when he had questions. When he had doubts. He should've trusted that she was doing what she needed to do. Instead, he got on his high horse and ripped into her, and for that, Levi was not very happy. It was a stupid thing to do. Of course, it had taken his older brother to show him the way.

Feeling like the little boy he'd been accused of being, he slowly made his way to Dani's office, only to find it empty. He took a deep breath and realized that if he had to apologize publicly that was a punishment he well deserved. He made his way to the main buffet area and saw both Levi and Dani sitting on the deck outside in the sun. Levi was holding Dani's hands in his. It was a jolt. Nothing could've made Aaron feel more like a heel than seeing his brother comfort the woman who Aaron loved. He felt like such an asshole.

He approached them quietly. Levi looked up and glared at him. When Dani saw Levi's face, she stiffened. Aaron knew he wasn't exactly welcome. He ignored that and stepped forward.

"I'm sorry, Dani. I had no right to blame you or to push you into telling me who my donor was. But to me, it was yet another betrayal. I didn't think I could handle that again. Not from you. So Levi brought the truth home to me this visit. I am sorry." He took a deep breath. "I don't need any more physio or medical treatments that I can't get locally. I'll pack my bags and leave today."

He turned and walked away, but she interrupted him. "How could you think you're the only one dealing with betrayal?" Her voice was low and hard, but he could hear the pain in it. She pointed at Levi. "You know your own brother's story."

She stood and faced Aaron. "Now here's mine. My last relationship ripped me apart physically and mentally, but I put myself back together, and I recovered. *Here.* In a hospital bed. Just like you. But what you said to me ripped me apart emotionally, down to my very soul. I'll take a lot longer to heal from that. Betrayal is *not* a two-way street. Just because you were betrayed doesn't give you the right to treat others the same way." She glared at him. "This center is where we give to each other. Where we accept that we *all* need help. It's a place where we're free and comfortable to both give and receive charity. There is no debt. There are no checks and balances here. We're all here for one thing, and that is to help people move forward," she snapped. "The problem with you is *you.*"

Spinning on her heel, she turned her back on him and stalked away.

Aaron turned to look at his brother, but Levi was already up and following Dani.

Aaron didn't think he could feel any worse than he had before, but he was wrong.

# Chapter 16

I N FRONT OF the center, Dani watched Levi get into his rental and waved goodbye to him. He would come back tomorrow to give the good news to Aaron, but Levi had refused to share that today. As far she knew, Aaron would be gone by then, but Levi said he had faith in his brother. He was an asshole, but he wasn't that big of one.

Dani didn't believe Levi. Not after what she'd seen and heard. The little boy in her heart was gone, and the man he had become was not somebody she wanted to spend any time around. Not any longer.

"Stay strong," Levi called out to her as he left.

That she could do. She had been doing that since forever. She returned to her office. At least she had a never-ending supply of work. About two hours later Stan called her.

"I think you should come down here," Stan said quietly. "It's Aaron."

He hung up before she had a chance to say anything. She stared at the phone in her hand for a long moment. She wanted to tell him she wasn't coming, but she had no choice. If Stan had called, then it was major.

Hating the nervous panic and worry forming in her stomach, she made her way to Stan's office. She stood in the doorway. "What's up?"

He motioned her to one of the rear treatment rooms.

"Go see for yourself."

She was about to refuse, but from the look in his eyes, she figured it was easier to take a peek. She walked down to the last treatment room and looked in through the window in the door. Aaron was busy fitting a new leg onto Helga, but the dog was having none of it. She was barking and running away excitedly as he tried to strap on the prosthesis. She didn't know why Aaron was in there all alone and not with Stan, but she assumed Aaron had a decent reason.

Stan stood beside her. "He's been designing new prostheses for her."

She nodded. "Good. Maybe that will be a career option for him in the future."

"Maybe." His voice was noncommittal. He nudged her arm. "Keep watching."

She studied Aaron again and saw when he caught the dog and held her close, he hugged her tight. When he let the wiggling bundle go, Dani caught a glimpse of his face, saw the tear tracks down his cheeks.

She closed her eyes and bowed her head. Was there anything like seeing a strong man cry to make her heart break?

"He told me an hour ago he was leaving. That everyone would be more than happy to see him gone." Stan sighed. "I don't know what's going on between the two of you, but I thought you should see this." He patted her shoulder and left.

Stan's words played on her mind. Yes, she would be happy to see Aaron go, only because having him here was a painful reminder of what she had lost. And he needed a stress-free environment to finish his healing. No matter how hurt she was, she wished him well.

She realized now how long she had cared for Aaron. She

closed her eyes. She prayed that it was a year later … so she didn't have to cope with this hurt, the pain … the loss. Opened her eyes. Saw Aaron with Helga. He smiled at the dog. But Dani still saw the hitch in his breathing.

She wished Aaron could somehow wipe away her agony. She almost laughed at the absurd thought. He was the one who had caused this agony.

She didn't think he had the words in him to mend her, to fix what he had broken.

Then she saw his face as he hugged Helga close again. His tears.

Maybe he did realize how much he had hurt Dani.

Maybe he was hurting, just like she was.

Maybe he wanted her to wipe away the agony he felt. Even knowing full well it was his fault.

Wanting love with no judgment.

*Oh, my … Just like the animals give us.*

Here she had been preaching about two-way charity and missing this deeper point. *Wow.*

Both of them had to get over this for any hope of a reconciliation to come about.

Some harsh words had been spoken. Hurtful words. Definitely something she never wanted to go through again.

Either way, she couldn't let Aaron leave like this. Not with so much anger and pain. Instead of knocking, she opened the door and stepped inside, closing it behind her. Helga raced toward Dani. She laughed and dropped to the floor beside Aaron, hugging the dancing dog. "You don't even need your spare, do you, girl? You just feel so free and unencumbered without the prosthesis. You're just happy to be alive and well."

"And to be loved."

She stiffened slightly at the pain in his voice. She nodded. "I think that's what we all want," she said quietly.

"Do you?" His tone was bitter. "I'm sure any number of people who want that would love a chance to love you."

"Apparently I don't want any of them," she said, tears choking her voice. "Seems I only like pigheaded, stubborn men."

"You're better off without those types."

This time she looked directly at him. "Maybe ... but don't count on that. Because I've liked this one *very stubborn* male for a long, long time."

His gaze was deep and fathomless. For a protracted moment, silence lay between them, as if neither knew what to do, what to say.

"I'm sorry."

She studied him carefully, looking into his eyes, searching for the truth—and finding it. She sighed. "I know you are. The thing is, that was your one shot. That was the one and only time you are allowed to blame me or hold me in any way accountable for the shit in your life. No more, do you hear me?"

A slow, tentative smile dawned on his face. "I was in pain, lashing out. I didn't mean what I said."

"You drew blood. Like I said, I'm not tolerating that anymore."

"Anymore? Does that mean you have forgiven me?" he asked, hope evident in his voice.

She looked at him for a long moment, then smiled. "I was afraid you'd react this way, right from the very beginning. I wanted to tell you, but Levi was adamant. For good reason," she added drily. "You just might be a tad sensitive on that issue."

He chuckled, then snaked an arm around her and pulled her close. "Thank you," he said against her ear. "You're a very warm, loving, generous soul."

"Don't you forget it," she said with spirit.

They sat on the cold hard floor in companionable silence for several long moments, just happy to no longer be at odds with each other. "I owe my brother an apology too."

She nodded. "You'll get the chance to tell him tomorrow morning."

He looked down at her. "He's coming back?"

"Yes. He has some good news for you but figured today wasn't the right day."

"If it's good news, I have no problem waiting," he said quietly, his tone one of acceptance. "Besides, if I get to hold you in my arms like this, I'm happy to wait forever." He dropped a kiss on her temple and just held her tight. "I still won't be a good bet for a long time, you know?"

"I wasn't asking for you to be a good bet," she said. "You have a lot of decisions to make moving forward. You have a lot of things to consider. I was just hoping to be one of the things you kept in your life."

His arms tightened around her. "If you have enough patience, give me a year, or maybe longer, to get back into a proper career. I have money. Not enough to pay for this treatment, but I do have money to keep myself going. I did speak with Stan about veterinary school, and I'm certainly considering it. This could be a five-year process."

She turned to look up at him, happy for him that he was considering such a move, and unintentionally repeated Stan's earlier question, "Were you planning on doing anything else in those five years?"

He looked down at her and smiled. "Maybe one thing

I'm hoping to do soon."

She frowned. "What's that?"

He dropped his head and said, "This."

He tentatively kissed her lips, as if testing the waters. Maybe it was too soon. But when she kissed him back without feeling hesitation or fear, he proceeded to kiss her passionately and thoroughly.

When he lifted his head, she said, "Yeah, we can do lots of that but not until the doctor clears you."

Aaron snickered. "I asked him a couple days ago."

"I'm sure he got a kick out of that." And Dani would never live it down. But it wasn't going to happen here. There were some lines that didn't need to be crossed. Not when she had a house of her own close by.

Aaron shook his head. "No, I think he was half expecting it." He fell silent again. "Do you think if I phoned Levi, he'd tell me?"

She studied his face and realized he had a lot riding on whatever Levi found out. No point in waiting. That was torture. She pulled out her phone and dialed Levi's number. When he answered, she said, "Your brother wants to speak with you." She handed the phone to Aaron.

HOLDING DANI CLOSE in his arms, Aaron took the phone. "I'm sorry, Levi. I had no business acting the way I did."

Levi said, "Good … Glad that's over with."

Aaron laughed at his brother's evident surprise. "Well, not quite. I'm still groveling to get in Dani's good graces."

He dropped a kiss on her forehead.

"Keep groveling. That's one hell of a girl. You'd better

treat her right."

"I will," he promised. "She also said you had some good news for me, but you were coming back in the morning."

"I don't have to return in the morning," he said. "Now that your senses have returned, I'll tell you on the phone. We caught your buddy, on tape and over several beers, admitting to what he did."

Aaron froze and closed his eyes in relief. He'd wondered if this day would ever come.

Levi was still talking. "I've handed over the tape to the brass. They'll reopen the case and be in touch with you soon."

Aaron didn't know what to say. He choked out a simple, "Oh, thank God."

"Now think about what you'll say when they call. They owe you for this. You need to make sure you get something out of this."

"Like what?"

"Like money, for one. You don't want to owe me for your care? Then you can pay for the next man. If you need to get retraining, let the military pay. Don't enter into any conversations or negotiations without someone watching your back. Do you hear me?"

Aaron smiled. "I hear you, but I don't have anyone like that to help out."

"Yes, you do. Me." With that, Levi hung up.

Aaron slowly passed the phone to Dani and told her everything.

"Oh, that's fantastic! That should take a weight off your shoulders," she cried.

As he stared down at her, he realized how much his life had changed since he'd arrived here—and all because of her.

He realized another very simple truth.

He tilted her head up slightly and gazed into her huge chocolate-brown eyes. "I love you."

Her eyes widened, and a little gasp escaped.

"I wanted you back then too. But I wasn't the man you needed yet. It took this experience to grow me into the person you really need."

She threw her arms around his neck and hugged him close. Against his ear, she whispered, "I love you too." She pulled back slightly, tears coming to her eyes. "Since we were teenagers, you're all I've ever wanted." Dani kissed him, pouring her love and passion into that kiss.

Humbled, he could do no less than give it right back. Exactly as he'd always wanted to do.

"We have so much to talk about," he whispered in her ear. "I feel the need to prove myself to you after all this. I have ideas, plans, to run by you."

"Like what?" she asked. "I'd love to hear about them. You can tell me anything, you know?"

"I'll get better about communicating." He motioned to Helga, sensing their happiness and wagging her tag wildly, circling around the two of them, still sitting on the floor. "I'm good with animals. Not so good with people. But the only person I really need to share things with is you. So …"

At his hesitation, she frowned. "Yes?"

"Here's what I've been thinking. I should probably finish my rehab here, and my team thinks I need another month …"

Dani nodded, a big smile on her face.

"And no telling how long the navy will take to decide on the Cain matter …"

At this Dani's eyebrows rose.

"But Levi thinks they owe me some money. Maybe between that and some educational grants I hope you might help me find …"

"Of course I'll help," she said.

"I want to be a veterinarian. And since A&M is so close, I was hoping to drive back and forth."

"You could take my car. It's an automatic. Plus maybe you could run some errands for me and the center while in town? You'd really be helping me out."

He kissed her on the nose. "You bet. I've got a little money saved, but it's not enough, so I'll barter my time for your vehicle. And, in that vein, I'd like to help Stan in the vet clinic and also you in the office—I *am* a bit of a computer geek—to offset my room and board, since I'll be staying long-term. That is, if it's okay with you?"

"Yes! This is so wonderful." She was in his lap, kissing him again.

He stopped to stare at her in wonder.

"What?" she asked.

"Who knew I'd end up here with you after all these years?"

## *Epilogue*

---

*Six Weeks Later …*

DANI WALKED TO where Aaron sat on the fence. He still couldn't believe they were together. She was so damn special. And he'd been such a heel… Still he was strong and fit and looking forward to a future with her and hopefully going to veterinarian school.

He looked up and smiled, accepting the mug. "Midnight is enjoying being around the little one."

"Midnight loves everyone," she said with a chuckle. Then held out two pieces of mail.

He took a sip as he eyed the bigger envelope, from the DOD. He flashed it to her, and she nodded, patting his cheek this time. He opened it to find a licensing contract for his patent on Helga's special prosthesis. He showed Dani. "Sweetheart, I'm getting paid!"

She gasped and tried to focus on the document Aaron waved before her.

"I'm so proud of you, Aaron." She snuggled closer to him, dropping a kiss on his lips.

Then he saw the small number ten envelope with the navy's return address. He ripped it open, found the check and was speechless.

Dani raised her head. "What is it, honey?"

He held it before her eyes.

"Oh, my God."

He nodded. Looked at it again before he faced her. "I know exactly what to do with this. I want to use some of it for someone with no insurance or donation help to come to the center."

Tears came to Dani's eyes as she heard those words.

"And I want to choose who gets it. You've got four coming in a few days, right?"

She nodded, too choked up to speak.

"Any pro bono cases?"

"Yes, two," she said with a sniffle.

He smiled at her and kissed her forehead. "I'll let you know which one then." He waited as she reached for a tissue and blew her nose. "And one final piece of news."

She checked his hands, probably looking for more mail. Instead she saw the small jeweler's box. And gasped.

"Dani Hathaway," Aaron said, "you've been here for me during the worst of my days—and my out-of-control temper and ego. Now I want to spend the best of my days with you. Will you marry me?"

She was full-on crying now, hugging him close, trying to breathe through her mouth. And she was the most precious thing he had seen in his life. "Will you marry me, Dani?" he asked again.

She nodded, sniffling. "I've been waiting for you for most of my life."

THE FOUR NEWEST rehab patients arrived several weeks later, and Aaron and Dani—still staring at her engagement ring—were there to meet them. Along with George, Shane,

Dr. Herzog, the major, plus Helga, Racer, Tipler, Maggie and Molly. And so many more …

"Welcome to the Hathaway House," Aaron said, his arms spread wide. "We are all here to help in your healing and recovery. Yes even me…"

The four injured men seemed as dazed as Aaron probably was on his first day here. Then the three friends Dani was hoping to have in at the same time hadn't happened. Only one was here. But it was the one he knew. He perused the four and found him.

The first guy asked, "Where are we?"

"Texas," Aaron said with a smile.

The second guy took a 360-degree turn in his wheelchair, a blanket covering his lap but not hiding the fact he was missing a leg. He checked things out with a disapproving frown firmly in place. "You can't possibly know what I'm going through," he nearly growled.

Aaron raised his pant leg to show off his newest prosthesis. "Designed by yours truly."

The third guy was all stoic machismo silence, his one arm crossed tightly over his chest.

But it was the fourth man who asked, "What the hell is this place?"

Aaron whispered to Dani, "That's Brock. He's my guy." Then Aaron stepped forward to address all the newcomers as the words he was given on his first day came back to him. "Right now you hate this place. You want to be anywhere else but here. However, in a couple weeks, you'll never want to be anywhere else." He studied the men in front of him. "Are you ready?"

BROCK ONLY HALF listened to the conversation as he studied the man in front of him. A different man from the one he knew. Then major trauma changed a person. He didn't know the first thing about this place. And maybe that was a good thing. Maybe—if they also didn't know about him— he could start fresh.

Brock knew Aaron. Not well like many others he knew, but Aaron was a good man. A solid fighter and someone Brock could trust. If Aaron had done okay here, then maybe … And if that was the case then the rest of Brock's unit could also come. Cole, Denton, Elliot—had all been injured in a mission after Brock had been hospitalized. Brock knew Elliot the best. But doubted he'd like Hathaway House. Not his style.

Then again, Brock's unit had all changed. Who knew what lay ahead of them? What he did know was there was no going back. This was his life now—no matter how he felt about it. So far it had been ugly as sin.

He waited a moment, then gave a decisive nod. "Let's do it."

# Brock

## Hathaway House, Book 2

## Dale Mayer

# Chapter 1

SIDNEY MORNING WALKED into Hathaway House and smiled. Nine months was a long time to be away, and she was happy to be home.

She spotted Dani, the owner and manager of Hathaway, behind the front desk and made her way over. Why she was working the desk was anyone's guess, but knowing Dani, it was because somebody else had had to step away, so she'd stepped in. Dani was like that. But clearly, she needed to hire more staff to handle the administrative side.

Dani finally lifted her face and looked at her a moment, her gaze confused, before she suddenly lit up. She bounded to her feet, came quickly around the counter and threw her arms around her.

"Oh, my goodness, Sidney! You're back!"

Sidney fiercely returned the hug. That was another reason she was happy to come back. These people were her family. She didn't have many blood relatives, and the ones she did have didn't remember her, anyway. That was the sad truth of Alzheimer's. Her mom had early onset, and even though she was only in her late fifties, she had no clue who Sidney was when Sidney visited her. It just made the visits harder and more bittersweet. There was a part of Sidney that said she didn't need to bother going because her mom didn't know who she was, but then she realized there was nobody else to make sure her mom was getting the care she needed, and that if Sidney didn't keep an eye out for her, anything could happen, and nobody would be the wiser. That couldn't be allowed to happen. She loved her mom. The memory of the woman she had been couldn't be allowed to be forgotten.

She stepped back from Dani's hug and smiled. "It's so good to be back. What's different?" She leaned forward and peered into Dani's brimming eyes. Tears? But happy ones, by the looks of things. Sidney glanced around the entry and reception area, but everything appeared to be the same. She shook her head and turned back to Dani. "Okay, give. What happened while I was gone?"

Dani beamed. "One of the nicest things that could possibly happen," she said in a low voice. She glanced behind her. "I met someone." She shrugged. "He's everything I could've hoped for." Then she added, "And, I broke my own rule … he was a patient here."

Sidney's eyebrows shot up to her hairline. Not only was that something Dani had firmly said was against the rules, but many of the people here for treatment were not in the right frame of mind for a relationship. Therefore, she was hesitant in her optimism for her friend's sake. "What kind of shape is he in?"

Dani grinned. "He lost a leg in the accident that sent him here and has some damage to his back."

"And mentally?" Sidney asked bluntly. She'd never been one to hold back, and she wasn't about to start now. Sure as hell, anybody who respected and cared about Dani wasn't going to either.

"He's in a good place. I'm certain of that."

"Okay. Have you had any word from the asshole, since?"

"No," Dani said, her voice tinged with relief. "None."

"Good." Sidney had been the second one to find Dani after her last boyfriend had beat the crap out of her. She hoped to never see such a thing again, especially not when it was somebody as nice and genuine as Dani. She gave her friend an optimistic smile and said, "Well, then, I look forward to meeting this new guy."

"I want you to meet him, too," Dani replied happily. "He's visiting his brother right now but should be back in a few weeks."

Sidney glanced down at the room chart, which was open on the other side of the reception desk, and asked, "How full are we right now?"

"Full," Dani said with a heavy sigh. "Aaron moved into the house with me so we could use his room," she said blushing. "I'm really glad to have you back. We have a couple of people coming back in, looking for short-term assistance on top of a full house."

"That's unusual," Sidney said. "Of course, that means business is booming, and that's a good thing for the center but sad for the state of the world." She glanced outside to the fields surrounding the center. "The animals?"

"Well, that's increasing, too. Stan is taking on an assistant, and they're going to be doing more surgeries downstairs," Dani said with a smile. "Aaron, my fiancé, is actually finishing his schooling to become a vet."

Sidney's eyebrows popped again. Then she grinned. "Sounds like you just might like him because he can help you make the center bigger and better."

The two women chuckled. "Not likely," Dani scoffed. "Although he's helped out a ton at the center too. Been great at getting some of the new arrivals settled in. What about you, are you settled in?"

"I am. I got in late last night and headed straight to my room. I'm glad it's still there," she teased.

Dani shook her head. "I'll tell you, it was close. We were getting to the point I was tempted to set it up as a patient room."

"Yeah, but you know I always come back," Sidney said with a smile. "Is my roster full?" It was one of the things Sidney loved most about Dani and Hathaway. Employees were strongly encouraged to continue training and education when possible—and jobs were always waiting when they came back.

"Oh, is it ever!"

"You know I like the toughest ones," Sidney said with spirit. In fact, she really did prefer them that way. She was a very warm-hearted, compassionate person, but she had no compunction about pushing these men and women into doing what they had to do, especially when they needed it.

"Well, you get to start with Brock," Dani said with a groan. "He's pretty well worn everybody else out."

"What's his problem?"

"He was injured in a car accident at work, but on US soil, and he hates the fact he wasn't injured while fighting. He's done two tours in Afghanistan and one tour in Iraq and then he came home and got in a crappy car accident, which has caused all kinds of hip, back and arm problems."

"And of course, psychologically, he feels guilty and stupid."

Dani sent her a sharp look. "He's not very open to talking about it. He's big. He's strong. He came here voluntarily, as his progress had stalled, and he did better, but then almost immediately, he's plateaued."

"Lead on, Macduff. I'll see how we get along."

"Actually, I just assumed there was no getting along. You need to go in and take charge. He's pretty much sent everybody else out of there in tears."

"Oh, good. He's perfect for me then because I'm ripe and ready to get back into some butt-kicking. He won't be sending me out in tears."

It wasn't that Sidney thought she was beyond breaking down over a patient, because she definitely wasn't, but she'd do it in a different time and place and certainly not where they could see it. If he was badgering, or in any way being hostile, well, that would just get her back up.

"Do you want to meet him first or see his file?"

"I want to meet him."

Dani sent her a conspiratorial smile and said, "Let's go."

They walked down the hallway, took a left and headed down around the corner.

"He's got one of the last rooms on this side?" asked Sidney.

"Yes." Dani nodded. "He's a very heavy snorer. The patients here have enough trouble sleeping without that on top of everything else, so we had to move him down here."

"Nasal cavity issues?"

"Yes, and he sleeps on his back. It's not his choice, but with his injuries it's about the only way he can knock himself out. He doesn't sleep well."

It was often a problem with those types of injuries. People had favorite sleeping positions, but after major trauma it was often not possible to lie in that position again. Their balance shifted, affecting natural pressure points. Everything changed, and sleep often suffered. She'd have to see if that was one of the things they could get Brock to improve. A good night's sleep was worth its weight in gold.

Dani rapped smartly on the door of the last room. A growl, and then a sigh, came from inside.

Sidney heard him and snickered. It was just way too cliché. She followed Dani into the room to see a big bear of a man lying fully-dressed across his bed with a laptop across his thighs. He raised his gaze, nodded to Dani, and then looked at Sidney and frowned. She frowned right back at him.

Like hell she was going to force him into doing anything she wanted. He was going to do it because he was here, and that was what he came for.

"Good morning, Brock. This is Sidney Morning. She was away, upgrading her training and thankfully she's back again," Dani said with a smile. "She will be taking over your physiotherapy."

Brock's frown deepened. "She doesn't look strong enough to do anything. And why the upgrading? Is she not fully certified?"

"Looks can be deceiving, because clearly, you look like you should be strong enough to do everything asked of you, but you're not," Sidney retorted.

She heard Dani suck in her breath in shock. But there was no way in hell she was backing down. Brock's eyebrows rose, and the look in his eyes turned from a steely glare to a hardened glint. She smiled at him. "Now we understand each other perfectly. I'll go grab your file, update myself on how far you've gotten and I'll be back in about twenty minutes."

With that, Sidney turned and walked out. She waited for Dani in the hallway and overheard an exchange in the room.

"Sidney is one of the best physiotherapists there is," Dani said.

"Does that mean she's allowed to have a lousy bedside manner?" Brock's voice was a grumble.

Sidney snickered out loud at that. Inside, she was revved up and ready to go. She rubbed her hands together gleefully. This was going to be fun.

Dani joined her and shook her head at the big grin on Sidney's face. "You really want to do it this way?"

"Oh, yeah. We'll see how he's doing in a couple of weeks."

"Okay, if you're positive. Let's get a cup of coffee, and I'll get his file and all the others for you."

The two walked through the cafeteria where lots of people sang out greetings to Sidney. She'd always loved the people here, and they seemed to love her in return. As a homecoming, it was perfect.

They got their coffees and headed back toward Dani's office.

Once inside, Sidney sat down in the visitor's chair. "I'm really glad to be back."

Dani smiled, picking up a stack of files, including a very thick one on top, and handed it to her. "I'm really glad to have you back." She nodded at the top folder and added, "And not just because of Brock."

"You have others like him?" Sidney laughed. "Sounds like I returned just in time."

"You know normally we only have one this difficult at a time." Dani groaned. "He's the most difficult, but there are a few others that need a little something extra." She smiled at Sidney. "You have that something extra."

"I'm just me."

"That means you are just perfect for here."

BROCK STARED AT the empty doorway. He wasn't sure what to think of the new therapist. There hadn't been anything wrong with any of the others. But he certainly hadn't been motivated to do his best or give his deepest efforts. He knew there was something wrong inside him, but he'd given acting normal a good shot. He'd thought he had them fooled but apparently not.

Or they were bluffing.

Instantly, he tossed that idea out. They were all professionals here. He'd seen it over and over again. It was really himself he was trying to fool. But why? He stared down at his big hands. His big mitts. That was what his sister had always called them. He supposed they were, especially when compared to her small, long, slender fingers. But his mitts were meant for hard, physical work. Shovels fit perfectly in his hands, as did hammers and saws and any other kind of tool, but especially weapons. He'd always reveled in his physical strength—his ability to do the hard work. So many hated it, but he loved it. His body rejoiced in using his muscles, using his strength. He'd grown fast and tall and hadn't really been aware he was the tallest in the family and still growing. Then, he'd started to fill out. While he was in high school, he'd taken on several part-time jobs. Roofing was one of them, and that was because he loved carrying the big packs of tiles around the roofs. If he did nothing else but carry them up and down all day long, he was content.

His appointment to the military had been perfect for him. He'd reveled in the physical training, and he'd excelled at the mental discipline. It had been a really good fit until his accident. But now he was no longer active. They might be able to find a job for him at a desk, or in some supply office, but how did one go from being the best of the best to being … almost nothing at all?

He certainly didn't want to mock those not in the navy. It wasn't for everyone. But it was for him.

As for him, a desk job would kill him. It wasn't what he wanted to do—it wasn't what he could do, and it wasn't what he should do.

But his active military lifestyle was over. The phone call had finished it. He shook his head, staring out the window. He had been doing fine until that. It wasn't that he had felt self-pity, or had self-doubt, it was more about apathy. A lack of caring. It was like his wellness was over, so now, who gave a damn? Like he wanted to beg for a tour in Iraq he would just not come home from. Surely that would be better than the slow wasting away here.

He'd spoken with his counselor several times, but he hadn't managed to tell him about the phone call shutting down his last avenue in the military. There would be such finality if he actually verbalized it. While nobody knew, it seemed like it wasn't real. There was hope of something changing it. But of course, he was only fooling himself.

Besides, the counselor had mentioned antidepressants earlier as well. That was the last thing he wanted. That was just going to put a pretty mask on a sad situation. It was nothing he couldn't handle, but he wanted to solve the problem—permanently. That meant finding another purpose in life. He couldn't go back to the straight physical work he had been doing. And he was nowhere as young as he had once been. He was thirty-three—the navy had been the best of the best in all things. He'd been a SEAL. Achieving that status had been a crowning glory of his life. Now, it was over. He'd had six good years there. At thirty-three he hadn't been ready to leave. But life—and the brass—had decided otherwise.

It wasn't that he was fighting his physiotherapy, because he wasn't, but neither was he actively working toward his recovery. In high school, one of the classes they'd been forced to take was several weeks' worth of meditation. Now, the world was so stressful if he could relearn the basics, maybe it could help him get through this stage more easily. There had been one particular exercise that came back to him now. They had to imagine themselves in a cloud, completely surrounded by a white fog and unable see the ground or the sky. All they could see when they looked down was a few inches of tiling underneath their feet. The instructor had said they had to take a step forward. Brock had asked her how they could take a step forward when they had no idea what was ahead of them. She'd smiled and said that was the point of the exercise. One had to have faith.

He'd never managed to complete the exercise because he didn't have faith. Not in himself. He'd been raised without religion. A cocky young man who hadn't needed it. Faith was for other people. In time, he had understood. It wasn't so much about faith and religion, as it was about being able to trust. Trust that there was going to be something, or someone, there to catch him if he should fall. Trust that if his feet were standing on something solid he could find the next step he needed to take. And here he was, lying in bed again, trying to surround himself with that cloud. He needed to step forward, but because he couldn't see where he was going, he didn't know how to take that step. It was all because, of course, he had no faith, no trust that something would break his fall. He didn't even know if the direction he was going to choose was the one he wanted to be traveling in.

He knew there was something deeply personal in all of these musings. He had yet to find a truth that would help him navigate these troubled waters. He knew the new therapist was going to arrive soon, and he wasn't sure he was ready for her, either. She reminded him of one of his old military superiors. Someone so high and mighty he tried to force everybody to do his bidding just so he could feel all-powerful.

In the military, he saw all kinds of people. He had to work with all kinds of people. Maybe that was a good thing. He didn't need to do that anymore. He didn't have to take her attitude if he really disliked her. He could complain. Have one of the others again.

Yet, he'd accomplished little here so far. He had only pushed himself to a point. He had done what he was supposed to do, nothing more. He realized that as far as he was concerned, he was still standing in a cloud. If he pushed himself any harder, it was going to force him into the unknown. In which case … what if he fell?

# Chapter 2

SIDNEY STUDIED THE thick file in front of her. She was still sitting in Dani's office going over the material. There was a packet of X-rays in the back, too. She realized Brock had sustained more injuries than she'd expected. She frowned as she read the notes about the original damage. He'd been to hell and back. A wrenched back, several broken bones, ripped tendons and severed muscles. The damage extended from his central spine around to the side and even his hip flexors were a mess. She shook her head. "How long has he been here?"

"Four weeks," Dani said.

Sidney nodded. She flipped back to the beginning of the file to see the other therapy reports. He was a hard worker but only to the point he was pushed. He never gave any extra. It was like he was doing what he had to do, but no more. If they told him six feet, he made sure it was six feet, but he never did six feet and a quarter. And that wasn't good because it meant he wasn't engaged in his own healing.

She sifted through the papers, looking for the psychologist's report, and studied several of the notations on it. He had his own file he kept on every patient, but when it was necessary for the team to understand what was going on, he'd add notes to the generic case file.

Sidney didn't want to have to point out these revelations

to Brock. That wouldn't help him heal as much as if he figured it out himself. That was what this place was about—healing on all levels. Being told what to do, and actively engaging in doing what needed to be done, were two different things.

She stood with his file in her hand and said, "I'll go talk to Brock now."

Dani looked up and nodded. "Take it easy on him. He's had a rough couple of nights. Nightmares again. He hasn't been able to tell anybody about them yet. That will happen over time."

"It would be good to know if there was a specific trigger for their return." Sidney held up the file. "Not that nightmares need a trigger. They sit in our subconscious ready to rise at any moment."

"You can always ask if you find the right moment. Maybe you can get it out of him." Dani gave her a bright smile. "If anybody can, you can."

Sidney shook her head with a laugh. "Such confidence."

"And well placed."

With a last glance at Dani, Sidney walked out and headed toward Brock. It was now nine-thirty in the morning. Hopefully, he was up and doing something active. It was up to her to get him moving. She knew he wasn't going to want to be tested, to be pushed, to see how far he could go. There might be an easier way to figure out why he was holding back. She'd read every note and understood the others' take on it, but she was coming at the problem from a slightly different angle. She specialized in these big guys. They were all stubborn, but they usually had huge hearts. When they shut that down it was like everything else stopped working. If their heart wasn't in it, nothing was going to move.

She stopped at his doorway and studied him. She couldn't help the pang of disappointment to see he was still lying on the bed. At least he was fully dressed. He was ambulatory, unlike so many others at the center. He could walk on his own somewhat, with the help of crutches to ease the pain in his back. But right now he was doing nothing but staring out the window. His fists clenched repeatedly in a rhythmic movement. She didn't think he was deliberately trying to do an exercise—rather, it was emotion driving them.

She plastered a bright smile on her face, rapped sharply on the door and walked in.

"Okay, I'm back. I've got this monster of a file here, and I've flicked through some of it, but obviously, I don't have time to read it all at the moment. I will later. What I do want you to do is tell me one of the aspects you like about the physio you've done so far and which part of it you don't like."

Instead of sitting in a chair beside him she sat down on the end of his bed. He didn't shift his legs to give her more space, just stared at her with that deep, dark gaze.

As she studied him she saw the first sign of the emotional weakness. Grief.

Seeing that, she changed her approach. She went from domineering and powerful to something gentler. She didn't understand what was going on inside him, but there was something so dramatic that it had worked its way through every part of his psyche. They were going to have to get to the root of that, but she couldn't do it without him trusting her.

"It's important to discuss what you like and what you don't like, so we can work together on a program that you will push yourself on." She kept her voice neutral and in control. She studied his gaze, but it had switched back to looking out the window. "I certainly have a program we can start with, if you prefer."

Again, no answer. She bounced to her feet and said, "Or, I can be a hard-ass."

Her reward for that was a tiny sniff.

She grinned. "I guess you don't believe me."

At that, his gaze shifted back to look at her. His eyes swept her from her toes and back up again.

"You're about a hundred and fifty pounds, nowhere near my 'mean.' For all your talk, you're a marshmallow on the inside," he said. "I've been brutalized by the best. Go ahead and do your worst."

"I don't have any intention of trying to force you into a wheelchair or into doing exercises. That's not what I'm here for. I'd rather spend my time with somebody who is trying than waste it trying to get somebody to give a damn. I thought you were a former SEAL. All-in, all the time. But I guess not. You're just dead weight." She stepped forward and put herself into his line of vision. "If you don't want to be here, I'm sure we can get you the hell out." She looked down at her watch and said, "I'll be back in an hour. You make your decision. You're either in that wheelchair, ready to get down to the exercise room, or I'll tell Dani you're looking for a transfer out."

Without waiting for an answer, she turned and walked out. Like hell she was going to deal with that shit. He was either in here or he was out, but she needed to know right from the beginning. As she went down the hallway she meekly pinched the bridge of her nose and realized how quickly he had gotten to her. She could see why Dani was happy to have her back. She'd had several other difficult patients before, and they'd often refused to do very much. This wasn't a holiday. His bed was needed for somebody who wanted to have an active part in their own healing and recovery.

She poked her head into Dani's office. "I'm still standing."

Dani chuckled. "Didn't get too far the first time?"

"Actually, I told him that if he wasn't going to be taking part in getting into his wheelchair and getting ready to go do what we needed to do, then I'd tell you that you needed to do a transfer."

"If he wants to transfer out," Dani said, leaning back in her chair, her expression thoughtful, "then of course, he can do that."

"Then can you start looking into that?" Sidney replied.

Sidney walked out of Dani's office with heavy sigh. She understood they wanted everyone here to do well, but Sidney was more of the opinion they needed to help those who were ready to help themselves. This wasn't a rest home for those who wanted to retire from living. She walked out onto the deck and grabbed a cup of coffee. Yet another that she probably didn't need. Then she caught sight of the Major. She had no idea if Dani's father had officially obtained that rank, or if it had been tossed onto his shoulders as a joke at some point, but it just stuck. His face lit up when he saw her, and he opened his arms.

She put her coffee cup down on the closest table and hugged him.

"Oh, my goodness, it's so good to see you," she said with a big smile. And indeed, it was. He was brimming with health and vitality. "I can see you haven't had a bad day since

I left," she said in admiration. "You're looking very fit and relaxed."

"Doctor's orders," he said with a big grin. "Now that Dani is happily together with Aaron I can relax a little bit."

Sidney laughed. "Is this a temporary situation, or do you really think this is it?"

He lost some of his humor, and instead she saw a deeper satisfaction in his gaze. "You know, I think they just might make it. Aaron is a good man and more than that, now that he's got his own health back, he cares about others. Those here and those that want to come … He's a huge asset to both the center and a great partner for Dani."

"Then I'm jealous," Sidney announced. "Wish we could all be so lucky."

"Stick around here. I'm sure you'll find somebody to love." He nodded behind him and said, "There are a lot of men here looking for a good woman."

Sidney shook her head and smiled. "But that's against the rules, you know."

The Major waved a hand in the air dismissively. "Pshaw. Rules are sometimes meant to be broken. People are always looking for love."

"Most of the men here are looking for new lives. They'll take them any way they can get them, and that doesn't necessarily include love."

He chuckled. "Bring your coffee over my way and sit for a minute," he said, motioning to a table out in the sunshine. "Bring me up to speed. How was the course?"

She took her coffee and joined him. The Major had always been interested in everybody in this place. When Sidney finally checked her watch, she saw she'd been there longer than twenty minutes.

"You have to be someplace?" the Major asked in surprise. "Are you working already today?"

"Absolutely. Dani's a slave driver." They grinned at each other, because, of course, it was just the opposite. In many ways, Dani was too easygoing, but she had people working for her that were independent, self-motivated and driven. They didn't need mothering. They just needed to be let loose to do their thing. Sidney could count herself at the top of that list. Suddenly, her phone rang. She clicked on it to see Shane's name.

"Hello?"

"Hey, girl, I heard you just got back, but it's not like you to be late."

"Late?" She didn't have a place to go. "I have no place to be late for."

"Your patient's here. He's already set up on the weights."

"Brock?" she asked slowly. "Is that who you're talking about?"

"You got it. He's been here a while, and we don't seem to get along too well. So, you may just want to come down here and help us out."

She knew he was only half joking. They were professionals, and everybody did the job they had to do. But like in any small community, there were those they got along with better than others. Brock had made a point of not getting along with anybody.

Nobody liked to carry dead weight.

"I'll be down in a few minutes."

She smiled at the Major and patted his hand. "Duty calls."

She put her dirty cup and saucer in the appropriate rack and contemplated what the news meant. Obviously Brock wasn't looking for a transfer. She wondered if she should tell Dani or wait until later. She decided later was probably a better idea. As she walked into the physio room, Shane gave her a high five and walked out. She hadn't exactly planned on starting here, but she took it to mean Brock preferred working on the weights. Then, of course, he was a big, strapping man, and likely used to having a big, fit body. This was going to be an important part of recovery. She could use that. Wanting … no, needing to get that power back, that sense of completeness, that sense of self was what this was all about. Sure, they were going to work on the injuries, and they would heal and strengthen every ounce of him they could. Mobility was high on that list as well. But all of it would come together much faster if he could ease back and be happy with who he was. He had expectations. *They* had expectations. But rarely did they ever go together. It was so important to be able to communicate and find that middle ground.

She dug up that bright smile again and walked over to him. "Now, this is a good place to start. Let's see if we can get that awesome body back."

He looked up at her and frowned. "I'm never going to get that back."

"You might not with Shane, there. But you will with me, if you're ready to do the work."

For the first time, she saw a hint of interest in his gaze. Good, she'd been right about that. She'd worked with several bodybuilders in her time. She knew how important it was for them to have that look, or maybe that feel. She didn't think he was bodybuilding material, a strongman competition would be better, but he'd been in incredibly good shape. So, he knew exactly what was required to maintain it. He was a long way away from that point. It was going be hard on him, but she could help him make a comeback—at least as much of one as he was ready to have.

SIDNEY WAS NOT at all what he had expected. She'd come off as such a hard-ass this morning. Some of what she'd said burned. And some rang with truth. He didn't want to transfer away, so here he was. And here she was, capable of seeing what he wanted out of this and trying to help him get it. He wasn't concerned about appearances, but he knew damned well that having a strong back was going to make a difference in his work life. That was what he wanted. He wanted to feel like he could do everyday tasks and chores with at least a certain amount of ability.

It meant a hell of a lot of muscle repair. He was up for it as long as the end result was the same goal he wanted. He wasn't even sure why he hadn't been able to work with the others. It wasn't that they hadn't wanted to help him because they had. Nor had they not seen that he needed help because they certainly had, and they were definitely professionals. But there'd been just something about doing the endless number of exercises, listening to them drone on and on about the body's muscle groups and the injuries that made him want to throw the weights across the room.

One thing he did know. He didn't want to leave Hathaway. So far, this seemed like it was the best place for him. He just needed somebody to help him get where he needed to be. Maybe his luck had finally changed—maybe she was going to be the one.

Two hours later, he was cursing her out—and she was

cursing right back at him.

"Come on. Push your sorry ass into that move. Don't you start wussing out on me, you little weasel." She danced in front of him as he pushed and tugged and pulled—moving the muscles, building the muscles, toning the injuries and forcing them to heal.

He glared at her and swore. "Don't take your frustrations out on me, you bitch."

She grinned. "Call me any name in the book. I don't care. You're not going to send me running. Besides, it just shows your lack of control."

"Goddammit," he roared and did one more set.

She laughed. "Now that's what I'm talking about."

"I'm so not happy with you right now." Sweat dripped, burning into his eyes. His body bowed over the weights and his back … Jesus! He hurt.

"No, but you can put that big mouth of yours into the job and make the next move."

And on it went. By the time he was done, he was afraid he really was done. He'd never been so goddamned sore in all his life. All those knots of the last six months, and the months of lying in bed, the workouts up until now—all of it had been nothing. He sat down with a sigh, realizing his whole body was trembling.

With any luck this torture was over—at least for the moment. However, he was quietly amazed. He had no idea that was inside of him. After completing BUD/s training, he'd felt invincible. The best of the best. He'd had a sense of personal accomplishment that had been the highlight of his life.

Now, all he wanted to do was make his way back to bed and stay there, pampering himself with room service and forgetting about getting out of bed again—ever.

Sidney had different ideas. With a sneer, she said, "Look at you, you're already finished. Down to the pool! Twenty laps, and then we'll consider a massage."

Shit. He glared at her in outrage. Had she read his chart? Did she know what he used to do? That swimming was a major part of a Navy SEALs career? Did she even care? "Twenty laps? Maybe I can't even swim," he challenged her. "Did you even think about that?"

She shoved her face in his and said, "Then it should be an easy walk on the pool bottom, Tank."

He stared at her for a few minutes, and then he howled. Not at just being called a tank, but at the image of him walking on the floor of the pool. He'd actually been really good at that when he was a kid.

Spirits high, and too tired to walk, he sat himself down in the wheelchair and headed for the elevator.

This might just work out after all.

# Chapter 3

BY THE TIME he'd made it through the pool session, she wondered if she'd overdone it. He was looking a little on the shaky side. However, his jaw was stiff, as if he was clenching it and refusing to break down and tell her. She could believe he'd had some of the worst taskmasters in the world. The military wasn't known for light, fluffy workouts. At the same time, she didn't want to be put in the same category. He did need to work, but he couldn't afford to overdo it. Strain injuries were way too common in this business. By the time she'd helped him sit down on the bench, he'd relaxed slightly. She grabbed some towels.

"Do you want your massage down here or back up in your room?"

His answer was telling. "My bed, please."

"Wheelchair or walk?"

Silence. He looked at the wheelchair, looked over at her and then stood. Instantly, he wavered. She moved the wheelchair into position behind him and pressed him back to sit down. "You can walk another time."

She didn't give him any chance to answer but wheeled him toward the elevator. Just because he was ambulatory didn't mean he was in the best position to make his way on foot all the time. Sometimes the workouts were just that much harder. Upstairs in his room, he was still dripping wet in his swimsuit, and she threw his dry towels down on the bed and wheeled him over to the side. She asked, "Do you need any help?"

She was fully expecting to walk out without doing anything more for him because she knew how stubborn he was.

There was fatigue in his voice when he answered, "Could you pull the bedding back?"

She could see the bedding had bundled up. She untangled it and folded it back. Then she took several towels and stretched them out on top of the bed. "You can put on dry trunks or lie down without any on," she said. "I'll be back in a few minutes."

With that, she walked out of the room. She headed into the office the physiotherapists shared where she had her own desk and dropped her towel on the back of the chair. She sat down, brought up his file on the computer and quickly updated it with the day's efforts. He'd done a hell of a job so far.

He was going to need a massage, however, to stop the muscles from tightening up too much.

She'd picked up a couple of really good creams while she'd been away this last time. Some had special ingredients to help make the muscles heal a little faster. When she was done at the computer, she went to her locker, found the cream she wanted and returned to his room. He was lying on his stomach without a pillow, completely flat, with his eyes closed. A towel lay across his backside. She could tell he had no trunks on. Good, she didn't want anything to impede her work. She opened up the cream, rubbed some on her hands and put the tube back onto the table. She kept the lid off in case she needed more. She hadn't worked on him before, so she had no idea how dry his skin was.

She started on the big trapezius muscles, gently at first. Mentally, she tested the tightness, the muscle mass from the injuries and his pain tolerance levels.

"You can go a lot harder than that," he murmured.

"All in good time," she said.

Every therapist she knew had their own individual system. She liked to work lightly to loosen and warm up the muscles. Then, she dug deeper and deeper, working at the knots, working at the tension, trying to ease everything up so the muscles relaxed. Staying focused, she worked her way through his back, his upper arms, shoulders and neck. Then she slowly worked down toward the bed of scars on the left side. She'd seen a lot of injuries in her life. Particularly working here, but these were some of the largest expanses of soft-tissue injury she'd ever seen.

Compassion filled her as she gently eased back the pressure where the muscle layer thinned down. His recovery would have been painful as hell. As soon as she touched the area above his hip, she could feel him tensing up again. With one hand working the top of his neck, helping him to relax, she gently worked through the hip into the lower back. He was missing so much muscle development on that side it was almost painful for her to massage. She worked the whole area, refusing to give in to his pain, or her own, and then she slowly moved down. She pulled the towel off slightly to see part of his glutes had also been damaged. One side of his cheek was deformed. She grabbed some more cream, smearing it over her hands.

"Not very pretty, is it?" he said in a gritty voice.

"Pretty is not the issue," she said calmly. "It must be a pain in the ass not to be able to sit flush."

That startled a laugh out of him. "I hadn't actually noticed that being an issue."

"Good. Let's see if we can build those muscles up, at least enough that you won't sit lopsided." With that, she went back to work. By the time she was done and easing her hands up and down his spine and neck once again, she could feel his breath dropping into a smooth, calm, heavy breathing instead of being tense and waiting for more pain.

As she stepped away and pulled the blankets on top of him, she smiled.

He'd nodded off to sleep. She stooped and picked up the wet towels he'd dropped on the floor and tossed them into the laundry basket. She grabbed her cream and walked out. As she left, she flicked the light switch off and closed the door. She didn't want him to sleep too long because lunch was coming up. However, if anybody deserved a nap, it was him. As she headed back to the office she caught sight of Dani.

The other woman changed course and headed toward her. "How was it?"

"Well, I don't think you'll have to find a transfer for him," Sidney said with a big smile. "He's asleep right now. He worked hard—he deserves the rest."

Dani's shoulders slumped with relief, and a big smile flashed across her face. "Oh, my God, I'm so happy to hear that. He's such a good guy, but he just wasn't getting anywhere."

"Sometimes just changing the personalities is enough," Sidney said with another smile. She patted Dani on the shoulder. "Have you got time for lunch today?"

Dani glanced at her watch. "Sure. Let's go and eat."

Back in the dining room, there was another round of greetings from people who were seeing her for the first time since her return. Sidney picked up a Caesar salad, a sandwich, and a big yogurt, and carried the tray out onto the deck. Feeling welcomed and happy to be home again, she sat down and relaxed.

While she waited for Dani to join her, Sidney flexed her fingers, feeling the ache of a job well done. That was another issue she was potentially going to have to look at down the road. Often, massage therapists had to change careers by the time they were forty because of their own physical injuries—arthritis being one of the biggest. She was licensed in both physio and massage.

"Sore?" Dani asked as she sat down. Her tray was full with salmon, soup and a salad.

Sidney laughed wryly. "Yes. But I worked hard this morning." She leaned toward Dani and added in a conspiratorial voice, "Not as hard as he did, though."

With that, they both grinned and dug into their food, enjoying the conversation and just being back together again.

"You know," Sidney said, "as much as I really like this place, it was the animals I missed the most."

"The animals are both good and bad," Dani said. "We have a few easy cases—several needed to be spayed or neutered, and that's something we subsidize for the rescue shelter. Of course, Stan is also very interested in prosthetics for the animals, so he has a couple of people working there helping him out, too. Aaron has expressed interest in that field as well." She nodded toward a young horse in the field beside an older one.

"Her name's Molly. She came here with a badly cracked hoof. She'd actually been living in the owner's house as a pet." Dani shook her head. "The owner seemed to think she was going to end up as a dwarf of some kind. But instead, she's got a full-sized lineage."

Sidney laughed. "That must have come as quite a shock."

"When Molly came here, she had never met another horse. Now she's attached to Maggie, and the two of them are pretty much inseparable."

"Good. It's not like you're going to get rid of Maggie," Sidney said with a smile. "Molly is a very lucky filly. And speaking of lucky, tell me about Aaron," she added with a grin.

"As I mentioned earlier, Aaron is going to school to become a vet. Stan gave him an awesome referral, but he worked damn hard and got great grades on the courses he needed to pick up. He's planning to come back and work here." Dani lowered her voice, looking around to make sure nobody was listening. "It was pretty hard not to fall in love with him at that point."

Sidney laughed.

"And you? Whatever happened to John?"

Sidney had been waiting for that question, but now that it was here, she really didn't have an answer. "Nothing. That's the problem," she said with a sigh. "He didn't want to move forward because he didn't care enough."

"Ouch."

Sidney looked up to see Dani staring at her. She dropped her gaze to her food, unable to speak.

A moment later, Dani reached across the table and covered her hand with hers. "I'm so sorry. You're better off without him."

"I know that, but ..." Sidney glanced around at the very large seating area.

Dani had turned this place into a multi-functional, multi-purpose room that worked so well for everybody. Those who wanted to be inside could sit inside, and those who wanted to be outside could sit outside. There were large doors that could close in case of cooler, wet weather, but most of the time the weather here was perfect. There was a lot to be said for this part of Texas. She had had high hopes John might want to move here permanently, but apparently, permanency wasn't high on her ex's list of priorities.

Sidney shook her head. "It's been a while anyway. It happened when I first got back to class. I spent most of the term getting back on track again."

"Well, things have eased slightly here, by my own making." Dani gave her a gentle smile. "Not that I'm advocating matchmaking or anything."

"Oh, my God, no!" Sidney lowered her voice, glaring at her friend, who was grinning at her impishly. "Absolutely no way is that going to happen."

"Sure, I was just kidding." But her eyes didn't stop dancing.

Sidney stared at her in trepidation. "Just because you're so happy doesn't mean the rest the world has to be the same way," she cautioned. "I'm totally okay to not have any romance in my life for a while."

"I believe you." But then she snorted, letting Sidney know there was no way she believed her.

And Sidney knew that if Dani had a chance, she'd find somebody for Sidney.

Which was so *not* what she was looking for right now.

THE SUDDEN KNOCK woke Brock from his nap. He opened

his eyes, feeling disoriented. He was in his bed, covered up with a blanket. And he hurt. Oh God, he hurt. But it was a different kind of hurt. Not like after the first injury or the weeks he'd spent in hospital numbed with morphine. It was the type of hurt he used to feel. The burn after a hard workout where he knew his muscles were functioning like they were supposed to. The burn that spoke of tiny microfiber tears in his muscles before they could build up bigger, better and stronger. As he lay there, the memory of the morning flooded through him. Somehow, she had gotten him to work like he'd never worked before. He had to give her kudos for that. They had settled into a rhythm of swearing and cursing at each other, and somehow, he'd risen higher and higher and done more than he ever thought possible.

The hard knock came again. He let his head roll to the side and called out, "Come in."

He had to wonder at himself. Before his accident, he could never have imagined a point when he would lie in bed and let somebody come into his room. He would've hopped up and answered the door.

But now, he just couldn't be bothered. He also didn't know if it mattered. He'd changed in so many damned ways. The door opened and his doctor walked in, a frown crossing his face as he saw him.

"Are you sick, Brock?"

With a wry smile, Brock replied, "No, just tired."

Still frowning, the doctor clicked on his iPad and studied something on the screen.

Brock figured Sidney had updated the reports, so the doctor was likely reading them over. For some reason, he felt protective. He didn't want her to get in trouble. Not when she'd done so much good for him. He threw back the covers, deliberately keeping his face straight and not making a sound as he sat up. "I had a terrible night last night." He glanced at his watch. "It looks like I missed lunch."

"There's no such thing as missing lunch. Just tell one of the chefs to get you something. There are probably tons of leftovers anyway."

Brock nodded. The doctor was still studying his chart. He wanted to get up and walk to the door to find food, but he wasn't sure he could do it without making a sound. The first couple of steps were likely to be as painful as hell. But he hadn't been a SEAL for nothing. Gritting his teeth, he stood and slipped his foot into the slippers he wore at the center, only to realize he was nude. With sheer willpower, he dressed in shorts and a tank. Turning to the doctor, he said, "If you need to talk to me, come and have a coffee while I grab some food. But I need food right now."

And he walked out, leaving stunned silence behind him.

When he was in the hallway, he took a couple of deep breaths. He was amazed that with all the work he'd done this morning, he wasn't screaming in pain. He didn't look to see if the doctor was following him but continued on in a slow, steady walk—under his own steam. And wasn't that something?

He made it into the dining area in time to see the kitchen staff starting to put away the food. Tray in hand, he walked over to the buffet and served himself a large Caesar salad and fried chicken.

Dennis, who worked behind the counter, said, "If there is anything you need you can't find, just let us know. We're cleaning up and getting ready for dinner."

"I'll be fine with whatever's here," Brock said with a

smile. "It looks great." He made his way along the line and snagged a piece of apple pie. Finally, he added a coffee and turned to slowly look at the large room. There was a table between him and the hallway, and it was probably the easiest one for him to reach. He picked up the tray, and with careful, deliberate movements, he walked to the table and set the tray down. He could almost feel a sense of approval whisper throughout the room. He thought he was alone, but there were still a few stragglers.

As he sat down, a little too heavy, a little too hard for his own sense of comfort, he realized he'd actually made the trip on his own for the first time. No crutches or wheelchair. For many that would be nothing, but for him it was a huge accomplishment. He looked up, and his gaze landed on a group of his peers on the other side of the room, many of whom he knew at least by name. They smiled and nodded at him—he got a sense of approval all over again. It made him feel damned good, but embarrassed. He could feel the heat rising up his neck. He turned to stare down at the food in front of him, deliberately ignoring the discomfort. He didn't want to make a spectacle of himself, and he certainly didn't want to be on show, but if there was ever a time and place to put in a good effort, it'd been today.

Now, he was starved. He dove into his lunch and polished off the salad and chicken. By the time he got to the apple pie, he was starting to feel more human. Taking his time with the pie, coffee in hand, he stared out across the fields. In the weeks he'd been here, he had never yet made it to the animal center below. It seemed so weird when he first got here to think there was a full animal therapy center and veterinarian clinic below. It sounded very confusing to him. As he understood it, the hospital was in charge of transition for animals as well as humans. They were bringing in prosthetics for the animals and had opened up another surgery down there. They did a lot of rescue work for some of the local shelters. He was sure that was a never-ending job.

It would be nice to see the animals, though. He'd always loved dogs. Never been much of a cat person, but he hadn't been around them enough to find out if that was something that could change. He knew he had done more than enough today, but he was hoping maybe he could do something about that this weekend. Maybe go down and visit. The doctors told him the animals were always in need of love and care, and anytime he wanted, he could go down and comfort the ones currently in residence.

He could see horses in the fields and beautiful green rolling hills. The countryside was stunning. He'd heard bits and pieces of the history of the place, and he knew there'd been a brochure when he moved in. Something about it originally having been a veterinarian school that the Major and his daughter had transformed. That in itself was a small miracle. That they kept the animals was just kind of an odd but wonderful touch.

At first, he'd wondered if it was even sanitary to have injured people and injured animals together in the same building, then he realized they were both animals and they both needed the same kind of clean and caring environment to heal. As a plus, both could benefit from being around the other.

He really wanted to see the animals. But it was going to be a bit much today. The weekend was possible, if he made it a goal. He considered the possibility and decided it was doable.

"What's very doable?" his doctor asked, standing beside

him, a fresh cup of coffee in his hands. With a smile, Brock motioned to the chair opposite.

"I didn't realize I'd spoken aloud," he said quietly. "I'm trying to set goals for while I'm here."

"Goals are an excellent idea," the doctor said, pulling a chair back and sitting down.

"I was looking for three to achieve in the next week." Brock's ideas weren't big. In fact, they were very small. But they were something.

The doctor leaned forward. "Interesting. Tell me what they are."

"They aren't major," Brock warned. "The first is to just make it to the dining room for three meals in one day on my own." Considering how tired he was now, he didn't think he would make it back today for dinner. In fact, getting back to his room was already starting to look like a daunting prospect, but he was glad he'd tried. Now he had a better idea of what he could do when he put his mind to it. He'd need days before he tried it again.

"The second goal isn't much either," he said. "I just want to put in as much effort as I did today again."

"So today was a good day?" the doctor asked. "And putting in consistent effort is key to progress."

Brock nodded. "A hard day but one I feel good about." He knew from experience, that a great effort on one day was almost impossible to repeat on the second day. Even though he went in with the right attitude mentally, it just wasn't possible. His body needed a break afterward, and it needed to slowly build up to that level of achievement again.

"And the third?"

"The third goal was to make it down to the animal hospital every day." He smiled. "To find a dog or two to pat or even a horse. Maybe even a cat. Something with fur. Something that could use a bit of love and gives back unconditionally."

As he considered the three goals, he added a fourth. This one was harder, but it was something he needed to do. *Be more social. He needed to get out and visit with the other men. There were also a few women here, but the gender divide landed close to ninety percent on the men.*

He just needed to get out of his shell and return to life. He'd spent a lot of time locked away inside his own walls, holding the entire world responsible for his issues. Or maybe holding himself responsible for the issues and then not feeling like he could reach out to others. As if everyone would know about his guilt and therefore not reach back.

He didn't know—and he was too damned tired to work his way through it right now. The bottom line was that either way it didn't matter. Change had to happen. He had done nothing but hide since the accident, and it was time for that to stop.

# Chapter 4

I T WAS ODD being at Hathaway House again. Sidney had done this back-and-forth dance between working and school for a few years now. Normally, she adjusted fairly quickly, but the last school session had been a bit rougher, thanks to John. Now, being back here again, she felt freer—more alive. It was a sobering thought how much a relationship could pull her down—make her less than she had been.

Dani had been to hell and back with her relationship before this Aaron guy showed up. Sidney was a little worried about that, to be truthful. But she hadn't been here for any of the courtship, so she wasn't sure how the guy had come across. It was always a danger to fall in love with a patient. Sometimes their situations were just so tear-jerking your heart literally went out to them. That wasn't good for them, or for you. She had always been very wary of something like that. She knew several others that had managed to pull it off and have relationships that lasted many decades afterward, and all the more power to them. But personally, she wasn't sure she could separate her professional life from her personal life in that instance.

It was almost dinnertime when she walked downstairs to see Stan. She'd hoped he was still there. He was a mainstay of the center, too. She pushed open the double doors of the veterinary clinic to still see several patients of all furry natures in the waiting room. He must have had a hell of a day if he was this backed up. As she walked across the reception area the assistant looked up and frowned at her. The name tag said Rebecca.

"Hi. Is there something we can do for you?"

Rebecca's voice was full of dread. Sidney smiled reassuringly and said, "Nope. I'm one of the therapists from upstairs. I just came down to see how you guys were doing. Actually, I've been away for nine months, and I wanted to say hi to Stan."

"Oh." Relief washed over the young woman's face. "It's been a heck of a day. He's having quite the time." She motioned with her head toward the full waiting room. "He's behind at the moment."

Just then the door opened, and Stan walked out, talking with a woman holding a small dog. As the woman left, Stan looked at the waiting room and shook his head. He turned, his gaze landing on Sidney. His face lit up, and he opened his arms. She gave him a big hug.

Sidney stepped back and said, "As much as I'd love to sit and chat, apparently you're really bogged down. Do you want me to give you a hand?"

"You so can. My assistant had to leave early today, so we're running behind."

She didn't know the ins and outs of the veterinary world, but she'd helped Stan before in the past. Between the two of them, they managed to get through the full waiting room in the next hour. When they were done, Stan slung an arm across her shoulder and hugged her close.

"Talk about good timing. I was afraid we'd never get through this day."

He walked over to one of the waiting-room couches and

sat down. Sidney studied his face, hating the fatigue in his expression. She didn't know how old Stan was but thought he appeared to have aged ten years while she'd been gone. "Sounds like you've had a rough year."

He laughed. "Rough day, yes. A rough year? No, it's been pretty decent." He looked around the room and said, "All the animal patients and their owners are gone at least, but I still have several animals that are staying overnight I have to attend to. Can you spare another half hour, then maybe we could go have dinner together?"

"I'd like that," she said with a smile. "Come on, let's get the work done first."

The first patient was a rabbit with a bad slice to its ear, which he'd had to stitch closed. While she watched, he took off the old covering on the wound and re-bandaged it. The rabbit didn't appreciate the attention it was getting, so it was Sidney's job to help keep it quiet. He was obviously a well-cared-for and beloved bunny, and quite a character. Next was a tomcat that'd had his mind changed and wasn't appreciating his new status.

"Do you actually keep these here overnight?" she asked.

"This one's a rescue. They were supposed to pick him up but asked if I could keep him overnight because they didn't have a volunteer to do the drive."

She nodded. "Makes sense."

By the time they got to the little filly outside in the fenced yard, she was immersed in the joy of being surround-ed by animals. The filly walked right up to Stan and nudged him with her hand. He laughed and pulled out chunks of carrot from his pockets. He fed her a couple of smaller ones and then walked over to the older mare standing a little farther back. While Stan fed Maggie the older mare the rest of the carrots, he quickly checked over the little filly. He explained what the problem had been to Sidney. "It's a case of when people don't understand the difference between house pets and farm animals."

"I can certainly see the attraction to keeping this little one close," Sidney admitted. But it was obviously short-term thinking. She reached up and stroked the mare's long forehead. "There are more horses now, too. As usual, Dani's been busy."

"Not only are there a couple of new horses, we also have a couple of new dogs and a goat," Stan said. "I just worry she's biting off more than she can chew."

"Then it's our job to make sure she doesn't. And to help support her and this place in any way we can."

Stan laughed. "It's good to have you back, kiddo."

"Good enough that you'll feed me, now?" she asked in a teasing voice.

He reached out an elbow and she hooked her arm through his. "Shall we adjourn upstairs?" he asked with mock courtesy.

She chuckled. "Why don't we have dinner on the deck?"

They walked around the center to the back where the pool was and climbed the large stairs on that side of the center. Once again, she marveled at how much Dani had managed to do here. Not only did they have top-of-the-line equipment, but that pool really made a huge difference to the care and treatment the patients received.

The kitchen was a busy place, and the dining room was also full. At least the worst of the lineup had finished by the time they were in line. There was a large buffet, but there was always someone on the other side of the counter to help serve if needed. She chose a platter of roast beef and vegetables. She waited until Stan had pulled out a selection almost twice as large as hers, and then they carried it over to the end of the patio, down to the pool level. They listened to people splashing happily in the water, as it was open and free for everybody once therapy had finished at four o'clock. She glanced over at Stan's full plate.

"How come you never get fat?"

He chuckled. "I work too hard."

"So not nice. If I ease up on my own workouts, then all this food will go straight to my hips."

"You could use a few pounds," he said comfortably. "Besides, you're gorgeous—I wouldn't worry about it."

She wasn't sure if he was joking or not, but inside, it was nice to hear.

"Rumor says you and your boyfriend broke up already."

"Rumors." She shook her head. "I forgot what the grapevine was like here."

"Actually, I think I heard about it at the time it happened, nine months ago," he said with a wry laugh. "Sorry to hear about it, though. Any pain like that is hard to get through."

"Especially when I had such high hopes he was the one." She bent her head and focused on her full plate.

After a few minutes he said, "How's Brock doing?"

She lifted her head and looked at him silently for a few seconds. "Have you met him?"

He shook his head. "I know he's got some bigger issues than some of the guys here, but he hasn't been down to see the animals. I was kind of thinking I might be able to take Helga upstairs and pop in to say hi, but I haven't had time yet."

She sat back and stared at him. "Who is she?"

He grinned. "You can thank Aaron for that. He's been instrumental in house-training a few of the rescues—like Helga. I tell you, that dog. We're constantly building her new legs. But since Dani sprang for a 3-D printer for the center, it's actually been a lot easier than we thought it would be. Helga is a Newfoundland cross, and a huge hit with the patients. Aaron's been the one taking her around as much as he can to meet everybody."

"I don't think I've met Helga," she said.

"There's just something very appealing about her," Stan said. "Of course, there's always Chickie."

"Is Chickie still here? When I left, his owners hadn't come by to pick him up, but they said they'd be in the next day."

"They never did show up." Stan's voice was deliberately neutral.

She understood the pain. He did a lot of work for injured animals, and when the families just gave up on the animals, he was hard-pressed to find new homes for them. Sometimes it just broke his heart because the animals went into such distress and depression after they were deserted by those who had once loved them.

"Chickie is so tiny, he's perfect for carrying around to the patients as well."

"I remember him."

Stan smiled. Then he looked behind her and raised an eyebrow in question. "Hello. We haven't met." He stood and reached out a hand.

She didn't need to turn around to know who was behind her. She watched quietly as Stan and Brock exchanged handshakes. Nice and crisp—maybe a bit of measuring. There was nothing between her and Stan. They had never been anything other than kindred spirits who seemed to be hooked on the center and everything that went on around inside. She motioned toward the spare chair at the table. "Join us, Brock."

"If I may?" Brock looked over at Stan.

"Sit down." Stan resumed eating, but he kept an eye on the two of them.

Sidney made the introductions. "Anytime you want to do any work or visit with the animals, it's Stan's world down here," she said with a smile. "What that really means is, he wants you to come down and help out anytime you have a moment."

"Hey, it's not that bad," Stan protested. "It was just bad today because my assistant had to leave early."

"How many animals do you have down there?" Brock asked curiously.

"A bunny, a Maine Coon, a couple of dogs, and a snake that might end up being permanent additions, and of course Molly is out in the fields with Maggie." Stan motioned toward the pair of horses.

"Do you keep other pets here, year-round?" Brock asked, his gaze going from Stan to Sidney.

"There are several that live here all year round. Dani keeps a certain number temporarily, until we can find homes, and when they can't find homes for them, she often ends up keeping them."

Brock went still. "That's got to be a full-time job, trying to find homes for the animals, particularly if they have special needs."

"Not for her. She has the time, the patience and the inclination. But there's a very large sector of society who think we should just shoot them."

Sidney lowered her gaze, studying the lines of his face. "Are you one of them?"

"Hell, no. I'd just as soon shoot people and leave the animals in control," he said. "Anybody who can help animals gets my vote."

"Well, Dani's always looking for help. So if you're bored and you want to volunteer somewhere, there's always stuff to do."

He studied her carefully. "What kind of volunteering?"

Stan laughed. "That's what got Aaron into trouble. Now, he's going to be a permanent fixture." He pushed his chair back and stood. "If you want to come downstairs and help in my section, you're always welcome to. Every one of those animals needs to be loved and cuddled the same as every human. Then, there's always the issue of cleaning cages, taking animals for walks, taking them outside to do their business, etcetera. There is never a shortage of things that need to be done around here."

Sidney watched him walk away.

"He seems to really care," Brock said.

"He's been here for a long time, and he really does care. He's helped thousands of animals that would've otherwise been put down."

"It's a very strange place here, having animals and people together." He played with the handle on his coffee cup and then raised his gaze to Sidney. "Not bad … just … unique."

Sidney nodded. "There needs to be more creative thinking when it comes to healing," she said. "I've heard of several old-folks' homes opening day care on the premises. Having little children around isn't for everyone," she said. "But for many seniors it's been a godsend. It's poured new life into their lives. As long as it's open, and people can come and go when they want to, and it's not overwhelming with the noise and the crying of younger children, it seems to work out well. These are just a few pilot projects, but I'd love to see similar ideas spread across the country. I think the same applies for animals. Just as we have therapy dogs and therapy pets we bring into old-folks' homes and day care, hospitals and hospices, there's no reason not to have them on a more permanent basis, like here. In fact, this was originally a veterinarian school. Then Dani's father, the Major, altered it. It was a slow process, but this is the end result."

"The Major?"

Sidney laughed. "If you haven't met him yet, you will know him when you see him. He makes a point of stopping in to talk to everybody. He's in his late sixties, and he has white, bushy hair and a big, white beard."

A comical look came over Brock's face. "I've met him. I just now realized who he was."

"He and his daughter Dani, who you've met, as she was the one that would've brought you in and set you up originally, worked together until he eventually turned the reins over to her. She handles all the transfers and the company side of stuff. Every time I turn around, she's expanding and bringing on more staff." Sidney laughed and shook her head. "Actually, I'm blessed to be here. I've been doing training back and forth, and updating my own skills. And thankfully, every time I'm done, there's always a job here for me."

"That says a lot about how they feel about you, then," Brock said. "I have to admit that after what I saw today, you're very talented."

"Talented?" That surprised her. She sat back and studied Brock. "What we went through today took talent?"

A small smile played at the corners of his mouth. "You got me to work today," he said. "You let me put out effort I didn't realize I even had inside anymore. That took talent."

She laughed. "That took motivation—on my side and yours." She glanced at his cup and stood. "I'll grab a second cup for you while I get one for myself, if you like."

SHE SAID IT so casually, he didn't feel like it was being done because he was incapable of going to get it on his own. Because of that, he nodded and said, "Thank you." He also didn't want to curtail the social visit. She was a fascinating woman. It seemed like it had been a hell of a long time since he'd seen anything other than that cloud over his head. Not that it was gone. And it certainly wasn't likely to ever go away completely, but for the first time, he'd left it in a corner. He was able to see little bit more of the world than when he'd locked himself in and away from it all. It was something he hadn't even been aware he was doing, but somehow he'd put up all these walls and kept the world out.

It had taken a very interesting and magnetic personality for him to even realize what he had done. He knew how wrong a relationship between a patient and therapist would be in many cases, but he also knew of several that had worked out. It was also way too early to consider anything beyond having a cup of coffee. But he had to admit that she pricked his interest, like no one else had in years. Even in the years before he had his accident. His last long-term relationship was four years ago. That hadn't ended so much as dwindled away into nothing.

As he sat, pondering the changes in his circumstances, he

couldn't say if it was the location, or the change of venue, or even Sidney herself. But there was a small kernel of hope inside. Maybe he would see his way out of this mess. It always irritated him that people who weren't depressed had the best of advice for those that were. None of it made any difference because when you were depressed you couldn't see a way forward, no matter whether you did all the stuff people seemed to think you could do or not. You couldn't just force yourself to be happy. That just made you mad and angry and more depressed.

"Here you go." A cup of coffee was placed down in front of him.

He smiled. "Thank you very much."

"No problem." She put her own coffee down, and then turned and walked over to the other side of the deck. He watched her go. There was a very large black man, missing both legs, sitting, basking in the warm glow of the afternoon sunshine. Sidney reached down and gave him a hug. The two laughed and joked for a minute before she turned and headed back toward Brock. He didn't want it to seem like he was watching what she was doing, so he turned his attention to the rolling, green hills around him.

He swore he could be anywhere from California to Kentucky from the look of the place. It was stunning—the simplicity and healing energy. Maybe that was what made the difference. Maybe just being around people who had a different attitude made a difference. People came on the clock and did whatever they had to do and they left. Just as he was reaching for the cup of coffee, Sidney stepped in front of him.

His gaze started to move up to her face but stopped halfway. In her hands, she held one of the smallest critters he'd ever seen.

"What is it?"

A tiny little bark came out of it in reply.

"He's a very small Chihuahua cross," Sidney said with a smile. "He's had a really rough couple of years. His bones didn't grow properly, so he doesn't walk or jump well. But being here is bit of a godsend in that sense, as he doesn't ever seem to be on the ground. Somebody is always carrying him."

She reached out her hands. "Brock, meet Chickie. Chickie, meet Brock."

Brock stared at the small dog with its massive chocolate eyes. The little dog barked, but it came out as a tiny yelp. He shook his head in wonder. Instinctively, his hands reached out, taking up the little dog and bringing it closer to his chest. "He's so small."

"He's fully grown. Chickie's four years old."

With a satisfied smile, Sidney sat back down across from Brock and picked up her coffee. "Isaac over there tends to have Chickie on a full-time basis, but Chickie really belongs to everybody. He lives here full-time. He's a special-needs dog, and Stan looks after him. The staff here have incorporated him in with the therapy animals."

He could hear the words floating across the room. He understood what she was saying, but his attention was completely fixed on the tiny animal in his arms. His heart broke and proceeded to melt all over him. He gently scratched the animal behind his ears. Chickie had no problem cuddling in against his chest. He didn't do anything but drop his head and stare up at Brock. In fact, if Brock didn't know better, he would have been sure Chickie was saying, "More please, more." He couldn't imagine an animal being this content. "He has some very un-dog-like qualities," he said. "I'm half expecting him to purr."

Sidney laughed. "You're not the first to mention that. He's got a very laid-back personality, and because he doesn't jump and bark much, and has a fairly sedentary lifestyle, he's very catlike. He's quite content to curl up on your shoulder or sit in your lap—he does like it to be warm. One of his health issues is his body temperature is a little harder to regulate, so he's a happy camper when he's tucked up against somebody's body."

"He's beautiful," Brock said. He was horrified to hear his voice break. Moisture burned in the corners of his eyes. Oh, dear God, he hadn't cried in a decade. He certainly wasn't about to break down over a tiny dog. The instinctive impulse to give him back to Sidney was so strong, but at the same time, he couldn't bear to be parted from the small animal that was so damned accepting.

"We do have one rule here regarding the animals," she said. "Please don't feed any of them table scraps. With so many of you, the minute that becomes a thing, it's almost impossible to stop the animals—particularly the dogs—from eating everything in sight. In Chickie's case, his system is very delicate."

Brock raised his gaze and studied the number of people in the kitchen area. "Not to mention every one of them would have a weight issue within seconds at this place." He gently stroked a hand down Chickie's back. "It's a habit for most humans to share with their pets."

"Which is why I'm very specifically telling you we can't. The last time somebody fed Chickie a piece of meat off their plate, he ended up with a bowel blockage. That's not fun for anybody."

Just when he thought he should hand Chickie back, the little dog dropped from a sitting position, and curled up in his lap. That just broke his heart a little more as Chickie tucked his head to the side and went to sleep.

## *Chapter 5*

E VEN THE NEXT morning Sidney was holding that picture close as she headed into her office—Brock cuddling Chickie. Chickie had been the happiest dog ever, and who could blame him? He was protected and loved—the two basic needs for any living thing. It was nice to see Brock in another light, as a big softie. But she knew he hadn't been brought to this place because he was a great patient. They had replaced his therapist four times already because he hadn't been a motivated man. That he'd worked for her yesterday was not something she was prepared to count on happening again tomorrow, or the day after. People often gave their all, and then backed off. Some things were just too hard to deal with on a regular basis. It was her job to keep him going.

Maybe she should bring Chickie into the sessions.

She smiled at that. Several times they had been tempted to bring animals up from downstairs. To show these men and women just how an animal was forced to deal with many of the same problems without all the support systems people had. Animals adapted much better than humans.

She snagged another cup of coffee on her way back to her desk, even though she didn't really need it. It was probably the fourth cup today, already. That was something she should look at trying to control. Too much coffee was never a good thing. She had broken the habit before, but going back to school had started her drinking it again.

As soon as she sat down, Shane walked over and placed his hands on the desk, leaning over to stare down at her. "You've been back a whole day, and I've hardly even seen you."

She leaned back and smiled up at him. Shane was one of those all-round nice guys. That didn't mean he was dull as dishwater, but for her, he was definitely not a super-exciting type of person. He was a friend, and a good one, and she had needed to cry on his shoulder more than once before. She propped her chin on her hand and said, "I haven't had time to do anything but breeze by."

He laughed. "Yep, we're pretty busy. You came back at a good time."

Sidney nodded. "So Dani said. She's already setting up interviews to bring more people on. There is a chance that Willa might come back."

Shane straightened at that. "That would be awesome if she could. I thought she was going to med school or something like that."

"I'm not sure if it was med school," Sidney said. "I do know she went back for more education but thought it was more therapy stuff."

"We probably don't need more therapists, but we could sure use some more physios."

"We never have trouble getting new people. This is an awesome place to work."

Shane walked back over to his desk and sat down, propping his feet up on the corner of the wooden surface. "You've been here for years now. It's been five years for me, almost six I think."

"Only six years," she joked. "I arrived just before you. I can see you being here for decades."

At that moment, two more physiotherapists walked in. The conversation turned to the general care of individual patients. As she participated in the conversation, Sidney was interested to hear nobody brought up the subject of Brock. Was he that difficult that nobody wanted to talk about him? Or was it because she was now handling his case, and they were waiting for her to bring him up? She didn't have a lot to say yet. Not until things got into more of a routine. Then maybe there'd be something to talk about.

She checked her watch and realized it was time to start moving. She stood and grabbed a manila folder off the desk. "Back to work for me."

As she walked out the door, Shane called behind her, "Don't forget, paperwork counts as work, too!"

She waved back with a smile. "Yeah, but that's the kind I don't like doing."

With the file in her hand, she headed down the hallway toward the large exercise room. She walked in and noted it was empty, which meant Andrew, her next patient, was running a little behind. She walked over to the large floor mats and double-checked everything was arranged and clean. She brought out two large exercise balls. Andrew had done phenomenally well since he'd arrived. He been here four months already and was looking forward to leaving in the next couple of weeks. She was fine-tuning his core muscles— even more important in his case, as he was actually missing both legs. But unlike a lot of patients, his attitude had always been excellent. Then again, he had a loving, supportive family who adored him—a wife and kids. He had a lot to live for. They all wanted him home in whatever shape he came in. It was his choice to go home as best as he could.

"There you are," a deep voice rumbled. "I'm Andrew."

Sidney turned to see Andrew walking in. He had running blades on the bottoms of his legs.

"Nice to meet you, Andrew. I'm Sidney." She grinned. "Look at you go. Aren't you the pro?"

"I've been wearing these for weeks. You just haven't been here. You were off lazing about in school, instead of being here where the real work was being done."

She laughed. "I know I wasn't the one working with you before, but I can see your progress from your file. You've done some awesome work."

He sat down on the ball as she watched, seeing confirmation in his gait she'd hoped to see. "What are we doing today?"

"Lots, but first take off both your prosthetic limbs."

He stared down at his metal legs. "There's just something really unnerving about not having them on now."

She nodded. "That's because they have become a crutch. Good ones, but a crutch nonetheless. They're great tools, but we tend to forget you have a lot of work to do without them." She opened his file. "I see you've done a lot of work on the upper body, and that's awesome. Obviously, you've done a lot of work on your thighs, and that's great, too. What I really need to see and test is how you are doing without them."

He looked at her and grimaced. "It's not very comfortable to work without them, anymore. I can, but it's much nicer with. They've become an extension of me."

"Exactly, that's the point," she said quietly. "We just have to make sure the base is as strong as can be, so if you don't have them you are just as strong."

He groaned, but he reached down and unclipped both of his prosthetics and dropped them to the side.

She walked over and picked them up carefully, and then laid them on the empty desk they had there for occasional use. She started him off doing simple core exercises on the ball while she watched. As she suspected, he'd been very good at hiding the weaknesses. His shoulders moved well, his arms and upper body strength were great, but every time he tried to do crossovers, or anything involving the lower back, there was an ever-so-slight pull, or he winced when he had to bring his other, stronger, muscles into play. That was what she needed to see. Because the body compensated, she needed to get the weaker muscles to step up and do their job. Most patients tried to avoid pain. They became very adept at making it look like everything was just perfect for the therapists. She had the benefit of fresh eyes. She could see where he was getting away with not doing the full job he needed to do.

That was too damned bad because he was going to hurt soon. But by the time he walked out of here in a couple of weeks, he would know what she meant. In the meantime, she sighed. She wondered how many times he was going to ask to go to the other therapists. They worked in teams here but sometimes a patient had a preference and the center tried to accommodate as much as possible.

She found out soon enough because his first request came at the end of that day. Daunted and tired, she walked out onto the deck and slammed down the stairs. Her day was done, dinner was ready, but she was too damned tired to even go over there. She could hear splashing in the pool below and thought maybe a swim would help.

"Hard day?" Dani asked with a light laugh. She sat down

in the chair beside Sidney and held out a cup of coffee. "Here."

"I think this is like my sixth cup today," Sidney said, accepting the drink from her friend. "I need to find something else to drink."

"There are lots of non-alcoholic options to choose from."

Sidney laughed. "I know there are. I'll find something." She glanced at Dani and her concerned expression. "What's up?"

Dani frowned slightly. "You had a session with Andrew today, didn't you?"

Sidney closed her eyes and then let out a half laugh. "I was working with him. I wondered how long it'd be before he asked for a change of therapists."

"Well, he's asked. What's the problem with him?"

"He's very good at hiding his weak spots," Sidney explained. "He's worked the most with Marsha, and I guess she didn't notice, but there's a whole muscle group that needs to be worked and strengthened. Otherwise, when the big muscles fatigue there will be nothing to hold him up structurally. Because of the lack of legs, he can't count on those to be there for him when times get tough."

"Do you think you were fair with him today?"

Sidney shook her head. She needed to explain this in layman terms. Dani was incredibly knowledgeable, but some of this was more medical than anything.

"Honestly, no. I had to be hard-ass. Because everyone had done such a great job on what they focused on that he looks great. Of course, it's easier to work the big muscles. Motivation-wise, he obviously wants to work the muscles that look good. Nobody wants to work on the muscles that hurt, and only some work has been done. The other team members have done a good job—to a point. The weaker muscles on the inside, the core, that need work, are for stability. He's done such a hell of a job that everybody looks at him with admiration now. His ego is pumped. He believes his muscles are fine, but they aren't. Not even close."

"He's planning on leaving in two weeks." Dani studied her carefully. "Are you saying he's not ready?"

"No. He's not ready. But if it matters that much to him, I could get him closer to being ready." She shrugged. "He can continue the same work at home, easily enough."

"Is this something anybody else could do?"

Sidney knew what she was asking. There was no way they worked together—with this many patients—without understanding that every therapist had a strength and every patient had a weakness.

"Absolutely. But they have to see what I've just seen and not take offense at not having seen it themselves earlier."

"Do you want me to talk to Andrew?"

Sidney shook her head. "No, it's my job. I'll do it. I'll talk to him today, and he can make a decision tomorrow."

Dani reached across and clasped Sidney's hand, giving it a light squeeze. "I'm so happy to have you home."

Dani rose and left Sidney there, sipping her coffee. That was the thing about Dani. She called it as she saw it, and in a nice way. That type of management skill was a gift. Sidney had been here off and on for years, but every time she came home the place became embedded more deeply in her heart. But even at home there was strife. One had to make com-promises.

She stood, coffee in hand, and walked back to Andrew's room. She knocked on his door, pushed it open and walked in. He was sitting on his bed with his laptop. As soon as he saw her, his face shut down. She leaned against the doorway and smiled.

"When I was working with you today, I wondered how long it would take you to ask for a new therapist."

She caught the look of surprise on his face.

"Is that why you were so hard, then? You didn't want to work with me?" There was no ego involved in that question, she was happy to see. It was curiosity.

"No, not at all. But you have to understand that when you do really well, it's much easier to focus on the parts you're doing really well at. Everyone likes success. You want to make the bigger muscles stronger, but because of your accident and internal injuries and the lack of legs … that's not enough.

"Stability is a massive factor for you. That means your core muscles, and not just that muscle group, of course. You've done some work—enough that the package is working well," she said. "But your body fat percentage is very low, so your muscles are shiny and bright, and you look model-perfect. If that's what you want, great. But I'm not concerned about the looks of the big, bad-ass muscles you're sporting because they aren't doing just fine."

She took a step inside. "I'm concerned about the days when you're really exhausted, the days you walk in and collapse on the couch because you just can't handle any more, and your back is killing you. Your stomach hurts, and your arms and shoulders hurt, and it's all because your core muscles are incapable of putting in as hard and long a day as the rest of the muscles that don't require 24/7 performance. As soon as those central muscles fatigue, every other muscle in the body has to compensate. When they have to do that, you have a cascading effect of damage. So, yes, I was hard on you. I could see what you needed to focus on. It's okay though, that you asked for a different therapist. I'm fine with that." She shrugged. "I've already spoken to Dani about it. But what you also have to decide is, do you want to leave this place the prettiest or the best you can be?"

She watched the glint in his eyes turn to anger, and she nodded. "You have overnight to make a decision. Dani has several other options ready for you. Talk to her in the morning, and she'll set you up."

"If you know exactly what I need, why didn't the others? Why didn't Marsha?"

She smiled. "Because they had become your friends and let you off easy."

With that she turned and walked out.

BROCK HAD HEARD about Sidney's afternoon with Andrew. First, it was in muted whispers then he happened to be sitting behind several of the therapists having lunch.

At first, he'd been slightly amused by her homecoming issues. Then he realized how much guts it had taken to buck the system and to step in to say and do what needed to be done. It was likely at a cost to herself. The other therapists weren't holding back in their comments, either.

"She just got back. She doesn't know what's been done or what was planned to be done. She's got no right to step on toes like that. There is such a thing as professional boundaries."

"She didn't actually do anything wrong," Shane protested. "She was asked to work with a patient, she saw a problem, and with her typical focus, she dove in to solve it."

"Easy for you to say," one younger woman snapped. "He wasn't your patient."

"No, but everyone here is everyone's patient," Shane reminded her. "We're a team, and we work on many people together. If there was a problem, someone else should have caught it, too."

"Exactly, but no one did," the same woman snapped.

There was an odd silence at the table.

By now, Brock was fascinated at the inside look he was getting into a profession he'd never really acknowledged as being full of the same human trials as every other industry. Of course, there were people that did better than others in every job. There was always someone seriously gifted. It amazed him to see how different employees worked. There were always those he hated to work with and those that were fine, and then there were those that were desirable co-workers. They had a gift to see things from a completely different perspective that allowed him to open up his way of seeing things. His buddies were like that. They had unique perspectives on the world that he appreciated. Very often, people liked to live behind their closed-door perspectives, but every once in a while, there was somebody that just made you want to jump through the window and see the world in a whole different light.

He knew both sides of it all. His two friends Denton and Cole had been injured in an accident recently. He hadn't heard all the details yet as his buddies didn't like to talk about it. Of course now that he was here they only had text and the phone. Cole was actually in pretty decent shape, but he was pretty closemouthed, so Brock couldn't know for sure. He'd wanted the three of them to recuperate in the same hospital, but that hadn't worked out. He was supposed to be that much farther along in his recuperation. He just wasn't sure he was.

Then again, maybe he'd had the wrong therapists until now. As he listened to the table ahead of him still wrangling over Sidney's involvement in a case she had just taken on, and then he compared that to the work she'd just pulled out of him, he realized he really was blessed.

She was one of those gifted ones, with the ability to sense something was not quite right. She wasn't going to tolerate him holding back, and that was what he needed. He needed a kick in the ass. He'd never seen himself as a slouch, or somebody who would slack off his work for somebody else to do, but there was something about Sidney that made him step up and be present. He hadn't seen that in another therapist, yet.

He wondered if he should talk to Andrew about it. Because with all this gossip, he could see several of the patients might become worried maybe they had the wrong therapist, too. The only problem was he didn't know this patient. He'd not made any attempt to get to know the others, either. He realized this island he lived on was by choice. He didn't have to be alone. There were a lot of people going through the same things here.

He'd already tuned out the physios' conversation, but just as he was about to leave, he saw Sidney walk into the room. Instantly, the conversation at the table ahead of him froze. Silence fell. Then the younger woman who had been so upset snapped, "Well, it's time for me to leave."

"Marsha, don't," one of the other women murmured.

Marsha picked up her cup and walked past Sidney, completely ignoring her. Brock happened to be watching

Sidney's face as it happened. He saw the wry smile on the beautiful woman's lips. Of course, she knew what the other woman had done. Just as she'd made him face up honestly to his reality, he suspected she wasn't somebody to shirk her own. As he watched, she walked along the food line and picked up some yogurt and a bottle of juice before heading out to the sun. She made no attempt to join the others. She probably knew the reception would be less than warm. Brock contemplated going out to sit with her but realized this really wasn't his place, either.

He suspected there was a lot going on behind her beautiful blue eyes. Still, she looked so alone. As he slowly got to his feet, Shane, the big physiotherapist from the other table stood, ignoring the others, and strode across the room to sit across from Sidney. Sidney's face lit up and she smiled.

Brock was too far away to hear the conversation, but it was animated. Good for Shane. He glanced down at his hands and the crutch he still carried for safekeeping and slowly made his way back to his room. Shane was a big, strong, healthy male. Maybe there was something between the two of them. Lord knew, he didn't feel like he had much to offer. Seeing the two of them left him with a bittersweet taste in his mouth.

He really liked Sidney. He admired her. He had clearly seen it from the conversation around him and had already realized there was a lot to be said for her strong character. Because he knew if he had somebody that enabled him all day long, he would probably give the same poor performance himself. That wasn't what he wanted. This team needed to push him. Same as he would want a partner to push him. To support him but not to sit there cosseting him so he could step back and not face reality. As he neared his room, his phone rang. He stopped, leaned against the wall and pulled it out of his pocket. "Hey, Cole."

"Are you at Hathaway House?" Cole asked. "If you are, how is it? I've been offered a place there."

"What?" Brock asked, astonished. "That's awesome. It would be fantastic if you came."

"Really, buddy? Are you sure? You wouldn't lead me down the wrong path, right? It wouldn't be just the two of us against the place, would it?" Cole's voice held humor, but at the same time, there was a note of anxiety.

Brock laughed. "No, man. This place is different. Nothing like I've seen before. Goes to show you how different the military is from the private sector. You'll see the minute you arrive."

"Well, that's good to know. Because I sure as hell didn't want to go from this institutionalized living to something worse. I understand Denton has already applied to come to Hathaway, too, but I don't think he has coverage."

"Having the three of us together, well, that would be awesome. But you're right, I didn't even know I had all the coverage for this. I'm not sure how I got in at all, actually. I applied, but I was totally surprised when I was accepted."

"Are you sure this is a cool place to be?"

"Do you like animals?"

"You know I do, especially dogs."

"Well, they're all over this place. There's a veterinary clinic on the lower level. So, there are therapy animals in the building, and patients upstairs get to spend time with all the animals downstairs."

There was shocked silence on the other end of the line. "Damn," Cole murmured.

"You have to come and see for yourself."

"I will. And it could be earlier than you think."

On that mysterious note, Cole hung up. Brock chuck-led. Life would be so different if Cole were here. He didn't know what was happening with Denton, but damn! With a lighter heart, and hope spreading through him, he made his way back to his room, feeling truly happy for the first time in a long while.

## Chapter 6

"**I**T'S ALREADY ALL over the place," Sidney said in a low voice.

"Of course, it is. Like any workplace, rumors and gossip happen sometimes."

Sidney nodded and scooped up a bite of her yogurt. "Yeah, I probably wasn't the most subtle person on the planet. Came out like an elephant in a china shop."

Shane gave a big belly laugh that had several other patients looking over at him.

She shook her head. "It's not that funny."

"Oh yes, it is. It's not that you're an elephant in a china shop, but you call it as you see it in that direct, forthright way that is not terribly welcomed by everybody."

She nodded. "I stepped on people, and hurt their feelings, right?" Damn, she hated doing that.

"I'm not so sure if it's you, or if it's professional courtesy—or lack thereof."

She leaned back. "Well, there are a lot of things I'd apologize for, but that's not one of them."

"Do you really see a problem with Andrew?" Shane asked curiously. "I never worked with him myself."

She studied him and said, "If you have a slot open, maybe you should. He'd probably get along well with you. He should not be around young pretty women."

Shane's eyebrows rose. "What, am I a mean old ugly troll?"

"No, but you're not likely to be susceptible to his charms."

Understanding slammed into his eyes. "Then maybe I should ask to take him on. He's only here for another couple of weeks."

She nodded, feeling better. "That would actually be a very good thing." She sighed. "Do I have to apologize to Marsha?"

"Honestly, I'd leave it. You don't think she did the best job she could. I'll find out myself tomorrow morning, but at this point, if you bring it up with anyone it will make it worse."

"As long as I'm not taking on any other people she's been working with," Sidney said. "That's not likely to work out so well."

"That's another thing I'm wondering. I'm not sure, but I think he managed to request her for the entire duration, which is not a good thing. I know they became great friends, but that's not always the best situation."

Sidney frowned. "That shouldn't have happened. Every therapist has their strengths and weaknesses."

"We have teams for each patient," he reminded her. "But members do shifts. The therapists always rotate through." He frowned as he looked across the table at the group of therapists he'd left. "At least, normally, we shift them around. If not, then we need to have a talk with Dani about doing more of that. I think it's been kind of loose up till now."

Sidney was silent for a moment. "I think you're right. I think we do need to switch around." Then she laughed. "But

I rocked the boat enough for one day."

She finished her yogurt and coffee and stood. "Thanks for coming over, Shane."

He was sprawled lazily in his chair, his long legs stretched out along the deck. "Not a problem."

She brought her dirty dishes to the shelf in the kitchen, and then made her way back to her room. Her quarters were on the far side of the building, and on the lower level. Several staff members lived on the premises, and a number didn't. It was a personal choice, and, of course, it also depended on space. She'd given up her small apartment when she went back to school, but it'd been recently vacated, so she was back in her same digs. She walked into the studio and collapsed on the bed. She rubbed her face with her hands. She really had to handle things better. That was her fault. She should've considered the previous therapist and not been quite so adamant. But like everything else, it was over, and there was only so much she could do now.

What she could do, however, was go for a swim. She got up and changed into her suit and cover-up, grabbed a towel and made her way to the pool. There were a lot of advantages to living on the premises—not only the meals but also the exercise facilities. After the day she'd had, her own muscles needed a bit of a workout. She'd love a massage, too, but that wasn't likely to happen. Often, the therapists worked on each other on an exchange basis. However, she figured she was probably out of the loop right now, and not likely to get back into it anytime soon.

There were several people on the pool level when she got there. She ignored them all and dropped the towel and cover-up on one of the chairs in the sun, walked to the end and dove into the water at the first lane.

As soon as the cold water closed over her head, a sense of peace and serenity filled her body and soul. She broke the surface to gasp for air, and then struck out strongly for the other side, once again filled with that sense of rightness. She'd never been one to not rock the boat if the boat needed to be rocked. Hopefully, now that she'd caused whatever turmoil was rolling on around her, things would work out and ease back down again.

There was always an adjustment to getting back to work, the same as it was going back to school.

She just wanted this adjustment to pass by quickly because she'd like to settle down and get to work again. That's where she excelled.

Although, apparently, she didn't excel quite so much in her professional and patient relationships. Suddenly, she felt slightly overwhelmed, wondering why she'd ever bothered coming back. She swam faster.

She really hoped tomorrow was going to be better.

BROCK SETTLED INTO his room, feeling a sense of peace and quiet. Now that he knew his friends could possibly be coming here to be with him, he felt energized. In need of something to do, he grabbed his crutches and left his room. He knew that his body had taken a hell of a workout today, and he didn't want to trust losing his balance and falling.

He hobbled over to the elevator and headed down to the vet clinic. He smiled at Stan, who was talking with a couple of patients holding cats in cages. He grinned and headed to Rebecca, the receptionist.

"Stan said he wouldn't mind having a few volunteers. I

don't have a ton of energy, but maybe there is something small I can do to help out."

The middle-aged woman looked up at him and smiled with a wide happy-go-lucky grin on her face. He immediately fell under her trance.

"A little bit of energy for hugs?" she asked. "Or a little bit more energy for cleaning cages? Depending on how ambulatory you are, we have a couple of dogs that need to go outside to do their business …"

He glanced down at the crutches and said, "I probably could take the dogs out to do their business as long as they don't knock me down."

She stood and glanced at the crutches. "Two of them are recovering from surgery and should be going home in a couple of days, so they're not exactly jumping around and hyper. I'll bring you one and see how you do."

He waited for a few minutes while Stan said goodbye to the two women, and then turned and walked over to say hi to him.

"Hi, Brock, it's nice to see you down here." He motioned at the crutches, "How are you doing today?"

"I'm doing just fine. I had a hell of a workout today, so I'm feeling the effects, but I was still a little too keyed up to spend the rest the night in my room."

"Who's your therapist?"

"Sidney." Brock watched as Stan's face lit up. "She took more out of me and made me pull more out of myself than I've ever had any therapist do. I gather she's going through a bit of a tough patch right now, but I've never had a therapist like her."

Stan's face cleared. "I'm really glad to hear that. She's a hell of a girl. She really cares about her patients, but she'd be the first to say she's less concerned about her relationships with everybody than she is about fixing what's wrong with the body."

"You know, I'm okay with that," Brock said. "I've listened to enough platitudes and empty promises, so when I find somebody who actually means what they say and does what they say, well …"

Just then, Rebecca came back with a Basset hound walking at her side.

"Oh, I think I can handle this guy." He was kind of relieved because he didn't want a dog that would trip him up, or a big one that might decide to drag him down the yard. He had been half afraid he was taking on more than he could handle.

"This is Marshall. He had a cyst removed, so he isn't moving superfast. But he has the same need to go outside as everybody." She turned to look over at Stan and said, "Do you want to grab Major and take him at the same time? That was the last patient for the day so …"

"Sure, I can do that." Stan started to walk in the opposite direction, but he turned and called back, "Just give me a minute."

Considering Brock had no idea where he was going, that was probably a damned good idea. He idly glanced around at the clinic and realized just how open and friendly it all looked. He turned back to Rebecca.

"How long have you worked here?"

"Years and years and years," she said with a laugh. "And I hope to be here years and years more."

"That's a hell of a good reference for coming here," Brock said. "It seems to be a thriving business."

She nodded. "It is, but we do a lot of charity work too."

Stan walked out leading a very large Great Dane. It was a little sprightlier than the Basset hound but not much. Brock let the Great Dane and Stan go ahead, and then he followed behind. The Basset walked slowly at his side. He realized he needn't have worried. In this case, it was the injured leading the injured. He was glad to be able to do it. Outside, there was a large dog run. Stan walked to the gate, opened it and held it open while Brock walked in.

"Just unclip the dogs and let them wander. There are only the two of them today."

It took a little bit of coordination, but Brock finally managed to unclip the leash from the Basset hound. He hobbled to the side of the pen, watching the two dogs carefully explore. They truly seemed to enjoy being in the fresh air. He agreed—he felt the same way. He glanced around to see several horses in one paddock, and beside them were a little, tiny foal and an older mare. Someone was talking with them. As he watched, Sidney threw her arms around the little baby and hugged her. Then she let it go, to watch the little horse dance and prance around her. Her laughter floated on the wind. He smiled.

That was what she needed. She couldn't have had an easy day. She turned and caught sight of them and waved. He waved back. He turned to see Stan grinning like a fool.

"She's quite something, isn't she?" Brock asked. In his heart, he was hoping there was no relationship between the two of them. There'd be at least more than a decade of age difference, but he'd seen many that had a lot more. Still, he couldn't imagine anybody telling Sidney that was a no-no because of some nefarious rule she didn't believe in. He knew she'd go where she wanted to regardless.

Stan nodded. "She's a really great lady."

Frowning Brock turned back and watched her reach over and hug the mare. "She seems to be comfortable with the animals."

"She comes down here a lot. She spends all day helping people up there, but who's to help her when she runs into trouble?" Stan's voice was sad.

"You know her well, don't you?"

"There are not too many up there I don't know. But for those who have been here as long as I have," he corrected himself, "we're family."

Brock knew he shouldn't say anything but was unable to help himself. "Is there anything more than that there?"

Stan shot him a look, and then he laughed. "No, not at all. She's like a little sister to me. They all are. For all the relationships that have come and gone, I've never met anybody here for me, unfortunately." He shrugged his shoulders and gazed straight back over to Sidney. "Her last relationship broke up on the first day of going back to school. It was pretty rough timing."

"That would be," he said sympathetically. Inside, Brock was elated. If she didn't have a partner, then that meant the field was open. He didn't even know how she felt about him. He sure as hell hadn't given her a great impression at the beginning, but he was starting to understand she wasn't going to be all that easy to care for, either. But sometimes one had to work for the best things in life.

He had a few months here. Maybe they could make some progress. At least he hoped so because he realized he'd been thinking about her all day long. As she walked over to the two of them, he brightened.

She stopped on the other side of the fence and crossed her arms on the top rail. "I'm surprised to see you here,

Brock. I'll have to work you harder next time," she teased.

But the smile didn't reach her eyes. Instead, he could see the deeper concern. He finally realized what Stan had been talking about. He was right. She looked after her patients all day long, but when she had a low spot, who was there for her? Taking a chance he said, "I'm enjoying gaining comfort from the animal world."

She raised one eyebrow and nodded. "So …" She looked down at the Basset and smiled. "Who is this guy and what happened that he's here?"

The three of them looked at the Basset as Stan went over Marshall's medical history. "He's come a long way."

The Great Dane wandered around and didn't appear to be interested in doing anything other than enjoying the fresh air and being with people. That, and he was probably in a cage for most of his time here, which wasn't nice for anybody.

"Do these animals have homes?"

"Both do," Stan replied. "They have families that love them. But so often we are the home for those that don't."

"Right, the charity work here the receptionist mentioned."

"I do a lot of that. But we couldn't manage to do it all without Dani. She somehow gets us funding when we run short. She has a charity set up and receives donations through that. Luckily, she seems to know a lot of money-people willing to donate, and that keeps the place moving, both upstairs and downstairs."

## Chapter 7

S HE WAS GLAD to see Brock here, although she shouldn't be. The animals were a hell of a tug on the heartstrings. He'd been tired out, but now he looked … content. So, something had changed in his world. She wished something had changed in hers. She knew tomorrow was a whole new day, and she wished it was tomorrow already.

"You've been swimming?" Stan asked.

She felt Brock's glance as she nodded. "Even then, I was still too keyed up, so I decided to come out and walk around to reacquaint myself with all my old friends." The old mare had followed her over and nuzzled her hand. She laughed and stroked the long velvet nose. "This is Maggie."

Twisting, she wrapped her arms around Maggie's neck. "She's been here as long as I have—much longer, in fact."

"And shall be here for a lot longer still," Stan said with a smile. "She's in great health."

Sidney turned and headed back toward the gate. "I'm going to head back to my place. I'll see you two tomorrow." She watched as a flash of something that looked like disappointment crossed Brock's face.

Impulsively, she said, "Unless either of you want to join me for a coffee?"

Stan shook his head. "I'm not done for the day yet." He turned to Brock and said, "You go on. I'll take both dogs back in."

"Are you sure?"

"Yes, you go ahead."

Sidney laughed like a little kid as Brock tried to hobble quickly behind her.

Somehow, she knew this was going to be fun.

And it was. Like two kids, they enjoyed a cup of coffee and conversation. No pressure. No strings. Nothing but two people who enjoyed spending a quiet hour together. She didn't keep him long. She was tired, too. And by the time she headed to her room, she was smiling.

The next day dawned bright and cheerful with a blue sky and sunshine. She'd gone to bed in a much happier frame of mind. As far she was concerned, yesterday was done and over with. With any luck, she could just move forward and get into a normal routine of being here. She checked her watch and realized she didn't have enough time for another swim. That was something she was going to have to adjust her schedule for. Fitness was important, particularly with all the food readily available.

She dressed quickly, walked upstairs and grabbed a coffee, then stepped out onto the deck. Standing at the railing, she studied the rolling hills and the animals. They really could bring in twenty to forty more horses without any difficulty. The lush grass could certainly support them. It might actually be a way to bring in income for the center, too. Rent out the paddocks and pastures. There were a lot of horse people around town. The only thing was, someone would need to keep an eye on them, and that was going to require yet more staff. Therefore, it might not cover the costs. She wasn't sure how a business plan would work.

The eating area was still empty except for one or two

people. Turning back to refill her coffee, she sent up one more silent wish that today would be an upswing day. At that moment, Shane and Marsha walked in. Marsha stiffened, grabbed a coffee and turned her back on Sidney. Shane smiled at her. "Good morning."

Grateful for his friendship, she said, "Good morning back at you. It's a beautiful day today."

"It is indeed." He grabbed himself a coffee, snagged a muffin and followed Marsha.

There was no invitation to join them. Sidney shrugged. Why would there be? She supposed it didn't help that she still felt more like a guest than an employee. Walking back to the buffet, she picked up a selection of yogurt, granola, and fruit, and took it back out to the sunshine. She sat down to enjoy her food with her back to the dining area. When a shadow fell across her, Sidney stiffened apprehensively.

"Can I join you?" Brock's deep voice smoothed over her.

She beamed a smile up at him. "Sure."

"You didn't look like you wanted company, so I wasn't sure." He pulled out a chair and sat down.

"Not to worry. It's fine." Always the therapist, she studied him critically. His color was good, but she could see the heavy lines of fatigue on his face from the workout the day before. She'd already known that today would have to be an average day, not another hard-working one. "Did you have a good night?"

He nodded. "Not bad. Still woke up a bit on the tired side, though."

"Is that so?" She smiled at him crookedly and went back to eating.

"This'll blow over," he said in a low voice, pointing with his chin to the other physiotherapists inside.

"Maybe. Maybe not." She turned to study the table were Marsha and Shane were sitting. "We're all professionals here. Some of us just have different techniques, and some of us are a little more abrasive than others." She gave him a lopsided smile. "You know which of these applies to me."

"It's what makes the world go round." He smiled at her, a lopsided grin that tugged at her heart. He was a good-looking man. Now that they'd gotten over their initial dustup, she looked forward to a solid, working relationship.

She checked her watch and said with a grin, "Are you ready for me to crack the whip?"

He snorted. "Yes. But I have forty-five minutes first, and I want every damn minute." Then he laughed. "Hopefully not too much cracking."

"It won't be quite so tough today."

He raised an eyebrow at her. "Getting soft on me?"

She chuckled. "Not a hope in hell. But every muscle needs a chance to recover." She waggled her eyebrows and leaned forward. "Just think—there's lot of muscles we can still work on while those are resting."

He winced.

She went off into gales of laughter. Finally composing herself, she added, in a conspiratorial whisper, "That's okay, baby, I'll be gentle." She stood and walked away, still chuckling.

"Promise?"

Sidney froze. Then, she turned and shot him an uncertain look, grateful to find his gaze fixed on his coffee cup before she hurried out the door. Only, the thought wouldn't leave her alone.

It seemed like for the last few days and weeks, all she had seen were couples kissing or exchanging special smiles, hands brushing against cheeks, wonderful loving gestures. Just the knowledge that the two people in question were in a special relationship. The world really was built for twos. As a single, it was an odd feeling to see so many other happy couples, particularly when she didn't have anybody coupled up to her. Did she want to be? Maybe. It had been nine months since her relationship had gone to pieces. It was certainly long enough to get over it, but she also hadn't found anybody else who attracted her. Immediately, her mind drifted toward Brock. She really liked him. She could tell a lot about the character of a person when she worked with them. So far, she'd found absolutely nothing to not admire.

He was also sexy as hell. So many men felt their sexuality went out the window when they'd lost a limb, when they were so badly injured there were physical deformities. She worked with injured men and women every day, all day. To her, the beauty of a person came from the soul inside. She could sympathize with the injuries, but it was her job to help make the person as strong, fit and as capable as they could be. To do that, she connected with the inner spirit that was unique to each person. Brock instantly came to mind. She had to admit he was unique.

She smiled as a tiny tingle went down her spine. She'd love to spend more time with him. But he needed to heal and strengthen, so he could move on. And then Brock would leave. So what good would it do to start a relationship now? Unless they were going to end up in the same town down the road, the chances of them being able to have a relationship weren't very good. Plus, she wasn't into clandestine affairs with patients. Even if Dani had opened the doors to that possibility.

Sidney understood because love was like that. Now, it

also allowed her to pursue a relationship with Brock, if she wanted to. And, she realized belatedly, she wanted to. Her thoughts were constantly on this man. And she knew he was of the same mind, with the same heartstrings tied in knots as she was.

Being in a relationship where one person settled sucked. She understood the theory, the philosophy that in every relationship somebody settled, but she didn't agree with that. She thought there were lots of relationships where people came in as equals. She wanted to believe that because if it wasn't true when she went wholeheartedly into a relationship and felt one hundred percent committed, that meant the other person was settling. And that was not what she wanted. She wanted someone to look at her as being good enough without any of the other limiting factors. She wanted someone to look at her and to feel humbled to have her in their life. In the same way as she had felt humbled to have her past relationships be a part of her world. The last thing she wanted was to consider that somebody had *settled* for her.

IT WAS SEVERAL days later when Brock returned to his room after a particularly testing morning trying to sort himself out. The counselor had not been one bit of help. He also hadn't liked the news from the doctor this morning and had been trying to reach his buddy Cole all day, with no response. He sat down on his bed and stared, dispirited, out the window. For all that had happened, this was a great place to be, yet his life right now still sucked.

He had just enough time to get a shower before lunch. If he didn't get to lunch early then there was going be a huge line. He headed into the bathroom and refused to give himself a chance to just stand under the hot water as he wanted to do. Finally redressed, he was about to pocket his phone when it buzzed in his hand.

He pulled the device out to see who had texted him. Cole. He read the message. **Where the hell are you?**

He answered back. **I'm where the hell I always am. Where the hell are you?** He frowned, confused by the message. Another text popped up on his screen with a soft ping. **Maybe you should come to the dining room and see for yourself.**

His heart jumped. **What?** He bolted down the hallway as fast as he could, making his way to the dining room. As he stood in the doorway, he scanned the huge room full of people. Was he really here? Why didn't he tell him when he was coming in? They'd been friends for decades. They had been in high school together. They'd taken different paths for a while, but then both had ended up in BUD/s training together. Seeing Cole and Denton in the same training camp at the same time had been both unnerving and hugely comforting. They'd supported each other all the way through the brutal training. But they'd passed. They'd actually survived, and they knew it was partly because of the support they'd given each other.

BUD/s wasn't the kind of training one did on one's own. Not that you couldn't, but the journey was a ton easier if you had somebody to help you get there. He'd put his own success down to having his friends there. They'd ended up on different SEAL teams over the years, and they'd gone on several missions together, but not as many as he'd have liked.

His gaze landed on the beloved, scarred face in the sunshine. He hobbled as fast as he could.

By the time he reached Cole, his buddy was standing, one crutch under his arm and tears in his eyes.

They hugged.

Damn, his heart was breaking with joy.

# Chapter 8

GOOD NEWS TRAVELED fast at Hathaway. Often, patients created friendships there that survived even long after the individuals had returned to their normal lives. Sidney didn't remember ever seeing two patients that had been friends beforehand coming here together, though. It would prove to be an interesting dynamic. Would they help each other or enable each other to do less? She was looking forward to finding out, particularly when one of them was Brock. She knew he'd had a hard adjustment here. A friend might be a good answer. At the same time, part of her was sad and maybe a little jealous. Her time away had isolated her somewhat from the other staff and until now, she'd enjoyed spending the time with Brock. Now he was going to want to spend his time with Cole.

Maybe that was good. A new perspective on his care and their relationship couldn't be a bad thing. She walked into his room with a bright smile pasted on her face. Already, she noticed a change. He sat on his bed, his back and shoulders straight, and a smile on his face as he texted on his phone. She had no doubt who he was talking to.

"Don't you look bright and happy this morning."

He looked up, and his grin brightened. "Absolutely," he said with a laugh. "A buddy of mine is here now, too. It's so great to see him."

She smiled. "Does that mean you can work harder and better and faster now?"

He laughed. "Well, I don't know about that. I seem to do plenty of that as it is when I'm around you." He motioned at his phone. "It's just nice to see somebody you know. Somebody who understands where you've been, and what you're up against. And know the same about them. It's not that misery loves company, but everyone needs …" A slight grin slid out. "… maybe understanding."

"That's normal. As much as we do understand, in that we see people like you day in and day out, we are not in your position," she said lightly. "So we can empathize and commiserate, but we haven't walked in your shoes, so we can't really understand."

"Exactly," he said, nodding his head emphatically. "You actually get it. More than I expected."

"Well then, you understand it's time to get to work."

He gave her a mock salute. "Lead on, commander."

She shook her head. "It's the other way around. You lead on. We're going to start in the weight room this morning. Let's go see what you can do today."

He hopped up easily, then he strode out of the room. He didn't take a crutch for balance or safekeeping. She smiled behind his back as she walked. He was doing so well. With any luck, he'd be out of here quickly. Not that that would make him terribly happy, if his friend had just arrived. But she didn't know that for sure. He did have a lot more to do on his back, that was for certain. She set him up with some exercises to get started. Light warm-ups, then she'd start checking out some of the muscles.

"Sidney?"

She turned to see Shane in the doorway.

"Give me a minute." She turned back to see how Brock was doing.

He waved her off and said, "This is just a warm-up. I promise, I won't hurt myself."

She raised her eyebrows at the cockiness in his attitude. He certainly had a lot more energy and a lot more enthusiasm this morning, and that was a good thing. She turned back to Shane and said, "What's up?"

"Andrew is being discharged in a couple of days," he said. "I wanted you to see how he's doing."

"There's no need for me to see him," she said. "I trust you to do a good job."

Shane laughed. "Actually, I think he doesn't trust anybody else now. Not that he would admit it."

She frowned at him. "What do you mean?"

"You were right," he said simply. "A couple muscle groups hadn't been given enough attention, and they needed work. Once he realized the truth of what you had said, he got really angry. Then he buckled down to work."

"He seemed like the kind of guy that would do that." She nodded. "I'm glad you took him on."

"Now he doesn't want to listen to my take that he's doing much better. He knows he's leaving in a couple of days and is afraid there hasn't been enough progress. But it's not required, and the cost of the bill would land in his lap if he stayed longer than prescribed."

She studied his face. "And?"

Shane leaned against the doorjamb and crossed his arms as he looked toward where Brock was working. "It's actually a request from Andrew. He would like to know if you could possibly come and take a look, to see where he might still be lacking."

Sidney blinked, and then she laughed. "So the guy that sent me away, complained about me and wanted to change to yet another therapist now wants me to make sure the work's been done properly?"

"Absolutely," Shane said with a crooked smile. "As you're the one that found the problem before, he would like to know you approve of the changes and you don't see anything new that concerns you."

Amused, she grinned. "Where is he now?"

"He's in the room next door."

She turned to look back at Brock. "I don't want Brock to be alone. Give me ten minutes, and we'll move over there. That way, I can keep an eye on both of them." She gave him a wry smile. "It's going to feel weird, though."

Shane squeezed her shoulder. "You did what you needed to do, and he had to learn." He turned and left the room.

She walked back to Brock and pushed him through the rest of the set she had established.

"So, we're changing rooms?" he asked.

Of course, he'd overheard the conversation. "Do you mind?"

"Nope, as long as it doesn't change what we're working on."

She grabbed his gear and motioned for him to go ahead. By the time he reached the door, she'd given the equipment a quick wipe-down and followed him.

In the other room, she could see Shane and Andrew standing and talking.

She studied Andrew, assessing his balance and his relaxed stance. Then, when he saw her, he straightened. She noted his stiff bearing but also that he stood strong. There was no leaning to the side.

"How much work is there to be done this morning?" she asked Shane.

"About an hour."

She nodded. She studied Andrew for another long moment. She walked around him. She knew he was a little confused, but she kept a smile on her face.

Brock reached out and shook Andrew's hand. "I hear you'll be leaving soon."

Andrew shook his hand warmly in return. "There are definitely worse places to be, but there's no place like home."

Brock chuckled in agreement. He nodded at Sidney and said, "I'll head over to the balls and do some more stretching before you come over and give me the drill-sergeant routine." With a goodbye smile at Andrew, he walked over to the chairs on the other side of the room to give them a bit of privacy.

Shane laughed. "I see he knows you well."

She gave him an amused smile. "Apparently I have a bad reputation here." She turned back to Andrew and said, "If you don't mind, can I get you to walk toward the door and then turn around and walk back to me. Walk straight and as naturally as you can."

He raised one eyebrow but obediently turned and walked toward the door and then, using the doorjamb, he turned around and walked back to her.

"Did you need the doorjamb for support?" she asked. "Or was it just habit?"

He frowned at her in confusion, then he looked at the door. "I'm not sure. I guess I have to figure that out." He turned on his own just fine and walked back to the door again. He passed through the doorway back and forth several times and said, "I think it's a habit."

"But you are favoring your left leg. Did you hurt it?"

He glanced down at his leg and said, "I accidentally cut it with my fingernail last night. It was surprisingly deep and irritated me. It surprised me how sensitive it is."

"Any injury on the stumps will take longer to heal. Until you build up the eventual callus there, you'll notice every little bump and scratch," she said calmly. She glanced over at the exercise balls and back at him. "Are you up for a few exercises?"

He winced. "I guess we're back to the same ones I did originally for you?"

She nodded. "I want to see how much improvement there is."

Andrew glanced over at Shane.

"It's all good," Shane said.

Andrew walked to the balls and removed both prosthetic limbs. She led him through a series of exercises to determine what the inner abdominal muscle groups were doing. Finally, he sat back up, his breathing strong and his face flushed. "Damn, this is hard work."

"Hard work it might be, but you did fine." She walked over to Shane and held out her hand for his clipboard. "You're still favoring the left side, but you've come a long way. I knew we would be able to get you there, but without some extra work, you aren't going to be able to maintain it. Going home will throw you off. There, you will twist and turn, bend and use muscles in ways you haven't in a long time, so that's going to put strain on your system. You need to maintain physio for several months. Shane will give you a set of exercises to keep you strengthening that muscle group."

She finished writing down the notes for Shane's chart

and handed it to him. She smiled at Andrew. "Other than that, you've done a lot of work and it's paid off. You're looking good." She reached out and shook his hand. "Congratulations. I hope you have a great future."

She patted Shane on the shoulder and turned to head over to Brock.

IT WAS HARD not to hear their conversation, but Brock focused on his workout, trying to give them privacy. There'd been enough rumors going around for the past week, and he realized this was a happy conclusion for Sidney. And for Andrew, by the looks of it. He wondered how he would feel if another therapist had said there was something missing in his workout, and that his current therapist hadn't done as good a job as possible. It would be scary. In Andrew's case, he was heading back home without the support he'd had here for so many weeks, if not months. To think that at the last minute something had almost been missed … well, that was one of the worst scenarios he could imagine.

For him, he had been assigned to Sidney on her first day back, and she'd done a hell of a job with him. Still, he had to wonder—what if a different therapist did see something else? Should one have multiple therapists because they each would see something different?

He knew it was that way in many industries. What one chef knew, another one didn't always know. What one editor saw wrong in a project, another editor would see differently. It wasn't bad, it was just the way the world was. He'd had other therapists before coming here, and he hadn't done well with them. Now that he was supercharged and starting to feel like his old self again, did it mean another therapist wouldn't see something different?

He had had Shane before. Apparently, Shane and Andrew had gotten along well, if what he'd seen these last several weeks was anything to go by. In fact, Shane and Sidney seemed to get along fine, too. A little too fine for his liking.

Brock gave his head a shake. He had no business thinking like that, but he was a single, healthy male, Sidney was stunningly attractive, and it was pretty damned hard not to. He'd spent a ton of his spare time with her. He couldn't wait to talk to Cole about her. Just the thought of seeing his friend at lunchtime made him move into his workout with a ferocity he hadn't seen in himself since Sidney's first day.

"Hey, killer, what's the rush?" Sidney asked with a smile.

Brock could see she was truly happy. Something had been settled inside. She was happy with Andrew now and the outcome of the problem. He had no idea how the other therapist would react, but he hoped none of it would come back on Sidney.

"I'm meeting Cole for lunch today," he said happily, pushing away that train of thought. "I can't wait."

She smiled. Hmm. Maybe things weren't perfect, yet. She was a little subdued. He gave her a bright smile, hoping he could infuse some of his good humor into her for the day. He was feeling fantastic. The happy mood kept up all the way through the morning workouts. By the time they broke for lunch, he was feeling damned proud of himself.

He headed back to his room and had a quick shower, then made his way to the dining area. He grabbed a chair at a table out in the sunshine—his favorite—off to the left by the horses and texted Cole. **I'm at lunch and I've got a**

**table for us.**

And he waited.

And waited some more. Frowning, he rose and headed to the buffet. He was hungry and really didn't want to wait any longer. Besides, he had no idea what was holding his buddy up. He hadn't even texted back. So … was there a problem? He cast his mind back to his first few days at Hathaway, and the teams he had to meet, and all of the testing that had to be done. He realized that if nothing else, Cole was likely exhausted and possibly asleep.

He could also be eating in his room.

Sobered, and remembering the harsh adjustment at the beginning of his own journey, Brock returned to the table he'd chosen out in the sun and ate his lunch alone.

Chapter 9

S IDNEY SAT ON the first table on the deck side of the dining room, watching as Brock walked in and took his place. She wondered about joining him for a moment, then remembered he was waiting for Cole. When he got his own lunch and headed back alone, she pondered for a second time if she should join him. But there was something going on between him and his friend, and she didn't want to get in the way. She was happy to support him if there was something there to be supportive of. But she'd have to wait for him to tell her about it. Shane dropped down in the chair opposite her with his tray full of food. She jumped in surprise.

"At least you're still talking to me," she said wryly.

"Of course. But then I'm a male."

She snorted. "There is definitely a difference between working with a group of females versus a group of males." As a female, she understood her own sex well. She had little tolerance for a lot of their foibles. But there were a lot of good things about women that men just couldn't compete with. Shane did a very good job of dodging bullets with all the women as it were. In fact, she wondered why he was single. He was gorgeous, compassionate, extremely professional and very good at his job.

"How come you've never hooked up with anybody

here?" she asked.

Startled, he stopped with his fork in midair, and then shook his head, popping the food into his mouth, a big grin on his face. When he finally could speak, he said, "Sidney, you need to work on your interrogation tactics."

"Why? It's a simple question." She picked up her coffee cup and studied him over the rim. "You're good looking. You're personable, and you're very professional. What's not to like?"

He gave a small shrug and said, "You tell me. There have been a couple women here I've liked, but it didn't work out."

She nodded. "That's too bad."

"I'm not too bothered. I figure I'll find somebody sometime. In the meantime I'm more than a little busy with my career."

She glanced back toward Brock, only to find he was laughing at something on his phone. "I hear you. With all the people coming and going in this place, it's a steady job just keeping up with the names."

"Speaking of people coming and going, Cole had a rough adjustment."

She looked over at him. "How rough?"

"He won't be doing therapy for a week or two. The doctors need him to regain his strength, first. The trip here took more out of him than anyone expected. And he pushed it as soon as he got here."

"Which means he hasn't fully recovered from his latest surgery. I'm sorry for Brock. He was so excited about meeting his buddy for lunch. But when he didn't show up, I see he ate alone."

"There could be many days like that."

"It happens." She made a mental note to have a talk with Brock later. Just because he was moving in leaps and bounds didn't mean his friend was going to follow. One had to be very respectful of everybody's progress. She spent a few minutes sitting with Shane while he ate, and then made her excuses. She took her cup of coffee and snagged an apple as she walked out. She had fifteen minutes before she had to go work on schedules and reports, and then she had a full afternoon. She walked to Brock's room to find the door shut. She stood in the hallway and frowned. Not wanting to see his mood affect his performance, or put his recovery in jeopardy, she decided on knocking.

"Who is it?" came the voice from inside the room.

"It's me, Sidney."

There was kind of an odd silence, then he said, "Come in."

She turned the knob and stuck her head inside. "Hey, you doing okay?"

His expression was a cross between frustration and disappointment. Something wasn't right, and she was willing to bet it was Cole.

He gave a shrug. "I'm fine."

"Well, you're not, but that doesn't mean you're ready to share." She took a step into the room and waited. "This is about Cole?"

His gaze flew up to her. "What do you know about Cole?"

"I know he's had a rough introduction, and it's going to take several days before he is likely even allowed out of bed." She was surprised at Brock's dark eyes and could see the myriad possibilities whirring away in the back of his gaze.

"I haven't seen him myself," she rushed to say. "But as

far as I know, there is nothing major. Sometimes traveling and the change can set people back for a day or two, and they just need time to adjust—time to breathe. That's what I would suspect is the issue with Cole."

"He's a good guy." He gazed down at his bed and nodded. "But he also isn't the best at following orders."

Her heart went out to Brock. He was really worried about his buddy. "I'm sure he is. Chances are, he's sound asleep and will likely sleep the bulk of the next two days to recover."

When he looked up at her again, she could see the hope back in his eyes.

"I can probably check on him for you, if you want."

He brightened. "Yes please. He's not answering my texts."

She turned to walk back out of the room, but then she stopped. "I wasn't here when you arrived, but do you remember how difficult it was when you got here?"

"Oh, yeah. That's why I thought it would make it easier on him to have me around."

"But when you felt like shit, and everybody around you was bright and happy and doing so much better than you, how did you feel?"

Comprehension hit his gaze. "I'll give him some space. Just let him know I'm here if he needs me."

She smiled. "Bingo." She turned and exited the room, heading toward Dani's office. As she walked around the corner she spotted several people she recognized as kitchen staff inside Dani's office. She was about to turn away and come back later, but Dani caught sight of her.

"Sidney, come on in."

"I don't want to disturb you if you're busy."

"Not at all—we're finished." The group in the office made their way out, some smiling and greeting Sidney. Then Dani motioned at the seat between them and said, "Grab a chair. I was just going over the menus and the purchasing bill with the kitchen staff." She made a grimace. "Budgets— never a strong point for me."

"It must be a strong point because you keep this place running," Sidney said. "Honestly, I could never do that."

Dani laughed. "I certainly do try." She smiled at Sidney. "I hear Andrew spoke to you today."

"Yes, he did, and I think all is fine between us."

Dani nodded. "That's what I heard, too. He will be leaving here within the next twenty-four hours. He came in and signed the discharge papers after you saw him. He's pretty excited to go home."

"I suppose his bed has already been filled, ten times over?"

"It has, indeed." Dani watched her curiously for a moment. "But that's not what you're here for, so what's up?"

Dani was very observant. She didn't have any counselor or medical training, but she understood people. She was way better at that than Sidney was. "Actually, I came for an update on Cole. Brock's worried about his friend. Like, seriously worried."

"With good reason."

BROCK'S PHONE BUZZED in his hand. It was an incoming text from Cole. He smiled and settled back.

**Sorry bro. Missed lunch. Trip was a bit more hazardous than I thought. Feel like shit.**

**Want company?** he texted back.

**Not today. I want to get knocked out and wake up in six months when my body no longer hurts. My heart, my mind and my soul are wanting to give in.**

**Sorry, Cole. Just rest. It takes a few days to adjust.**

**I'll need every one of those. Goodnight.**

Feeling bad about his friend, but not knowing how to help him, Brock checked his schedule for the afternoon. That was one thing about being at this place, his days were pretty damn full. If it wasn't physio, it was doctors, check-ups, testing, counseling, therapy, career discussions about his future and discussions about how to adapt into society with his current handicaps. That was one session he'd originally hated to go to, and now, he didn't mind at all. Everybody sat in a circle and discussed their plans for after they left this place. It gave him a chance to see how many physical handicaps everybody had. It helped him to realize he wasn't alone. He wasn't the only one struggling. Just being around different people with different mindsets was positive and helpful.

Determined to make the best of the day, he finished off his afternoon on a positive note and tried to keep up the same attitude for the next few days while Cole stayed in his room and rested. That Cole didn't want friends visiting was a little worrisome. But as he'd been pretty antisocial himself when he arrived, Brock could understand. And he honored his friend's wishes.

After three days, Brock was finally determined to stop by and see Cole. He walked down the hall to find the door shut once again. He'd walked in this direction a half a dozen times already, and it was always shut. He knocked and got no answer. He wasn't sure what to do. Cole was no longer answering his texts and didn't appear to be answering the door, either. Determined to find some answers, he walked back to the front reception desk and the manager. He'd spent enough time talking with Dani to at least know who she was but not enough to be especially friendly. He knocked on her door, and when he heard the call to enter, he pushed the door open and walked inside.

Dani looked up and smiled. "Hello, Brock."

"Hi. Do you have a moment?"

Dani set aside the file folder she was holding. "Of course. What can I do for you? And by the way, you're looking great."

He smiled self-consciously. "I'm certainly doing a lot better. I'm not there yet, but I can now see that I'll be up to going home when my time is up."

"Where is home again?" She looked up. "I should remember but with so many patients I do forget the details."

He shrugged. "It used to be California, but I don't have any family there anymore. I do have friends in Texas, though. So, I thought I might stay local."

Dani nodded, a big smile on her face. "That sounds like a wonderful idea. Maybe we'll get to see you often, even after you leave."

He wondered if that was actually a teasing note he heard in her voice. Did everyone know he was sweet on Sidney? Should he ask? He gave himself a mental shrug. No. Thankfully Dani spared him further anguish.

"What can I help you with?"

He motioned toward the spare chair. "Do you mind if I sit down?"

"Yes, of course, please sit."

He pushed the office door closed and sat. He turned

back to Dani, who had a slight frown on her face.

"Is there a problem?"

Then, he remembered the last time he'd dealt with Dani, before Sidney had come into his life. He shook his head. "No, not the way you mean. I'm actually just worried about Cole."

Enlightenment crossed her face. She folded her hands together on the desktop. "I'm sorry, I should've come and said something to you." She glanced down at the papers on her desk, then back up again and said, "Cole is in the hospital. With any luck, we're hoping he'll be up to returning to us in a couple of days."

Brock stared at her. He didn't know what to say but managed to force his mouth to work. "Is he badly hurt?"

She shook her head, and his fear subsided somewhat.

"No, but obviously he wasn't quite ready to be here."

Brock nodded. He stared out the window and felt the four walls closing in on him. "I'm so sorry for him."

"It happens. Not very often, but every once in a while, we get a doctor who signed off on a transfer a little too early. Or the new arrival thinks he's better than he really is or knows better than his medical team, and he relapses. He's not bad. But his fluids were low, and he was starting to run a fever. It was the prudent decision to put him in the hospital for a couple of days until he is stabilized again."

"Of course. Anything to keep him safe." He jumped to his feet, needing to get out. Like way the hell out. "I haven't been out on the grounds yet," he said. "But I have to admit I'd really like to get out there today."

"A day trip can be arranged. Or if all you're really looking for is a chance to get out and visit with the animals, make sure you tell somebody where you're going and give them an estimated time so if you don't come back we can come looking for you. It's better if you have somebody that can go with you."

He could feel her searching gaze, but he didn't know who he'd take with him. "I'd be happy to ask Sidney, but I'm sure her day is full." He rubbed his arms anxiously and shook his head. "I'll be fine on my own. I just need to get out."

"Understood."

He mumbled his thanks, turned and bolted from the room as if the walls were actually pressing in on him. Well, as fast as anybody with his damned legs could. He was so much better, but there were so many twinges and pains and things he couldn't do yet. Just the simplest of things, such as bending and picking stuff up off the floor was such a hardship when you didn't have the right muscles working and the right body parts in place. He'd had no idea he was looking at something like this when he was first injured. Recovery had been an eye-opener.

He shouldn't be surprised about Cole because, dammit, that man had probably pressured his doctor to release him early. And he'd probably ignored the warnings to take it easy. That was so Cole. Knowing that Brock was here would've just added to it. And Brock had been pushing him hard to try to get a spot at Hathaway because he'd been lonely. How very selfish of him.

Grateful for the break in his schedule, and feeling small, and hating that his friend had had such a setback, he made his way outside to the pasture where the horses were. The long grass was wonderful to walk in. Even just being outside in the fresh air was healing. Being on the deck was one thing, but walking or hobbling on the property itself was great. He had both crutches with him just for safety—the last thing he needed was a fall at this stage. He walked slowly down the fence line as the horses came over to check him out. The soft feel of their long noses and their beautiful, gentle eyes almost broke his heart.

He'd never had a chance to be around animals—at least, not very much. He remembered he'd also offered to volunteer downstairs at the vet clinic, but he hadn't returned—so much for a new start and helping others. Suddenly feeling like he needed to make up for his halfhearted start, and for Cole's problem, he slowly made his way back to the vet clinic. There, he set about cleaning cages and feeding animals with the help of the assistants. He could understand the terrified cat that hissed and howled and climbed to the farthest corner of his cage. He had felt like that when he got here. By the time he made his way through the cages and got to the bunny who was just content to be picked up and cuddled, he realized that was where he was now. He'd come a long way, just as these animals had too.

More settled, he headed back out to the waiting room and found Sidney chatting with the receptionist. Her face lit up when she saw him.

"Hey, I heard you were down here helping out."

He nodded. He figured everybody knew—they kept tabs on all the patients, which was fully understandable. If something went wrong, getting immediate help would be appreciated. Right now, while he was upset about Cole though, the care and attention was a little hard to escape. Still, it was Sidney, and she could come looking for him anytime.

He smiled at her. "I'm done now."

"Good. How about a swim?"

He stopped and looked at her. "That's actually a great idea. I just felt hemmed in earlier and needed to get out, so I went outside for a bit, then came back in to help with the animals, thinking that might switch my mood."

"And switch your mood, it does. It's one of the best ways to get out of a funk. So is exercise."

He gave a short laugh. "Good point. Okay, a swim it is. Then I need some food."

Sidney glanced at her watch. "A swim will take us right up to dinnertime."

"You're on." Feeling much better, he headed to his room to grab his trunks and towel. This was just about a perfect way to end a crappy afternoon.

# Chapter 10

SIDNEY DIDN'T WANT Brock to think she'd been keeping an eye on him, but Dani had given her a heads-up about his feelings over Cole's setback. That was something she didn't want to see him get depressed over. Everybody was entitled to a day when they didn't feel one hundred percent. She'd had enough days like that herself. She kept an eye on him, though, going from window to window to see where he was. When she saw him heading back toward the building and then didn't come upstairs, she had called down to the receptionist and had been told he was in back helping out. Which was a perfect answer. When one was feeling lost and alone, helping somebody else who was in a worse condition was always a good way to return to center.

Sidney headed into the women's changing room and found a locker. She changed and grabbed her goggles before heading back out to the pool. This swim was something she was looking forward to. Her own muscles were feeling generally fatigued. Dealing with a lot of people on a daily basis pulled her down sometimes, too. Sometimes people got the wrong impression—that she was cold and hard. But that wasn't the way she was. Sometimes she just had to be a hard-ass to get people to do what they needed to do. At that moment, Marsha walked past, curled her lip in a sneer at her and kept going.

Sidney stopped. She wasn't going to let this low-lying, toxic situation continue. It had to stop. She spun around. "Marsha, what is your problem?"

With that Marsha froze, turned and snapped, "What's my problem? You."

Sidney shook her head. "You shouldn't have any problem with me. I didn't do anything."

"You're the one who pointed out I hadn't done my job." Her lips curved downward in a scowl. "Because I was friends with a patient."

Sidney rolled her eyes. "Do you think you're the only one who ever made that mistake? We all have. It's part of the business. You see what you want to see. You aren't always the best person to give diagnoses. We're supposed to be working as a team. We're supposed to always make assessments for each other. You're not perfect. None of us are."

Marsha frowned at her. "You didn't have to go to Dani about it."

Sidney's eyebrows shot up. "What are you talking about? I didn't go to Dani. I don't have to go to Dani. Dani somehow ends up hearing about everything anyway. I'm not a tattletale. If that's what's got your panties all twisted, then know it wasn't me." She turned and stalked off.

Sidney went to the deep end of the pool, put on her goggles and dove into the water, cutting cleanly through the surface. Her encounter with Marsha had been just enough to fuel the angry embers inside.

Pouring her frustration and anger into each stroke, she forced her body to move as fast as it could down the long lengths of the pool, flip-turning at each end and swimming back. She took a good eight laps as fast as she could before she came to a slow stop and just let the water wash around her.

Exhausted, she floated on her back and tried to catch her breath. She couldn't believe how drained she felt now. But it was a good fatigue—there was peacefulness inside. She floated for a long moment until she felt somebody come up beside her. She still didn't want to talk, so she just stayed where she was.

"You okay now?"

A wry laugh came out of her. She rolled over to look at Brock. "I guess that was a little display of temper, wasn't it?" she said calmly.

"Maybe. But maybe it was justified. The thing is, it doesn't really matter either way because you obviously needed the outlet, so you took it and you used it. You're looking better now." He reached across and stroked the few straggling hairs back off her face. "In fact, you look incredibly beautiful."

Sidney's skin tingled where he had touched her, and her eyes opened wide. "Brock, are you flirting with me?" she asked teasingly.

A wicked grin flashed across his face. "I don't know. Will it work if I do?" He swam closer. "You know if we were all alone …"

She smiled. Inside her heart warmed and swelled. He was such a nice man. "If we were alone, it'd be a different story, is that it? Instead of flirting you'd be mocking me?"

"Hell, no," he protested. "As you know perfectly well." He drifted his thumb across her full bottom lip, stroking it gently.

She couldn't help herself. She kissed his thumb on its second pass. His eyes darkened with that slumbering look. She glanced around and saw that except for them, the entire pool area was empty. The corners of her mouth kicked up. "You know, for the moment, we are alone …"

Instantly she was tugged forward into his arms, and his lips came down on hers. They barely treaded above the water as he kissed her with the heated passion she knew was inside him. She'd seen that same energy, that same passion for life in his workouts. Now, when it was fully focused on her … Wow. She slipped her arms up around his neck to slide her fingers through his hair. Dimly, the sound of voices reached her ears. She went to pull away, murmuring, "Someone's coming."

Instead, he whispered, "Take a breath." He gazed deep into her eyes. Curious, she took a breath, and he sealed her lips with his own, and they sank below the water. Down, down, down.

Such a magical feeling. Underwater where no one could see them—at least, not yet. Avoiding the world around them. Just the two of them lost in each other's arms.

She succumbed to the magic of the moment.

THERE WAS A time and place for everything. This was certainly not it. But in its own way, this moment was perfect. Brock's heart and mind were fully engaged with a beautiful woman whose body was pressed tightly against his. As they floated, and rolled, and kissed and tumbled in joy, he realized just how absolutely unique the situation was, and he wanted so much more.

The need for oxygen strained at his lungs, but he didn't want to let her go. He'd happily drown, if he could do it in this togetherness. He'd breathed into her mouth, and she into his, as they exchanged kisses and the life force of the very air they'd taken with them. But like all good things, it had to end. Slowly they broke apart and floated to the surface. As each gasped for fresh air, they stared at each other in wonder, realizing something special had started. Not just started but had crossed that initial awkward series of first steps. At least, he hoped so. They were obviously physically compatible if the last few minutes were anything to go by. He couldn't wait to hold her again.

Making love was one of the most glorious things when the person in your arms was also the person in your heart.

He knew he wasn't a perfect specimen anymore, but he also didn't think in Sidney's case that was an issue. She'd spent a lot of time working with men in various stages of health and life. He didn't see the same repulsion or the same distaste in her he'd seen in other women. It was as if she didn't even recognize his shortcomings. Even though he knew that wasn't true because she was the one that always pinpointed them and then forced him to work on them. That in itself was unique.

As others made their way toward the pool and the coffee tables on the deck, they floated away from each other. He knew this was more to give an appearance of normality than anything else.

Besides, a few minutes to cool the ardor of his body was a good thing. But now there was frustration thrumming through his soul. He'd known going into that kiss it wasn't the time or place, but to think common sense might have stopped him. That would have been a shame. Yes, he wanted her. Yes, he wanted her more than he'd ever wanted another woman. Especially now.

But those few minutes had also been something he'd

never experienced before, and for the moment, he just wanted to savor her. There was no need to force his body into heavy physical exertion just to wear off the frustration eating at him. Instead, he simply floated on the surface of the water, just existing in the aftermath of such joy.

Something he had never expected to experience because he didn't even know it existed. Now that he knew, he couldn't wait for another opportunity to go there. Of course, his mind immediately set about trying to figure out how to make that happen. They both lived here. She worked here. His lips quirked at that thought. At some point, he was no longer going to be here. But he was also footloose and had no future locked down. In a way, if he wanted to pursue a relationship with Sidney, that was an option. Part of his talks with counselors was about a career. What steps he was going to have to take to return to a normal life.

The only family he had left was a sister, and they were no longer close. It was his friends he was closer to. If he thought Cole and Denton were going to settle in Texas, then he'd settle beside them in a heartbeat. He'd love for the three of them to do barbecues in the backyard over a beer, watching their toddlers play in the grass. In a way, there was just nothing better for a man like him. Of course, to have the toddlers, he had to have the mother. His heart immediately zoned in on Sidney. She'd be perfect for that role. She was caring and empathetic, and yet she was also the most kick-your-ass-when-you-were-down-because-you-needed-it  type of female he'd ever met. Strong when she needed to be and yet caring all the rest of the time. Those were qualities anybody would admire.

"Are you going to just float around?" Sidney joked.

He lifted his head and smiled. "I thought we came for a

nice, relaxing swim."

"Relaxing being the operative word here. I've already done a few laps and burned off some of that lovely energy. How about you?"

"And here I was, just enjoying the after-burn, and not wanting to burn it away." His gaze met hers in a knowing way. He watched the pink flush spread over her neck and cheeks, but she smiled.

In a low voice she said, "That's a nice way to put it." She glanced around at the other people sitting at tables. "Some tea might not be a bad idea."

"Are you okay? Are you ready to leave?" he asked. He wasn't. He'd only been in here a few minutes. But if she was leaving, then he would.

"I'm more than okay," she said in a low voice. "I'm not quite ready to leave. I'm going to float for a while. Stay with me?"

At the invitation, his heart shouted, *yes*. In a quiet voice, happy and content, he said, "Absolutely."

And he watched a smile start in the back of her stunning eyes before it broke through to her lips—and his heart.

## Chapter 11

THE NEXT MORNING, Sidney glanced up as Dani walked into the physiotherapy office. "Good morning, everyone."

There was a hail of good mornings back her way.

Sidney caught Dani's eye. To make it look like she expected the meeting, she grabbed her notepad, pen and coffee and said, "Inside or outside?"

"Outside, always." With a laugh, the two women walked out of the office and proceeded through the building to the big back deck. As they approached the dining area, Dani said, "I'm going to grab a coffee. Pick a table and I'll join you."

Sidney chose her favorite far corner where the morning sun hit. There wasn't enough heat in the day yet to make it uncomfortable but just enough warmth she sat there with her face turned into the sunlight and relaxed. Really, right now, her world was pretty amazing. Aside from the whole Marsha issue, of course, but she'd weathered worse.

"Don't you look happy this morning," Dani teased as she returned with a cup of coffee and a fresh cinnamon bun.

"I don't know why I would," Sidney replied. "I didn't sleep well."

As if on cue, Dani held up two forks. Sidney grinned and grabbed one, and the two enjoyed the warm treat.

When they were done and sipping their coffees, Sidney cleared her throat.

"Am I in trouble?"

"Not any more than usual," Dani said with a chuckle.

At that, Sidney laughed out loud. "Ain't that the truth," she said dryly. "Apparently, I can get into trouble without trying."

"I did hear from Marsha. Not once, but twice. Apparently, you insulted her and upset her yesterday on your way into the pool. Then you supposedly had a lovemaking session in the pool."

Sidney's eyebrows shot up to her hairline. "Wow. All of that just from Marsha?"

"Absolutely."

"It certainly wasn't a lovemaking session, or anything indecent. However, I will confess there was a kiss exchanged. But only a kiss." Inside, Sidney winced. Marsha was correct in that it was completely unprofessional. But so was taking a simple kiss and blowing it up into something lewd and inappropriate. Did the woman hate her that much? Apparently. That was too damned bad. Maybe she could have handled the session with her and Andrew in a different way, but Sidney had just come back from school and hadn't adjusted herself. Not that that was any excuse for Marsha's poor on-the-job performance.

"That's what I assumed. How bad is the relationship between you and Marsha?" Dani asked.

"Apparently bad enough that she's coming to you with tales like that."

"She feels you've been very mean to her. That she was criticized unfairly." Dani sighed. "Of course this has to be investigated."

"I didn't mention the issue with Andrew to you as I knew I could switch up his program. I should have brought the problem to you earlier," Sidney admitted. "Maybe that would have avoided most of this."

Thinking to herself, Sidney had to wonder if she really had been that mean? She didn't think so. But if she'd hurt Marsha's feelings, then that wasn't right, either. She considered this a professional issue. Marsha had been sloppy in her work, and that wasn't acceptable. She needed to be able to take professional criticism. They all did. Not everybody was on their game one hundred percent of the time. Sometimes, it took other people's perspectives to see the truth. However, positive reinforcement was also important. She was not Marsha's supervisor. She glanced over at Dani.

"Has Shane mentioned anything to you?"

"I've already spoken to Shane. He's backed you up. He stated he took over the patient's care after agreeing with your assessment. He did speak to Marsha about it, and about her behavior toward you, but had thought it would die down. Instead, she came and made a formal complaint." Dani's smile was wry. "Of course, that gave me an opportunity to discuss her work performance."

"Of course, that was her and your right," Sidney said. "It's far better that she get a chance to air her grievance than hold it inside. Otherwise, it's going to fester and cause a very negative work environment for all of us."

At the relief crossing Dani's face, Sidney realized she'd been little worried about that. She reached across the table and patted Dani's hand. "I've been here a long time. We've weathered lots of ups and downs. This is just another one."

"I know." Dani's smile was sad. "It's always hard when it happens."

"Am I being disciplined, then?"

Dani shook her head. "No. I'm just going to ask you to add a little bit of oil to your tone when you speak with her. I've already spoken to Shane. I do have to go back and speak with Marsha again."

"As always, I'll try. Incompetence is something very hard to ignore. No matter whom it involves."

"Isn't that the truth. I will be monitoring Marsha's work for the time being, along with Shane, to make sure other patients are receiving the best standard of care."

They sat in companionable silence for a moment until Dani spoke again. "How serious is the relationship with Brock?"

At that, Sidney dropped her gaze to her hands on the table. She sighed and looked up at Dani. "I don't know. I'm not even sure what it is we're doing. In all my years of work, I have never met anyone that affected me like he has."

"Oh, I do understand that," Dani said with a sigh. "We've always held to that unwritten rule about no relationships between patients and the medical team. But that's shifting, and I guess that's my fault."

"I wouldn't place blame," Sidney said. "And I think the shift needs to happen. You're putting people with big needs up against people who have the ability to help solve those needs. We have men and we have women, many of them single and attractive, and temperaments will collide. Both positive and negative."

"So true. I guess it hasn't happened very much before."

"I think it started to happen when you expanded. Bringing in thirty extra patients and the extra fifty staff to deal with them means there are many more temperaments to come to terms with. More interactions, more friendships and relationships blossoming.”

"Of course, my own world is changing in that same way.” Dani's smile was mischievous. “I appear to have led the way this time.”

"You are our leader.” Sidney's grin was wide and happy for her friend. “You're going to have to put together a policy on staff and patient relationships, so there can be rules to follow.”

"Another thing to add to my ever-growing list.”

"I hear you.” Sidney grinned. “I can't wait to meet Aaron, you know.”

"He's all heart. I have to admit, it would have to take somebody like that in order to tolerate what I do here.” She gave a wistful smile. “He'll be back after his exams next week, I believe.”

Sydney smiled. “Is he on board with Hathaway House?”

Dani nodded. “He is, indeed. And looking forward to helping Stan out downstairs.”

"That would be terrific when he's finished his training. But he has what, three or four years to become a veterinarian? That's a huge commitment?”

"More. Four or five I believe. He's looking forward to it, and it's lovely to see him with such purpose—passion for his future again.”

Sidney watched the blush of pleasure cross her friend's face. She grabbed her hands. “I'm really happy for you, Dani. It couldn't have happened to a better person.”

"What about you and Brock?” Dani asked with a laugh. “You deserve happiness, too, you know.”

"Ha, we've only kissed so I don't even know what we are yet. At the risk of overthinking the situation, I have no idea what his plans are, and I've been here for a long time. I wasn't really looking to leave, yet."

Dani patted her hand gently. "I definitely hope it won't be for a while, but if it's time for a change, I would certainly understand."

"I would too. But at same time it's not where I want to see my future."

"How's Brock doing with his emotional issues?" Dani asked.

"That's actually a good question. He was very angry when we first met. That's eased a lot now. I'm not sure he's totally dealt with the problem though."

"Sometimes we deal with stuff up to a certain point, and then it takes a trigger to push us over the edge."

"The trouble is, those triggers can be damned painful."

"Absolutely. But maybe having Cole here will help."

"Actually, I'm afraid having Cole here could make it worse." Sidney didn't really have any basis for that thought, but instinct said it wasn't going to be as smooth a ride as they'd hoped.

"That's not good," Dani said. "I worked hard to bring the men together."

"So far, I think it's been a great reminder that he's lucky to be who he is and where he is. But I know he's also really worried and, for now, until Cole's back and settled in and doing better, he's going to be very stressed and focused on his friend's return."

"Why's that bad?" Dani asked. "Particularly when you consider what some of his issues were?"

"Because he's not talking about it. This is going to allow him to transfer his anger and his hurt and whatever else is going on inside his head to this new target and let him avoid looking at his own issues."

Dani sat back with a frown. "Maybe that's something that needs to be brought up with the rest of his team?"

Staring out at the green fields and the horses in the distance, Sidney nodded. "It's something I need to do. I just haven't gotten to that point yet. I don't want to jump the gun and assume anything in terms of his treatment and his recovery. At the same time, I can see a potential problem, but as long as it's only a potential problem, then it's not something I need to bring up."

"Unless it is a potential problem that you can't stop from becoming a bigger problem without intervention."

"Decisions, decisions." She gave Dani a warm smile. "Here I am up against the same problem as Marsha, which puts me in an interesting spot. As much as I want to go and talk to the team, I don't really want it to get back to Brock that I was the one who brought it up."

"You don't want Brock to worry?"

"I don't want Brock to think I betrayed him."

"I think in this instance, it has to happen. I don't like the word betrayal, as it doesn't really convey the right meaning, but you're right. He's likely to view it that way, at least at first. I do understand what I'm asking. I think it's a professional understanding of a potential problem that could be averted if somebody would bring it up and discuss it with him. That's partly your job. If he's going to hold that against you, and I know how difficult this is, then you don't have what you think you have with him."

"Oh, I do understand that, and I have considered all of it. The trouble is that reality is a bit of a bitch. I'm not exactly sure he's ready to hear the truth on that issue."

"No, but if you were talking to any other physiotherapist right now, you know exactly what you would say."

"I know. That's why I'm talking to you. Because I know that ultimately you are going to tell me to go and do what needs to be done and not what he would like to think needs to be done."

AS NIGHTS WENT, last night had been perfect. Brock had gone to bed with a smile on his face, and when he had woken up, the smile was still there. After all, he'd spent a fantastic hour in the pool with Sidney last night. He never expected to find somebody who mattered so much in a place like this. He'd not been against the idea. He just thought maybe professionally it wasn't the best for both parties. And even now, he wondered. He understood the problem had been with Andrew becoming friends with his physiotherapist, and that when that little bit of doubt crossed his mind, he wondered if Sidney would get in trouble for the same thing. He could see himself doing what she'd done, if the roles were reversed. Hell, everybody would want to do the best for their friend. Look at him and Cole.

At that reminder, the smile was wiped off his face. On his way to breakfast, he headed to the front room and the reception desk where he spoke to Melissa.

"Any sign of Cole coming back today?"

"Cole will be back tomorrow morning," she replied with a bright smile.

Instantly, he felt just that much better. "Thank you," he said. "That's the best news ever."

His heart lighter, he made his way out to breakfast. On the patio, he saw Sidney and Dani sitting together, clearly in intense conversation. He didn't know if something else had gone wrong, but he hoped it didn't involve him. He wanted to keep getting top-quality care, because ultimately, that was what he was here for. He wondered about the idea of having a different therapist. Or would that happen as he progressed? Would that be something that would benefit him? He didn't know. He'd been through a lot of physiotherapists before Sidney arrived. As soon as he'd met her, everything had changed for the better.

Still, a good night's sleep and a bright, cheerful morning had given him a raging appetite. The aroma of the breakfast made his stomach growl. Brock loaded his tray higher than ever, and he stared at it, feeling bemused. Then one of the kitchen staff behind the counter walked over. He picked up Brock's tray.

"I got it for you, man. You must be hungry today."

"Honestly, I'm starving," Brock replied as he led the worker to his table. He stared down at the pancakes, sausages, hash browns, toast, orange juice and coffee and smiled. This was something he could get behind.

And maybe it would help him to clear his thoughts as he started his day. His gaze lifted, and he caught sight of Sidney again. He smiled. Really, all he needed was to see her to get a better start to his day. He was a fool to worry so. He just needed to focus on the important things ... and one of those was how she made him feel.

## Chapter 12

THE NEXT FEW days fell into a regular pattern, and it was a pattern Sidney liked. She wanted the routine and the safety and comfort of knowing she was back where she belonged. It hadn't been an easy adjustment. Not with Marsha and Andrew. But also, a level of discomfort had developed in the relationship between her and Brock. Before, they had just been friends, but she managed to keep her own perspective. Now, for the first time, she wondered if she was being as detached as she needed to be with his care. Was she falling into the same trap Marsha had fallen into? That would be the worst. Particularly after everything she'd been through already. It was something in the back of her mind she couldn't quite let go of. Because of that, she kept her personal time with Brock as impersonal as she could. It was friendly and polite, but not loving. Maybe that was wrong of her, but she felt she needed the distance to make sure she wasn't falling down that same rabbit hole.

Maybe it was because she was afraid she worked him a little harder than she had to, but he seemed to thrive on it. There was just something about seeing a big man come back fully into his own that gave such a sense of accomplishment for both of them. After one particularly grueling session, instead of tears in his eyes, which she had seen in the past, his gaze shone with a sense of achievement. "I'm doing much better, aren't I?"

She flopped down onto the mat in front of him and laughed. "That's not the word I would use. You're doing fantastic."

Shane, who'd been working on the other side of the room, came over to talk to them. "Hey, Brock. I didn't know you had that in you."

Brock laughed, clearly a bit uncomfortable with the attention, but it was obvious to everyone he was pleased with the compliment. "Thanks. It felt like a long road to get here. I sure as hell wouldn't have made it as far and as fast without Sidney, though."

Sidney laughed. She handed Shane her clipboard.

"Are you doing anything for the next hour?"

Shane looked to his patient who was being wheeled to the pool for a therapy session with somebody else.

"Actually I have a bit of a break. I don't know about an hour, though. Why, what's up?"

"In the spirit of making sure I'm not missing anything," she said with a smile at the two of them, "is there any chance you could run through a few exercises with Brock and assess him for yourself?"

Shane's eyes lit with understanding. "You know it isn't a bad idea if we set something like this up on a regular basis."

"I was wondering that myself. I mentioned it to Dani."

"What's going on?" Brock asked.

She smiled. "I just thought that having a change of perspective on your treatment and your development, from someone who has worked with you earlier, could possibly point out something I'm not seeing."

Brock leaned forward onto the machine where he sat and said, "This is about Marsha, is it not?"

She flushed ever so slightly, heat washing over her cheeks. "Maybe, but regardless, it's a good idea."

"It's not your fault, you know." Brock grabbed the towel beside him and wiped his face and shoulders, tossing the towel over his neck. "I don't have any objection to Shane putting me through the paces. Although I'm not sure I'm up for it today, considering I'm as tired as I am, but you shouldn't let her erode your self-confidence."

Surprising herself, she blurted out, "But I eroded hers."

Both men stopped and stared at her. She shrugged. "I didn't mean to say that. I just realized how much it bothered me. She complained to Dani, so a formal investigation had to be opened." She motioned at the clipboard now in Shane's hand. "Before it comes to something and it gets any uglier, I would like you to take a look at what I've been doing, and what Brock's been doing, and see if I've missed something."

Shane nodded. "Happy to. But I don't want you to let Marsha get to you. She did miss something, but it never even crossed her mind to ask for help. At least you try to be open and honest about it, and you look for a second opinion. That's normal in our business. That's why I think we should make some changes. We all have multiple patients. There should be discussions on the best treatment for each of them between us. We aren't islands here. We should be a team on an island together."

Sidney liked that. She gave him a big, quick hug and said, "I will leave you two for the next half an hour. I'm going down to make that suggestion to Dani right now." With a bright smile, she turned and walked away.

Shane was one of the easiest people to get along with. He was always open to ideas, and he often saw where problems were that needed to be fixed before anybody else did. She really appreciated working with him. She'd grown as a physiotherapist here because of him. Sidney worried Brock had dominated her thoughts a little too much. What if she had missed something herself?

She peered into Dani's office, to find her friend on the phone and buried in paperwork. She frowned, considering whether she should walk away and come back later, but then she saw her folder was on the top of the stack and realized this needed to happen now. So, she waited.

BROCK MOTIONED AT the clipboard in Shane's hand. "I can't imagine she could possibly have done anything wrong, when I personally know how much I've improved since she took over my care."

"She's all heart. Therefore, she wants to make sure her relationship with you hasn't affected her ability to be detached enough to see what you need and don't need. I approve of what she's doing, and I certainly understand it. Because of Marsha there's been a lot of bad blood, and that's something she's very uncomfortable with, too."

He couldn't help himself. "My relationship with Sidney?"

Shane shot him a knowing look. "I know exactly what's going on between you two, regardless of all the rumors about that little lovemaking session in the pool."

Brock's heart stalled, and then raced. He opened his mouth to speak.

But Shane was still talking. "I happen to really like Sidney. I know she had a bum deal with her last boyfriend, so

I'm hoping what you're feeling is more than just a fly-by-night attraction because she's a long-term girl. She is one of those that you take home to your mom. I know that her heart is already engaged, so I'm really hoping you aren't going to mess her up."

As much as Brock loved to hear that his attraction to Sidney was reciprocated, and he already knew she was the take-home kind of girl, he was still stuck on that "lovemaking session" bit. "You do know we only shared a kiss in the pool, right?"

Shane studied him searchingly. "You serious?"

"Yes. I kissed her, but that was it. Believe me, I wanted to do more. But obviously, it wasn't the time or the place."

Shane let out a rumble of laughter. "Absolutely not the right time or place, considering somebody's passing rumors about her screwing around with you in the pool and making it sound nasty and kinky and very much something she wouldn't want other people to see."

"I'm certainly not into having other people watch," Brock said in horror. "I can't imagine Sidney would appreciate anybody passing rumors around about her."

"No, locker talk is not something any girl likes. Especially not somebody as sensitive and simple as Sidney is. She's very straightforward and honest. There will be bloodshed over this if she ever finds out."

"Then I'm presuming she doesn't know yet, or she has heard some but not the whole story."

"I assume not, too, but I don't know for sure." Shane looked back down at the clipboard. "Now, if you're up to it, I could run you through a couple of tests that will give me a good idea of where you're at."

"After what you just said, absolutely. I feel like I need to pound something into the ground, but I'll take it out on the equipment, not my body, then a little bit out on Marsha."

"Relax about her. That kind of behavior always has fallout. She'll get her own. You don't have to do anything about it." Shane dropped the clipboard and turned to look at him. "Just so we understand each other—it would be much worse for Sidney if you did try to defend her."

Brock clenched his jaw and glared at Shane. He understood what Shane was saying, but it was going to be damned hard to let anybody else say something nasty about Sidney.

"Brock, do you understand me? If you make this a big deal, it's only going to get worse. Dani won't have much of a choice but to step in hard. Do you understand that?"

"Yes," he bit off. "But it's not fair. Sidney didn't do anything." His glare deepened. "Neither did I. That's just as upsetting as thinking somebody is attacking her. It's also my honor."

"I hear you. So let's get to work and make sure there is nothing here that Sidney can be held accountable for."

On that note, Brock gave him a hard nod. "Where do we start?"

Chapter 13

---

D ANI LOOKED UP as she replaced the phone on her desk and smiled at Sidney. "I was just about to call you."

"Oh, good. I came because Shane and I were discussing some of the issues between physiotherapists and patients and friendships. We were thinking that as a common practice, we should check in on each other's patients—just to get a new perspective, a second professional opinion." Sidney exhaled, realizing she was babbling. But her employee file had been open on Dani's desk.

Dani's eyebrows rose. "This is because of Marsha?"

"Shane asked me the same thing. In a way, yes, it is, because it did illustrate the fact that we have a flaw in the system. Nobody else had seen her work, and in the work she did with Andrew, there was either a mistake or simply poor work being done. If another physiotherapist had been working with Marsha, it would be quite likely problems would have been noticed sooner. But she did the bulk of the work with him exclusively."

"You're saying that the team system we have in place isn't enough?" Dani asked as she leaned forward and propped her elbows on the desk, studying Sidney.

"I do think the team system works well," Sidney said. "But I think we need more team-based physiotherapy relationships as well."

"So, you're suggesting doubling up on each patient?"

The frown was almost instant, and in that moment Sidney shook her head and smiled. "No, no. I'm not talking about needing to have twice as many physiotherapists or booking in twice as much time with each patient. I can certainly understand the budget being your primary concern."

"It's not that it's a primary concern, but it's definitely a constant concern so if you're suggesting we need to do something like that, the budget just does not allow for it as it stands."

Sidney shook her head again. "That's not what I'm saying at all. I'm just saying that in the days and weeks that we plan out our work with each patient, we need to have somebody come by on a regular basis to see how things are working out and to give a professional second opinion. Honestly, it's no big deal. It's just something that Marsha, and now my relationship with Brock, has brought to the forefront."

"Is it something I need to set up, or is this something you need to set up?" Dani sat back.

Feeling better about the whole situation, Sidney said, "It's really something that we physiotherapists can do between us ourselves, maybe with Shane taking the lead on it. I just wanted to run the idea past you."

"Consider the idea run, and I approve. Anything that helps to improve patient care is the bottom line."

"I figured that's how you'd feel, and I'm quite glad, actually. Shane is currently putting Brock through a couple of exercises to see how he's doing. I wouldn't want to think my own feelings had gotten in the way of Brock getting the best care here he can get."

"I understand your concern, particularly with what happened with Marsha, and I guess it's certainly possible, so thank you for getting Shane to step in and take a look. Having brought up your relationship with Brock, maybe I can bring up something else."

"Sure." Sidney settled back in her chair, feeling much more relieved about the entire situation. She wondered if Dani was going to ask about their future, and she really didn't have too many answers for her, but she didn't want to leave the center if it wasn't necessary. If Brock decided to stay locally, she could continue to work here, and she'd be a happy camper. But she had to understand that maybe Brock needed to move elsewhere. If that was the case, then she had to consider her options, too. She had certainly left enough times and come back, but what she didn't want to do was leave for a relationship that was going to end, and then come back.

It would really suck to leave with her boyfriend, and then find out that it wasn't what she thought it was.

"I told you about Marsha and the pool."

"Right. The famous kiss." Sidney grimaced. "Who thought that such a simple thing would make me notorious here?"

"Unfortunately, apparently Marsha didn't tell just me." Dani spoke slowly, but her gaze was direct and her tone firm. "It seems like she may have enhanced the story, and she appears to be spreading it in buckets."

Sidney stared at her, stunned. "Why?"

"I don't know for certain, but my guess is it's probably because of what you did about Andrew."

Sidney slumped in her seat. "This is why I don't have many girlfriends," she said. "That's just not something I could ever see myself doing. I might be pissed off at myself for having not done as good a job as I could, and I might be pissed off if somebody else pointed it out to me. But I'm sure as hell not going to blame the other person and go so far as to get revenge."

"That's why we *are* friends," Dani said with a brilliant smile. "I can't do that to anyone either. But we do know that not everybody thinks or acts the way we do. Right now, I have a situation on my hands that I have never had to face before."

"I just gave her more fodder, didn't I?"

That startled a laugh out of Dani, and she leaned forward conspiratorially. "That said, it was a good kiss, right?" Her eyebrows rose and fell suggestively.

Sidney giggled. "Oh, my God, it so was."

Then she collapsed in big, boisterous gales of laughter. No matter what happened with Marsha, Brock was in her life. She didn't know where that was going to take them, but she wanted to give it as much of a chance as she could. "Too bad there isn't any way to prove what happened."

"Actually, there is. People tend to forget I have security cameras everywhere in this place."

Sidney gasped, heat flushing over her cheeks. "Now that could have been embarrassing."

Dani looked at her with a sideways smile. "This is where we go back to that question—is there anything I'm going to find on that tape other than a kiss?"

"No. But let me tell you, it was *some* kiss."

"Having brought it to the head that she has, I don't have any choice but to view it to make sure I understand exactly what went on and when," Dani said. "Then I will have to deal with Marsha."

"I'm sorry about that. It never occurred to me somebody would have that kind of vindictiveness. She's right, though. We shouldn't have kissed like that." She leaned her head back and stared up at the ceiling of Dani's office. Not as passionate a kiss, at least. She frowned. It looked like the situation was far from over.

IT WAS LATE in the afternoon when Brock made his way to his bed. He hadn't had to use crutches for a long time, but his left leg was cramping, and he felt weak today. It was a setback he wasn't impressed with. He'd been walking pretty decently, with a limp and one crutch under his left arm, but still managing to mimic a fairly natural movement. However, today he was dragging that damned lame foot. He understood progress came in stages. He also understood, from the team meetings, how much mental processes affected the healing ability of the body. All that was fine in theory, but it was a different story when you were dealing with a setback. Resting the crutches along the bottom of the bed, he lay down with a sigh. It was such a relief to get his sore leg up. For the first time in a long time, he wondered if maybe he should just have dinner in.

He wasn't sure what had gone wrong, but today he just felt like crap. Had the extra testing with Shane worn him down that much more? Maybe that was all it was—just a bad afternoon. Who knew? He'd read all kinds of journals about diet affecting healing and joints and what not, but he wondered how it was possible to learn to do everything. He suddenly felt disappointed with where he was at the moment. He certainly couldn't blame Shane because the things he'd had him do hadn't been that strenuous. The only good thing about today was the fact Shane was pleased with his progress. And Shane would know, since they'd worked together earlier, prior to Sidney's arrival.

"Brock, you've come a long way," Shane had said with an encouraging nod. "You can put the success for that squarely on Sidney and yourself."

"So," Brock had asked in a low tone, checking to make sure nobody else was close enough to overhear him, "Sidney didn't pull a Marsha, then?"

Shane had smiled, patted him on the shoulder and said, "Sidney pulled a Sidney. Behaving as she always does—as a consummate professional. That she's also allowed herself to open up to something more between the two of you just makes her very special."

"Could she get in trouble for that?"

"That's a little harder to determine." Shane looked at him knowingly. "Maybe keep the little swimming pool scenarios out of the relationship for now. Actually, out of all public places."

"That leaves nowhere else," Brock said. "But I would never want to do anything to jeopardize her position, or her professional reputation."

"Both have been hit lately."

The conversation had dwindled after that.

Now Brock stared at the bedroom door. Privacy with Sidney? Today it seemed like a long way away. It wasn't, but as he'd had a physical setback, he was pretty darned sure she'd had a setback in this place, and for that, he felt guilty as hell. If only he had more energy to make his way down to Dani's to give an explanation. Not that there was much to be said. He wanted Sidney and had reached out and taken just a tiny delight in that kiss. He was sorry somebody had seen them. Sorry something so beautiful had become degraded. Determined to set things right, he reached for his phone and found Dani in the contacts. He hit dial and collapsed back onto the bed with the phone to his ear, waiting for her to pick up. Finally he heard a cheerful voice on the end of the phone.

"Hi, Dani. It's Brock. Can you come to my room for a moment?"

"Sure can. I'll be down in five."

Brock lay with the phone at his side and waited for her to walk down the hallway. He recognized Dani's footsteps as soon as she got close.

At the door, she knocked and then entered. She saw him and she said, "Oh dear."

He gave a half laugh and motioned her inside. "I'm fine. Just not as good a day as some days."

She nodded her head in commiseration. "That happens. Even for those of us that aren't injured."

"So true." He remembered those days well. One tried to be upbeat and happy, but there were just some days when you got out of bed and everything seemed like shit. "Thank you for coming."

"I'm always happy to see you. What can I do for you?"

"A couple of things. I understand Cole's return was delayed yet again. He will be coming back, won't he?" he asked hopefully.

She smiled. "Absolutely. I'm expecting him tomorrow morning."

He gave a heartfelt sigh of relief. "I've been very worried about him."

"We all were. We will take his adjustment slow."

At those words, Brock studied Dani with a wry smile. "Good luck with that."

"That's a very perceptive comment." She laughed. "We see it a lot. Everybody has their standards of what they think they should be doing, but the body is completely disconnected from that expectation. It will do things in the timeframe acceptable to it. That's often difficult for people to accept."

"Like me." He stared down at his leg. "Progress has been phenomenal," he said. "But after all this talk about Sidney, I was getting disturbed."

"Oh dear, I'm sorry to hear that. Rumors are always something we try to stop, but it's not possible. Not when there are more than two people around." She pulled his chair over and sat down next to the bed. "What is it about Marsha's situation that bothered you?"

"It actually made me concerned Sidney was doing the same thing—with me. Overlooking important signs that would impact my progress." There. He had brought out the relationship between him and Sidney for the first time.

Obviously she knew because she nodded. "It's a valid point. It would never be a good thing to have your confidence in a professional team around you eroded because of something like that." She paused. "Are you asking for a new therapist?"

"Oh, no. No." He shook his head. "You're misunderstanding. Actually, I was going to talk to Sidney about it, but she brought it up herself this morning at our session. Shane was there, working, and she called him over and asked him if he could take a look at me running through some exercises and some tests to see if she had missed something."

Dani's eyebrows rose in surprise. "Now that's very interesting."

"I was quite surprised, too, however, as I had already been wondering if it's something I should've brought up with her, I was actually very happy to have her bring it up for me."

"How did Shane feel about it?"

"He asked if this had anything to do with Marsha."

Dani's face clouded over. "It is amazing how one incident can permeate a professional culture and cause trouble."

"He was happy to do it. He did tell her it wasn't necessary, but she said she would like him to do it because *she* felt it was necessary."

"I'm very glad you told me about this," Dani said. "Are you happy with the diagnosis Shane gave you?"

Brock grinned. "He said Sidney was doing a damned good job. There were no concerns."

At that, Dani laughed. "Yes, that's what we like to hear." She stood as if to leave.

"I don't want to get Sidney into trouble," Brock said. "So please don't tell her I told you what happened."

Dani looked down at him, but there was a gentle smile on her face. "That's the thing about Sidney—she's a professional through and through. She already came to me and told me she asked Shane to spend some time with you, going over what she'd been doing."

At the look of relief crossing Brock's face, she laughed. "We try to be a family here. Some members of the family are willing to do what is necessary." She walked toward the door. "Sidney suggested there needs to be checks and balances between the physiotherapists. Something they should carry out amongst themselves on every patient." She turned to look back at Brock. "So, thank you. It's nice to know the team is developing better ways to serve everyone." With that, she turned to the door.

"Wait," he called out.

Dani turned, a questioning look on her face. "I'm sorry, I didn't even ask if there was anything else bothering you."

He motioned at the door. "Could you close it? What I have to say next is a little private."

Dani closed the bedroom door and came back toward him. "You've been worrying over lots of problems. Feel free to talk to me anytime."

"I know. I just realized this has become a bigger issue." He took a deep breath. "I want to apologize."

The faintest frown crossed Dani's face. "Why would you have anything to apologize for?"

"The kiss in the pool."

He could see the understanding dawn on her face. He hurried on, wanting to get the words out.

"I also understand other people saw us." He shook his head. "I thought for sure nobody was around. I never considered the position it would put Sidney in." He swallowed hard. "I have to admit, given the same circumstances, it would be damned hard to not do the same thing. I'm really falling for her. It's just that given the circumstances I crossed the line."

"Did she push you away?" Dani asked, her voice serious but a smile playing at the corner of her lips.

"No, she didn't. She responded wonderfully."

Dani's smile widened.

"Moreover, I couldn't have expected what would happen."

"We do know it won't happen again in such a public place, don't we?" she asked.

He grinned, realizing that apparently this wasn't such a

big deal. "I would hope not."

"So then you have nothing to apologize for because if Sidney responded, then she was not upset either. Now, if you had forced her, then that would be different."

"She definitely wasn't unwilling." He gave her a lopsided grin. "And for that I'm incredibly grateful."

Dani laughed—a beautiful, chiming sound that rang around the room. "That something so beautiful can happen between you and Sidney is awesome. It was after work hours, it was on your own time. It was in the pool where somebody saw you, and that is unfortunate. In most cases, it wouldn't be a problem. However, the person who saw you holds a grudge against Sidney, so things became nastier than they should have."

"Marsha?" He'd already heard from Shane, but Dani confirmed it.

Dani nodded. "But you don't have to worry, I will deal with it. Now, was there anything else bothering you?"

Her tone was teasing, and he took no offense. He'd like to think they were moving past the formalities to friendship. He'd been here long enough now he considered many of the people here friends. Of course, he considered Sidney a whole lot more, but as these people were her friends he didn't want to alienate anyone. He shook his head. "I think that empties all the bits and pieces bugging me."

Dani stood up. "Good, because healing will not happen while all of those issues are festering. So I'm glad you felt free enough to tell me about you and Sidney. As Sidney's my friend, I'm delighted for her." She gave him a big wink, turned and walked out, leaving Brock grinning like a fool.

He collapsed back with a smile on his face. So everything he thought about Sidney was true. His confidence, although slightly eroded by Marsha's comments, went up.

He glanced down at his leg, realizing the throbbing had stopped, and although it was sorer than he had expected, his mood and spirits were up, and he was no longer feeling such a heavy burden. In fact, he was seriously thinking of a swim and shower before dinner. He desperately wanted to meet up with Sidney for dinner.

*Chapter 14*

S IDNEY STOOD AT the entrance to the big, open dining room and studied the noisy population already in residence. The last thing she really wanted at this point was more people. She definitely didn't want to have anything to do with the physiotherapists she worked with, one of them in particular. She was feeling very anti-people this evening. As she glanced outside at the late-afternoon sunshine and the green grass, she thought about what she really wanted.

"Sidney, what can I get you today?"

She smiled at Dennis, one of the guys working on the other side of the counter, and said, "Do you have anything to take out? I just want to get outside onto the grass, maybe sit in the pasture with the horses."

Dennis's face burst into a big grin. "You want a picnic? That's awesome." He glanced up and down the line of hot, steaming trays already out. "Is there anything here in particular you're looking at for dinner?" he said. "I can pack it up for you. You can just bring the containers back to be washed."

"Thank you. It all looks wonderful. But something that's easy to eat would be better."

Dennis pointed at the beef bourguignon. "How about a main dish of that, and a big green salad?"

"I don't know how easy it would be to eat but it looks

delicious, so yes. Thanks." She studied the desserts and said, "I'll come back for coffee and dessert afterward."

"Give me five." Dennis disappeared into the kitchen. While she waited, Sidney picked up a bottle of water to go with her dinner. Dessert was going to be a piece of divine-looking chocolate cake.

Dennis returned a few moments later with a plastic bag. He came around the buffet and opened it up to show her. Inside were a knife and a fork, and two very large containers.

"Wow, that's a lot of food."

"You can eat. I've been serving you for years. I know this is probably just round one for you."

She laughed and added her bottle of water to the bag. She thanked Dennis, then turned and headed downstairs, stopping in at the vet's to say hi to Stan on her way out.

"Did anybody else come to visit today?" she asked him.

"Dani's out in the pasture. She's brought in a new horse—an old mare heading for the glue factory."

"Perfect, I brought a picnic dinner and I was going to head out to the pasture. Where is she?"

"She's in the same pasture with Molly and Maggie. All three of them are getting along just fine."

"I haven't visited with little Molly in a while," Sidney said. She could sense Stan studying her face. She gave him a smile. "I'm fine. Honestly. I just need a bit of food and fresh air."

"You always know you're welcome down here," he said. "If you want company, I'll bring out coffee in a little while."

"I'd like that. Thanks." She grabbed her bag and headed out back. Heading out through the corral system was the easiest and fastest way to get to the pastures.

Of course, almost as if they knew she was coming, Maggie and baby Molly had made their way to the fence, a big silver dapple mare behind them. But there was no sign of Dani. Sidney'd forgotten to ask Stan what the new horse's name was. She walked over and hopped up onto the corner fence to give them each a big cuddle, and then she pulled out her hot dish. It had cooled somewhat, but now it was the perfect eating temperature. With the sun shining on her face, and the animals surrounding her and the whole of Hathaway House behind her, she dug in to enjoy her dinner.

IGNORING THE WEAKNESS in his leg, Brock proceeded toward the dining room. He stood at the entrance and studied the big open room. There were a good fifty to sixty people sitting down and eating, the rumble of conversation bright and cheerful. Not at all what he wanted. He studied the faces, recognizing a lot of the people he'd come to know. There were a lot of good people here. But although he tried, he couldn't find Sidney.

He pulled his phone out and sent her a text. **Where are you?**

The response surprised him. **Out in the paddock with the horses. I brought dinner out here.**

He studied the phone in his hand, and a slow smile came over his face. A picnic. What a great idea. Could he join her, though? What Sidney was allowed versus what he was allowed was the difference between employee and patient, but it was worth a try. She had told him where she was, so maybe that was already an invitation? He figured there were enough problems that he was much better off giving her a chance to say no. Then he stopped with that thought. What if she wasn't being honest? He shook his head, feeling like a dithering fool.

At that moment, Dennis walked over. "Hey, what can I get you tonight?"

Brock raised his gaze to the other man and smiled. "I'm just trying to figure that out."

His phone rang just then. He excused himself and answered the call.

"Hey Brock," Sidney said. "When I said I was out by the horses, I meant it. I actually had Dennis pack me several containers and am sitting out here having dinner."

"That sounds wonderful. Are you interested in company?" He tried to keep his tone neutral.

"Absolutely. Come down to the vet's, and then head out along the hall toward the horse stalls. You'll see me there."

He ended the call and turned to face Dennis. "A little bird told me you packed a picnic for her. Any chance I could get the same for myself?"

Dennis flashed him a wicked grin. "Are you going to take it to eat with her?"

"Absolutely."

Dennis laughed. "Good for you. In that case, tell me what you want, and I will pull it together."

That was easy enough. Brock walked along the counter, hearing his stomach start to growl. His energy was picking up at the thought of food, too. He was no longer anywhere near as tired as he had been. He ordered a decent-sized dinner, and before long, Dennis was standing beside him with all of the food packed up in glass containers. He handed the bag over.

"Here. Just make sure you bring all the containers back so we can get them washed up for tomorrow."

"Awesome." Brock glanced at the coffee and desserts and said, "I guess I can come back for the second course?"

"Exactly what Sidney said."

With conspiratorial grins the two men parted ways, and Brock headed down to the vet's office. The elevator opened up on the vet's level, and he took a left down the hallway toward the horses. He didn't want to waste any time in conversation with the others, so he headed straight outside.

As he walked out into the sunshine, he blinked at the bright light. It took him a moment to find where Sidney was. But then he saw her. She was at the corner of one of the pens, sitting on top of the railing, eating—the horses stood right beside her.

"What a perfect idea."

She laughed, her voice happily trailing across the open air. "I just couldn't stand to be inside anymore. Walls were closing in on me, and there were too many people."

"I had the same thought looking at how jam-packed it was. Even though the atmosphere seemed happy, it just felt too confining."

"Exactly. And Dennis was a sweetheart." She nodded at the bag in his hand. "Apparently, he did the same for you."

Brock hobbled closer. "Yes he did. I probably have ten times more food than you do."

"Good. Then I can share yours." She grinned at the look of bemusement on his face.

He studied the railing and frowned. "I sure would like to sit down on the top, though."

She glanced at his leg and at the logs. "I could shuffle over, and you can have the center seat at the corner here."

He hated to make her move for anything that would show him as less than capable, but the last thing he wanted was to end up falling and causing his glass containers to shatter all around them. That would be a little more embarrassing than accepting her offer to move.

He handed her up the bag, and then, laying his crutch against the railing, he swung himself up to the top of the fence post. Sitting straddled, with his back leaning against the fence to support himself, he settled in. With a big smile, he reached out a hand to Maggie, who'd walked over to check out his arrival. She gently nuzzled his hand, giving a tiny nicker.

"She's beautiful, isn't she?"

"They all are," she said quietly. "I just love the animals here. Every time I get upset or sad or lonely, I can come here and know they accept all without judgment. They are really beautiful to have around and to be available to hug and hold."

"You've had a couple of rough weeks, haven't you?"

"So have you," she tossed back. "But Cole will be back tomorrow, so that should help."

"It'll be nice to see him again," Brock admitted. "But I have a different understanding now. I get that he tried to do too much too fast, and the traveling and adjustment were something that set him back. As I've had setbacks of my own, I will do a lot to encourage him to not go that way again."

"The opposite effect can happen, just because of that," Sidney said softly. "Sometimes, we nurture people too much, and then they don't strive for more. It's important to do what you can, so your body will allow you to do more without causing injury or stress. Internal tension is just as bad as external. All the applied forces should be even. That's very hard to attain or maintain."

"Very philosophical."

Sidney looked off across the green hills. "Well, for the first time ever, I was looking at quitting."

He stared at her in surprise. "Because of Marsha? Please don't let her upset you to that extent."

"It's a lot of things. It's Marsha. It's crossing a professional line. It was getting caught and having somebody spread gossip. It just leaves a bad taste in my mouth."

"It can and likely will happen anywhere. Not just here."

She nodded. "True, but for the first time, I guess I'm open to the idea of leaving. This was always my place to work. I felt at home here and that everybody here was part of my family. It just feels odd now."

"You've really only just arrived, still haven't had time to properly adjust, and you're ready to leave? What's it been, a month? Six weeks?"

She nodded. "About that."

"It's not enough time. You've just barely settled in, and yes, some trouble started."

"It's more than that. I also have to think of my future. What is it I want to do in ten years?"

"I thought you told me this is where you want to be in ten years."

"True, but what if I want a family in the future? How do I handle that?"

"Don't most of the doctors and nurses and patients and staff here have families and relationships?"

She appeared to mull that over for a minute, then nodded. "I guess they do. For some reason, I was thinking I was going to have to leave in order to have a future."

That jolted him into silence. So, did that mean he wasn't anything she wanted in her future? He stared down at the food in his lap, and it suddenly tasted like sawdust. He took a deep breath. He had to know the answer. "Does that mean you're not interested in a relationship with me?"

She spun and looked at him. "No, that's not what I meant at all. Why would you think that?"

"Because you just said you would have to leave to find your future."

She stared at him, her eyes round, and then she frowned. "Because you're going to leave."

"Am I?" He tilted his head and studied her. Looking for some truth on the inside that would tell him they were both heading to the same place. "I can work in Dallas as well as I can work anywhere."

"What work?" she asked with curiosity. "I don't think we've ever discussed that."

"That's because so many people think when you're a military grunt that's all you are, but I'm actually very good with computers. I'm sure I could get an IT job in the big city."

"Won't you need more training?"

He shook his head and smiled. "No. This is what I did in the military."

Understanding flaring in her eyes, she said, "In that case, that would be perfect for you. Dallas is a massive city. I'm sure you'd have no trouble getting a job."

As she said that, their eyes met and held. Heat flashed at that sudden knowing they were on the same page. They were skirting around major issues, looking to see how closely their lives might fit together. He started to lean forward, seeing her stretching toward him. Just before their lips touched, the door to the vet clinic slammed open.

"Hey, Sidney?"

They broke apart and turned to face Stan.

"There you are." He ambled toward them, two big mugs of coffee in his hand. "Hey, Brock. I didn't know you were here or I'd have brought another cup."

Brock smiled at the friendly doctor. He was a man he'd be happy to call a friend. He was a good-hearted soul. A flash of relief glimmered through him that Stan didn't have any interest in Sidney on a personal level because he really wasn't up for a competition.

Brock held up the dish in his hand. "I'm still eating—not quite ready for coffee yet, thanks."

Stan handed Sidney a cup. "This is a great idea, you guys. I should do this myself. Sometimes it's just nice to come out and enjoy the sunshine."

"Isn't that the truth?" Sidney said with a smile.

Maggie trotted a few steps closer to come and see Stan. He reached through the fence post to give her a good scratch. Brock watched as Stan interacted with the horses, seeing that same natural affinity and an innate joy to be one with the animals.

"You have a special relationship with the animals and a very special place to work here," Brock said. "Not only are you working with the animals all day long but when you take a break, you naturally come out to visit and socialize with them as well."

"Actually, it's often a lot nicer," Stan said with a smile. "The reason they are in my place is because they're hurting and need help in some way or another." He patted Maggie on the nose. "These guys are all in good shape—fit, happy, healthy and enjoying life. Sometimes it helps to get away from the pain and come and see the joy."

He glanced up at Brock and added, "The same goes for

you two. You're dealing with your own pain. Sidney's dealing with the pain of a lot of people. Coming out here is all about renewal."

Brock smiled warmly. "We all need that."

*Chapter 15*

SIDNEY AGREED WITH both men. In fact, that was exactly what she was here for. It wasn't that she wanted to move, it was just that the first upset of returning home again had disrupted her life so badly. It was honestly the first professional dispute she'd had since she first came here. Then again, she may have avoided a lot of drama by her frequent absences for school. There were a lot of people here, along with a lot of personalities. She had to remember that fact. And if she was staying, she'd have to find a way to get along with Marsha. At the same time, it also took a lot of pressure off her shoulders to think maybe she wasn't going to have to leave.

With that thought, the grass suddenly seemed greener, and the sun a whole lot brighter. She realized the thought of leaving was more difficult than she'd imagined. She would've made peace with it, but it wasn't necessary, and therefore, Marsha was not going to be allowed to be an excuse. That meant she had to make peace with the situation somehow.

When the three of them had finished the food and drink, they walked back into the vet's office and spent the next half hour cuddling the animals. She picked one up, hugged and kissed and cuddled it a couple times, then put it back down again and picked up the next. It just went with part of her mood. After they were done, she and Brock made their way upstairs to the kitchen to return their dishes. Dennis saw them coming, and his face broke out into a big grin. They handed over the leftover containers and thanked the man profusely.

His merry laughter rolled through the big room, which was almost empty now. "It was a great idea. If you want to do it again, just let me know."

Sidney no longer wanted a coffee, but she definitely wanted dessert. Brock was likely to want some, too, so they moved down to the dessert table where Brock picked up a piece of the chocolate cake she'd been eyeing earlier and a coffee. They walked back out on the deck and into the mellowing, early-evening sunshine. As she sat there at the empty table, her face lifted to the setting sun, she realized just how absolutely perfect this place was.

"You look like you're feeling better," Brock said.

"I am. I just had to make peace with a few issues. It's stupid to let something small ruin something so important to me."

"Marsha and this place?"

She nodded. "Of course, it helps to know you might be staying close, too." She shot him a teasing glance. "Apparently, privacy around this place doesn't exist."

He laughed. "I see that. It might be easier if people know we are an item."

She nodded. "It might."

"Are we an item?"

She turned to look at him, her eyes flashing with delight.

"Are you asking me?" she teased. "Aren't you going to be a macho male and make it a fact?"

Something in his eye glinted. "Who, me?"

She chuckled. "I get it, I'm just teasing. You don't need

to be tough, here. But I'm pretty sure that's not a big part of your personality anyway."

"Well, I used to be tough. I just don't know that I still am. Maybe, but I don't really feel like it. Once I get back on my feet and into independent living, things might change. Who knows? On the other hand, a lot of who I am here is a result of all that's gone before. I'm different now. Better."

She looked over at him and smiled a slow, gentle smile. "I'm really glad I'm with this person here. Too often there are layers to our individual personalities we never let anybody else see. It's only through struggle that we get to see the inner person. I really admire and respect the man I've met here."

"Damn. I do feel like I need to confess, though. Because after all that kiss and your stuff, I did start to wonder if I should be asking for another therapist."

Silence.

"I guess that's normal," she said in a low voice.

"I didn't ask. You brought it up before I had a chance to. I was going to talk to you about it first to see if you felt it was an issue. But then when you asked Shane to look after me, I realized that you'd already considered the issue."

"What did he say about your care?" Her gaze focused on him. "It's been a hell of a day, if I forgot that."

"It has been a hell of a day. But he was very happy. He said that—you'd been your usual self—a consummate professional."

Heat flashed up her neck with pleasure as she heard his words. "I'm glad to hear that. But I also went to Dani and had a talk with her about it. I suggested all the therapists should do some round-robin checking up on patients, just to see how they are doing. It makes sense. We're all going to have a different view of each injury and how to proceed."

"Yes, Dani told me."

Sidney sat back in her chair. This whole situation was snowballing. Not only were other patients second-guessing their own therapists, but some of them had gone to Dani with their questions and concerns. She sighed. She was going to have to talk to Marsha one of these days. At that moment, Marsha walked into the dining room. She caught sight of Brock and Sidney and froze.

*Shit.* It looked like that future conversation was about to happen now.

Sidney glanced at Brock to see if he had noticed Marsha's arrival. "You might want to go to your room. I don't know if Marsha's looking for a fight, or what." She sighed and added, "I do need to talk to her."

Brock studied her face, turned to look at Marsha and said, "I'll stay right here, thanks."

She winced. "I really don't need an audience."

"And yet, you might. Maybe with a witness, the truth will come out."

She studied his face and nodded gratefully. "Good point."

Her heart started to pound inside her chest. She was so very non-confrontational. Yet, she was also the one known for calling a spade a spade. She wondered for a moment if there was even a chance Marsha would just brush it off, but when she glanced at Marsha again, the woman was stomping in their direction. Before Sidney could take one more breath, Marsha was already standing in front of her, hands on her hips.

"So, there you are."

Sidney straightened in the chair. "Yes, I'm here, did you

want me for something?"

"I've reported you're fraternizing with a patient to Dani."

"Fraternizing? Interesting phrase." She smiled at Brock and said, "If you mean the friendship developing between Brock and me, that's fine. Dani already knows."

Marsha's lips thinned. "So, it's okay for you to be friends with a patient but not for me?"

"It's okay for all of us to be friends with patients," Sidney said. "It's not okay when that friendship affects how we do our job."

Marsha's lips turned into a sneer. "So, of course, you haven't had any problems being detached in your work with Brock?"

Sidney barked out a short laugh. "Of course, you're perfectly right. I'm not perfect. I'm not detached. When you care about somebody, you can't be detached. However, as professionals, it's our job to do the best we can, and when we can't, we need to rely on others and ask them to help out."

"That's not likely to happen." Marsha shook her head. "It appears you have the complete run of this place."

"I'm sorry you feel that way. I was hoping we could find a decent working relationship moving forward."

"It's got to be you or me," Marsha said. "There's no way in hell I am working with you."

Sidney nodded wearily. "Again, I'm sorry to hear that, and I wish you luck with finding another job. You're very talented—I'm sure there's lots of places that would be happy to hire you."

Marsha looked at her, nonplussed. "I'm talented?" She shook her head. "How does that fit in with everything else you said about me?"

"I said nothing about you. I told you that you weren't being detached and had missed seeing some things that needed to be seen. All you had to do was ask somebody else to see if your perspective was skewed because of the relationship."

"Oh, sure. It's not like you've ever done that."

Sidney was damned happy to reply to the woman's accusation. "Yes, in fact, I have." She motioned at Brock. "I had Shane run Brock through the paces, to see what I might've missed." She paused. "For that matter, moving forward, that is going to become common practice between all of us. To be discussed at tomorrow's meeting. It has already been cleared with Dani."

"What's going to be common practice?"

"More teamwork. Having another therapist see how the work is going, so it's not just one person's prognosis, because each of us sees progress in a different way."

Marsha's face was an interesting play of emotions. It was as if she liked the idea, but she didn't want to like the idea.

"Oh."

"Every time something like this happens, we have to learn from it," Sidney said. "I didn't expect to have a friendship with Brock, but once I did, I realized I hadn't really understood what you were up against."

"I wasn't Andrew's lover," Marsha sneered.

"That's good because Andrew is happily married. However, Brock is not, and I'm not his lover, either."

"Oh?" Marsha's face was a study of consternation as she looked between Brock—who was sitting back, quietly watching the two of them—and Sidney. "But I saw you in the pool?"

"Absolutely, you saw a kiss between two people who are

fond of each other. Between people who are looking to have a relationship, and who were caught by surprise at just how much there was already between us," Sidney admitted. "A kiss that was probably too passionate, but it was past work hours, and I was not on the clock. It was our own personal time, in a pool we are entitled to be in. I'd have preferred nobody saw us, of course. But I would have also preferred those that saw us would not have tattled or severely embellished the story out of malice. You also have to understand Dani has security feeds all over that area. So of course, she checked out the videos to see for herself what happened."

"Oh," Marsha said in a small voice. "I didn't know that."

"In the many years Dani's been running this place, she's been up against almost every possible scenario between two people. When she runs a complex of this magnitude, with hundreds of people—employees, patients and visiting staff, not to mention all the support staff—including the veterinarian clinic—she needs to know what is happening."

Sidney had no idea how Brock was feeling about all of this, but she didn't dare take her gaze off Marsha. She had to get this all out and dealt with now. "All Dani expects from us is a professional environment at all times while on duty. Our private lives are, as always, our own."

She stood, towering way above Marsha. She didn't intend it as a power play, but she wanted to let her know exactly what she needed from her. "That's what I would like to see. My private life is my life, and you're entitled to yours. If it doesn't cross the line in terms of patient care, it's neither of our business. As for that mistake, hopefully this new system will prevent it from happening again because I don't believe you did it on purpose. I just think it was one of those blind spots that can creep up on us when our focus is elsewhere."

Marsha nodded. "I didn't do it on purpose. I wouldn't hurt Andrew. Of course, I wanted to give him the best care possible. I won't do it again."

"I'm certain you won't," Sidney said warmly. "But at the same time, the way you dealt with the problem and the way you've dealt with me since is not something I'm happy with."

Marsha looked very uncomfortable. Clearly, she'd come over intending to blast Sidney and make a few demands of her own. Now she was in the hot seat, and it was not a very nice place to be. Sidney took pity on her.

"If possible, I'd like to put this behind us and move forward as the two professionals we are."

She waited, watching the expressions twist and turn across Marsha's face. Then the woman relented, and her shoulders sagged. Sidney let her breath out slowly. It could've been so much worse.

Marsha looked up at her and gave her a small, fragile smile. "I'd like that. Have a nice evening." With one more smile, she turned and walked away.

Sidney fell back down in her chair and looked to Brock. "Oh, my God. That was hard."

He reached across the table, grabbed her hand and said, "It might've been hard, but you did a damned good job."

IN FACT, SIDNEY had done better than good. She had been professional, but easygoing, and somehow, she had taken Marsha's ire and turned it into something completely

different. He knew in that moment, he should never have
had any doubts. He hadn't really, but there always had been
that question in his mind about whether she was right for
him. Now he knew. There was no one more perfect for him,
ever. Just that simple act of trying to make something of a
relationship with Marsha made him love her all that much
more.

It made him realize how hanging onto his own feelings
of bitterness about his accident and the sense of defeat had
hurt him. He hadn't actually seen Sidney's magic, but it had
worked on him just as it had worked on Marsha. He felt
whole again. He had let all that anger go, and he was so
much better for it. He just hadn't understood how far he'd
come, but now he did as he watched Marsha picking up
coffee and dessert. Even her bearing was different now. She
had a bounce in her step, a swing in her hips, a smile on her
face.

That's how he felt—as if something inside had been settled, been resolved. It was put away in his past where it
belonged. Dealt with, so he could move forward. With his
own miracle—Sidney.

He stared down at his coffee cup, stunned by the realization. He had no idea his feelings were that deep, but they
were. Like a slow river moving way below the earth. When
they popped up, it was certainly a surprise. He had no doubt
about the validity of the experience, the reality of his feelings.
She was somebody he could really relate to. He wanted her
like he'd never wanted another woman. She reached across
and stroked his hand and said, "You're so quiet. Problems?"

He smiled into her eyes and said, "Yes."

She raised an eyebrow. "What's the problem?"

"You," he said with a smile. "I don't think I've ever met

anybody more admirable than you."

Clearly self-consciously pleased, she gave a laugh. "No, not true. This place is full of them." She motioned around them. "You're just looking through rose-colored glasses."

"No," he said with a smile. "I'm just now seeing the truth for what it really is."

She frowned, and he could see the little bit of worry coming into her gaze. Hell, he was feeling a little nervous and worried, himself.

"This is the truth, and I want you to be happy about it," he said. She was starting to push back, leaning against her chair. He knew she was doing what she usually did. When there was an unpleasant truth coming out, she was trying to step away. So it wouldn't hurt so much.

"Well, I hope you will," he said. "Because it's really something major."

She studied him and waited. He took a deep breath.

"I just realized how much I love you."

Tears came to her eyes. She reached across the table and grasped his hands in both of hers. "Maybe it's been really fast. Maybe you don't know really how you're feeling. Maybe it's more a case of being grateful you're healthy and strong now, and you can leave soon."

"Stop," he ordered. "I'm an adult. I have a very good idea of what I feel, how I feel, and why I feel this way. I understand you might be nervous, a little scared. But then, hell, so am I."

She stared at him, and then, in a small voice, she whispered, "Really? Do you?"

That note of vulnerability was his undoing. He picked up her hand, brought it to his lips and kissed it.

"Absolutely, I love you."

She leaned forward, her hand going on top of his. Although it seemed they were in a small, private bubble of their own, he knew that wasn't so. She'd gotten in enough trouble because of his actions.

Not anymore.

Then, she surprised him. She leaned forward, squeezing his hand, and said, "You'd better. You'd better be sure because I love you, too, and I don't think I could stand it if this was misplaced gratitude."

Not giving a damn if anyone saw them or not, he leaned across the table, tilted her chin and kissed her. He wanted the whole world to see. Wanted them to see she was his, and he was hers. Forever. When he slowly withdrew and leaned back in his chair, he said, "Convinced?"

A smile played out on the corner of her lips. "A little bit. Because that was just a *little bit* of a kiss."

He grinned boyishly. "Now, if we had the time and the opportunity, I could show you a whole lot more."

She smiled once again, tears coming to her eyes, and said, "I look forward to it." She stood, then he did, too. She threw herself into his arms.

"Dear God, I love you so much," she whispered. "I've never been happier."

His arms closed around her, and he knew exactly what she meant. Because neither had he.

## *Epilogue*

*The Next Day ...*

COLE SAT IN the wheelchair in the doorway to the dining area and studied his best friend. Brock had never looked happier. In fact, he couldn't imagine love sprouting from such a horrific event. There had been so little joy in Brock's life lately. Cole was really happy for him. It also gave him hope for himself. He'd been single for a long time. Of course, he'd been married before, then divorced. His being in the military had been brutal on his wife. She'd been terrified he would never come home. Finally, she couldn't stand living with it any longer. He'd understood, but it broke his heart. Five years later, he had a broken body to go with it.

He wondered if he was ever going to become whole again.

Brock had been filled with guilt and anger. But it looked like Sidney had a way about her because he was no longer the same bitter man Cole used to know. For that, he was grateful.

Maybe Hathaway House did perform miracles. He'd heard wonderful things about it before he'd applied for a transfer. Of course, his own arrival had been much less than stellar with him having to be transported right back to the hospital. But he was back now, and he was prepared for the fight of his life because he now saw hope in front of him. He saw a chance to become the man he had been.

Maybe not the exact same as he had been, because that likely wasn't possible, but he had a chance to become a man that was as good as he had been. Brock was living proof of that.

Cole wanted that for himself.

He hoped Hathaway House had just one more miracle to deliver. And if Cole was lucky, it had his name on it.

# Cole

## Hathaway House, Book 3

# Dale Mayer

# Chapter 1

C OLE MUSTER LEANED against the headrest of his hospital bed at Hathaway House and stared out the window. Acres and acres of verdant green pastures cordoned off with white fencing met his gaze. He couldn't imagine how many acres were here, but he assumed at least forty, and that meant the property alone had cost a ton of money. Several horses grazed nearby, and even a goat bounced through the various paddocks. Outside his window was a stunning picture. After being in a sterile city hospital room for too long, this was a luxury.

A luxury he'd lost—temporarily anyway. A luxury he wouldn't take for granted again.

He realized now how much he'd been fighting to get back here before he nearly lost it all. That he was given one more chance brought a sense of relief almost overwhelming in its intensity.

He understood what the doctors here had said about his setback. Something about too much stress, a swelling bladder, too much exertion, sleeplessness due to the onset of PTSD and the abrupt cessation of his meds. They didn't even mention his initial injuries. Then they did tests, inserting catheters and whatnot, all over again.

And just like that, he was back at that city hospital, almost in tears when he woke up there. He'd been terrified he'd lost his one chance at Hathaway House. Of attempting that miracle recovery he'd heard about from friends—which he so desperately wanted for himself.

*Depressed* was too minor a word for his mood—*devastated* was more appropriate. The doctors had promised he could return to Hathaway as soon as he stabilized. At the time he hadn't believed them, but now as he looked around his bright, cheerful cream-colored walls and tiled floor, with that beautiful expanse of horse pasture outside the window, he believed. And he'd do anything to stay. He'd only been here for a couple hours, but he just wanted to lie in bed and rest, regroup after his travels and remind himself never to take this place for granted again.

Yet, he was petrified to do too much and end up in the hospital a third time, essentially banning him from Hathaway House. Overdoing it was what had done him in the last time. He'd been so determined to meet up with Brock again, to set some serious goals, to make a life for himself that Cole thought he had to give it his all and do as well as his friend had, or he'd lose the prize—getting his health and strength back and losing this damn wheelchair.

He had been so cocky and so sure of himself that he had *chosen* not to take several of his medications and had worked to exhaustion with disastrous results. The cumulative effects had spiraled quickly, his body shutting down various vital functions, resulting in an ambulance ride to the hospital.

He wouldn't make that costly mistake again. As someone who'd survived BUD/s training and spent six years as a SEAL, Cole knew exactly how damaging mistakes could be. He hadn't been ready to walk away from his military career, but being in a truck when a landmine blew up was a hell of an exit strategy. He'd been flung free and then speckled with shrapnel. He'd lost the lower half of his left leg. After that, infection set in and required several more surgeries. Now he had an outrageous-looking purple-and-red stump that, so far, refused to accept any weight on it.

He looked forward to increased mobility and knew that eventually enough scar tissue would form so he could use a prosthetic limb, but right now it wasn't an option. He had also taken a hit with all the bits of shrapnel in his back and shoulder, plus his landing had broken his hip. Thankfully his sciatic nerve, although bruised, hadn't been badly affected. But it'd been painful as hell.

Recovery was a bitch, but that was why he was here—to strengthen his back and to get his hip fully functional again. Then, of course, there was his leg and shoulder. Crutches worked but not for very long and not for very far, yet he felt like using the wheelchair was giving in, even though it was easier on him.

Cole had always had more than his fair share of stubbornness. But he also had more than his fair share of fear, and that still bothered him because one of his biggest fears facing him now concerned his future. He had no idea what he would do from here on out. He could probably return to the military and take a desk job. But once you'd been at the top, office work wasn't really an option. He had several friends who'd left the service to work at private security companies, but they weren't a busted-up, beat-up, old piece of shit like he was. Every time he thought about holding down a job or of eventually being independent, his mind shut off, and his fear took over.

Still in denial mode, he couldn't face it all yet.

He'd had hopes and dreams growing up, but they had all been focused on the military. And he'd worked steadily to make that happen. Now he had no idea what to do for a second career. The thought made his gut bubble with acid.

He took a deep, ragged breath. Time to get this show on the road. As his mind took that leap, he heard footsteps in the hallway. Sure enough, they stopped at his door, and then there was a light rap.

"Good morning, Cole."

He smiled at Dani, the manager of Hathaway, who'd been nothing but gracious regarding his ultimate failure at his first launch. What if his second was just as bad?

He tried to drop that kind of thinking, sitting up straighter, and smiled at her even more brightly.

She walked in and studied him.

He could feel this most critical test—the assessment of his health. She might not be a doctor, but she was hell on wheels as a first-alert system.

"Glad to see you're awake, Cole, after your transfer here. It's almost lunchtime. Good timing on your part," she said with a big grin. "I believe the chefs are doing a Greek-themed meal today."

"That sounds wonderful. I am pretty hungry," he admitted.

"That's a good sign." She lifted her tablet and jotted some notes.

Curiosity flared in him. He knew he wasn't allowed to see what she wrote, but that didn't stop him from wanting to know. Besides, notes would be a part of life here. They would all keep track of his condition, including her.

"Your team will drop by this afternoon," she said with another smile. "We'll take this morning as a complete reboot."

He brightened. "I was hoping you'd say something like

that," he confessed. "I felt quite the fool for having made a mess of my first time here."

"Don't feel like a fool about anything. But please remember, it's very important that you follow your plan exactly. You do have medications, and you do have exercises, and you do have very important meetings to attend." She patted his hand gently. "If you are concerned about anything, then first and foremost, discuss those issues with your team."

Abashed, he nodded again. "I'm sorry. I didn't mean to cause so much trouble last time. I thought I was doing so well, and I got cocky."

"It's nice to see you were feeling so positive and enthusiastic," Dani said, "but it's very important that you don't do too much, too fast. Your rehab plan is put in place for a reason. You need to trust your team to know what's best for you."

He winced. This was probably the first of many recriminations he would have leveled at him, especially once his team arrived. "I've learned my lesson." He turned to stare out the window. "I promise it won't happen again."

"Good. So, a few changes have been made in your team because of some staff shifts and patient discharges, not because of what happened earlier." She handed him a sheet of paper. "These are your team members. Once again, everybody will stop by this afternoon and say hi. Not until after lunch though. If you have any questions, you can talk to them or me."

Once more she studied him for a long moment. "I can get someone to take you out in a little bit. But not on your own power today."

"Good." He smiled at her look of surprise. This was the

new him. Careful. Someone who listened to instructions and his body. "I am tired. I'm not sure my legs feel up to it." He glanced around the room. "If I can't get around, do I call for somebody, or should I get into the wheelchair on my own?"

"Today, somebody'll help you."

He laughed. "Fair enough." He glanced at his watch. "Do you think I could text Brock and ask to meet him today?"

She beamed a beautiful, bright smile. "He would like that." She turned and made her way to the door. "Sit tight. I'll send somebody in right away."

SANDRA DENVER CARRIED her now-empty medication tray back to the pharmacy. She carefully locked up the tray as she did every time. She took one last look around the room, then pocketed her keys. It was almost lunchtime. So far, the morning had been routine. It wouldn't stay that way though.

Cole was back. That was enough to send butterflies flitting through her stomach. Initially she had been attracted to the man, but she was also furious at him. She knew she shouldn't take it personally. If he hadn't wanted to take his medications, then that was his right. He was a legally consenting adult.

But he'd signed up to follow the programs here.

She was also following his doctor's orders. She'd been the one to give Cole the medications and to trust he would take them. When he hadn't done so, without letting everyone know, she'd felt responsible.

Even now, this burning red ball of rage was in her. She'd received a verbal upbraiding from the doctor, and she'd taken it as she did everything—with a stoic expression and an apology. Afterward an unknowing innocence had disappeared. Up until then, it had never occurred to her that people here might hide something from her, like not taking their medications. But from now on, no way could she be complacent about her patients' actions.

Since that day, when Cole had been rushed to the hospital, she took an extra five minutes with each patient, ensuring all their medications were completely swallowed before she left the room. Many of them objected. Quite possibly she should have been double-checking all the time, but people came here voluntarily and signed up and paid big money for their recovery. All they had to do to make a change in their medications was talk to their doctor. She wasn't in charge of that.

As she walked into the main hallway, she caught sight of Dani coming toward her. "Good morning, Dani."

"Morning, Sandra." Dani tilted her head toward the dining room. "On your way to lunch?"

Sandra nodded. "That's exactly where I was heading. I'm looking forward to the souvlaki and whatever else the kitchen made today. The last time we had Greek food," she said, "you had to get there fast before it was all gone."

"Well, I believe the chefs are doubling the amount to-day," Dani said. "But you're right. He who is late gets only leftovers." She turned and looked down the hall. "Would you mind helping Cole into the dining room? He's planning on meeting Brock for lunch."

Sandra stiffened and tried to cover her reaction. "Brock's a great guy," she said warmly. "I can do that."

But something must have been in her voice because Dani turned suddenly and studied Sandra's face. "Cole's been a slightly disruptive presence since he arrived, but he's trying to make this second transition as smooth as possible. If this is a problem, please let me know."

Sandra would have to face him eventually—this would be a relatively easy way to break the ice. She shook her head and forced a smile. "I'm fine. I'll go get him. I presume we're taking the wheelchair?"

Dani nodded. "Yes. He's not ready to walk with his crutches yet."

With that, Dani continued toward the dining room. Sandra took a deep breath and turned resolutely in the direction of Cole's room. He was damned lucky Dani had let him return. After that stupid stunt of his, Sandra would've shot his ass back to the VA hospital and left him there.

Chapter 2

---

SANDRA APPROACHED COLE'S bedroom slowly. The door was open, which was a good sign. She knocked and stuck her head in. "Hey, Cole."

Cole turned to look at her. He smiled. "Hey, Sandra."

"You're looking better."

He grimaced. "Be hard not to, considering the shape I left this place in the last time."

"Not taking your medicine will do that to you." She couldn't resist saying that. His shamefaced look made her realize she'd been hanging on to something he probably wasn't. Everyone always thought they knew better. It was something she dealt with daily. "I met Dani in the hallway. She asked if I'd make sure you meet up with Brock for lunch."

He straightened, almost as if insulted. "I'm sure I can get there on my own."

"I'm sure you could too. But not today. It's very important you start off as slow as you can." She waited. "So is that a yes or a no?"

He nodded. She guided the wheelchair to his bedside and watched as he slid to the floor on his good leg, grabbed the wheelchair arms and shifted his body into the seat. She walked around to the front and adjusted the footrest for his leg.

"You may want this," she said, grabbing his lap blanket and throwing it onto his lap.

He tossed the blanket back to the bed. "I hate the blanket. It always makes me feel like an invalid."

She sighed. "In that case, the blanket can stay here, but if you get cold …" She let her voice trail off in warning. "Remember, no lack of communication of any kind this time, please." She pushed him toward the door.

Normally he'd be strong enough to wheel himself to the buffet, but they would all be watching him closely for the next couple weeks. It was incredibly easy to overexert, particularly when accommodating the loss of his lower leg. Plus, his body was still dealing with the surgical aftermath from his most recent time in the hospital. His medications had also been increased, and he tired easily.

She didn't want him to be so exhausted he couldn't get back to his room. He was stubborn enough that he wouldn't ask for help and would do it alone anyway. She'd seen pigheadedness in all its forms here, and it usually came from the men. Something about the male ego didn't like asking for help. She could understand that, but sometimes egos had to be put in check.

"I'm ready for lunch myself," she said. "I hear it's Greek today."

"I didn't have a chance to try the food that much last time. My visit was so damn quick."

"That's too bad, because the food is great around here. They never skimp."

"And for you guys too, right?" Cole craned his neck to look up at her. "The staff eats here also, don't they?"

"Oh, absolutely, we do. It's one of the perks of working here."

"I imagine there are a lot of those. Brock told me about the pool, but I never made it there."

"There's the pool, the food, the horses and living accommodations for those of us who might need them. Yes, there are a lot of advantages to working here."

He nodded. "I thought so. Is the environment always so happy? Everyone seems so upbeat all the time. That's very unusual."

"That's because it's a good place to be." She pushed him through the entrance of the large dining area. "Did Brock tell you where he would meet you?"

"I never thought to ask. I forgot how big this room was."

"I'll take you to the deck so you can sit in the sunlight, and we'll look for him as we go." She pushed him out to the deck where the sun was high enough to produce some good heat, but not be unbearable quite yet.

There was no sign of Brock as they made their way to the far end of the deck. "Maybe you're early."

"Maybe." He kept twisting and turning in his seat to look for his buddy. "He said noon. He should be here by now."

Sandra understood how Cole felt. "Once he shows up, I can either fix a plate for you or you may want to see all the offerings on the buffet line. Let me know." As she settled Cole at his chosen table, she heard someone call out.

"Cole."

There was Brock, making his way over—smooth, agile, and stronger than Sandra had ever seen him before. She caught Cole's reaction—the whisper of envy on his face— and felt a rush of sympathy for the man. She patted his shoulder. "Don't forget. He's been here for a few months now. You'll get there."

He glanced at her and said in a low voice, "Well, I'd be damned happy if I end up looking like how Brock is now. He was more broken than I was."

Unbidden, a gentle smile made its way to her lips. His eyes held hurt and fear, and she was damned sure he wouldn't want to know she'd seen either.

"I'll bet you on it. You follow your regimen and listen to your team, and it won't be long before you'll be like him."

Brock threw his arms around Cole and gave him a big hug. "Damn, it's good to see you again." He sat and stared at Cole, a big grin on his face. "Man, I was afraid you weren't ever getting back to this place."

"So was I," Cole admitted. "You don't know how happy I am to be here."

Brock grabbed Cole's hand. "This is the best place. You'll be a whole different man by the time you're done."

"I hope so. I was admiring how well you're doing. I didn't expect to see you looking so healthy and fit."

Brock laughed. "Well, there is the physical side, and there is also that lovely healed emotional side."

When he caught that particular grin on Brock's face, Cole studied him for a moment. "Don't tell me you've found a woman too?" He didn't want to sound as shocked as he felt, but damn, he was shocked. He shook his head. "Only you, dude. You come to a place of healing for a bunch of broken-down old farts, and you end up with a partner. Talk about luck."

Sandra rolled her eyes at the macho banter and then watched Sidney walk toward them, carrying two cups of coffee. Sandra would be leaving Cole in good hands now with Brock and Sidney.

Sidney stopped beside Brock and looked at Cole. "Ready

for round two at Hathaway House?" No malice was in her voice, only sympathy and a touch of gentle teasing. She shared a telling look with Sandra.

Cole winced visibly. "Could we forget about round one? That would be really good if we could."

Sidney put the two cups on the table and said, "Considering you're Brock's buddy, maybe. Maybe, just for you, we'll let all that slide." She faced him squarely. "You probably don't remember me, but I'm Sidney."

Cole shook his head. "I don't actually. Sorry."

Sandra looked at Sidney, a smirk on her lips. "He had just commented on the fact that Brock found a relationship in a place like this."

Sidney laughed, pink washing over her cheeks. "It was touch-and-go for a while there, but we made it."

Sandra saw the questioning expression on Cole's face as his gaze went from Sidney to Brock and then back again. When he glanced at Sandra, she nodded. "Yes, it is possible."

He dropped his gaze to the wheelchair and his partial leg. "Maybe for some people."

Cole's mutterings caught Sandra's ear. She walked away then. Cole would need time to adjust. He also had to shake off some of his self-pity and his downcast attitude. Brock had done a lot of work to get into the condition he was in. It was important Cole saw that effort for what it was—effort he would have to put in himself, at a pace his own body could handle. There were no shortcuts to this.

However, with Brock's rehab months ahead of Cole, maybe he would use that as his inspiration to move forward. She certainly hoped so. Cole had the ability to completely turn around his life. This place had so much to offer, as he'd said. She'd like to see him ready to take on the challenge. But it was all about mind-set.

*His* mind-set.

She wasn't sure he was there yet.

COLE WATCHED SANDRA as she walked away. Her attitude had changed over the last few minutes. He hadn't been as sure of his welcome when he had met her earlier. She'd been friendlier with Sidney and Brock. He remembered what she had said about his medications, and for the first time considered how not taking his medications might've affected more people than just him. He'd taken the physical hit … but maybe she had too in another way. Right. She had probably gotten into trouble.

Goddammit. That was not what he wanted.

No wonder she hadn't been as friendly when she came to his room.

"Hey, buddy, what are you thinking about?"

He turned his attention to Brock. Bigger than life and looking like he had a whole new lease on it.

"You are looking incredibly well." Cole shook his head. "I hope my recovery is just as good."

"It will be, but it's not easy. You've got to put in the work but not overdo it. Find the right balance." Brock grinned at him. "And having Sidney as my trainer didn't hurt."

"Hey, I'm not a personal trainer. I'm a physiotherapist," she said to Brock. Then turning to Cole, she added, "He likes to put me into the gym-model role regardless." She shook her head. "Talk about demeaning, Brock." Her light and happy tone belied her words. Sidney rose then. "You guys can talk all you want, but I'm hungry. And I've got to get back to work in an hour. Time to get some food."

Cole watched as she walked away. "Hot damn, Brock. She's dynamite."

Brock settled back with a satisfied smile on his face. "Yes, she is. But believe me, it's more than just looks. She's got a huge heart, and it's all mine."

"You are one lucky guy."

"Lots of women are here. Maybe you'll find one for yourself." Brock looked toward the buffet. "Sidney is right. We need food." He hopped to his feet. "Are you freewheeling, or do you want a hand?"

In that moment—that one sentence with no judgment, only acceptance—he knew Brock did understand what Cole had gone through and what he still had to go through. And he knew Brock wouldn't judge him for not getting there on his own.

"If I want to stay on Dani's and Sandra's and Sidney's good sides, then I could use a hand. I promised I'd do as little as possible this morning," he admitted. "And that includes wheeling myself around here."

Brock chuckled. "It's important to not get on anyone's bad side here," he said. "Come on. Let me do the honors. You'll be running around this place in no time."

"Lord, I hope so. I'm just worried about doing too much again only to land in the hospital." He lowered his voice. "You said it yourself. You were afraid I wouldn't return. Well, I'm terrified that, with one wrong move, I'll be kicked out of here forever," he admitted.

"That would suck," Brock said, his voice equally low. "So we have to make sure you start the right way and build on that. These are good people here. Give them a chance. They'll do right by you."

# Chapter 3

SANDRA HEARD THE last part of Brock's advice. She hadn't planned on sitting so close to them, but by the time she had filled her lunch plate and had found a table of her own, there wasn't much choice. She had been forced to sit closer to them than she'd wanted, and their voices carried. Still, it was good advice Brock had handed out. Hopefully Cole would use it. She could see he had the makings of a decent, and probably wise, man. Everybody was out of their comfort zone when it came to major health issues. How people reacted during a crisis said a lot about who they were inside.

She'd seen grown men cry in despair, and other men showed such inner strength and character through their adversity. This place had it all. Yet, what you arrived with didn't mean that was what you were stuck with. Being here transformed people, or rather they transformed themselves. The patients had a lot of support at Hathaway House, but it was up to them to take the required steps. That was what she wanted for Cole. Originally Brock had been one angry person too. Then Sidney had gotten hold of him. Even before they had started their relationship, she'd shown him what he could do if he put his mind to it.

That was the difference, having an entire team working on a patient's care, and Sandra was a part of Cole's team. She wasn't a therapist—she wasn't someone who had an active hands-on role to play. She was a nurse. She came to see people on a daily basis, but she was one of a lot of people not just working with one or two patients. Three permanent full-time nurses were on staff, and then they had several aides who came in on a part-time basis and that was just the day shift. Everyone still had plenty of work. There were dressings to be changed and stitches to be checked, and there were often catheters and other various physical issues to be attended to. She was happy to do it. She enjoyed her work.

The medication rounds gave her nightmares now. Amazing how one incident, such as Cole's, was enough to underscore she'd not been as diligent as she should've been. She was lucky that something much worse hadn't happened before. Now it woke her up in the middle the night, chilled and sweating, the "what ifs" running endlessly through her mind.

When she was alone and in the dark, and no one else was around to hear, she often found herself crying in fear. She never wanted to be responsible for the deterioration of somebody's health. She was always extremely careful with her medication distribution. It was one of the areas that had been really impressed on her throughout her training. She'd had a mentor through all the years she'd worked in hospitals, and they'd always stressed the same thing. She'd been here for four, maybe five years now, and a situation like that had never come up—until Cole.

Oh, she'd had her own various struggles. She'd had people who argued with her, not wanting to take a specific medication. That was fine. She had them talk to their doctor. She only adjusted the medications as per the doctor's instructions.

But to have someone, like Cole, deliberately fake taking his medication to avoid letting anybody know what he was doing—well, that was scary. She hoped he'd learned his lesson, and she knew she certainly had. These days her rounds took longer because she waited for people to swallow their medication in her presence. Several had commented on it. She half expected somebody to complain, but so far, nobody had—or none that she'd heard of.

The complaints may have stopped at Dani's door. Sandra should probably find out. Better to know up front than to wait for a second complaint to come through.

She finished off her lunch, having successfully blocked out the rest of Brock and Cole's conversation, and carried her dishes to the busboy's cart. She smiled at Dennis, one of the kitchen staff, standing near the buffet. "Dennis, that was absolutely fantastic. I'm all for Greek food every week."

"You're not the first to say that."

"How about we go global? Take a two-week period and pick a country and then do something different every day?"

He laughed. "I can mention it to the chefs, but they've got their own ideas too. Although I honestly think you will like what they've got planned."

"I know I will. What you guys end up doing is awesome." With a smile, she picked up a cup of coffee, snagged a cinnamon bun—which she didn't need but couldn't resist—and headed toward Dani's office.

Dani looked up and smiled. "Hey, Sandra, how are you doing?" Her gaze dropped to the cinnamon bun. "Oh, my God, that looks absolutely fantastic."

"I know, but it's way too damned big." She asked Dani, "You want half?"

Dani glanced at her, then back at the cinnamon bun

wistfully. "I shouldn't …"

Sandra stepped in, closing the door behind her with her foot. "Neither should I." She sat, split apart the cinnamon bun and picked up her half, nudging the plate closer toward Dani. The two women sat in secret enjoyment and polished off the treat.

"By the way, the Greek lunch today was absolutely divine," Sandra said.

"It was, wasn't it?" Dani licked her fingers and then reached for her coffee cup to help wash down the dessert. "I wanted that bite of something sweet. Thank you." Dani focused on Sandra, her eyebrows raised. "Is there a problem? Did you need to talk to me about something?"

Sandra shook her head. "No problem. I wondered if there had been any complaints about me."

Dani's expression turned to surprise. "No. Should there be?"

"I guess I deserved that." Sandra laughed and reached for a napkin on the desk to wipe her fingers. "Since Cole's slip … I stand by to ensure patients actually take their medication now." She shrugged. "I felt horribly guilty when he deteriorated so quickly. I couldn't figure out what the hell was going on."

"That wasn't your fault though," Dani said. "Cole brought that on himself."

Sandra nodded. "Oh, I totally agree. But it doesn't make me feel any less responsible."

Dani tossed her pen on her desk and leaned back in her chair. "That's the thing about living at this place. We're not responsible for everyone else's actions. We live with these people. We watch their growth. We see their failures. It's damned difficult sometimes." She stared out the window.

"Learning to separate guilt and responsibility, placing it firmly on the head of the person where it belongs, can be a challenge."

"I agree. I just wondered about any complaints," Sandra confessed. "I try to be super nice about it. I bustle around to make myself useful, but I am always watching like an eagle to make sure they pop those pills. A couple people have commented on it."

"Have they? Well, they don't appear to mind that much because nobody's been to see me." Dani sank in her chair a little deeper. "Most patients here are very amiable. Every now and again, we'll get somebody who's much less so, but so far, I haven't heard any complaints."

Sandra bounced to her feet and picked up the empty plate off Dani's desk, relief flooding her body. "That's good to hear. I won't pester you any longer. Have a nice afternoon."

"You too," Dani said. "Thanks for the treat."

With a big smile on her face, Sandra headed back to her office, feeling much better until she found Kenneth, one of the more troublesome patients, in the staff offices, studying the whiteboard with this week's schedules. What Cole did was harmful to himself. But what Kenneth did was harmful to others.

"Kenneth," Sandra said, "you are not allowed back here. This is for medical personnel only. The door is clearly marked."

"You have a weekend off coming up. I'll take you to town for dinner, a movie ... a nightcap. Breakfast on Sunday morning."

"No, Kenneth. I don't date patients."

Thank God Shane showed up right then as Kenneth did

not take her rejection well. Shane seemed to understand what was going on. He patted Sandra's back but his focus was on Kenneth. Motioning toward the door, Shane said, "We've talked about this before, Kenneth. Your lack of respect for boundaries. Your inappropriate behavior with the female staff."

"It's not like that," Kenneth said. "Sandra and I are dating."

"Stop it," Shane said with authority, his voice loud.

"Kenneth, that's a lie. We are not dating," Sandra said, happy to hear more footsteps coming their way.

"Like I told you before, Kenneth, only male staff will interact with you because of your treatment of the female medical personnel here. Now I'll have to report this latest incident to Dani." Shane shook his head. "This was your second strike. If you continue with these unacceptable actions, you'll be banned from Hathaway House."

By this time Dani and Stan and a couple male orderlies had appeared.

"I didn't do anything wrong," Kenneth shouted as he was led away.

Sandra shuddered. Kenneth was the one patient in hundreds that was difficult. And all because he wouldn't follow the rules. She couldn't wait until he left.

"I THINK I'VE shown you everything on the top floor." Brock stopped and stepped slightly in front of Cole. "Are you up for more? I can take you downstairs and show you the vet's clinic and out by the pool, or I could take you back to your room."

Cole tried to assess his condition. "I *am* a little tired, but I'd love to go downstairs. If I can see it all today, that will give me something to work toward. I saw a little the first time, but I'd been so focused on getting better I never paid any attention to my surroundings."

"Good enough." Brock pointed the wheelchair at the elevators. After he pressed the button, one of the elevator doors opened immediately. He pushed Cole inside and sent the elevator down again.

"There are stairs here too for your use later in your recovery," Brock said. "A challenge you can set for yourself is to make it to the animals or the pool on your own power."

Cole chuckled. "I like the way you think. I should get a notebook or something, so I can write down some of these ideas."

"If you don't have one, Dani's got some she keeps in a filing cabinet."

"I hate to ask."

"If you have a problem asking, I'll get you one."

The double doors opened, and Brock wheeled Cole from the elevator. "We'll take a right and go to the veterinary clinic. Probably a couple human patients are inside and easily a dozen furry ones. Everybody, patients and medical staff alike, come here whenever we need that connection. You like animals, don't you, Cole?"

"Absolutely, especially dogs." Cole watched with interest as they entered the veterinary clinic's waiting room.

The vet was saying goodbye to a customer leading away a golden Lab. "Hey, Brock. How's your day going?"

Brock smiled. "It's going awesome. This is Cole." He turned toward Cole and said, "Cole, this is Stan. He's the vet here."

"Nice to meet you, Cole."

"Nice to meet you too. So, according to Brock, we're allowed to see some of the animals?"

"Absolutely." Stan turned. "For that matter, I've got someone you should meet." He came back a moment later with the biggest, fluffiest critter Cole had ever seen.

"It's white, and it's huge. I have no freaking idea what it is, but I love it," Cole said with a laugh. It was placed in his arms very gently. He wrapped his arms around the creature and hunted for its face.

"What is it?" Brock asked, fascinated.

"It's an Angora rabbit. One of the longest haired ones I've ever seen. His name is It, after the character on *The Addams Family* show."

"What's wrong with him?"

Brock and Cole were busy petting the animal, whose ears could now be seen, followed by a pink nose. The rabbit lifted his head and sniffed. Cole laughed. "Keeping this guy clean has got to be a full-time job."

"He's actually a show animal who had trouble with a couple of his claws, so I gave them a good clip and disinfected one toe that was looking like trouble."

After a moment of holding the rabbit and enjoying having an animal in his arms, Cole lifted him up and handed him back to Stan. "I'm a dog person," he said, "but I've never spent much time around other animals to know if I like them or not."

"Stick around here long enough and you'll get lots of opportunities to find out." Stan held the rabbit carefully in his arms. "Anytime you want to go outside and spend some time with the horses, feel free. Just make sure to tell the staff where you're going and for how long, and also don't open any gates if you can avoid it. Slip through the fences or climb over the top instead. If you have to open a gate, make sure you close it really fast behind you."

Cole smiled. "Sounds fantastic. I won't be taking any chances with gates for quite a while, but just the thought that I could even go out there … now that is something to strive for."

Soon afterward Brock steered Cole's wheelchair down the long hallway and through a door to the outside. "In this direction, we have access to all the pastures and the horses. There are times," Brock admitted, "that Sidney and I come here for picnics. It's a great spot to sit outside and eat."

It seemed like way too much effort for Cole now, but the concept brought a smile to his face. "It's nice to know it's a possibility too."

Brock moved the wheelchair in the opposite direction. "I'm taking you this way, so you can see what the staff uses after hours, and we can too in our private time, and during therapy."

As they approached, Cole could hear laughter and splashing. "Is this the pool you were talking about?"

"It is."

Suddenly, there it was in front of them. Cole gasped. "Wow, it's huge," he exclaimed. "I didn't expect to see anything this size."

"That's because it's for therapy and fitness. So it's got some serious lane length. I'm not even sure how long it is, but I wouldn't be at all surprised if it wasn't twenty-five yards. Although it's probably closer to twenty."

Cole studied the beautiful blue water. "Half is under cover?"

"Yes, that makes it the best of both worlds." Brock continued to push Cole alongside the big patio. A couple people sat off to the side, having coffee. "This is open to everybody, but only once a patient is cleared to come. There is no lifeguard on duty. So most need an orderly and that means part of the therapy."

"That makes sense. A lot of people here are not in the best physical shape. Accidents do happen." Cole studied the ramp at the far end. "The ramp's helpful too, I'm sure."

"Yeah. Be careful around it though, and you're only allowed in the pool after the doctor okays it and you've advanced enough to handle yourself." Brock took his buddy around one edge of the pool. "I've never seen it in operation, but there is a lift here to help some patients into the water."

"Thankfully that's not my problem."

Brock squeezed Cole's shoulder. "I hear you. I wasted a lot of time in bed, thinking about how shitty my life was and how stupid my accident was. Now I look around, and I think, damn, I'm in great shape."

"I need to remember that. I'm feeling stupid about everything I did in my first attempt. Now I just want to reboot and move forward and make a go of this."

"Then you can. But you must depend on your team. Let them know you're working with them because they're working for you. If one of you gets off track, well, it can get ugly." Brock kept them moving around the swimming pool, past a hot tub, and then around the far side. "We'll head all the way around to the ramp out front," he said. "After the tour, I'll take you back upstairs."

"How does the food work again?" Cole should know this, but he'd forgotten.

"There are always drinks and snacks available. If you're hungry, you can ask for food. Otherwise, it's three meals a day. Breakfast from six to nine, then lunch from eleven until one, I believe—although I've been there later, one-thirty, even two o'clock, and had no problem getting food. Dinner starts at five and runs until seven."

"Good. I'm looking forward to that. One of the worst things about being in the hospital was the food."

"You're right. That was *the* worst." Brock laughed. "That won't be your problem here." He pushed Cole up the front ramp, and before Cole knew it, they were at the double doors of the entranceway. Brock rolled the wheelchair onto the large Welcome mat and waited for the glass doors to open automatically. Instantly, cool air hit them.

Cole nodded at Melissa manning the front desk.

"Good afternoon. Giving Cole a tour," Brock said.

Melissa smiled at the two of them. "Good afternoon to you two."

Brock left soon after they returned to Cole's room as he had a meeting with his doctor to check on his own progress.

Moving carefully, Cole got from the wheelchair to his bed and was damned grateful to lie down and collapse. Who knew how tiring sitting up could be? Inside, he felt a hell of a lot better. This place offered so much more than he had first thought.

Cole had dozed off when there was a rap on his door. He opened his eyes to see a tall man walk in with a tablet in his hand.

"Good afternoon. I'm Dr. Herzog. I stopped by earlier, but apparently you were out and about, having a social hour."

No recriminations were in his voice, but it reminded Cole he and the doctor were both probably on a schedule.

"Sorry. Brock took me on a tour of the place. I understand I have a schedule around here somewhere, but I haven't had a chance to settle in yet."

"True enough. But after the last time, I don't want to delay your rehab too long, so that you get in the shape you need to be in. Are you ready for an exam?" He raised an eyebrow at Cole.

Cole rolled over and nodded. "As ready as I'll ever be."

# Chapter 4

S ANDRA NEARED COLE'S room as the doctor walked out. She waited for him in the hallway. "How is he?"

Dr. Herzog smiled. "He's in the best shape we've seen so far. I'm feeling quite encouraged, but it's his turn now."

She sighed with relief. "That's good news. I was a little worried we'd have another repeat."

He shook his head. "I don't think so. I've noticed a strong shift in attitude. He has a lot more gratitude about being here now."

"I'm glad to hear that."

"I'll go over the changes in his medication with you now, Sandra. We'll start him on the first round this after-noon."

She nodded and checked his tablet and then pulled out her own. Together they synced the medicine and dosage information and updated Cole's file.

"Okay. I'll make the changes on his next dose. He should be in meetings all afternoon."

"Yes, he should be, but he's been out and about this af-ternoon, so he's missed a couple. I had to circle back to see him. I'm the first one to touch base with him," Dr. Herzog commented. "We need to be on this."

"I took him down for lunch, and the last I saw of him, he was with Brock. I'll go over Cole's schedule with him and make sure he's doing okay and he didn't do too much on his first day back," Sandra said.

"You're the one who insisted on the wheelchair?"

She nodded. "And Dani."

"Good. It'll take him a couple days to adjust. He has to build up that leg and his arm too, not focus only on his back."

"The surgical scars don't look all that great either. Did you notice?"

"Yes. I noted a small amount of inflammation, but I've given him a topical ointment to put on daily, so with any luck, the redness and swelling should soon go down." With that, Dr. Herzog smiled and headed off to see his next patient.

Sandra tapped on the door.

"Come in."

She walked in, stopping near the bed. "Hey, Cole. Where did you and Brock go?"

Cole looked up and smiled at her. "We went all around the compound. It was good. I really like that pool."

"Hey, this is Texas. Everybody likes pools."

He chuckled.

"The doctor gave you your checkup," she said, "but I need a baseline set of measurements, like blood pressure, for example, and to run you through a standard checkup for my own records."

He lay back with his tablet on his belly. "Do what you need to do."

That was a change in his attitude. He hadn't exactly been this easygoing before. In fact, he'd clearly not seen the point. He'd wanted to start his physiotherapy right away. She was happy to see this compliance. "Did you see the animals outside?"

"Outside and inside." He smiled up at her. "It's quite a place."

"It is, indeed." She ran through her checklist, marked down his results and added a few notes about his attitude and general condition. "You need anything else this afternoon?"

"No, I believe I have people who I'll be seeing later."

"Yes, you will. Your tablet should have your schedule of appointments on it. Let me know if there are any problems."

"I will." He glanced over at the bedside table. "I forgot to get a cup of coffee to bring back to my room. Is that something I can get on my own at any time?"

"As far as your team allows you. For now, I'll grab you a cup. Cream or sugar in it?"

"Thanks, I like it black though."

She nodded. "Back in five."

It was not part of her duties, but she'd always found it a simple thing to be nice to people. Besides, if it kept Cole in bed a bit longer, then that was fine with her. Her instructions were to keep him as calm and low-key as possible, so grabbing a cup of coffee was not exactly a hardship.

In the dining hall, Dennis was cleaning up after lunch. She snagged a coffee cup from a fresh tray of hot mugs that he'd set down and then took another one for herself.

She made her way back to Cole's room and found him almost nodding off. She tiptoed inside and set the cup on the table, turning to leave.

"I'm not sleeping. Honest."

She chuckled. "You could have fooled me. It looks like you were two $Z$s away from being gone."

"It's a shock to see how tired I still am," he admitted.

"I think one of the biggest challenges for the big strapping young men when they arrive here is to recognize the limitations of their bodies. Major illness and trauma are hard to adjust to. However, this isn't forever. This is what you must deal with for the moment. Every day it will get better and better."

On those words, she tiptoed out again. Hearing no response, she figured he'd fallen asleep, but he called out after her, "Thanks."

She smiled. "You're welcome."

Maybe it *was* a completely different Cole this time, and that was a good thing. She headed to her office to update files before she saw her next patient. That was one of the things about her job—there was always paperwork. She started with Cole, taking the opportunity to write down a few additional observations she'd realized since leaving his room. These were notes she kept for herself, but his doctor could read them as well.

She'd come to trust her own judgment when it came to patients, until the incident with Cole. Thankfully Dr. Herzog had come to trust her judgment too. One of the reasons why she liked working here. She never felt like her opinions had no value.

In fact, it was just the opposite. She felt the doctors had come to rely on her quite a bit. She never wanted that to be taken the wrong way or for their trust to be misplaced. Not ever again.

AS MUCH AS Cole tried to brush it away, Sandra still seemed less open than last time. That was too damned bad because he really wanted to know her better. It had never occurred to him that she might have gotten into trouble over him. If she had, then he needed to apologize for that. However, at the same time, he wanted to move on, to move forward and to forget about his first attempt to stay at Hathaway House.

He studied the cup of coffee beside him. The best way to make it up to her was to do well this time. He knew more team members were due in this afternoon. He shifted on the bed until he was sitting up, leaning against the headboard. He wished he had a notepad. He still preferred paper and pen over his tablet. And Brock was correct. Cole needed to make some goals. He pulled out the phone he'd been given and was happy to see it was similar to the one he'd had here before. All the same contacts were in there, and he'd already added Brock.

He dialed Dani's number, and when she answered, he said, "Brock suggested you might have a notepad for me to use to write down a few goals and notes to help me do things a little differently this time."

"Absolutely. I'll be your way in a few minutes. Any idea which size you want?"

The question surprised him. He had been hoping for something to write on, not anything specific. "No, just something you don't need. Even a few pieces of paper would be helpful."

"I'll find something for you," she said.

With that call ended, he put down his phone and lifted his coffee.

Shane walked in as Cole set down the cup again. "Hey, Cole. I don't know if you remember me, but I'm Shane Roster. I met you the last time you were here."

Cole nodded. "You're my physiotherapist?"

"Absolutely." He placed his tablet on the end of the bed. "I saw you getting the tour from Brock, and Dani's given me her word you were warned not to overdo it these first few days."

Cole chuckled wryly. "As much as I'd like to forget about the last time, it appears everyone wants to keep reminding me."

"Only for today," Shane said with a smile. "We have to make sure we're all on the same page. It's good timing too. The notes just came through from your last hospital visit." He opened his tablet again. "You've been doing a series of exercises, but you're struggling with the stump. Is that correct?"

"The lower part of my back and my left underarm were damaged by shrapnel," Cole admitted. "That makes crutches very difficult."

"So, you'll be in the wheelchair for a while as that stump heals, and you're prepped to get a prosthetic limb on it as fast as possible. Then we'll get you on two crutches until you can handle just one as you adjust to your prosthesis. Ultimately you won't require crutches at all. Mobility is one of the greatest joys and rights of the human form." Shane glanced at Cole. "Obviously this will be an awful lot of work, and you need additional help to stabilize your frame. Some of the muscle tissue is gone forever, and we can't do anything about that, but your body will compensate. Particularly if you lean sideways for prolonged periods or for any repetitive movement that you do. So we must ensure that you don't fall into that trap." He studied him. "Case in point is the way you're sitting right now. Close your eyes and tell me how you feel in terms of balance."

Cole closed his eyes and tried to assess where the pressure points were. "It feels like I'm leaning to the right and the headboard is hitting hard on my right shoulder. There's pressure on my right hip, more than on my left."

"Now open your eyes and look at the way your body is sitting and leaning. See it from my perspective."

Cole opened his eyes and frowned. "It *looks* like I'm straight. So why does it *feel* like I'm so much heavier on one side?"

"Because you're still subconsciously protecting your injured left side. Now, while you're looking at me, imagine yourself with your body as you were before your accident. Equal muscles, both sides strong, both toned, and then shift your seating accordingly."

Cole frowned. "It sounds odd, but … I have to close my eyes to do that."

"Then close your eyes."

He shifted his weight in his mind, seeing his body as it once had been. Entirely strong, he prided himself on his left and right sides being equally balanced. He'd been a gym junkie and worked his left side extra hard to match it up with his dominant right side. In his mind, he saw his body as it used to be, and he used his hands to shift his position and then leaned against the headboard. He opened his eyes. "Is that better?"

Shane walked over and picked up a small mirror from the top of the dresser. He held it up, and Cole stared in surprise. "I swear to God, I shifted over." But it wasn't visible.

"That's because, in your mind, you still can't trust your body to keep you from falling. Imagine sitting in the middle of a bed surrounded by cushions and then shift your weight so you're sitting upright, using the mirror."

Cole shifted and leaned until he sat straight. He shook his head. "I feel like I'm falling."

"That's a trust issue. You must get to where you can do this without having to consciously think about it. But imagine if you spent your whole life leaning to the right, even when you're sitting in bed and propped up. Imagine what happens to the muscles on the right and to the muscles on the left."

Cole winced. "Yeah, not a pretty picture. I used to do a lot of bodybuilding," he said. "It was hard to get the two sides to match."

"Obviously you're right-handed, so a lot of work had to be done to balance out the left side."

"Right. So, is it a mental impression that I'm not secure or am I really not getting it?"

"It's both. Your perception is of having an injured left side, and you don't trust it can hold you. That's what we'll work on." Shane put down the mirror.

"It's a bit of a relief," Cole said, "because it's quite a shock to see how much I'm protecting that side."

"That's why I want you to do this, starting today, for ten minutes of every hour that you can." He looked at his watch. "Over the next five hours or so, sit in this 'uncomfortable' awareness position for ten minutes of every sixty. Then go back to what you were doing. You must retrain your body to understand this current position is natural and what you've been doing before is not natural. But you can't do it all at once. It becomes easier and easier as we slowly build up the muscles on the left side."

He made a few more notations on his tablet, and then he said, "I'll be back to see you in the morning. Have a good afternoon."

As soon as he had left, Cole shifted into his usual position. "That was at least ten minutes," he muttered.

Yet, he could see what Shane was saying. It was a little disconcerting. Why the hell had nobody mentioned that before?

Cole had known he had to get back here. These people would help him. He felt like the last place had been overrun with underpaid staff. Although the hospital people had cared, they had so many to tend to that damned little got done. Cole didn't want to be mollycoddled. He didn't want somebody to pat his hand and sympathize. He wanted somebody to kick his ass and push him to step forward.

Like what Brock had. That's what Cole wanted for himself. He wasn't sure that Shane would be that kick-ass guy, but he had already noticed something that nobody else had while Cole had been hospitalized.

And that was a damned good thing.

## *Chapter 5*

WHEN HER DAY was done, Sandra got yet another cup of coffee. She should probably cut back—just as she and Sidney had said all too often—but for whatever reason, she drank more caffeine than she liked. Habits were hard to break. Instilling new healthier ones were more difficult. Case in point, she had yet to address her fear of water, or maybe it was a lack of confidence in her swimming skills, even though her on-site apartment was only steps away from the magnificent Hathaway House pool. Shaking her head, she took the stairs to see Stan and the animals. She'd heard talk of a large Angora rabbit but didn't know if it was still here.

Besides, she hadn't been to the vet clinic for a couple days. She felt better when she visited on a regular basis. There was always a dog or a cat that needed a cuddle.

Nobody was at the front desk, and nobody was in the waiting room. She frowned and checked her watch. Normally Stan was still here. Sure enough, the door opened then and Stan walked out. He took one look at her and smiled. "Hi, Sandra. How are you doing?"

"I was feeling a little on the blue side, and I hoped to hug an animal …" she said, her voice trailing off.

He opened his eyes wide and smiled. "How about me? Will I do?"

With a big grin, she stepped into his arms and hugged him. Stan was like a resident big brother. Although he was only fifteen years her senior, there was nothing other than friendship between them. As far as she knew, he had never had a relationship with any of the staff here either. She wasn't sure how she felt about relationships between staff, but she figured that if the two people were consenting adults, it was nobody else's business. However, if it did affect the work environment, then that would change things.

"There was talk of a very large rabbit?"

"Did Cole tell you about that? Yes, that was It. He's back home already, but I'm sure you can visit the ones still here."

She brightened. "That would be nice."

He led the way into the back, and thankfully, most of the surgical recovery cages were empty.

She glanced at the sedated dog with tubes running in and out.

Stan noticed where her attention was and nodded. "That's Jojoba. He had a tumor on his hip I removed. He'll be fine though." Stan walked to the rear wall where the cats were. A big mama cat and her kittens were in the same cage.

"Oh, my gosh! They're so tiny."

"She was brought in pregnant. So now we'll keep her until the kittens can be weaned. Although, if I find a foster family, that would be good too. We'll find homes for the babies and fix the mom, so she doesn't end up in this situation again."

Sandra didn't want to take one of the babies from its mother. She glanced around. "No other dogs or anything?" She shook her head and smiled. "Quiet day for you."

"Exactly. Have you been out to see Molly lately?"

She shook her head. "Molly? Not sure I've met her at all," she confessed.

Stan laughed. "Let me show you." He took her through the back way and out the side door. He pointed. "There." The little filly raced up and down the meadow near the two older mares. "Molly's the baby."

They walked to the fence, and all three horses came over right away. Stan kept a plastic container at the corner. He opened it up and pulled out a handful of grain, which he gave, open-handed, to the older two. Sandra did the same for the baby.

"Oh, my God, she's adorable."

"Innocent and fresh, with the whole world ahead of her. Sometimes we have to remember that."

"I know. It's easy to forget that, isn't it?"

"Sounds like you've had a rough day."

"And yet, I didn't. I do seem to be in a down mood though."

Stan nodded. "Sometimes we don't need a reason. Sometimes the color of the sky is just gray, not blue. Sometimes there is no laughter, just talking. That doesn't make for a bad day. It just makes it another day."

She grinned. "Words to live by."

COLE STARED AT the four walls of his room. Overall, his day had been good. However, keeping his energy expenditures to a reasonable amount, he still wanted to get out for a bit. He wasn't sure how anybody would react to that, but if he took his wheelchair, maybe it wouldn't be too bad. He was tired, but it was doable. Even to sit by the pool would be nice. It was hot today, and the air-conditioning blew through the room, but it gave him a closed-in feeling. He wanted sunshine and warmth, but at the same time, he didn't want to be in the killing heat. The pool might be a good answer. He'd love to get in the water, but he knew he wasn't allowed to do that yet. And he sure as hell wouldn't go against anybody's wishes. This time.

Maybe Brock was up for it. Cole sent his buddy a text message. **Hey, interested in going to the pool or sitting outside somewhere?**

**Absolutely. Be there in five.**

Perfect. Even if they just grabbed a cup of coffee. Although, he seemed to be slugging that back pretty hard. He was sure other choices were available at the coffee bar or in the buffet line.

It wasn't long before he heard Brock's footsteps coming down the hallway. Cole managed to sit up, and using the headboard as he had done before, he sat in the wheelchair. He smiled at his buddy. "I hope you don't mind. The walls were closing in on me."

Brock nodded in understanding. "They do that real fast here." He stepped up behind Cole's chair. "Where would you like to go?"

"I was thinking the pool area because it would be cooler but still out in fresh air."

"That's possible. But there are also the animals. How about we take a walk around and look at the horses first?"

"You sure you're okay pushing me?"

"Hell, yeah. Sidney's got me on some pretty awesome strength-building exercises. My back and shoulders are stronger and better than they've ever been before," Brock said. "I can't wait for you to feel the same thing, buddy."

Cole wanted the same damn thing so bad. He also knew that going too far, too fast … "I do too. All in good time."

"That's the attitude." Before long, Brock had them downstairs and outside in the fresh air.

Cole tilted his face to the waning sun. "It's beautiful here. I haven't seen so much green grass in one place."

"Something to do with the underground springs. Water in Texas is worth its weight in gold. Hathaway seriously has an incredible irrigation system, but I imagine—in the hot, dry season—it can get pretty tough to water all this."

"Isn't that the truth? Still it looks like pictures of Kentucky."

"Agreed." They wandered the grounds in silence.

The majority of the grounds surrounding Hathaway was wheelchair accessible, to make it possible for all the patients to get around outside easily. As they walked to one of the pastures, a goat ran alongside them and jumped on the top railing of the fence.

"I gather they're not trying to keep *them* inside," Cole said.

Brock laughed. "Not sure you can."

Cole studied the goat—it was very small, almost pygmy size. But it was friendly. It jumped off and came to visit. Cole reached down and gave it a good scratch behind its ears. The goat jumped up and landed in his lap. Cole laughed.

"Is that okay, or do you want me to take him off?"

Cole laughed again. "Nah, it's good. I don't remember the last time I had a goat in my lap."

He wrapped his arms around the fuzzy creature and gave it a hug. The goat *baaed* at him and jumped off.

"I guess he didn't like the hug much."

That little touch of nature in its purest form put a lightness of spirit back into Cole he hadn't even realized he lacked. He and Brock stayed and watched the goat as it danced and pranced and jumped along the fence. A moment later, an older goat called to it, and the baby took off.

"Was that a kid or a pygmy?"

"I have no idea," Brock replied. "All I can tell you is that it's very active." He grabbed Cole's wheelchair and pushed forward again. "There are the horses." He pointed out the big ones, and then Cole saw the little one.

"Hey, another baby."

"Yeah, that's Molly."

Cole listened as Brock told him what he knew about the little filly's history.

"They tried to keep her as a pet? Why would people do that?" He stared off at the obviously contented horse, eating grass and sticking close to the two bigger horses. "And the other horses?"

"One is Maggie, who's been here since forever. She was a rescue. I'm not sure about the history of the other one," Brock admitted. "Dani also has her own horses here. Midnight's on the far side by Dani's house, and I think she has another one also. Of course they are all hers essentially."

"There's a house on the property?" Cole twisted to look but couldn't see anything.

"Check the tree line and look closely." Brock pointed to the left.

Then Cole caught sight of it. A beautiful house nestled, almost hidden, in the trees. "Wow, that's nice. Is that hers?"

"Her father owns all this. He built this business up from nothing. The Major had a lot of adapting issues from his own military injuries when he bought this place, and he and his daughter built it up as much for his own project as to help others. Have you met the Major yet?"

Cole shook his head. "Not that I remember." He cast his mind back, and then an older man with white hair, a white beard and a big smile came to mind. He'd gone from table to table in the dining room, busy talking with everybody. "I think I know who you're talking about though."

"If you haven't met him yet, you will soon. The Major delights in getting to know everybody here. This place is more about family than being an institution."

Cole could see that. "If he's beaten back his own demons, then he'll have a good idea what everybody else is going through. It's not easy sympathizing or empathizing when you can't relate to how others are suffering."

"I believe he understands more than most," Brock said. "I haven't spoken to Dani about the Major's recovery, but Sidney's told me some. They had quite a struggle with his health for years. He was depressed to the point of being suicidal at one point in his life. He had PTSD plus physical injuries that held him back from living a full life. But if you look at him now, he's a completely different man."

Words to live by. *A completely different man.* That was Brock too. Cole remembered seeing Brock in the hospital after his injuries and thinking how terrible his friend looked. It wasn't just physical—it was emotional and mental too. Now the buddy pushing him around this place was a whole new man all over again. That was Cole's goal in life—to be a whole new man because the old one sucked.

# Chapter 6

S ANDRA WOKE THE next morning feeling more at peace than she had for eons. For the first time in a long time she hadn't woken up in tears. Weeks had gone by since Cole's arrival, and he'd settled in well. The only recurring problematic factor showing up in the team's weekly meetings regarding Cole's progress came from his psychiatrist and his therapist and dealt with his inability to open up. Which was a shame as any psychological findings could benefit the therapist's ability to help Cole deal with any false beliefs that may be holding him back in reaching his goals. The psychiatrist was still looking for the root issues in Cole's life, which his therapist would then help him deal with, but Cole avoided the trauma of his IED explosion, even more earlier events in his life, only wanting to face forward with no resolution of past dramas. The psychiatrist was not giving up and kept prodding each week.

As for Cole's therapist, Kimmy was happy to see Cole's forward-facing mentality, yet Cole was unfocused as to his second career. In one of the team meetings, Sandra had asked if maybe Cole would respond better to an informal conversation, like with her, and how he might feel pressured with these recurring themes when seeing his psychiatrist and his therapist. The two doctors conferred and agreed. Sandra would pass on any further insights she discovered.

Except for the two mental blocks noted at several team meetings, Cole was making good overall progress, not overextending himself physically, yet following his doctor's orders, taking his medications as prescribed. Sandra and Cole were in a routine now, and that was a good thing for everyone. In a place like this, routine kept everything moving forward.

She was still hesitant around Cole, but a bond was forming, and that was the way she liked it. It was nice to become friends with these people when they were here. However, on a day like today, it was harder. Isaac would leave this morning. She was so happy for him, but still it would be tough because she probably would never see him again.

It happened that way most of the time. Patients talked about keeping in touch, but in her experience, it was rare—the odd email, maybe a thank-you card. But as people integrated back into their real, normal lives, the stages of their recovery faded into insignificance. Maybe it was supposed to be that way, but it left her without that sense of any long-term continuity of that friendship, and she was sad for that reason.

She waited at the front entrance. Isaac's cab ride was here, waiting for him to make the final walk out the front door. He would leave under his own steam, walking on his own two feet and carrying his own two bags. If there was ever a change, it was this man who had shown up in such bad shape. This was one of the biggest and most startling transformations she had witnessed.

She stood and watched as Isaac, who'd lost both legs, walked toward her, a massive grin on his face. He'd have been a hell of a football player with the size of his chest and shoulders. He had taken his injuries hard, but unlike so many others, he hadn't gotten depressed—he'd gotten even. He was the best he could be right now. He even walked normally. It would take a skilled medical professional to spot the shifts of his prosthetic limbs. Isaac was doing so well.

When he saw her, his grin widened. "I was hoping to see you before I left."

"I wouldn't let you go without saying goodbye," she said, and damn it if there weren't tears choking her throat.

He put down his bags, opened his arms and gave her a gentle hug.

That was the thing about Isaac. He was a giant physically, but his personality had been that of a teddy bear. They would miss him. She stepped back to wipe the tears from her face. "It was a delight working with you, and you will be missed."

He smiled. "Don't take it personally, but I hope I never come back."

She laughed. "And we hope we never see you as a patient here again."

"Don't worry. I'll stay in touch."

She smiled because she'd heard it all before. He said goodbye to several of the other residents, and then he walked out into the sunshine. His sister wanted to pick him up, but he had said no. He would start his new life the way he intended to go on—independent. As the taxi drove away, she turned toward the hallway, but she still wiped away her tears.

"You okay?" Cole asked as he appeared in front of her.

She stopped in her tracks. She smiled at him, maybe for the first time with a free, open, happy smile. "I'm sad and happy at the same time. Someone who was here for months and who had an incredibly difficult recovery just walked out of here carrying his own bags. He's flying out to California on his own. He'll make it."

Cole looked at her and then smiled. "I guess that's the ultimate joy for you."

"Joy and sadness. We're a part of the stage of their lives that they don't ever want to remember. So we all ..." She shrugged and took a deep breath. "In most cases we are forgotten." She continued past him and then froze. "Oh, my gosh. You're not in the wheelchair."

COLE LAUGHED. "YOU noticed, did you?" He kept his voice light and carefree. Inside, he was beaming because he was on crutches. He hadn't gone very far yet, but it made such a difference to be fully vertical and mobile. Besides, when he'd seen her walk past, he'd made a special effort to reach her, just so she would see him. So silly. Yet, he couldn't stop himself from thinking about her. She most likely didn't even notice him most days. He'd been a problem for her in the beginning, and now he was sure she was keeping her distance. She maintained a professional eye on him, but that was it.

The last couple weeks he had developed an interest in Sandra, but he knew that was foolish. Still, something about Brock and Sidney's relationship made Cole realize his physical form wouldn't necessarily stop him from finding somebody he liked. Only one person in this entire place made his heart race and his gaze stare at the doorway every time he heard footsteps in the hall. She came into his room two to three times a day, and although these were profession-al visits, he couldn't help but wish they were something more.

Immediately she frowned. "Are you sure you're not doing things too fast? I know you think you're getting that much better, faster ..."

"I am getting better, faster. And yes, I do have permission to be on crutches. Although I can't go very far. This is my first run. I don't want to screw anything up and over-stress other parts." He grinned at her. "But it's absolutely awesome to be on my feet again."

She beamed at him. "It's a huge mental shift that we see a lot here. I'm so happy you've reached that point."

He grabbed her hand, brought it to his lips. "So am I."

Sandra's expression was stunned, and a knot formed in Cole's stomach. *Play it off, dude.*

He winked at her and turned, then said, "Race you to the other end of the hall."

He had no idea what made him say that. He knew she stared after him with that surprised look. Escape was the only option. But when hobbling around on crutches for the first time, he wouldn't likely escape quickly. Maybe his challenge would give her an excuse to run away. Hell, that was what he wanted to do.

"Hold up," she called out. "No running."

He tossed her a disbelieving look, and the twist of his torso was just enough to throw his weight off-balance. He quickly stuck out one crutch to catch himself before he went down. At least he was still standing. But his back was screaming.

She gasped and raced to his side. "Are you okay?"

He closed his eyes and bowed his head. "I'm fine. Just doing too much." Then he heard the same damned echo in his head, all over again—*going too fast, going too far, going too soon.* Jesus, when would he ever learn? In his own embarrassment, he'd "run away," and he had done more damage than if he'd just casually walked off.

He gave her an embarrassed smile and took ownership. "That'll teach me." He nodded at his room one doorway down. "Good thing I'm almost there." He left her and made his way to his room where he sat on the bed and laid his crutches across the end. Using his arms, he shuffled up the bed and collapsed. He knew he hadn't hurt himself badly. But at the same time, it had been a jolt to his senses. A fall might've been good. It might've stopped him from trying something like that again. "What the hell was I even thinking?" he muttered.

He could sense her in the doorway. He willed her to disappear. The last thing he wanted was her pity, her sympathy or even her amusement, although that would be a hell of a lot better than the other two.

"I'm fine," he said, waving an arm at her to go away. "You don't have to worry."

"I'm not worried. I'm just a little concerned."

"There's hardly a difference." He rolled over to face the window. "I always like to make a fool of myself. It's a great way to meet girls." Only the words came out more sarcastic than he'd intended. He shook his head, but he didn't hear any retreating footsteps. Instead, she laughed.

Then he heard her soft voice from the doorway. "There are lots of ways to meet girls. Please don't hurt yourself as one of them. If you want coffee sometime, I'm certainly up for that."

Then all he heard was her footsteps, almost racing down the hall. He lay there on the bed with a slow, wide grin growing on his face. Hell, he'd fall to the floor anytime if it meant getting that response.

# Chapter 7

WHAT HAD POSSESSED her to do something so foolish? Sandra raced to her office. She glanced at her watch, now a bit behind in her rounds. Seeing Isaac off had put her behind schedule, but that moment with Cole had set her back even further. On the other hand, she'd also seen something that tickled her pink. She had deliberately held back from getting too close to any of the patients over the years, but she could blame Dani for any shift in that now. Dani and Sidney. They both had relationships with men who they had met here.

That was both good and bad. Good in the sense that she was delighted for them, but bad as it also highlighted what those without a relationship were missing. She'd liked Cole right from the beginning, but when his condition had declined and he'd gone back to the hospital, she'd been so worried about his health that she'd pulled back, not wanting to hinder him in any way. Sure, he was back again and doing very well, but from what she could see, he still appeared to be headstrong and driven to do too much.

It wasn't that those were bad traits, but they had to be held in check. That he liked her was obvious, and it made her feel good because she really liked him too. However, she wasn't sure she could live with his headstrong-and-driven personality. She was slow and cautious. She was a taking-safe-steps-forward type of person, whereas he appeared to dive in and damn the consequences.

Maybe that was his military training. She imagined it took serious guts to throw himself out of planes and to scuba dive in rough waters and all the other activities she'd heard the men did. Her world was built on routine, on a strict regimen. It was built on safety. She helped people get better. Any mistake on her part—well, it could kill a patient. Of course, any mistake on his part could also kill him. She shook her head at the contrast ... and the similarities.

At her desk, she updated her computer records. Her tablet would sync automatically. Then she set out the medications to dispense.

One of the biggest problems in her professional interactions with the male patients at Hathaway House was the fact they often viewed the relationship between the people who they worked with and themselves in an unhealthy light. They put too much emphasis on the gratitude, or whatever you wanted to call it, that they felt toward the people who worked with them every day. Like they latched on to that person and didn't see them in a real light. She'd seen that happen a lot. Take Kenneth for example. Some patients—and staff—found it hard to separate a healthy relationship from that type of dependent relationship here. Being a friendly and helpful caregiver should never be taken as something else. Which was Kenneth's biggest flaw. She didn't see that same problem in Cole.

Yet, Sidney and Dani were lucky to have healthy relationships with Brock and Aaron, who were both stable and solid. The two couples seemed very much in love.

Sandra would like to find a healthy relationship like that for herself.

For the first time, she felt Cole may feel the same way. But what exactly? It wasn't something she was prepared to push. She was all about moving forward slowly and carefully. Whereas, she could already see he was the guy who jumped into things—maybe relationships too. She wouldn't go there too quickly.

Still, the look of embarrassment on his face when he'd almost fallen and his comment when he lay in bed—well, she'd seen a side to him she hadn't seen before. She wasn't sure that was a good thing because it endeared him to her that much more.

She quickly finished selecting her medications, picked up the tray and made her rounds. She went from patient to patient, dispensing pills. When she came to Cole's room, she knocked on the door. He was still lying down, facing the window.

"Cole?" she said. "It's me again."

He rolled to his back, looked at her and smiled. "I figured I'd chased you away."

She grinned. "I don't chase away that easy."

"Glad to hear it." He propped himself up on the bed, motioned her over, accepted his medication and reaching for his water bottle, threw the whole lot down at once. He handed her the empty paper cup and said, "I'll be happy when I'm off these."

She nodded. "You and many other people." As she went toward the door, she glanced back and said, "No ill effects from the crutches?"

He laughed. "No idea. I haven't gotten up again."

She glanced at her watch. "I'm going for coffee in about ten minutes, if you want to meet me in the dining room. I like to sit out on the deck where the sun is. If you make it, great. If not"—she shrugged—"no problem."

*"IF I MAKE it, great. If not, no problem,"* he repeated. *Like hell.* This was his first chance to cement a small step here—so very necessary for the rest to follow. Sure, he was tired. But he wasn't completely done. He looked at the crutches, then at the wheelchair, and realized he might be better off in the wheelchair. Proving it was one thing—stupidity was another. He slowly lowered himself into the wheelchair and laid the crutches across the bed one at a time.

Settling himself into a better position, he placed his hands on the wheels and headed out the door. The hallway was empty, which was a good thing as his control of the wheelchair left a lot to be desired. He'd seen some guys do amazing things in theirs from climbing stairs to any number of other feats. They were all way beyond him. The trouble was, he also didn't *want* to be very good at maneuvering a wheelchair. This wasn't his life or permanent base.

This was his life *for now.* He felt better, more like his old self on the crutches, but he had to admit it was easier on his body to sit in the wheelchair.

It was early afternoon, which meant the dining area was quiet. He was thankful for that. It made it so much easier to get around when he didn't have to dodge people, even though there was plenty of room between the tables.

He was a little on the hungry side. He rolled up to the coffee bar and filled a cup. He studied the treats on offer and decided on a cinnamon bun, so famously delightful here. They appeared to be warm. He put one on a tray, along with his coffee, then picked up the tray and gingerly placed it in his lap. He reached over and grabbed a handful of paper napkins in case of accidental spills, then slowly turned the wheelchair and headed at what he would call a relaxed pace out to a table in the sunshine. To his surprise and satisfaction, he arrived without spilling anything. He grinned. Success was nice.

"That's a pretty happy smile on your face there, champ," Sandra said, coming around the table. She held a cup of coffee in one hand and a cinnamon bun in the other. She laughed. "Great minds think alike, huh?"

Still worried about dumping the coffee, Cole carefully transferred the tray to the table. Sandra moved a chair out of the way so he had room to wheel up against the table. He relaxed back in his chair.

"The whole way here, all I could think about was that damned cup. I was so sure I'd end up wearing it."

She grinned. "You wouldn't be the first."

He nodded. "That doesn't mean I want to be the last either."

"*Latest*," she corrected with a smile. "There will be many more. But take the successes as they come."

He removed the coffee cup and the cinnamon bun from the tray and set it off to one side. Something about trays made him think of hospitals. He hated them. He sat back and studied Sandra as she tucked into the pastry. She didn't take little delicate bites, but she ripped off part of the big coil in her fingers, and then she sat back and moaned. The joy on her face made him smile in anticipation, which had nothing to do with the cinnamon bun but more about the tightening in his groin, wanting to put that kind of smile on her face himself.

Dangerous thoughts, especially here. He gave his head a

shake and reached for his treat. She seemed to make it clear he was a patient and nothing more. And it was best things stayed that way. Right?

Pushing away those thoughts, he took his first bite of the cinnamon bun. "Wow, this is really good."

She nodded, her mouth too full to reply.

He grinned as he watched her slowly uncoil the entire cinnamon bun and eat it bite by bite while he took a chunk from the side like some wild animal. "I wonder if they've ever done any research on the way people eat cinnamon buns."

She glanced up, took one look at the way he ate his and said, "Yep, and you're eating it wrong." She flashed that grin at him again and peeled off another piece.

"I never really thought about it. I pick it up and bite."

"It's best if you unwrap it first. My favorite part is the very center."

"Right." His throat suddenly clogged as his thoughts became wayward once more, focusing on the best parts of her being in her center. He swallowed hard and turned to stare at the fields around them. "It's truly beautiful here."

"It's also incredibly rare. This is a green oasis in Texas."

He grinned and nodded. "Where are the dust bowls and the tumbleweeds?"

"Not for a few miles around here, that's for sure."

"Dani and her father could sell this property for millions."

Sandra shook her head. "Hopefully they won't. The center is doing a tremendous job helping people."

Keeping the conversation light and neutral, he asked her about her work. "How long have you been here?"

"Five years. And with any luck, I'll stay for another ten

to fifteen at least."

"What about marriage and family?"

She nodded. "Absolutely. But one doesn't preclude the other. I'd love to stay here, working, even if it's only part-time. I've seen a lot of my friends lose track of their careers and become very isolated once they have children, especially if they stop working full-time. It's hard at first, but once you get that work-life balance, it's nice to have an adult life and not days full of baby talk. Even if it's only for one or two days a week. We're close enough to Dallas that a lot of people here commute daily."

"Don't they all?" He glanced around and added, "It never occurred to me that staff quarters were available here."

She laughed. "They are, indeed. Not terribly luxurious but comfortable, and you get the advantages of the pool on the grounds and the food." She held up the last bite of cinnamon bun to emphasize her point. "There are an awful lot of pros and not too many cons about being here."

"I hadn't thought of it, but it's a great idea."

"A lot of the staff are married and have houses between here and Dallas. We also have a number of specialists who regularly make the trip from the big city too." She smiled. "I remember when a spinal surgeon from Dallas came to visit a friend of his, who'd opted to spend his recovery time here. The surgeon was dubious in the beginning, but he is a convert now. He sends us a lot of people. He also stops by to check on some of his patients occasionally. It's close enough for him to come in whenever he's a little worried."

Cole sat back. "That says an awful lot about the job that's being done here."

"Exactly." She glanced up and smiled. "Speaking of which, hello, Major."

The Major stepped around the table into Cole's view and held out his hand. "I'm Don Hathaway—or the Major as a lot of people call me—and of course, I'm Dani's father."

"Nice to meet you." Cole reached out and shook the man's hand, studying the cross between Santa Claus and Rip Van Winkle. Don wasn't quite as large as Santa, and Don didn't have the super long Rip Van Winkle beard, but the Major's contagious smile matched both images. "This is a hell of a place you've developed here."

"Thank you." The Major nodded, and Cole realized Don carried a small dog.

Sandra reached out and said, "Hello, Chickie."

There was the tiniest of yelps as the animal shifted in the Major's arms. Cole stared at the little critter, fascinated. "Is that a dog? Or maybe a rat? I'm not sure."

# Chapter 8

S ANDRA GRINNED. CHICKIE was unique.

The Major laughed—big belly laughs that rolled across the open porch. "This is Chickie. He's a four-year-old Chihuahua cross. He has stunted growth, and he's physically deformed. But he's extremely well-loved by everyone. Here." With a sudden move, the Major handed Chickie to Cole.

Sandra watched as Cole held out his hands but had no idea what to do with the dog. He lifted him to eye level, clearly studying the huge brown eyes that stuck out of a very small head. Chickie's eyes held so much trust. Intelligence. And hope.

As if unable to resist, with a reaction she'd seen time and time again, Cole bent and nuzzled the little dog's head with his cheek. Chickie's little *yip, yip* was audible from where she sat. Cole cuddled the dog close against his chest. Chickie laid his jaw against Cole's shoulder and snuggled in.

"Chickie is a special family member here," Sandra said, her heart melting to see this guy take to Chickie—and Chickie take to him—so easily. "He's well-loved, and although he has lots of his own physical problems, he is a mascot of hope for everyone here."

Cole nodded, and Sandra could see the faintest shimmer of wetness in his eyes.

"We always make a point of introducing him to everybody, and we let everybody know he's on a special diet and can't be fed anything off the table," the Major said. "The last time that happened, he ended up with a bowel blockage, and he had surgery to help him with that."

Cole looked at Chickie and shook his head. "I promise I will not feed him."

"He obviously would like it if you do," Sandra said with a big grin. "Like all dogs. But he doesn't jump well, and although he walks, he is so darned small that most people end up carrying him around. Which, as you can see, suits him entirely."

Cole nodded and gently rubbed his chin back and forth against the dog's small head. "Does he live here?"

"Several of them do," Sandra said. "Chickie has a basket in the front reception area. Helga lives here too. She's a big Newfoundland with a prosthetic leg. She makes the rounds to every room here at some point in time. She has an uncanny nose for finding people who might need a canine hug. An assigned member of the kitchen staff makes sure meals are brought to the dogs twice a day and that they have water available when needed. Other than that, we give them access to the outdoors. They're all house-trained as much as they can be, but there might be the occasional accident," Sandra said calmly. "We understand when that happens. For animals and people alike."

She didn't know if Cole got the message. This place was all about acceptance. He needed to know that. Even when people made false starts, it was okay when they got up and moved forward again. She expected Cole had a lot more setbacks coming. It was the nature of life, and it was very much the nature of recovery.

"A dog called Racer was here for a while. He had wheels.

I haven't seen him in a few days. I should ask about him."

"Wheels, huh? I guess that makes sense." He glanced over at Sandra. "It would be nice to spend some time with Stan and the animals. I've always been a huge dog lover." He cuddled Chickie closer. "Something about their ability to love unconditionally … and animals like this are so much smaller and yet so much more trusting. They can step in and comfort you when you're dealing with so much garbage," he said. "It's really special."

"That's one of the benefits here." She smiled. "In the beginning, a lot of people were concerned about the hygiene issues between animals and people. Infections are a problem anywhere, but the upstairs is sanitized on a regular basis. So is the downstairs, for that matter, because the animals are healing too. A lot of the animals, such as Racer, had to have surgery. This little guy had surgery as well, but that was a long time ago." She glanced at Chickie. "Are you okay with Chickie? Do you want him a bit longer, or do you want me to take him now?"

Instinctively, he wrapped his arms around the little guy to keep him close.

She smiled. "I wanted to make sure that he's comfortable here with you, and considering his delicate system that he doesn't need to go out."

"Right. Then I guess I should give him back." He gently picked up the little dog and kissed him on the top of his head before handing him to the Major. "If you don't mind, maybe I'll get a chance to visit with him later."

"Absolutely," the Major said. "If you don't see him around, go to the front desk. He could be sleeping in his bed there. He is in popular demand, but sometimes he is completely alone and looking for somebody to love too."

The Major scooped up Chickie and tucked him against his shoulder and headed back inside, into the dining hall.

Sandra turned toward Cole. "Two of our biggest icons in this place are the Major and Chickie."

Cole smiled. "I'm sure life would not be the same without having characters like those two in it."

COLE'S ARMS FELT empty without Chickie in them. He wanted to get a dog when he was in a better situation. He had had a small apartment in California, but his landlord had put his stuff in storage for him, rather than Cole continuing to pay the rent. He knew he probably wouldn't return to something like that anyway—one of those old buildings that didn't have an elevator. Right now, for all intents and purposes, he was homeless. That felt very strange. When he'd been living on base, he had housing. Then, for a while, he'd moved off base and had his own apartment.

Now he wasn't entitled to base living as he was no longer active in the military. He wouldn't ask to go back either. It wasn't his life anymore. No matter how much he wished things could have been different, this was his new reality, and he had to make decisions about his future. He'd been an IED man, but there was not a whole lot of work for bomb specialists in civilian life. With the physical requirements to be on a police force, he wasn't sure that was an option for him, now that he was physically disabled. He didn't see how any of his work history and SEALs experiences would help him in a second career.

That meant retraining. He had some funds socked away and could get government assistance, but he needed a goal to shoot for. It was also hard, if not almost impossible, to think about what his options were when he hadn't even healed yet, didn't know what his new physical abilities would be. Everything seemed so out of reach, and when he tried to reach out, he felt he was being left behind. Like with his much-older brothers when he was a kid.

Yet Cole *had* to move forward regardless, albeit slowly now, a little bit at a time, one step after the other. He couldn't start thinking long-term *yet*. Not until he was better, both physically and emotionally. He'd use Brock as a model. The man had been broken inside and outside for such a long time, but to see him now, well, he was just so different. Cole was so happy for his buddy, and he wanted that same success. He didn't know what Brock planned to do with his life now, but Cole was sure it would incorporate Sidney in some way.

Dallas wasn't very far away as Sandra had said. Lots of people lived there and commuted here. Hathaway House was probably only ten to fifteen minutes from the outskirts of the city limits and a half hour more from downtown.

He'd heard Dani's fiancé, Aaron, had applied and been accepted for veterinarian school, most likely with Stan's help, but that wasn't the life for Cole. He loved animals, but he certainly didn't want to be a veterinarian, dealing with sick and broken pets all his life. He had no idea what he did want to do, and that would be an issue—but not one for today.

He suddenly realized Sandra was still here, staring at him, a concerned frown on her face. He gave himself a mental shake. "I'm sorry. I'm sitting here, lost in my own worries, when I should be enjoying my time with you." He reached across the table and held out his hand. He was gratified when she reached across too.

"You're a very special woman. I don't know how you can handle all of us broken people as easily and as well as you do."

She smiled. But the smile didn't reach her eyes.

"I'm fine," he said gently. "I've got a lot of things going on inside that I have to realign to my new world."

She nodded. "How true. We see that a lot. Some people had lives before the military. Some people have lives they can go home to with skills they learned from the military, and other people are starting all over again."

He smiled wryly. "Put me in the starting-all-over-again category."

"But your counselor will give you aptitude tests and career counseling and things like that," she said. "You'll still have to make some decisions, but you may discover several options are available to you."

She smiled again, and this time her smile did reach her eyes.

He stared at her long fingers, her perfectly trimmed nails. She had the gentle, soft fingers of a nurse's hand. He reached his other hand across the table, laying it beside hers, and opened his palm with its large square calluses. The difference was instantly obvious.

"Even before I went into the military, I was more of a physical worker. Not like Brock, who was a roofer, doing any construction job he got his hands on. I was always into landscape, gardening." He smiled. "At one point, I thought I would have my own company. I like to build small walls, fences and ponds." He shook his head. "That was a long time ago."

"Maybe it's something you could go back to. There is something very nurturing and healing about working in gardens," she replied, making a mental note to share this with Kimmy.

"I'm sure there are at least a hundred, if not a thousand, landscaping companies in Dallas alone."

"That doesn't mean there isn't room for another one. Or that you couldn't work for one of them if you wanted to."

"But it's physical work," he reminded her. "That makes it not a great option."

She settled back thoughtfully, her fingers drumming on the table beside his. "Maybe," she said slowly. "But that doesn't mean you can't hire people. If you're the boss, you won't be doing a ton of the physical labor anyway. Physically, you *can* get back a lot of your strength. Look at Brock."

Cole nodded. "Brock is my idol right now," he said with a smile. "The fact is, he's also a good guy."

"Has he lined up his future career?"

"I'm not sure. We haven't spoken about that. But he was hell on computers before. So I imagine his job prospects are a bit better than mine."

"Maybe. But there is room in the world for everybody. Everybody has options. Even you." She stood and smiled. "As nice as it is to sit here and visit, I need to get back to work." She took several steps away and then turned. "I imagine you have something you're supposed to do now or someplace else you're supposed to be."

He frowned at her and then saw what time it was. "Oh, crap. You are so right." In fact, he was already late.

## *Chapter 9*

---

THE NEXT FEW days followed a gentle and routine pattern for Cole. Sandra stopped in to say hi during her rounds. They got coffee together midmorning, and she saw him again in the evening. She knew he didn't see the same improvement she did. Then again, she was watching for it. It could take weeks before that sudden, magical moment happened, where the patient saw the improvement.

But day by day, taking it slow and steady, Cole got squared away and built up some strength. He was working a lot with Shane in the morning and then swimming in the afternoon with Brock. She was happy for Cole. His mood had shifted as well. A team meeting on his progress was scheduled for this afternoon. She'd be interested to hear what the others had to say about him. A couple people had commented on the fact that she was spending a fair amount of time with him, but so far, she had tossed that off as a joke. She knew it was noticeable, but she hadn't made up her mind what to do about it.

Dani had not said anything to Sandra about relationships not being allowed. Dani was with Aaron after all.

Anyway, Sandra didn't think that was on Dani's agenda. No, it was more about Sandra and what she would do for herself. She wanted to be sure her job remained secure. And she was uncertain that she wanted to get involved with somebody who would just turn around and leave. She planned to stay here, and if Cole wasn't staying local, then that wouldn't work long term.

She walked into the meeting room, tablet in hand, and took her seat. When everybody was there, the meeting began with a number of patients to review. They went through several case folders without any disagreement. Then they came to Cole.

She brought up Cole's folder on her tablet, and Shane started.

"He's come a long way in these last few weeks. One thing I would say is that he seems to be holding back. I think his initial arrival and doing too much has stopped him from applying himself now. He's afraid to set himself back any further."

Cole's therapist Kimmy nodded. "He won't open up about some issues as well. Not that we need to know every deep, dark secret he has, but we don't want anything that adds stress or has a negative impact on his healing."

The discussion carried on around the table.

"Is he making any friends here?" one of the psychiatrists asked.

After a moment of silence, everybody turned to look at Sandra.

She flushed. "I'm friendly with him, yes, but I'm hoping he's making new friends with other people too." Several of them looked at their tablets, and she wondered what was going on. "Do you think that, because we're friends, he's not joining in with other people?"

"I wondered if that was an issue with him," Shane said. "He is, however, friendly with Brock. Because he has the two of you as his cornerstones, quite possibly he is keeping himself apart from the others. We do see that. Until the patient settles in, it's hard for them to integrate."

"Is that an issue with Cole?" Sandra asked bluntly. The last thing she wanted was for anybody to be concerned about this and not bring it up, then it come back to bite her later.

There was silence for a moment. Then Shane spoke again. "I think integrating would help. I guess I'm a little more concerned that he's not putting in his full efforts. It's like he's found his comfort zone, and he's stuck there."

"Oh." Sandra studied Shane. "Do you think that's because of a friendship?" She frowned. "I'm not sure how that would be."

"No." He shook his head. "I shouldn't have linked those two together. I don't think they are related. When he first got here, he pushed himself too hard and too fast, and he had a natural relapse. But when he arrived the second time, it was as if he was scared to try. At the same time, he could see Brock, and he wanted what Brock had." He held up a hand to forestall Sandra's question. "I don't mean that as Cole wanting a relationship. I mean how Cole wants Brock's very much improved level of physical fitness."

She settled back, realizing Shane wasn't saying anything derogatory. He was just laying out the facts as he saw them.

Speaking slowly, Shane continued. "But at the same time, there is almost a disconnect. Because he tried once and hurt himself, he is scared to give that full effort again. So I can see some discouragement in him right now. It's like he's got an issue of *before versus now*. If he tries too hard, he'll push himself back. If he doesn't try enough, he's not reaching his goal. Brock's the goal. Cole doesn't see how to get from where he is to where he wants to be."

"I can see that," Sandra said. She glanced around the

room at everybody else. "Anybody else have something to add?"

"It's all about fear," one psychiatrist said bluntly. "He's afraid he will fail. He's afraid he'll set himself back. He's afraid he'll never reach Brock's state. He's afraid he'll always be *half-as-good*. He was a SEAL. Brock was a SEAL. They are incredibly competitive, but there they were equals. Cole doesn't see himself as Brock's equal right now. He's behind the curve and is afraid he'll never catch up."

A flash of sympathy tugged at Sandra's heart, but she knew sympathy would not be helpful. "What's the answer?"

The psychiatrist faced her and smiled. "What did you do?"

She frowned at him. "I didn't do anything."

He grinned. "After you found out that Cole had tossed his medicines, how did you react and get back on track?"

She stared at him, not happy being put in the hot seat for her own behavior. But these meetings were all about making helpful and constructive progress moving forward, so she didn't have a lot of choice but to answer.

"I locked down and became more paranoid. I watched all the patients, ensuring they took all their medications, not just one. I still do that," she confessed. "It grabs a hold of you, and you're scared of making a mistake. The same as Cole must feel."

"So how do we help him?"

Maybe an answer to that question would be of help to her too. The more she thought about it, the more she realized she had eased back already on her paranoia. Why? Because of Cole's change in attitude.

"We give him time to let him work through the issues and be there for him," she said quietly. "We learn to trust him as he must learn to trust us."

COLE LOOKED UP as Brock sat beside him. Cole was constantly amazed at how good his buddy looked.

"How you doing, Cole?" Brock put his coffee on their table, sitting in the shade out of the hot sun. "How's the therapy work going?"

Cole winced. "Alternately painful and not bad."

Brock laughed. With a commiserating nod he said, "I think everybody here can relate to that. When you give it your all, it hurts like absolute crap the next day. But slowly, day by day, and with continued hard work, you can see the results."

Cole dropped his gaze to his coffee cup. He nodded as if he understood. The trouble was he understood something different.

"What's the matter?" Brock asked.

Cole shrugged and shifted in his seat. He stared out at the large open area. "I guess I haven't seen the progress I wanted to see."

"Keep at it. You'll get there."

"I don't think so in this case," Cole said quietly. "I like that you're here. Fact is, I want the healing results you have, but I'm just not getting them."

"How long have you been here now? Four weeks?"

Cole nodded. "Give or take a few days."

"And your first week was all about a slow start, right?"

Again Cole nodded. "But after that it's been steady."

"Absolutely. If you look back to your condition when you initially arrived, versus where you are today, you'd see the change for yourself. Instead, you're comparing yourself to me, and that's not good. I have been here working my ass off for months now. I'm almost free and clear," Brock said, "but not quite."

Cole felt a rush of pride for his friend. "Now that would be awesome." He smiled at Brock. "Did you do anything special? Was there any one thing you can think of that helped your recovery?"

Brock shook his head. "I don't know about *one* thing specifically, but I can list several. One was getting Sidney as my therapist because she took my motivation, which was nil, and supercharged it to a hundred percent. Then having Sidney come into my life in a personal way definitely helped."

"Well, that's not my case obviously." Cole slouched back in his chair.

"If she was your therapist, would you be motivated to do the work you need to do?" Brock lifted his cup and took a sip of his coffee. "Or are you scared of a relapse?"

Cole looked up and let out a slow breath. "Before the relapse, I was absolutely determined to get the exact same results as you. I would beat your time. I would kick your ass. I would make sure I owned this place," he said. "I wanted my body back in the biggest way." He picked up a spoon and stirred his black coffee, studying the swirling pattern in the cup. Then he continued in a low voice. "When I came back the second time, I was terrified. They warned me about not doing too much." He sighed. "Now I feel like I'm lost in the middle ground. I'm scared to give it my all because that setback scared the crap out of me."

"Understandable. It was rough on you at the time. Hell, it was pretty rough on me too." Brock smiled. "I was devastated when I heard you'd been taken back to the hospital."

"You and me both." Cole chuckled wryly. "From where I was, when I first returned here, to where I am today is a huge improvement, but it still seems like I am so damned far away. It's there within my grasp, but it's not. I can almost reach out and touch it." Cole grabbed Brock's arm. "I can see it in you. You made something magical happen. I'm looking for that same thing."

Brock turned his arm over so he could grab Cole's forearm. "But you weren't here to see my first three months as I struggled to get to where I am today. Plus, you don't see how you're actually making your own miracle happen right now. Because you're in the middle of the process, you can't see it yet. Remember when I was terrified of failing BUD/s training?"

Cole nodded. "It was easy to spot the fear because I felt the same damned thing."

"But we made it. We gave it our all, and we made it. What you must do is make that adjustment and understand, even if you give it your all right now, give everything Shane asks of you, you won't have a relapse. You could have a day where you feel like shit and think you can't do any more, but people like us, we can't say no." He stared into Cole's eyes. "We have to go all-in."

Cole smiled at him. "That was our motto, wasn't it? And so true. When we do something, we go all-in." He could feel something stirring inside him, the power that drove his desire to do better. It was that incredible competitiveness to do his best. "That's what I needed to hear."

Brock squeezed his buddy's arm and released him. "The other thing to remember is, when we were in BUD/s training, in many ways it was all about fighting the demons within yourself to find that best within you, so you could make it through the training. We did it as a team. We were together. We helped each other. We made it. There were days all of us were in tears, when all of us were broken, but *always* one of us wasn't as bad as the others, and that's what held us together. That's what pulled us up so we all made it."

"You're right. That's exactly it."

Brock nodded in agreement. "Before, when I was broken, I was at the lowest I could be. Now it's your turn to be down, and it's my turn to help you get back up."

"Too bad Denton isn't here."

Brock grinned. "That's something I wanted to talk to you about. I heard from Dent today. Dani called to tell him how things are looking good, and she hopes to have good news for him soon. It may be another three weeks until he knows for sure, but for however long I'm here, it'll be good to have the three of us together again, like old times."

"Good? Man, that is freaking awesome." That was the final clincher Cole needed to ignite the burning fire inside—it went from glowing coals to flames instantly. "You know he'll require a little help when he gets here, right?"

Brock nodded slowly. "That can be your job, dude. Like I'm here to help you, you can be here to help him. He'll see me and think that's too high a level to achieve. It'll be up to you to show him how very doable it is."

Feeling like Brock's words had rooted themselves somehow on the inside, Cole sat back in his chair, filled with determination. "Now *that* I can do."

<h1 style="text-align:center">Chapter 10</h1>

SANDRA REMEMBERED THE conversation from the team meeting many times over the next few days. In a way it was unfinished, incomplete. She disagreed that her friendship with Cole could be detrimental to his progress. That was like saying, hugging and petting the sick animals downstairs would hinder the patients' recovery upstairs. She wasn't Cole's therapist, and she wasn't a psychiatrist, but she was a nurse, and he was one of her patients who she looked after and kept an eye on.

But now that Cole was in much better physical shape, her role was becoming redundant. She barely stepped inside his room now as he was off most of his meds. When she did go to his room, it was as a friend, and friendship should add to any relationship. It shouldn't take away from it.

Of course, she'd already seen the beneficial results of a relationship in Dani and Aaron, and in Sidney and Brock. Even Cole's relationship with Brock. Sandra knew that had a much bigger impact on Cole than his relationship with her. Maybe it was supposed to be like that. If you stayed secluded and didn't have to deal with all these issues, you also didn't grow as a person. Even though the growing part could be painful, there was so much joy afterward when you looked back at how far you'd come.

Nobody at that meeting had suggested she step away

from the relationship. As she and Cole were only friends, she didn't feel she needed to. But a part of her worried all the same.

It was Friday afternoon, and she had a whole weekend off. She'd head to town tomorrow to do some shopping. She grabbed her tablet and a coffee and walked to the pool area. One of the advantages of her apartment was how close to the pool she lived. She sat in the sunshine, out of the way of the splashes, and brought up the list of things she had to do. When she heard her name, she glanced at the pool to see Cole swimming toward her side. She smiled. "You swim like a seal."

He gave a startled laugh. "I absolutely do." He hefted himself onto the side of the pool and sat there, the water dripping off him. She smiled, appreciating how much his body had grown and changed. He was no longer the same broken man. He wasn't completely fixed, but she could see the progress. She wondered if he could.

"What are you working on?" he asked.

"A shopping list of things I'll get in town tomorrow."

"Oh."

She glanced at him. "We do get weekends off, and this is mine." She shrugged. "We're on split shifts, so when I get a couple days off together, I'm happy to go to town."

He nodded. "Sounds like fun."

"You're welcome to come." She tossed off the invitation casually and then added, "But beware, I have a lot of shops to visit on my list."

He shook his head and said, "Not exactly my deal."

She grinned. "I don't know too many men who like to shop."

"I do if I need something," he said. "I'm not much on

window shopping."

"There are no windows on my list," she joked. "Do you need anything while I'm out?" She studied his face as he contemplated the question. Then he shook his head.

"In a couple weeks, I might enjoy a trip to town," he said. "But too many stops may be hard on me at this point, so I don't want to risk it."

"Still worried about doing too much?"

He shook his head, water droplets flying everywhere. A few of them landed on her legs, making her laugh and shift back a bit. "I'll take that as a no."

He grinned up at her. "Not worried about it. I just don't want to do anything that'll set me back. I know how hard it was to get here." He opened his arms and said, "And I'm a work in progress. I also know how hard it was mentally and emotionally with the initial setback." He shook his head. "I'll do a lot to avoid that."

"Very good thinking on your part," she admitted. "Make sure you're not holding yourself back from further progress out of fear."

He glanced at her. "Is that something you have dealt with before?"

She nodded. "I think we all have. Fear is a killer for so many of us."

"Fear is something I had to deal with throughout my training and when I went on missions," he said. "I can't say it's something I expected to feel during rehab. But it was one of the biggest stumbling blocks in the beginning. I wanted to do so well. I wanted to be a success story and was so afraid that, instead, I would be one of the worst-case scenarios." He flashed a tentative grin at her. "But slowly, step by step, as I see my own improvements, the fear abates, and in its place, I find self-confidence."

"As long as the self-confidence is in check, then everything's moving the way it should be."

He grinned at that. "Isn't that the truth? Overconfidence can be just as devastating as fear."

"It's all about balance," she said. She got up and walked to the edge of the pool, watching the blue water splashing up at the edges. "This pool is a genius idea."

"It is. I feel strong and vibrant in the water. The minute I get out, it's not the same feeling at all."

"I'm not a very good swimmer," she confessed. "I keep meaning to learn, but ..." She let her voice trail off.

"If that's something you would like to do," he said, "while I'm here, I can certainly teach you."

She glanced at him in surprise. "Really?"

He nodded. "I wasn't kidding when I said I was a SEAL. Water and I are best buddies." Then he rolled off the side into the water and did a series of laps, where he propelled his body up onto the surface and then let it flop back in again.

When he broke the surface, she was still smiling. "Okay, now that was very seal-like," she said. "I don't want to do that. Maybe the front crawl and the breaststroke."

"My daily schedule is done. I had my last therapy session, and it's like four o'clock. Go change and come back," he said. "We can do a quick lesson right now. Then you can practice any time after work."

She hesitated.

A teasing grin crept over his face. "Unless you're scared."

After their earlier conversation about fear, she glared at him. "That might have worked in high school, but it won't work on me now."

"Maybe, but it's also on your bucket list," he said.

"Knocking something off your list and learning a life-saving skill at the same time, that's well worth doing."

She studied the cool, refreshing-looking water and realized how much she'd always wanted to beat that demon. But she wasn't sure he was the right teacher.

"I don't know if I'm scared of the water or if I just don't know how to swim well enough," she confessed. "I've tried to swim in the past, but I never did it successfully."

"Go get changed," he ordered. "Then come back, and we'll find out. Come on. Don't make a big thing of this. Get into the water, and we'll sort it out."

She gave him a suspicious glance but then saw he was being sincere, so she nodded and turned and walked to her apartment. Once there, she changed into her bathing suit and grabbed a beach wrap and a towel and then walked back out. He was doing laps along the right-hand side of the pool. She walked to the shallow end and dropped her wrap and towel on a chair, feeling very self-conscious. She quickly slipped into the water.

As soon as she stood in waist-deep water, he appeared in front of her.

"Perfect," he said. "Now let's see how much you do know, and we'll go from there."

An hour of much fun and laughter followed as he taught her to float, something she still struggled with, and then he showed her the simple front crawl technique. She hated putting her face underwater and quickly realized that was one of her biggest hurdles. Then he switched to the breast-stroke. With her head out of the water, she had more confidence she could stay above water and yet still get from one end of the pool to the other. She managed six laps before her arms and legs felt shaky. She shook her head. "I had no idea I was so out of shape."

"It's not that you're out of shape, but you're pulling on muscles you don't normally use—and dealing with fear," he said quietly. "Both of those things stress you out more than anything."

She glanced at him and said, "I guess you know something about that."

He nodded. "More than I would like. Now let's go again. This time, do the front crawl again, and you can keep your head to the side so you can still see, but you will be getting one step closer to proper form."

The problem with that was she kept thinking. However, after she had made it to the other end of the pool and back again, she was improving slowly. When they finished that set, she pulled herself up to sit on the side of the pool.

"Now," he said, "you should practice every day if you can. If not, at least every second day for a few days. Then I'll come back, and we'll work on fine-tuning your technique. Once you get those down, it's all about practice and endurance. The more you do, the easier it becomes."

Feeling delighted with her progress, she dropped back into the water, threw her arms around his neck, and kissed him on the cheek. He hugged her close.

"I'm happy to give back," he said quietly. "Everybody here has treated me incredibly well."

She pulled away slightly and smiled. "It's easy to treat you well. You're a very special guy."

HE WOULD HAVE been happy to be more than just company for her—he wanted to be close to her. To build that bond and strengthen that little something they had into something so much more meaningful.

But if she thought he was a special guy, well, he wouldn't argue with her. If he could get another kiss as well, he wouldn't argue with that either. But neither would he put her in the same position Sidney had been in. No make-out sessions in the pool. He swam back slightly and whispered, "Last thing I want to do is get you into trouble, like Sidney."

Sandra wrinkled up her face and floated backward. "Good point." She shook her head. Then nodded to the side.

He turned and caught sight of Kenneth, another patient, and wondered how much he had seen, overheard.

She continued. "It's a sad world when somebody can't give a kiss of gratitude without certain people taking it the wrong way." She dove underwater.

He frowned. A kiss of gratitude? That was so not what he wanted. When she broke the surface again, he glanced around to make sure nobody was listening and said, "If this was a different place and time, I would show you a real kiss."

She threw him a startled look, and as if realizing what he meant, rich color rolled up her face. She dove underwater again.

Cole didn't blame her. He felt a bit antsy himself now. He probably shouldn't have said what he did. It was like stating his intentions. Putting the cart before the horse once again, pushing instead of pulling back. He sank underwater, pissed at himself for having taken such a step. He didn't want to scare her off.

He didn't want to make her nervous around him. He had meant his comment to be gentle, teasing and seductive. Instead, it had come off hard and critical and a little bit angry. Mind you, that was partly because of her comment about gratitude. He swam to the side and pulled himself up where he could sit on the edge of the pool. He glanced around, wondering how far he would have to go to get to his crutches.

Only somebody had moved them. Instantly, fear struck him inside. He didn't have his wheelchair here, his backup, for when he was tired. But without a wheelchair or his crutches, getting anywhere would be a lot harder. Sure, he could manage a few hops but only a few. He stared at his missing lower leg. He hadn't brought any of the prosthetics with him either. He was scheduled to get refitted for one Monday afternoon. Provided the stump was stable, free of infection and strong enough. He'd had a ton of trouble with that.

He glanced around, but he couldn't see anybody else nearby. His crutches now leaned against the changing room wall. Why the hell would somebody do that? Normally he was easygoing and laid-back about his property. He would lend stuff out and not be bothered if people were a little late returning things. But he had to admit he had struggled lately over having his own possessions in a specific spot. Moving his crutches though, well, that was just mean. He swiveled around and used the handles on the ladder to pull himself upright.

Of course water was everywhere—a hazard for those with two legs as well—which was one of the reasons the crutches had solid rubber bottoms. He could hop on one foot, but his crutches were probably twenty feet away. He couldn't afford to fall—that would be a failure. Yet, he also wanted to do this on his own, for even asking for help would be a draw in his mind, not an outright win. He wanted a success here.

With that thought uppermost, even knowing he would look ridiculous, he bent so his hands touched the ground and did a half-leapfrog action to his crutches. Not the debonair masculine can-do look he was going for.

With the crutches back in his hands, he headed to the changing room. The last thing he wanted to see was the look on her face. For sure, he wouldn't have minded getting his hands on the asshole who had moved his crutches. Once inside, he sat on one of the big wooden benches. He leaned back and closed his eyes. Every time he thought he was moving ahead, he hit something that sent him reeling backward. Nothing quite like the reality of not being able to walk from the pool to the changing room without looking like an idiot to bring a guy down a peg or two.

She would be so much better off with someone else. Someone whole. Someone who wouldn't embarrass her with the basic functions of life.

*Chapter 11*

S ANDRA BROKE THROUGH the water, happy to see
Kenneth nowhere in sight and in time to see Cole
making his way to his crutches in a rather unique manner.
Why were they so far away? She knew some guys laid them
literally alongside the edge of the pool, wanting the security
of their tools near at hand. Still others deliberately placed
things farther away to make it more difficult for themselves,
pushing their own limits. She didn't think Cole would've
done that, but she still didn't know him that well. She knew
from their weekly team meetings Cole had yet to open up
with his psychiatrist or with his therapist either. And it was
their job to get him to talk about his issues, so she shouldn't
feel shunned.

But she did.

When he didn't say goodbye to her or even wave at her
in the pool but headed straight into the changing room, she
wondered if he was upset with her.

She had kissed him impulsively. She was happy with her
own progress with swimming and pleased he'd taken the
time to teach her some basics. Instead, he'd seemed discom-
fited and afraid they might be seen. That she might get in
trouble. And what about his comment afterward? Did he
truly want to show her a real kiss, or was he teasing her
again?

Out of sorts herself, she climbed from the pool and grabbed her cover-up and towel and headed to her own apartment. No point in asking Cole if he needed a hand. At this moment, chances were he'd just snap at her.

One thing she had learned a long time ago—pride was a highly motivating factor for a lot of men. She'd do nothing to take that away from them. Especially Cole. He'd had several setbacks already. She refused to make that worse.

Showered and changed, she walked upstairs to the dining hall, thinking about grabbing a late dinner before the buffet closed for the night, and then maybe spending some time outside. A few of the staff rode a couple horses here, and she hadn't gone for a ride in a long time. She wondered who might want to ride with her. It was not just about the safety of not going alone. Although she was a good rider, it was much nicer to go with someone.

The dining room was mostly empty, and the food was running out, but she still had some selection. She smiled to see the hot pasta and vegetables. She loved the food here. Because they offered such a wide variety, she could pick and eat as healthily as she wanted to. She grabbed a large salad and asked Dennis to chop up a chicken breast with some shaved Parmesan cheese. She chose a table outside in the sun and enjoyed her chicken Caesar salad.

Returning her dishes to the appropriate rack, she picked up a granola bar and an apple on her way out. Dani was probably still in her office. Sandra headed down the hallway, making a short detour to pass by Cole's room. The door was shut, and she wasn't exactly sure what that meant. She'd been in there many times, and she couldn't ever remember seeing the door closed. However, if he was having a private conversation with a doctor or someone, it made sense.

At Dani's office, Sandra was happy to see her friend still at her desk. Dani was buried in work, not ready to shut down for the day. "Hey, Dani." Sandra gave a sharp rap on the doorframe and walked inside. She shook her head at the stack of files on Dani's desk. "Maybe it's time you got an assistant."

Dani tossed down her pen and chuckled. "If I take on an assistant, it's one less therapist or one less nurse or person for the kitchen or for housekeeping." She smiled. "The budget only goes so far."

"I get that. How do you feel about going for a horseback ride?" she asked. "The walls are closing in on me today."

Dani's eyebrows rose in surprise. She glanced around at the paperwork, then checked her schedule on her computer. "You know what? Hell, yes. I've got no more meetings today, so give me a second to shut down my system and to put away a few files."

Happy to have company for her ride, Sandra sat in Dani's visitor's chair and waited. When Dani was done, the two women headed out.

"I've already eaten. Do you need anything first?" Sandra asked.

Dani shook her head. "I had a late lunch. And now a horseback ride sounds like the perfect medicine." She led the way to the stables attached to the veterinary clinic, and before long, she had Midnight saddled. She glanced over at Sandra. "Who do you want to ride?"

"I'll take Rose." The dapple was a favorite of hers. She was always easy to catch, making it a short job to get a saddle on and get out. Dani rode Western, whereas Sandra rode English. Neither horse seemed to mind whichever they did. Midnight was Dani's, however, and she was the only one who rode him.

Within minutes, the two women were in the pasture and loping along the acres of long grass, heading for the open fields in the distance. They made for the gate and soon were outside the main grounds, in the freedom of the world beyond Hathaway House.

Sandra lifted her face to the sun. "I so needed this today."

"Tough day?" Dani asked sympathetically.

"Not really. I've had much worse days."

"Is it Cole?"

Startled, Sandra looked over at her friend. "Cole?"

Dani shot her friend a knowing look. "I've seen the building attraction. The smiles, the touches, the extra glances. You care. He cares. It's lovely to see."

Sandra let her breath out in a heavy exhalation. "Is it? Sometimes I think we might get somewhere, and then it's like right back to square one."

"I think that's standard for all the men here." Dani smiled. "I wasn't sure about Aaron for a long time."

"But you are now?"

Dani grinned. "Definitely. We don't select an easy path when we choose one of the men from Hathaway House. They come here for a reason, and we aren't it."

"True enough." Sandra thought about that. "They also come with a lot more emotional baggage. It's not as if we've picked somebody up off the street or that we met at a friend's."

"I don't agree with that," Dani said. "I think that, in those cases, the emotional baggage is hidden. With the men here, it's easier to see what their baggage is. At least the initial layer of it. Sometimes they have deeper issues, where you have to ferret out what's wrong and why. It can be anything from survivor's guilt to feeling like they caused or brought on the accident themselves. Many of them suffer from PTSD." She shrugged.

"The thing with the men here is," Dani continued, "with so much going on, sometimes it's hard to figure out the core problems. Our military patients have extra problems, over and above what a lot of civilians have, but we deal with them. It gets brought up in the discussions in group therapy, and they work through them. Often they find that once they start working through one problem, other problems pop up because so much of it's connected. Before I started working here, I had never thought about that link. I finally learned that, even with my own problems, they could translate into dealing with other issues."

Sandra nodded. "It makes a lot of sense. I guess that's one of the extra benefits here. Once people are in therapy, it's hard to confine healing to a specific area."

"I think it's actually impossible," Dani said. "Yet, when you meet all these other apparently healthy normal males in the rest of the world, so few are dealing with their issues. They've shoved them all inside, and they think they're fine."

"Even if they're not."

Sandra thought back to some of the other relationships she knew about, such as Dani's last one before Aaron, where her ex had beaten the crap out of her. Sandra had never faced anything like that. Her last relationship had broken down because her boyfriend spent all his free time on video games. What was the point of a relationship if he didn't spend time with her? But he wasn't even interested in addressing that question. When they'd broken things off, she'd been relieved. "And yet Cole is something else." Sandra flushed when she realized she'd spoken aloud.

"You care about him, don't you?" Dani asked.

"I do. I just don't know how much." She gave her friend a small smile. "He dominates my thoughts from morning until night though."

"That's a lovely start."

COLE WATCHED FROM the deck as the two women rode off in the distance. Both were so natural and comfortable on the horses that they were a joy to watch. Both were whole, healthy and happy. His hands fisted as he stared at them. They were the opposite of what he was.

He was damaged and conflicted, and although he'd been improving mood-wise every day, right now he felt like he was back at the beginning. He should walk away from being friends with Sandra. *No*, from attempting to be more than friends.

He really liked her. But she deserved better than him.

Someone bumped into him, hard. Cole was still getting used to his prosthetic limb but remained standing, then glared at the guy—no crutches, no wheelchair, all his limbs intact.

"Dani's taken, and Sandra's mine. Stop staring at my girl."

Before Cole had decided how to best handle this situation—without getting kicked out of Hathaway House—Shane strode over, and the asshole left.

"You okay?" Shane asked, his phone to his ear.

Cole just nodded, watching the lunatic scurry off. From Shane's end of the conversation, Cole heard this guy was infatuated with Sandra. Why hadn't she told him? Cole would have handled this creep for her.

"Sounds perfect. I'll corral him while we wait for the police to arrive. Be good to have him gone."

*So the guy was a problem*, Cole thought. At least Hathaway House had procedures in place for this sort of thing. *At least they were taking care of it now. Should lighten up things for Sandra and the others.*

"Sorry, Cole. He'll be gone soon and won't bother you or anyone else anymore."

Cole knew Sandra and the other medical personnel here couldn't share patient information with another patient, but Cole got the gist of it. And that guy had looked normal. *Whole*. When he wasn't pushing Cole around or spouting lies.

But looks could be deceiving. And just because some guy hadn't lost a body part didn't mean he was healthy. *Hmm*.

Cole glanced around the dining area. The same and other related thoughts were probably running through the minds of every man and woman who were patients here. How did they reconcile their current selves to *who* they used to be, and how did they make peace with that, when they had wives and husbands and children?

Did they think they should walk away? Or did they feel loved enough, safe and secure enough in the relationship to stay and work through the multiple future obstacles in order to come to peace with their physical disabilities?

In theory, absolutely nothing should keep him and Sandra apart. They were both adults. Relationships were allowed here. Even relationships between patients and staff as evidenced by several of the relationships he'd already seen. Was *he* keeping them apart?

Not to mention, he didn't know if she was truly interested. Not after her "gratitude" kiss. Self-doubt crippled him. She was special to him, but here in this place, he was one of many to her. He wanted to be strong, to be the best, and to show her that he was still who he'd been before he got injured. Not that she knew that version of him. Yet, he'd been proud of that Cole. This Cole was beset by doubts and insecurities. His self-confidence was at an all-time low.

How could she love that? Surely she wanted a man to walk beside her, not someone she had to bolster all the time. Every time he tried to stand up and prove he was different, he was unique, he was better, something happened, and he took a step back.

Then he thought about Sandra's stalker patient with all his disabilities hidden inside. Cole looked down the hallway where the guy had disappeared. Cole's subconscious now lectured him: *Just be yourself. Stop worrying about it. If it's meant to be, it will be. Enjoy who she is. Don't look for more. Focus on your healing, not on a relationship. You're here for one reason—make that reason count. You'll never get another chance at it.*

All of that was true. At the same time, he had found something he wanted more than that.

He could thank the crazy guy for this revelation.

Cole didn't want one or the other, he wanted both. He wanted to be healed, strong, fit and ready to take on the world again—even if from a damaged physical perspective—and he wanted her at his side. *That was asking for a lot.*

Still, he argued with himself. *Why not? Why not reach for what I really want?*

That settled, his brain focused on more practical matters. How would he take care of himself and someone else in the future? He had no job, no decent prospects of a good job, no house. He had his bank account from his years in the military and a pension—it was small, but at least it was something.

How the hell was he to train for a new career? During the military, the team had teased Brock for all his computer geekiness. But now, with Cole's lack of education and lack of training for the real world, he had to wonder if maybe Brock hadn't had the better deal after all.

Still, there was lots Cole *could* do. But what did he *want* to do? He could go for some retraining, but no way would he attend a university for four years. That was not on the agenda. He wasn't sure he could handle a lesser degree or the two years required to get an apprenticeship or some other kind of heavy-duty training.

The money being what it was, along with the time and effort required, he didn't think he was up for extensive long-term training. So, what *could* he do with a minimum of training, and even better, if that training was online? As usual, nothing came to mind. He pounded the top of the railing with his fist, and then slowly turned and made his way back to his room.

So much was unknown in his "new" world that it frustrated him. He needed answers. He needed a direction. He sat on his bed, opened his laptop and started searching.

When it came to career options, he found more than he'd expected. And immediately felt guilty for not listening more to his therapist and getting to this point weeks ago. What was he good at? Before his accident, he was said to be good with people. He'd been charismatic, and even now he would love a career that would keep him away from the 9-to-5 desk-job routine. Sure, some office time was fine, but he'd like to be outside and moving as much as possible.

Landscaping came back to mind. Could he make a go of something like that? He'd always been good with his hands, building and growing things. But there was hardly decent money in that for a one-man operation. But at least in Texas, it wasn't a seasonal occupation, like in many other parts of the world. Winter was a cooler season here, not for planting … but it would keep him outside and physically active. It was also a job that dealt with people. He was very good with money, and of course, he had to be very good if he planned to go out on his own. He wasn't so much a salesman, but he did know that people liked to get a good deal.

Real estate crossed his mind. He could become an agent. The only thing was, the market was volatile. Lots of time was involved, encouraging each potential buyer into signing a purchase contract, and it was not a stable income.

He could drive a truck—he had certainly driven a lot of them before. But did he want to do that long-term? Or make a clean break from his past and find something new?

He closed the laptop, got up and left his room. He went down the far hallway to give himself a little more exercise. His leg felt punchy today and in need of a little extra push. Like everything, he needed balance. Something he'd do well to remember moving forward.

As he walked past the row of staff offices, his prosthetic limb gave him some trouble. He leaned against the wall to adjust it slightly.

Then heard Sandra's name.

"Has she had a follow-up meeting about Cole not taking his medications that time?" a woman asked from the room he had just passed.

He froze.

"I think so. It's not her fault. Here people don't hide what they are doing. All the medical personnel stress the importance of honesty and truth from day one with each patient. So does Dani at intake time. It's in all the brochures too."

"Well, she should have looked," the woman said, her tone exasperated. "She's the one who gives out the medicine. None of us are here all the time, so we must rely on good and accurate and complete records. As far as we know, all medications have been taken. How are we to know any different? How are we to accurately assess our patients without this data?"

"How many times do you think, since Hathaway House first opened some seven years ago, somebody has tried to trick us like Cole did?"

"No idea—but even once is too many."

"Don't be so hard on her. If she'd never run into anybody like Cole, she wouldn't be expecting that."

"Yes, but it is still her mandate, not only to give out the medicine but also to make sure they take it. Anybody can hand out tablets. It's her responsibility to administer the medicine, not just dump it out somewhere and walk out."

"Don't you think she was punished enough?"

"Was she punished?" The woman's voice lightened slightly. "If she was, well, that's good. I don't mean a major punishment. I don't think she should lose her job over it, but a reprimand is certainly in order. Not to mention a follow-up to make sure she won't do that again."

Cole's legs suddenly felt very rubbery. He had asked her in passing, way back when, if she'd gotten into trouble over him not taking his medications. Of course, when he was originally here, it had never occurred to him to consult someone. He had figured he was an adult and he had the right to take his medicine, or not, as he deemed fit.

But now, he understood that the medical world did not view it the same way. What he should have done was had a discussion with his doctor about his meds, asking which ones he could stop taking and how to wean off them. That way everybody would have been on the same page. Obviously he must have known that what he was doing was wrong because he didn't do it openly. He didn't contact the doctor. He didn't mention it to Sandra. In fact, he'd hidden it from her.

And that made him feel even worse.

The conversation behind him turned to a different topic, and he slowly moved forward. Now he was damned sorry he'd taken this hallway. All he wanted to do was go back to his room and shut the door. How would he face Sandra again, knowing she still faced reprimands from his actions? She wasn't the one who had done something stupid. That had been him. He was 100 percent responsible. No way could he let her take the fall for that.

He grabbed his phone and found his doctor under Contacts. As luck would have it, his doctor answered and said he had about fifteen minutes between patients and would come to Cole's room.

Dr. Herzog was very patient and listened to Cole explain how wrong he was to stop his meds without telling anyone and how it wasn't Sandra's fault and that he didn't want her getting into trouble. The doctor smiled at Cole. "I agree with you. However, she was reprimanded, and notice of such is in her permanent personnel file." When Cole grimaced, Dr. Herzog added, "However, in my letter I count Sandra as one of my best nurses."

When Cole launched into more arguments about how

unfair this was to punish Sandra for Cole's mistakes, Dr. Herzog raised his hand. "The people who matter know Sandra's heart. Even though she has one strike in her file, she's already redeemed herself with her updated protocols. Just like you, Cole, have one strike in your file and have already redeemed yourself with your updated actions and mind-set."

When Dr. Herzog checked his watch and said he had to leave, Cole felt drained. And frustrated.

He would try again. He picked up his phone and called Dani.

## *Chapter 12*

SEVERAL DAYS LATER Sandra realized something really was wrong between her and Cole, and she wasn't just imagining it. She stood in his doorway and studied him. He had deliberately looked out the window as if to avoid her. She'd let him get away with it earlier but not a second time.

"Cole, may I come in?"

He turned, gave her a fake laugh. "Oh, I didn't see you standing there."

She leaned against the doorjamb, waiting for his permission to enter, and asked quietly, "What's wrong?"

He shook his head. "Nothing. Just tired. That's all."

Only he'd said that yesterday too. At first she'd believed him. But not now. Taking a chance, she strode in. "I don't believe you."

He opened his mouth to say something, but she quickly interrupted.

"Yesterday you said the same thing. Now you're ignoring me. Have I done something to upset you?"

His startled gaze focused on her. "No. Not at all."

"Then what? Why?" She motioned to the doorway. "I thought we were getting somewhere as friends." She swallowed painfully. She'd rather be upfront and honest. "I thought we were better than just friends."

His gaze softened. "It's me, not you."

She gave a sarcastic laugh and turned toward the doorway. "Right. Normally that's the woman's line." She walked out into the hall. She could feel herself shaking with hurt even while she tried to understand his attitude. Something was obviously bothering him, but what was it? And what did it have to do with her?

To bury the pain, she buried herself in her job, focusing on every detail, keeping thoughts of him, of them, at bay. There was no *them*, not really. He was just a patient, someone she'd once been friends with.

And that sucked.

COLE WATCHED SANDRA walk out, feeling like an idiot. His heart was full of regret, and he didn't know how to get back on track. He'd come here to pull himself together, but right now, he'd hit yet another major obstacle in the road. Instead of moving forward as a cohesive unit, emotionally and physically, he was breaking apart, becoming less than what he had been. He hadn't meant to hurt her feelings. He'd never do that. He really cared about her. The hurt in his heart right now made him realize he wanted more than he'd first assumed. For that reason alone, he needed to be the best he could be. She deserved nothing less.

There was a hard knock on his door. He found Brock standing in the doorway, his arms crossed over his chest, a frown on his face—not a welcoming look.

"Trouble?" Brock asked.

Maybe it was the timing, maybe it was Cole's lack of defenses. Maybe it was the new understanding about where he was right now, but he nodded. Normally he wouldn't speak about his personal problems. But over these last six months since the IED explosion, a lot had happened to change that. He could no longer be an island. He had the support of his medical team here. He would love to have Sandra's support plus he needed his friend's continued support.

"Just a really ugly realization." He leaned back on his bed and gave Brock a weak smile, who now looked the epitome of vibrant life and health. "Didn't I always compete with you? Always try to do better than you?" he asked his friend.

Brock chuckled and walked inside. He grabbed a chair, which he pivoted and sat on backward to stare at his buddy. "Not only did you always view me as competition but you always had to be of equal value." He shook his head. "No matter how I tried to convince you that you would find greatness just as you were, you didn't see that."

Cole shifted his gaze to the window. "Sometimes you have to wonder what makes a man who he is."

"Don't wonder. Accept who you are and work on changing what needs improvement. Not only did you always try to compete and to do better and to be the best," Brock said with a grin, "but you also used to hold me up as some sort of a role model. I was never that. I was never above you. I was never better than you or smarter or faster. Yet, you seemed to think that, and you always worked harder and harder to beat me."

Cole smiled. "Those were the days, weren't they?"

"They were. But you know something? I'm happy with these days too," Brock said. "I sleep in my own bed, and I have a whole new future. I have a beautiful relationship. I'm not fanatical about fitness, but I care enough to work out and to stay in shape. No, I'm not doing the same work, but I'll find something else." He shrugged. "The pressure is off right now. I hadn't realized how wearying it was being in the navy, doing what we did. We were always primed to be the best, to be in the best shape and to be ready to take on the world. Now I get to relax. I don't think I ever did that before. It never seemed like I wanted to. But I do now. Life operates at a new pace, and I like it."

"It's not the life we used to live," Cole said. "I feel different inside. When I first arrived at Hathaway, I still had that same strong drive to do bigger and better things. But there was a panic behind it. Almost a frantic need to prove I could do this." He nodded sheepishly. "And yes, I still had that sense of having to do at least as well as you did."

He motioned toward Brock, adding, "But it's also obvious this is one challenge I have to tackle differently. I don't need to be better than you," Cole said, "but I sure as hell don't want to be any less physically. I don't want poor results. I know this part is completely under my control, and yet in another way, I have no control. I can't get around the physical disabilities. Also, I was careless and hurt someone and caused trouble on my first arrival," he admitted. "I never once thought about anybody else. I never considered I would get somebody else in trouble." He shook his head. "I don't know how to fix this."

Brock raised an eyebrow. "Tell me what's going on."

Cole winced. "It's not very pretty."

"Nothing about any of what we're going through is pretty. From soiling the bed because we had no control when we woke up from surgery, to having catheters stuck up our dicks, to having nurses who wash us until we are capable of handling our own physical needs," Brock said in a harsh voice. "I've been there too, buddy. But you and I are both past that. There shouldn't be any embarrassment for either of us anymore. We know each other as well as we know anybody, so give. What the hell's going on in that head of yours?"

"It's stupid."

"It's all stupid. That also means it can and should be sorted out. Do you think I was any different when I came here, completely riddled with guilt that I wasn't blown up on the job? That I was injured in a car accident at home? Look at all the tours I did in Iraq and Afghanistan. How many opportunities I had to get some horrific physical injury. But no, I came back and got messed up driving from point A to B. I took it out on everyone," he admitted. "So don't tell me about stupid. I was stupid. Now let's hear your stupidity and see if we can get rid of it, and then hopefully you can heal that much more."

"I want to get better," Cole admitted ruefully.

Brock grinned. "Have you noticed something? It's like there are these little bars. We climb up to a certain point, and then something comes that we must deal with, and the bar falls a bit, and then we climb a little bit higher. The higher I went, the more I saw how much my personality and internal issues had to do with it. I felt like I was less than a man and not capable of being what Sidney needed," he said, shaking his head. "Wow, that was a big one."

Cole stared at him with rising hope. "I've been wondering about that myself."

"Sandra?"

Cole nodded. "We've been dancing around a lot of issues," he said, "but I hurt her, and this morning I brushed her away because I didn't know how to deal with what was in my head."

"From the beginning of your rehab, forget about every-thing else. Deal with one issue at a time," Brock said. He crossed his arms on the back of the chair. "We used to do this in the military. Hash out ideas, hash out our problems, hash out the little things so they didn't become bigger issues. Do it now."

Cole took a deep breath. "A few days ago I went for a short walk, feeling antsy. As I was coming back to my room, I went the long way around, past the offices. I was having some trouble with my prosthesis, so I stopped and leaned against a wall to fix it and overheard part of a conversation."

Brock nudged him along. "About you?"

"Indirectly, yes. But directly about Sandra."

Brock settled back. "Okay."

Cole continued. "About her making a mistake in her job or not having done her job properly or however it was worded. I don't remember because once I understood what it was all about, I felt really, really bad." He motioned with his hand around the room and added, "I did mention it to her at one point, weeks and weeks ago, but she brushed it off."

"She brushed what off? What did you do?"

"Remember when I first arrived, and I had that setback?"

Brock nodded. "Yes."

"Of course that setback was my fault because I was doing too much, too fast, right?"

Brock shrugged. "If you say so. I don't know the details. I know I didn't get a chance to see you. You were here and not doing so well, and then you were gone."

Cole winced. "I was so sure I knew what I needed. So sure I could handle everything that came at me. So sure that if you could do it I could do it," he muttered. "So sure that I stopped taking all the medications Sandra brought me."

"Without talking to anybody about it?" Brock leaned forward and stared at his buddy. "Without discussing this with your doctor or Sandra?"

Cole shook his head. "Exactly," he said. "Obviously it was wrong."

Brock settled back. "Wow."

"Exactly, *wow.*" Filled with a sense of relief now that he'd gotten the worst of it out, he tried to explain further. "I don't understand what was going on in my head, but I thought it was a good idea. I was on a medication cocktail at the time. I hadn't had any improvement for a long time, from my perspective, and the pills didn't seem to be doing whatever it was they were supposed to. I knew I was still on some antibiotics and a few other things." He winced. "Now, of course, after the setback, and after the warnings the doctors gave me, I know I shouldn't stop taking prescription medicine suddenly."

"You had a lot of internal injuries too. When you got here, they were a little afraid it was too early for you to be in rehab as it was."

Cole nodded. "Plus, I had trouble with blood coagulation." He smiled, embarrassed. "Let's just say it was not my brightest move. The fact that I did it for three days in a row and then collapsed and had to be rushed to the hospital, well, that was the height of stupidity."

Brock nodded. "All because you figured you knew better."

"I know." Cole lifted his hands in a bewildered gesture and then let them drop in his lap. "I figured I was here now for recovery, and I didn't want anything left over from the previous hospital, including the meds, and that I could do this alone. I thought, *I can be strong. I can be fit. I can be better than everyone.*"

"Instead, you did something that worked against you and your plans."

Cole gave a bark of laughter. "Yeah, when you look at it that way, it doesn't sound so smart, does it?"

"Buddy, I hate drugs of any kind. You know that. But when I'm here, and I'm recovering from a multitude of various surgeries, and they tell me I need to take something, I take it. I mean, if I was working with bombs and you told me to put this wire on this detonator and to hold my thumb there and not to take it off, you sure as hell know I'll do that until you tell me it's safe to take my finger off."

"I know. Believe me. I know. I had lots of time in the hospital to figure that out," Cole said. "It was quite an awakening to see how much of a brain fog I had been in about what my condition was and what my future looked like." He shook his head. "I look back now, and I want to slap myself for being so stupid."

"So, what's this got to do with Sandra?"

The corners of Cole's lips turned down. "She's the one who hands out the medications every day."

Brock looked at him for a long moment and then slowly nodded. "So, she's probably been given a reprimand for not having noticed or not having stayed behind to make sure she saw you take your medications."

Cole nodded. "Something like that. I did mention it to her, and I did apologize way back when, and she seemed to brush it off. However, in the hallway, I heard them talking about how she's doing her job since that event."

"And about you?"

"About me and other patients. I got the impression it

was whether she had changed up her procedure enough since the warning to get her off the hook."

Brock winced. "Sandra's been here a long time."

"All I had to do was talk to the doctor to find out how many of them were necessary, and why I was taking them, and which ones I needed to take, and which I could try to get off," Cole said. "But to go off drugs like that—it's not safe to go cold turkey."

Brock sighed.

"Yeah stupid I know, I've figured that out now."

"You always were a bit of a hard-headed 'jump first and think later' guy. But right now, I presume you're feeling crappy about what you did, and added to that, you might have gotten Sandra into trouble. Even if it's a done deal for you, it might not be over for her."

Cole slowly nodded. "It's not. Even though I spoke to Dr. Herzog to straighten it all out, I was too late. When I came back here the second time, all I wanted to do was to forget about that horrible start. Everybody joked about my restart, and yet it doesn't appear that Sandra got her reboot. I never meant to get her in trouble, Brock. You've gotta believe me. I would never do that. She's great at her job. She loves being here. She served all these people so well, and yet here I come along, and in three days, I completely mess up her life."

"But it doesn't seem like she's holding it against you. She's been more than friends with you for the last month. She's been your confidant and something a whole lot closer from the looks of it, and at the same time this has been going on in the background in her world."

"And she didn't share it with me."

"That's another part that's gotten to you, isn't it? She

knows more about you than you do about her, including that she was in trouble over this."

Cole lay against the headboard and nodded. "Exactly."

Brock crossed his arms over his chest. "On that aspect, you're not thinking clearly. She's in a position where she's the guardian of your health. She's the watchdog. She's got to make sure what she sees and registers as your results on a day-to-day basis is factual and truthful, so she does the absolute best she can to minimize any negative impacts on your health. For that reason alone, she wouldn't tell you, knowing guilt will have a detrimental effect on you and your healing."

Cole stared at him. "You see? I know that ... but my heart doesn't like it."

"Got it. It doesn't change the fact, however, that if I were in her position, I wouldn't have said anything to you either, bro," Brock said.

Cole stared at his buddy for a long moment, then slowly nodded. "I guess I see your point. If our situations were reversed, and I thought she would be injured by the information and it would slow her healing, I wouldn't tell her either."

"Do you understand how much of a chance she's taking, being friends with you and dealing with all of this? She hasn't had an easy time of it, and now you've made it harder on her. Maybe that's something you should take a closer look at. Because she's here and available doesn't mean you can hurt her willingly either."

"Not willingly," Cole protested.

"Unknowingly or not, your actions have a domino effect on others. Not just her either."

"Do you think she did wrong?" Cole hated that he had

to ask. He really hated that. He wanted to defend her to the ends of the earth, but he didn't know what he was supposed to do.

"No, I don't. She gave you the medicine, and you're an adult. You were cognizant and in your right mind. You were under no force, no duress. She shouldn't be in trouble." Brock shook his head. "However, you hid what you were doing, so she couldn't document anything. You didn't talk to her, so she couldn't report it either. The worst of it is that she wasn't as observant as she should've been."

Cole stared at the doorway. "She put it on the table and left."

"That's all she should have to do. Because, if you don't want to take it, that's up to you. Step up and take the responsibility for your healing, or your non-healing, and be responsible for your actions," Brock said quietly. "She's paying for the repercussions of your actions. She also must stand up and take the repercussions for her own actions. If it was not in her mandate to stay and watch as every patient swallows their pills, then she won't be in trouble."

"And yet, she does that now."

Brock looked at him and nodded. "Of course she does. As you came close to dying, she's not sure how your mental stability was back then, and as for the medications, well, you never talked about it with her. So, it's her responsibility now to make sure it doesn't happen again. She has changed her system, and because of that, she has taken on more responsibility to make sure patients are taking their medications."

Inside, Cole could feel his whole sense of complacency at being at Hathaway sinking. He leaned back and stared out the window. "Maybe it would have been better if I hadn't come at all."

"I have been there too," said Brock. "When we are in-jured and hurting, and we have that support network around us, it's easy to believe the world revolves around us," he said. "We are unaware of what our actions lead to and what it is that we set in motion, as well as how we feel about it." He shook his head. "That will work to a point. Then we switch from 'me' to 'we,' as the team helps us move through this process. But the medical staff are real people, just like us. They have weaknesses and strengths, just as we do."

"And is there another stage? Where it's back to 'me' again without the 'we'?"

At that, Brock bounced to his feet. "Absolutely. That's where I'm at. So just keep working through the process, and remember these people are here to help you, one way or another."

"What about my heart? What about when our heart is feeling a whole lot more than it should?"

"I don't know that there is such a thing as too much heart. Part of that 'me to we and back' transition is all about accepting help. About accepting friendships and taking the ones that matter the most and moving forward. It's not wrong to care. It's never wrong to care." He walked to the doorway. "I'm going to sit outside. Want to come with me?"

Cole stared at Brock for a long moment. "You know? I think I'll go to the pool. I love being in it, and I have stuff inside to be worked out."

Brock smiled. "Talk to you later then, my friend."

## *Chapter 13*

S ANDRA SAT AT her desk to attack some paperwork finally. Kenneth had left—an added bonus for her. Plus she'd spent so much time with Cole lately she had more recordkeeping backed up than she liked. She hadn't shirked her job, but she could have done more, and if she hadn't had other interests, she'd have done this already. Now was a good time to get caught up.

At least it gave her something to focus on, other than the hurt inside.

Shane sat on the chair beside her. "Tell me what's going on."

She looked up in surprise and caught sight of the clock behind his head. She'd been here for two hours already. She turned her attention back to Shane. "Nothing's going on. Why would you think that?" She tried hard to keep her voice calm and stable, but there was an ever-so-slight tremor. When understanding came into his eyes, she groaned and sat back, flinging down her pen. "Okay, so something is wrong but nothing major, and I'll get over it."

"Something to do with your meeting later this afternoon or did something happen with Cole?"

She frowned. "I've been trying to forget about this afternoon's meeting." And she had for the most part. It was a follow-up to the initial problem Sandra had had with Cole.

"Well, that answers that. It's Cole."

She shook her head. "Not so much about Cole as understanding that the men here are complicated."

Shane grinned. "I'm not all that simple myself."

She rolled her eyes. "You know what I mean."

He nodded. "Yes, I do. The patients all come here with an awful lot of issues. That also makes the price that much sweeter when you get there, reaching the goal."

She laughed wryly. "Well, that would be nice today as he said a few hurtful things this morning. I let him get to me."

"So maybe look at why he's pushing you away. What it is he thinks he's done, or in what way does he think he's failed? It's either that or he has decided you're better off without him."

She sat back in surprise. "Surely not all relationships can be reduced to those options."

He shook his head. "Of course not. That doesn't stop it from being true most of the time. In many cases, it is exactly something like that. Especially here. These men were prime specimens—big egos, big bodies, fit, capable and powerful—until an injury sidelined them. Some come with an attitude they can take on anything, and they do. It's wonderful to see them storm right through their healing and recovery process." He smiled. "Others charge ahead and fall back because they took too many big steps at once."

"Cole." Hence her upcoming meeting this afternoon. She shook her head. "But he won't do that again. He's not the same guy anymore."

"Good, glad to hear that. Do you think Cole got wind of your reprimand about his actions?"

"No. That's strictly a doctor-nurse thing. It's part of my job, and I screwed up."

"What if somebody mentioned it to him? What if somebody told him, either laughingly or jokingly, that because of him, you got into trouble?" He leaned forward. "Do you think that would make him feel good or bad?"

"With Cole, that would make him feel terrible. He's already thinking he's not enough. That if he hadn't driven over an IED, he wouldn't be here."

"That's a running theme with a lot of the men here. They were either taken out during a mission and feel guilty or injured during some stupid thing stateside and feel equally guilty because it wasn't on a mission."

"Of course that's Brock." She sighed. "I'm not even upset at Cole about his initial screw-up. It's just that when you open yourself up to a person, it hurts to get slapped back down again."

"And yet, you're coming from reasonably healthy relationships in your past. For you, opening up isn't such a big deal. That's your nature. Neither is that big slap in the long run as you evolve. Ignore your hurt for a moment. Look at the bigger picture and figure out why he's doing this. Then get him to explain it to you. Because that shows you trust him. He must slowly rebuild who he is, what he is and what he wants. He'll make mistakes along the way. As you build a relationship with him, you can make mistakes along the way too."

She gave Shane a warm smile. "How did you become so smart?"

COLE FELT A lot better after talking with Brock. He also knew he owed Sandra an apology. She had appeared so upbeat about the whole thing, but then again, he'd been so mired in his own thoughts and feelings he hadn't taken any time to see where she was coming from. He lay on his bed and stared out the window. One of the good things about being here was his sleep had improved. He realized just how much so when he looked back on the long journey he'd taken since the accident. In the beginning, he had regularly woken up in a cold sweat after recurring nightmares, but now things had calmed down.

He had turned that around and had made many positive steps forward. He was slowly moving away from the nightmares. People had warned him about PTSD and said the effects could hit him anytime down the road. It was awfully hard on relationships too. But so far, that hadn't been a big issue for him. Just that horrible feeling of having to catch up to others. Otherwise the world would leave him behind.

He shook his head. Maybe that was rooted in his childhood. He was the youngest of three brothers. Coming fifteen years after his next oldest brother, Cole had always felt left behind, which was true in a sense, and how they were years ahead of him, which was also true. He had little to no relationship with them, then or now. They already had girlfriends who later morphed into wives. But he'd spent so much of his childhood trying to catch up to them.

He felt that way when he had become a Navy SEAL too.

*How odd.* He hadn't made that connection before.

He'd made it through basic training, and they were some of the best days of his life. Afterward with Brock and Denton at his side, things had gotten even better—having buddies who accepted him was great. However, he always worried he was inferior and thought he couldn't compare to them. Then Brock had his accident. Brock appeared to fall so far down that, for once, Cole didn't fall short when compared to Brock. Cole didn't have to "catch up" to close the gap between how he saw the two of them.

He felt small admitting that about Brock. At least it wasn't a conscious thought. It was more a case of being able to relax because he didn't have to work so hard to catch up to Brock anymore. The same was true when Denton got injured.

Until Cole had his own accident. That led him to the same lack of self-confidence and acceptance he had known over his whole life.

So was he doomed to relive his childhood fears comparing himself to his brothers in all his later relationships in life?

Yet, his brothers were never really *in* his life, already moving on to lives of their own by the time Cole was old enough to have memories of them. His parents had "moved on" too, both dying months apart, shortly after he turned twenty.

He needed to book time with his therapist to work out some of this. Since he'd been here, and since he'd seen the shape Brock was now in, Cole was so far behind again, which was where his depression and angst came from. He didn't know if Sandra would understand this, and he didn't want to cry on her shoulder, to explain all this heavy stuff because he really liked her. He didn't want her to see him like this, weak. He wanted her to see him as a strong physical male with a can-do attitude. All this heavy emotional crap would be a burden on anybody.

The last thing he wanted was to dump it on her.

He picked up his phone and sent a text to his therapist. He didn't have an appointment scheduled for the next couple days, but it suddenly seemed important that he deal with this sooner rather than later. He grabbed the notebook Dani had given him and jotted down ideas. He could see how so much of this was rooted in his childhood, but that didn't mean he wanted to continue repeating this. What he needed was to stop feeling so inferior. To stop feeling he wasn't good enough. To stop feeling he had to constantly improve and be better to be accepted.

He had thought for sure that making it through BUD/s training would help him gain that self-confidence. Making the final cut for BUD/s proved that. Plus the BUD/s training had been plenty hard. BUD/s took only the best of the best, and he had been one of those. For a long time, it seemed like he'd been okay with that. Having Denton and Brock around had been a huge help too. Together, they'd formed a friendship that would last for life.

Yet, he didn't remember his current insecurities ever being an issue before between the three of them because they'd all helped each other. It wasn't him against the world anymore, nor was it about his older brothers being so far ahead of him, not waiting for their kid brother to catch up. With Brock and Denton, it was the three of them together against the world, and Cole had been happy there.

He had been comfortable, content. No—it had been— and he wrote down the word as it came to him—*secure*. He'd lost that feeling after the accident. He had lost his place in the world. It was like he'd lost his place in his SEAL family too. The family dynamics had changed when Brock had been injured and while he was gone, but Cole still had Denton. Although they had kept in touch with Brock, he wasn't there physically, and he wasn't there mentally. Yet, that had been okay. Cole's SEAL family unit had shifted and changed, but it was still complete.

And then Cole had been injured and Denton too, and Cole had lost that sense of family security. When he'd arrived here, he had immediately jumped forward, trying to "catch up" again—to his SEAL family this time. Trying to regain his place beside Brock. Chasing his brothers again. Only Cole had lagged so damn far behind, he panicked that he wouldn't make it. He had to give it his all. But of course, instead of talking to anybody about it, he was full of bravado and had dumped his medicine with the idea that he didn't need it.

He thought he could do this without any outsiders' help. Because he knew he could, because he was so macho and so male. Sure, in the past, in the military, that was the way things were done. SEAL teams against whoever else. But this was a whole new world, and he didn't know how to find his place in it. As he jotted down these notes, that was another key point. He had been left standing on quicksand. He had lost his footing, his foundation, and while that was one of his key points, he'd also lost so much more. Not only was he on shaky ground physically, but he was on shaky ground emotionally and mentally. He thought about it and added *spiritually* to that sentence too. He sat back, realizing tremors ran up and down his system.

Talk about home truths.

Talk about ugly home truths …

He shook his head. He hadn't expected some of this to come up. As he stared out the window, he wondered what it would take for that little boy inside to be comfortable with the man who he was now and with his position in the world. When would the little boy from his childhood stop trying so hard for all the wrong reasons?

Try? Yes.

Work hard? Yes.

But do it because it was important to him in his own world, not because he was "catching up" to be like the others.

There was a knock on his door. Inside he hoped whoever it was would walk away. He wanted to be alone right now. So much was going on inside him, like his support walls were crumbling. He was vulnerable. He opened his mouth to tell them to go away, but his therapist stepped inside and smiled at him.

Her gaze sharpened. She turned, closed the door and grabbed the spare chair. She reached out for his hand, and he grabbed on. She sat beside him. "I see you've had a breakthrough."

He stared at her, his fingers clenching hers. He was in his early thirties, and this woman had to be in her mid-fifties. But her grip was solid. It was like a lifeline at this moment in time when he felt like he was drowning.

"A breakthrough?" he said in a broken voice. "How is this possibly a breakthrough?"

She smiled and gently squeezed his fingers with her own. "Tell me …"

And the crumbling walls burst, and the words poured out.

## Chapter 14

S ANDRA GLANCED AT her watch. It was time. She'd avoided thinking about it for most of the day, her mind consumed with what was going on with Cole. She didn't know what the hell she would do about him. But she couldn't worry about that now. She got up, grabbed a notebook and poured herself a cup of coffee from the pot in the nurses' station before walking to her meeting. The doctor was already there ahead of her, as was Dani. Sandra smiled at them both and sat.

After the initial pleasantries, the conversation kicked to the subject of Cole.

"Personally I'm delighted with his progress," Dr. Herzog said. "After that rough start, he seems to be settling in quite nicely and is showing a lot of improvements on many levels."

He turned to look at Dani and Sandra.

Dani nodded. "I agree. He's approached me a couple times on things that were bothering him. I take his ability to ask for help and question some of those issues as a good step forward. He has taken responsibility for his own healing. He is looking at his recovery now with a more independent spirit. He's gone from 'me' to dependency on the team, but I do see glimmers that he is looking outward at the bigger world and his role in it."

"You always see the best things," Sandra said. "He is

looking at the world like you described."

Dani smiled. "Well, it's true. There are so many stages to the recovery process. Everybody doesn't go through all of them, but they all get to the healing part, eventually—we hope."

The doctor faced Sandra. "How do you feel about his medications?"

She nodded. "I'm making sure he's taking all of them, Doctor. I've dealt with the fact that I was partially responsible for his decline."

"It's good that you feel you have dealt with your part but not that you feel even partially responsible. He's a grown man who made his own decisions, and now he has recovered and moved on," he said. "Dani, I think we're done here, unless you have any concerns?"

Dani shook her head. "No, not at all. The issue was brought up. It was addressed. We moved on." Dani turned toward Sandra. "Cole's concerned about any ramifications his actions may have had on you."

Sandra's eyebrows shot upward. "Really? Must have been a few days ago then," she said drily. "I'm not even sure he is talking to me today."

"If he doesn't," Dani said, "maybe he'll tell Brock whatever is bothering him."

"That brings up an interesting point," the doctor said. "How do you feel about them being friends here? Has it been a benefit or a detriment? Does Brock's presence help Cole, or does it make it worse for him?"

"I think it makes things easier for him," Sandra said. "But at the same time, I think he held Brock up as a bit of an idol, with his progress as the goalposts. Brock has achieved exactly what Cole desperately wants to do," she said. "I think

Brock's improvement pushed Cole's competitiveness so far and so fast that that is why he made that error in judgment with his meds and all. I think he's moved past that." She glanced around. "Maybe we should bring the rest of the team in for that discussion."

"I've heard their comments at the weekly team meetings, and you two are currently seeing progress as do I." The doctor made several notations in the file and then handed it to Dani. "If that's it, I'm heading out." He gathered his things, said his farewells and walked out.

Sandra felt stunned. She leaned toward Dani. "That's it?"

Dani looked at her, a smile playing at the corner of her lips. "What were you expecting? Another reprimand?"

She frowned at her. "Frankly, yes."

"Have you had any further issues that are a direct result of the initial incident?" Dani asked.

"No, of course not," Sandra replied.

"Therefore, no new reprimand. We all trust you to do your job. Continue to follow your changed methodology. There is no need for anything else."

Sandra frowned at her good friend. "You do realize I've been a bit worried about this since Cole's original setback?"

"You do realize you should calm down about it and not worry?" was Dani's reply. "At least not to that extent. But it is to your credit that you are as concerned about it as you are. It's nice to know that you care enough to make sure you're doing what you can for your patients."

"I love it here," Sandra said. "At the beginning, I was terrified I would get fired, but apparently that's not an issue."

"Once again, only one person has to take responsibility

for this, and that would be Cole. We must look at his actions. And nobody ever once suggested you should be fired."

Sandra sat back in her chair, a sense of relief coursing through her. "I didn't expect that, but I did expect to be warned about that eventuality."

"Would you feel better if we did warn you that you could lose your job?"

Sandra thought about it. "That would be foolish. Like I hadn't thought of the repercussions myself. Like I was afraid to trust my own judgment as to how to correct the issue." She shook her head. "No, I definitely don't want that. I've had no problems here for five years, then one patient comes along, and everything goes to hell." She laughed. "Of course it would be Cole."

"One more thing I want to be clear on. Have you had any disparaging remarks from any of your coworkers as a result of this situation?" Dani asked.

At that, Sandra shook her head.

"Good. If you do, please let me know." Dani rose and said, "By the way, you may want to see this." She held out the file the doctor had given her, opened to the topmost page. Sandra could see right off that it was her personnel file because her name was on the side. At the bottom of the page, the doctor had written, "Excellent nurse. You would be wise to keep her here."

Dani laughed, closed the file and made her way across the room. She turned in the doorway. "If you're still out of sorts, maybe go see Stan. I know one of his assistants had to leave early today. I imagine he's a little on the short-staffed side."

Sandra checked her watch. Considering she had just gotten off easily—to her way of thinking—she could certainly help out Stan. He had been a huge support for her in this situation. She made her way downstairs to see Rebecca, Stan's assistant out in front, dealing with several frustrated-looking customers. She walked around to the back of the counter and leaned over.

"Is there anything I can do?" she whispered.

The assistant nodded with relief. "I'm all right out here, but Stan needs help in Exam Room 2."

Sandra smiled and pushed open the door to the room in question. Stan was inside with an owner and a very large dog, who was whining and squirming on the table.

"Oh, dear," she said as she approached Stan. "May I help?"

He looked at her with gratitude. "We've given Rocky his shots, but I could use your help in the back. We're behind on feedings and cleaning the cages. I don't have my assistant today, who normally does those two jobs. If you only clean out the cages, that'd be huge."

She smiled. "I'm used to cleaning up messes. No problem."

Sandra walked into the back to see that at least ten of the cages were full. She'd been here many times over the years and knew exactly what had to be done. She started with a female cat that had been spayed. She was still groggy, but she was scheduled to be picked up before the end of the day. Sandra gave her a quick cleanup, checked on her to make sure she was okay and left her to recover. Sandra could clean that cage once she was gone.

After that, it was a case of systematically going through, reading the charts and instructions, changing out newspapers, towels and bedding and checking on each of the patients to make sure they were recovering well. She also gave each one a little bit of love and attention so they would be reassured everything was okay. The animals were scared—some of them were in pain, and most of them were groggy from drugs. Two of them were on IVs.

Once she'd checked all bandages, she then changed each animal's water dish. She filled up food dishes, changed some cages, and before she knew it, she was done. The room itself also needed to be cleaned as some bloody towels were left on the table, and all kinds of paper towels were crumpled into a heap on one side of the floor. She took a moment to clean up the back room. When she was done, she walked out to the much quieter reception area. "Okay, cages done, back cleaned, rooms tidied up. What else can I do?"

Rebecca looked at her. "You're an angel. Do you have time to walk these two dogs?" She pointed to the two patient charts in her hands. "They both need to go outside."

"How long are they here for?"

"They both belong to the same owner, but he's been called away on a family emergency, so the dogs are staying overnight."

Sandra headed toward the dog pen on the other side of the room. She clipped leashes on both of the spaniels, and the two bounced around her legs in delight. Leading them through the back, she headed down the tracks toward the pastures. If she was taking them for a walk, she might as well enjoy it and be outside in the sunshine, walking in the areas where she could partake of the beautiful weather too. She didn't want to rush the dogs because they would be closed up again for the rest of the evening. Of course, somebody would take them out again in the morning, but without their owners and being in a strange place, it wasn't much fun for them either.

She took her time and let them sniff all around. When they had both done their business, she cleaned up with the doggie bags she had shoved into her pocket and slowly led the animals back to the clinic. When she got them in their cages, she stayed with them for a few minutes as they settled in. Then she washed her hands and returned to reception.

Stan came to say goodbye to a patient and to drop off two files at the front counter. He turned for the next patient and stopped. "Nobody else is on the list?"

The receptionist smiled. "You're done for the day, Stan."

He chuckled wryly and clapped his hands together. "Thank God for that." He turned to Sandra. "And I see you've been a busy bee. You managed to sweep up and wash down the back room as well as take care of our furry friends."

She laughed. "I needed to keep busy," she confessed.

A knowing look came into his eyes. "Problems with Cole?"

She grinned, feeling slightly embarrassed. "You say that like it's a common occurrence."

"Not so much a common occurrence with you," he said. "But a common occurrence with the women at Hathaway in general at the moment. I've had both Dani and Sidney down here with the same issues."

She winced. "Yes, your clinic has become quite the remedy for us when our spirits are low."

He shrugged. "I have nothing against that. I wish more of the patients would come here. They'd probably heal a lot faster."

"We do try."

"Why don't you take out that big tomcat in the back?

We did some work on his paws. He had an ingrown nail that we cut out. But that's fixed, and he's very relaxed. He would also appreciate the chance to get out, I'm sure."

"Is he good with people? If so, then maybe I'll take him upstairs to visit."

"He's very good with people. By the way, his name is Juicy."

"Why would anybody name him that?"

"Because he drools." Stan gave her a droll look. "He has a harness apparently, and he is quite accustomed to it, so he might want to walk, but he won't want to walk too far. Besides he prefers being carried." He chuckled. "That could have something to do with why he's on the overweight side."

Juicy was overweight, but he was also adorable. He was a cross between a Persian and some other breed, so his face was flatter than a normal feline's profile.

As soon as she picked him up in her arms, she wanted to show him to everybody upstairs. She hit the button for the elevator, and when it opened on the top floor, she stepped out. The cat looked around with interest. Sandra walked to the far side where she knew several men who had been here for weeks. As she approached, they looked up, and a big smile broke across one man's face.

"Isn't he a fine-looking boy?"

She chuckled. "I thought I remembered you were a cat guy, Connor."

He gave her a big grin. "I so am." He reached up, and she very gently put Juicy in his lap. Connor had lost most of one arm above the elbow. But that didn't stop him from cuddling the cat and scratching Juicy's ears.

"My, look at that. This guy has a bum arm like I do." Connor chuckled.

Connor was very careful to avoid the bandage on the cat, in case Juicy was upset about it, but the cat didn't seem to care. He was placid, and as long as somebody held him, he seemed to be happy.

Sandra watched Connor interact with the other men at the table. It was amazing what good news, combined with a little animal therapy, could do for a person.

Then there was Cole. His words this morning, well, those had bothered her a lot.

But what could she do about it?

IT SEEMED LIKE hours before Cole finally ran out of words. He lay on his bed, almost dripping with exhaustion. But he hoped that feeling was internal and that his therapist didn't realize how messed up he was. Going back into his childhood, then examining the various points in this pivotal year, moving forward at her nudging—it had been an exhausting and emotional journey. He lay here, staring at his hands, so mentally tired and emotionally exhausted he wasn't sure he could add anything more.

She straightened and smiled at him. "That's quite a breakthrough, Cole."

He raised his tired gaze to her. "Good. Hopefully I don't ever have to go through that again." He managed a weak smile. "Is a breakthrough supposed to take all the stuffing out of you and make you feel like you're limp, lying on the bed without a bone or muscle left to do anything?"

She chuckled quietly. "Sometimes, yes. Sometimes it's worse. But in any case, it's all good."

He shook his head. "Yet, I don't want anything to do

with anybody anymore. I don't want to talk to people. I want to hole up and hide away. I wish I lived in a cave somewhere, a long way away."

"That's normal. When you have a breakthrough like this, you come face-to-face with parts of yourself you haven't met in a long time. It's like finding out you don't want to be alone anymore, but at the same time, not liking the people you're with."

"I still need to talk to Sandra to clear the air," he said. "But right now, I don't want anything to do with her." He shook his head. "I know that sounds horrible but …"

"It's not so much about avoiding people as it is about you needing time to be with yourself. So you don't have to justify how you feel to me." She stood. "How about I let you rest right now? Do you need anything?" She grabbed the blanket from the foot of the bed and opened it up over him. "The best thing you can do is rest."

He nodded. "Can you clear my afternoon? I don't know if it's possible, but I'd appreciate it."

He snuggled deeper into the blanket, wishing she would go away now too. A lot of stuff swirled around in his head. Thoughts and emotions, actions, reactions, all that he had pulled out from dark, disturbed places he had to look at but didn't want to. They fascinated him but repelled him at the same time. He knew most of it was childhood stuff, painful memories from a long time ago. Instances that had made perfect sense at the time but now were the exact opposite. He truly wanted the world to go away.

As she walked to the door, he called out, "If you see anyone coming, tell them I don't want to see anyone."

He wasn't sure if the door was open already, but he heard voices outside.

She called back, "That's all right. I'll tell everybody you're not available today."

He curled up into a ball under his blanket. "Thank you."

He felt he should do something about Sandra, but he wasn't up to it. He also wasn't sure what to say now. Because of the thoughts in his heart, everything was in complete confusion. More than that, he felt so empty. Drained. There should be a sense of relief, a sense of renewal. But he didn't feel that now. He was still an empty vacuum on the inside. He wanted the world to go away. Or maybe he wanted the world to disappear with him in it. He could hear a conversation going on outside. He didn't know what the conversation was, and he didn't care. He wanted the door closed and everyone locked out.

"Please, close the door. Nobody's to come in," he called out. When he heard the *snick* as the door latched, he relaxed further. Perfect. All he wanted to do now was sleep, collapse, pass out, ignore everything and everybody. Maybe when he woke up, this would all be over, and he'd feel like a better person. Right now, he just felt like shit.

*Chapter 15*

---

SANDRA LEANED AGAINST the wall in the hallway outside Cole's room. She watched the therapist walk away. She had been told quite clearly nobody was welcome inside and Cole had mentioned her specifically.

The blow was visceral.

The therapist didn't have to say that because Sandra had already heard enough as she'd stood here at the doorway getting ready to knock. Hathaway House was well-built, but nothing could keep those harsh words from being heard where she stood. Cole didn't want to talk to her. He didn't want to see her or have anything to do with her right now.

That was hard enough.

She'd just come to terms with her own messed-up emotions and didn't need to hear that. Not only was it stunning in its timing but the effect on her psychological state was devastating. She forced herself to return to her office. To do something that could keep her mind off this morass of thoughts that threatened to break her into tears. He probably had a good reason for what he'd said. But … well, it was too much now.

She had the last of her files and stacks of paperwork to be done. She had medicine to give out, cabinets to be sorted and tidied and new stock to be ordered. She'd do it as she always had. It was her job. She'd be the same person she always was, happy and friendly to all the patients, but at the same time there was this gap—a disconnect between her heart and her soul. A place where Cole had existed. A place that was rapidly emptying. She didn't know what had happened or why Cole had been in his room for so long, but his therapist hadn't been upset upon leaving Cole, which usually meant Kimmy had seen progress on the patient's part.

That was good. But if Sandra was part of the problem, if she was part of the old stuff he was getting rid of, well—she knew how that worked.

Unfortunately.

Drawn and tired out, she worked like an automaton, quickly pushing through the work she had to do. By the time she finished up for the day, she wasn't sure she wanted food. She knew when she got to her room and lay down, it would be worse. So she delayed going to her apartment and headed to the dining room, but it was too early for dinner yet. Maybe she could pick up something in case she got hungry later.

She had to wear off this numbness, the sense of deadness inside. Cole had taught her some things about swimming, but the pool would feel lonely without him there by her side. Still, it was a good way to take what he'd had to offer and move on. That was what he'd done—what he was doing. She'd be a fool not to do the same. It would also help her work up an appetite for dinner. She went to her room, changed and grabbed her cover-up, then went to the pool. It was busy, but the slow lane was empty.

*That's just perfect,* she thought. She dropped her towel and her cover-up, went to the deep end and dove in, remembering all the lessons she'd been working on this week. Slowly she made her way to the other end. She could see that she had progressed somewhat.

If she could do even ten laps, that was something. She forced herself to empty her mind and to focus on her strokes, to focus on hitting the far wall, turning and flipping back, returning to the other side. She kept on moving, left arm, right arm, left arm twisting, take a breath, face down, next stroke and repeat. She didn't remember when she'd gone from swimming with her head above water to swimming with her face underwater. She'd had a breakthrough of her own.

She didn't even get a chance to show Cole. That was how life was. You learned something, you moved on. You wanted to show people so they could share in your joy, but at the same time, even if they weren't there, you still had to push forward. The joy had to be hers. She had to be proud of herself and not simply proud for someone else or because someone else seemed proud of her.

Trying harder to shake off her mood, she poured more energy into her strokes. She used a full-leg kick, like an otter. Getting to the far end of the pool was a bigger chore than she had imagined, so she shifted her strokes so she was above water and slowly worked on her less-strenuous breaststroke. When she hit the shallow end, she walked to the ladder, and then made her way to the nearby bench. There she collapsed with her towel wrapped around her.

A few people were still around. She smiled at several as they walked past. She grabbed a second towel and rubbed her face down, but she could feel tears burning in the back of her eyes. She hated crying. It made her face all puffy and red. It made her throat dry out. But worst, it made the rest of her feel like she had been pushed through an old ringer-style washing machine. It left her feeling rubbery on the inside. She stood, grabbed her cover-up and headed back to her room. There, she showered and got dressed.

A lot of daylight hours still remained, and she didn't know what she wanted to do. Food first and then she needed an avenue to heal the hole in her soul. There was so much pain involved in letting go. She walked to the dining hall and found the room a bit more full than the last time she'd been here. A hot dinner was already laid out. She would go to bed early tonight, so an early dinner would be fine. She still had no idea how she would fill her evening hours though, not expecting to sleep at all.

Normally that wasn't a problem here. She could walk, she could sit around and watch TV or read a book or visit with some of the patients or other live-in staff. But right now she didn't want to be around anyone. She grabbed a plate and picked out a few items. She was very hungry, yet nothing appealed to her. By the time she reached the end of the buffet line, she figured she had enough nutrients to get her through the rest of the day. She walked to the other side of the dining hall and sat with her back to the room. She stared apathetically at her plate. Suddenly a man stood beside her.

She forced a smile at him. "Hi, Brock. What's up?"

He motioned at the empty chair at her table. "May I sit?"

"Sure. What are you up to?"

"Waiting for Sidney to finish work so we can have dinner together."

Sandra dropped her gaze to the table. That word *together*. It was wonderful when you were a couple with someone. But it seriously sucked when you were alone.

She pasted another bright smile on her face. "I'm happy for you two. You look like you would do well together."

He chuckled. "I hope so, but I'm not easy. At least she's not scared off by me."

"Why would she be scared off?" Sandra asked, curious.

"Because I still have bad days," he explained. "Some days I'm irrational, then I get completely overwhelmed with a lack of self-confidence, a sense of defeat and a sense of hopelessness. If it wasn't for her standing by me through the rough times, I'm sure I wouldn't have made it this far. And I certainly would have scared off any number of other potential girlfriends."

Sandra wondered if some of this was a warning for her. "Sidney is a special person. She doesn't scare easily."

"Isn't that the truth? She's some woman."

He seemed to mean it. That he was so full of admiration and joy, and just to know he was together with Sidney, brought a true smile to her face. "I'm really happy for you," she said warmly.

He looked at her, his gaze piercing. "And I'm really happy for you too."

She sat back, mostly wanting to put some distance between the two of them. "Why?"

"Because you and Cole have the basis for exactly what Sidney and I have. The trouble is, you two are back where Sidney and I were when we started. Lots of doubts and insecurities, rough days on either side, rubbing up against each other, and then pushing away. Like trying to keep magnets apart."

She winced. "Yeah, that's a little too close to the truth."

He nodded. "But that doesn't mean it has to stay that way. Cole's going through some rough times right now."

She snorted. "You think?" She shook her head. "Of course he is. It's part of his healing process."

"Just because you know that doesn't make it easy when he doesn't include you in it."

She shot him a look of surprise. "That's very perceptive of you." She shifted her gaze to the horses in the fields. "Maybe I should go for a horseback ride again tonight."

He turned and glanced at the horses as well. "That would be a lovely idea. I guess I wanted to give you a vote of confidence," he said with a brief self-conscious smile. "I don't want you to give up on Cole. Because Cole might give up on himself then. That's the worst thing any of us can do—giving up on ourselves and that someone special in our lives."

He got up and left, leaving her to her thoughts. And what a mess they were.

She watched him walk away. Did he know about Cole's breakthrough? She glanced around the room surreptitiously. Did anyone else know? The only way anybody could know is if Cole or the therapist had spoken to someone, and they'd either overheard or been that person spoken to. She sure as hell hadn't said anything. Did Cole and Brock talk to that extent?

Maybe he knew what was going on with Cole's current condition. She wanted to call Brock back and ask him if he knew what Cole's breakthrough was all about. But that would be prying. She had had his door slammed in her face over that, quite firmly. There could be no asking questions and getting personal information unless it was from Cole now. That was tough too. Brock was part of his confidence group. She thought she had been. Obviously not. Rejection was a bitch.

She settled back and stared out at the grass and the sunset. As she sat here, she realized how much of an assumption she'd made over these last weeks as she and Cole got closer and closer. She had thought they were more than friends. Heading to something much more than that. Apparently, she'd overstepped her bounds and had been drifting down a fantasy road. But then she recalled conversations and touches, the joy of being with him, the glances, the smiles. It hadn't been all on her own that she had made those assumptions. He'd been as much a part of it as she had been.

As she sat, more than sadness and despair filled her. There was a kernel of anger. She might've been responsible for where she was now, but so the hell was he. That wasn't fair. She was exhausted after her swim, but now an anger that just wouldn't go away rippled inside her, and she'd no idea what to do with it. Where could she go to avoid her anger? How would she handle this mess?

She'd never availed herself of any of the professional services offered here. Right about now, she could sure use someone. It would have to be somebody she didn't know, somebody who didn't know her situation because she'd have to work with them afterward, and that would be very difficult. She was essentially a very private person. She never aired her dirty laundry in public. But right now, she hurt. Everything hurt. She wasn't sure how she would get through tonight. The evening stretched out ahead of her endlessly, and she couldn't even begin to imagine getting through the initial hours.

COLE WOKE TO darkness in his room. He slowly rolled over

to his back. He hadn't done anything overly physical, other than his normal therapy work. But he hurt. Everywhere. Joints he hadn't noticed in the last few months were now aching. His muscles hurt—even his gut throbbed.

"What the hell was that all about?" he mumbled.

How was it that letting go of emotions and old traumas could hurt on so many deep physical levels? Yet, he finally had a sense of freedom. A sense of openness. As if he'd dropped several huge weights off his shoulders.

Which he guessed he had. He slowly sat up and lowered his legs to the floor. Grabbing his crutches, he made his way to the bathroom. As he stared at his face, he saw he even looked different. He wasn't sure if that was an improvement yet. He still had that worn-out, been-through-the-fires-of-hell look. But not in a physical way—in an emotional way.

He checked his watch and saw it was just past midnight. He shook his head in astonishment. Talk about one helluva sleeping pill. He'd been knocked out and had stayed out. He'd missed dinner, sleeping all afternoon and into the evening, and now the whole place was asleep. Where the hell was he to go? He wasn't even sure if he was ready to get up yet. His body had forced him out of bed but couldn't he just go back to sleep?

He slowly made his way to the bed and realized he was still fully dressed. He hadn't been under the covers—he'd been lying under a single blanket. Then he remembered his therapist had thrown it over him.

He wasn't sure if he'd sleep anymore, but he had to try. He undressed to his boxers and this time crawled between the sheets. He rolled over and lay there a moment. But he wasn't ready to go back under. He grabbed his cell phone to check his messages, but there was nothing from Sandra. Why would there be since he'd run her off earlier?

Then he remembered hearing the voices before he collapsed this afternoon. Sandra had been there, talking to his therapist. He winced, remembering how adamant he had been about not letting anybody in, about not wanting to talk to anybody or to see anybody. With a sinking heart, he guessed she had probably heard him.

And had taken it personally. Why wouldn't she? After everything else he had said and done, it *was* personal. He hadn't meant to hurt her. He didn't know for sure he had, but if that had been him on the other side of the door, and her in the bed, saying, *Keep them away, I don't want anyone in here*, he'd have taken it personally too.

Not in the mood to sleep right away, he sent her a text message. **Sorry I didn't see or talk to you earlier. I had a pretty rough day and went to bed. It's past midnight now, but I am awake. Still feeling like crap but better.**

Not giving himself a chance to second-guess his actions, he hit Send.

# Chapter 16

H ER PHONE WENT off. Sandra stared at it in the darkness. She shouldn't answer it. There was no need. Whoever was texting could wait until morning.

Only … she couldn't ignore it.

She snatched her phone off the night table and quickly checked to see who had sent her a message.

*Cole.*

Her heart stuttered, then stalled, and afterward raced ahead at the sight of his name. Of course he had her number. Every patient had the contact information for everyone on their team. So far, nobody had abused the system, so it worked well when somebody needed to contact them. She certainly hadn't expected a text at midnight though. She read his message and then sank back onto her bed.

Well, at least that lined up with what she had already overheard or assumed. She didn't understand quite what was going on, but he was still talking to her. She put down her phone and lay here in the darkness, wondering what she should do. She wanted to answer his text, but it might be better if she didn't.

When her phone chimed again, she was afraid to pick it up. It was Cole once more. This time, his message was simple.

**I'm so sorry. I never meant to hurt you. I never**

**meant to get you in trouble.**

There was something otherworldly about lying in bed, reading his communication, discerning what he meant by the words. Was there more to those statements? Was he saying, *Walk away*, that he didn't want anything to do with her? Or had he really had such a crappy day, and he hadn't done anything on purpose, so, if she'd been caught in the backlash, he was sorry?

She didn't know how to answer him or if she even wanted to. If she did reply, he'd know she was awake. Did she want that? She shook her head. She didn't know what the hell she wanted.

*Wrong.* She wanted her life back the way it was a few days ago, when she was in this little fantasy world that they were both working toward a relationship. Something other than friends. Something other than patient and practitioner. She already knew that could go very wrong. She thought back to what she'd heard today and to the therapist's words when they spoke outside Cole's room.

Cole had had a breakthrough, but what had he broken through from? If it was old traumas, that could be incredibly devastating. Any breakthrough was good because those walls were what stopped people from improving and from doing the things they needed to do. Things they had locked away and were afraid of that directed their actions as they moved forward. So much of it was painful. But it was old pain.

This was a different kind of growth. It was spiritual and emotional, and if he was doing that, more power to him. It said a lot about his character that he was taking those steps. Sometimes those changes happened when you least expected them. Like a paradigm shift, when suddenly you saw things and realized how you'd been acting or how you'd seen things. Realizing how very bad things had been or at least how very improved they were now.

She hated to use the words *good* and *bad* because that always came off as judgmental. That wasn't what she wanted for her patients or herself. But there was this awareness of life afterward. As a child, you stuffed everything down inside, but it still directed your actions or words and your life ever after. As you added more and more events, more painful conversations and hurtful words and actions by others that you couldn't face, they all determined who you ended up being.

She was only guessing here that something like that had happened to Cole. She already knew he was competitive and afraid of being compared and found lacking, always wanting to be the best. She didn't know what else was going on. But one thing she did know was that regardless of how it turned out, she could not do any less than she always did.

He had reached out to her. If she didn't reach back, it was a done deal. She wouldn't have to worry about whether they'd be the professional patient and practitioner. That relationship would be finished. If she did reach out, it was no guarantee of anything more, but at least it would help his healing. And that was ultimately what he was here for.

And what she was here for.

If she did nothing other than her best to get him back on his feet and to move him out the door, she could look back on this stage and smile and know what she'd done had been the best thing for him. It might not be the best thing for her, but that was not the point of her being here. The question was, was she a big enough person to reach out to Cole? She stared at the text message. He probably thought she was asleep and would see this when she woke up. Instead, she was lying in her bed, unable to sleep because of him. Quickly she tapped out a reply. **No need to apologize. Life happens.**

She knew that was rather cold, but if she was sending it from her practitioner's point of view, he had to know he was off the hook. She certainly didn't begrudge him anything. After his words to her earlier, she decided to make something better out of all this instead of the stupid back and forth texting.

Nothing held them apart but themselves. That made her angry. Because that truly meant he wasn't ready. She was, he wasn't, and that was her problem, so she had to walk away. She'd always prided herself on having forthright conversations instead of endless drama. She was not someone who played mind games and twisted up words, reading things into them. Yet, here she hadn't had that clean, clear conversation she was accustomed to.

That was as much on her shoulders as on his. He was a good guy. He'd had a rough start, but he'd also had a great number of years where he'd done well in life. It was a glaring example of reaching the top, enjoying success, and then having your feet pulled out from under you. In his case, having his feet pulled out from under him had resulted in the loss of a limb. He could certainly bounce back from that injury with absolutely no ongoing problems. The damaged muscle could be mended. The physical lifestyle would be harder. But all of it was doable. He could be and do and have anything he wanted. He just had to believe in it. He had to want it enough to make the effort to achieve it. She threw down her phone, rolled over and tried to go back to sleep.

Her phone beeped again. "Shit."

She stared at the damned thing flashing on her bed beside her. It was Cole again. Hesitantly she reached out and clicked on the text.

**No, that's not life happening. That was me dealing with garbage. I think you heard something today that I didn't mean for you to. I wasn't sending you away, in particular. I wanted the world to go away. At least until I could restabilize and find my footing. Some old stuff came up today, and I let it all go, but in the process, it felt like I'd let go of my foundation. I was pretty shaky for a while. I was just trying to cocoon.**

Her breath gusted out of her lungs in a big rush. She stared into the darkness around her. It was hard not to be affected by his words. Because she too knew how that felt. Anybody could relate to it. Anybody who lived and had a relationship, or who had tried to do something and failed. Life was as much about adjusting as it was about progressing. Sometimes it was the same thing. Accomplishments for patients at Hathaway House could be measured in minuscule increments.

It wasn't the same for much of the world. But when it came to emotional healing, no cryptic signposts said how well you were doing. Usually, when something major happened to break through a wall following a trauma, there was hell. For Cole, there was quicksand all around him and a sense of newness and fear because now he understood what he'd been doing. So how would he stop himself from doing it again?

Supposedly the new patient perspective helped. But not always. He had done so well, and yes, she had heard those words. She'd reacted out of fear. She had been afraid he didn't want anything to do with her. Afraid he was shoving her away.

But he was right in telling the world to go away.

Slowly she typed her reply. **Understandable. Hope you're feeling better.**

She hit Send. She wanted to say so much more—texting seemed so cold and formal. Even though she'd used very informal language, it was hard to reach out through this medium. She stared at the phone and wondered if she should hit Dial instead.

But they were both lying in their beds, and that was an intimacy she wasn't sure he was ready for. As she rethought her decision, her phone rang in her fingers, startling her. Sure enough, it was Cole. With a soft smile on her face, she answered. "Hello, Cole. Aren't you supposed to be asleep right now?" she chided gently.

"I could say the same for you," he said.

His voice was both pained and harsh, as if his throat was sore. He'd probably been crying. For men who cried rarely, their throats were often sore afterward. "Did you sleep all afternoon?"

"Yes. I missed dinner, and now I'm lying here, wondering how long it'll be until breakfast," he said, a touch of self-deprecation in his tone. "I slept so many hours already, I doubt I'm gonna sleep again tonight."

"After that kind of emotional trauma and release, you'd be surprised. You're awake now, but in another hour or so, you could be sound asleep again."

"I hope so." There was an awkward silence, and then he added, "I think you were in the hallway earlier. I didn't mean to name you specifically, but I thought it was you outside, and I didn't want you to see me that way. I was hurting. I was confused. And I was crying. I couldn't handle you seeing me like that."

He'd been afraid she'd view him differently because of

that. She shook her head wildly. "Oh Cole, I wouldn't think any less of you. Trauma is trauma. It doesn't matter if you're male or female, young or old. None of us are strong enough to bottle up everything life keeps throwing at us without reacting. I wouldn't have thought any less of you if I had seen you go through that breakthrough. You have to deal with the pain, the loss, or the sense of disconnect that often happens afterward. I certainly would never think any less of you if I saw you crying," she stated plainly. "Any more than I would want you to think less of me if our positions were reversed."

"Guys aren't supposed to …" He fell silent.

"So it's okay for the so-called weaker sex to cry because we're supposedly less able to handle trauma? Because we supposedly cry at the drop of a hat?" She smiled as she thought how different the male and female psyches were. "I've seen many men cry, and all the more power to them. Much better to cry and let out that emotion than to bottle it up inside where it festers."

He gave a heavy sigh. "You're right. I couldn't deal with anything at the time."

"That was your right too. I did take it personally when I heard you say you didn't want anything to do with me and not to let me in. But then you've been acting strangely for a few days, and that was just one more blow."

She could almost hear the wince from his end of the phone. "I have a confession."

"What is it?" she asked slowly. She wasn't sure she wanted to hear this, but given that they were now talking honestly, she had to listen.

"The other day I walked around the floor, and I paused outside some offices to adjust my prosthetic as it's been giving me some trouble," he admitted. "I overheard a conversation about you. Something about a reprimand over me."

"Oh." She closed her eyes and reached up to pinch the bridge of her nose. "I'm sorry you heard that."

"It brought up all the times that I jumped too far, too fast, and fell. That up until that moment, I hadn't considered the impact my actions would have on anybody else, particularly you."

She shook her head, even though she knew he couldn't see her. "Don't worry about that. It wasn't even so much a reprimand as I made a change to our system because of that. I wasn't in trouble. I'm not in trouble. It's all fine."

He let out a breath, and even over the phone, she could hear the shaky tremor run through his exhale. He'd been worried about it.

"We mentioned it before briefly," he said. "But we never really discussed it, never went into the details of it. So, when I heard that, it brought up all my insecurities again. If we'd have spoken about it and if we'd have cleared the air the first time, then I could have brushed this off. But we didn't. Then today, with all that stuff that kept coming up, it seemed like this meeting was more punishment for you, and I didn't want to hurt you. Knowing you were in trouble over something I was responsible for—I couldn't deal with it."

She smiled. "Don't worry about any of that. Just focus on your healing."

"Yeah, I would, but my stomach is growling."

She chuckled. "If you want to meet on the deck, I'll see if I can rummage up some muffins and maybe something to drink. Hot milk or juice?"

There was silence for a long moment, and then he said,

"Can we?"

There was such hope in his voice she laughed out loud. "There are rules, but we're not prisoners. I'll get dressed, if you're up for it, and I'll meet you in the dining hall."

"Be there in ten," he said, and he rang off.

Her heart was lighter than she could've imagined when she had first laid down on her bed. She got up and quickly dressed in yoga pants and a light camisole top. Not sure how cold the night was outside, she grabbed a sweater and slipped on her flip-flops. She didn't have to get formal. It was midnight, after all. As she headed toward the eating area, she walked by the pool deck and thought of all the times she'd considered coming to the pool but hadn't. That would be a good idea tonight. It might help her fall asleep too. But first she'd spend a little time with Cole. Maybe they could patch up their relationship. If nothing else, her heart felt a whole lot lighter knowing he wasn't personally pushing her away.

COLE SLOWLY MADE his way through the dark hallways. A small series of running lights were along the edge of the hall, lighting up the floor so he wouldn't trip and fall. Although it was midnight, still the odd person wandered around. He avoided all the main areas and headed straight to the dining hall. He was still feeling pretty wrecked, but the thought of seeing Sandra right now, well, that was worth a lot.

He was grateful he'd reached out. He was even more grateful she'd responded. A quiet hum of activity came from the kitchen, and a few lights were on. He hadn't expected anything to be going on here at this hour but then realized a night staff was on duty. Maybe even kitchen staff, doing prep work or something. He didn't know. He did know there were a lot of people to feed, so it shouldn't be a surprise to learn about a night shift in the kitchen too. He wandered to the coffee island and studied the industrial-size maker. It was most likely the worst thing he should have right now.

"No coffee for you," Sandra said, her light voice coming out of the dim light. "I'll have a cup of herbal tea. What about you?"

"I haven't had warm milk since I was a kid," he said with a smile. "But hot chocolate might not be a bad idea."

She disappeared into the kitchen, with an air of somebody who lived here, worked here and knew the ins and outs way more than he did. He waited patiently until she came out again a few minutes later.

"One of the staff will deliver it to us," she said. "Let's go outside. I want to sit in the moonlight."

She walked ahead of him, leaving him to make his way behind her. He liked that about her. She didn't make any attempt to slow down. She walked normally and acted normally. It was up to him to become normal in the way he acted. There was a lot to be said for that.

Outside, the fresh air and moonlight made for a very special atmosphere. He stood there, absorbing the nighttime stillness, the silence broken by the odd chirp of a cricket or the croak of a bullfrog. The night was clear, and he could see the lights twinkling from the pool below. "I'd love to swim at this hour."

"The pool area isn't locked," she said. "But I'm not sure what the rules are for patients. I'm certainly allowed, as somebody who lives here and as part of the in-house staff." She shrugged. "We can check with Dani in the morning to see what the regulations are should you plan on swimming often at this time of night."

He nodded and took his place on one of the big benches that wrapped around the entire deck. "This is a good idea," he said. "Thank you for coming to meet with me."

"Thank you for texting me." She leaned forward. "Yesterday I'd just come to terms with whatever it is we were doing and needed to talk with you, which was why I was in the hallway outside your door. So, as for timing, it was pretty crappy on my part."

He winced. "Or rather crappy on my part."

She smiled. "But I'm fairly certain *this too shall pass.*"

He reached up and rubbed his eyes. "Like all this emotion. My eyes are hot and burning. My throat's dry and scratchy. My body aches in places that never ached before, even after Shane put it through all his workouts." Cole gave a half laugh. "Nobody warned me about this emotional and psychological stuff. I feel like somebody took a meat mallet and pounded me into the ground."

"That was actually *you,* doing that to yourself," she said cheerfully. "That was you pounding all that crap out of the recesses of your mind. In fact, you had to let it out. It's a principle in life that you find what you are, and who you are, in different places now."

He reached across to her and laid his hand on top of hers. "I don't want to think that I hurt our relationship."

He watched as she looked up in surprise, and then her gaze warmed. "That's what I came to talk to you about earlier," she confessed. "I was hoping we could get past whatever was going on between us and reach for something better."

He squeezed her fingers. "Yes, please."

He let go of her hand and settled back on the bench as

one of the kitchen staff came out with a tray. Not only was there hot chocolate for him but a variety of muffins and a couple pieces of fruit. He smiled. "Thank you very much. I was quite hungry."

The man nodded. "That'll happen when you miss dinner." He took the empty tray away and left the two of them in privacy.

Cole glanced at their surroundings. Nobody was in hearing distance. In fact, it appeared even the kitchen staff had left now. "It's really unique here when it's empty."

Sandra nodded. "The setting's very intimate right now."

He gave her a sideways smile. "Not intimate enough."

With that, she blushed in the shadows and gave a light laugh. "True."

As if that step of intimacy had been a little too far, too fast, they settled into a more general conversation. He shifted in his seat and finally said, "I feel like I don't know how to do anything anymore. You have to relearn everything in this situation, and things that I used to be good at, I have to start from the beginning again because apparently I'm no longer good at them."

She looked at him with a puzzled frown. "Like what?"

"Like flirting. Like having a relationship. Even basic day-to-day stuff."

She nodded. "I imagine that's because you see yourself as a very different person now, having to put your old skills together with the new body, and so far they probably don't fit for you."

"I don't want them to," he admitted. "I want to be the man who can get past this and reach for what he wants." Cole winced, knowing what her next question would be. Was he ready to answer it?

Maybe not but he wanted to. It felt like he'd been waiting all his life, playing catch-up and never getting what he truly wanted. And what he really wanted sat across from him right now. He didn't want to hurt her any more than he wanted there to be doubts between them. He didn't want to fail. He had to brave it out and tell her the truth.

She reached across and laid her hand, palm up, on the table. "What do you want?" she whispered.

He took a deep breath, gave her the most caring and loving smile he possibly could, grabbed her hand in his and whispered in the darkness, "You."

*Chapter 17*

TEARS CAME TO her eyes. How long had she waited to find a man who would care for her the way she cared for Cole? So many of her friends had partners, had dated men, and she'd been envious the whole time. She'd always wondered if her time would ever come. She wondered what was wrong with her, why she hadn't been attracted to any of them. Until Cole. It was all about Cole.

Still holding her hand, he asked, "Should I take that back?"

She looked up at him, startled at the tears pouring from her eyes. She sniffed them back and snatched one of the napkins off the table with her free hand, quickly wiping her eyes. "You can't take it back," she whispered. "You'd break my heart if you did."

He squeezed her hand so gently and slowly drew her inexorably closer. But the table was between them, so she got up and moved to stand at his side. Instead, he shifted on the bench and tucked her down until she sat in his lap. She snuggled in and wrapped her arms around his neck, simply holding him close.

"Are we past all that ugliness now?" she whispered.

"God, I hope so," he said. "I never wanted to hurt you. I never want to hurt you again. I'm a bit of a mess. I've still got lots to learn. I will get angry sometimes. There will be

497

nights when I can't sleep because of the nightmares."

She reached up and placed a finger against his lips. "I know that. I understand that. I still want all of you anyway."

He crushed her to him. "You can't take that back either." He tilted her head up, so he could see the truth in her eyes. She held nothing back. They'd been at crosscurrents for too long. Somebody had to take the chance of being honest and open and walk across the water that separated them to the freedom that togetherness would bring.

He lowered his head and before he kissed her, he whispered, "Please don't take that back."

Then he crushed his lips against hers. Instantly passion rose between them. But a sweet, tender passion, more like the sealing of a promise. The tenderness of the kiss that meant forever. This wasn't about taking the moment just for them. This was about enjoying the moment as if it were the first of many more to come. She drew her arms tighter around his neck, holding on tightly. She couldn't think of anything she wanted more.

When he finally lifted his head, he asked, "Are you sure?"

She nodded and smiled. "I'm sure." She studied him and then gently dabbed away the moisture in the corners of his eyes. "Are you okay?"

He cuddled her close against him. "Never better. I've finally found what I've been racing toward. I finally understand why I have always been playing catch-up. Because they all had something I've never had. I didn't understand it until today. Now I finally do."

She leaned back, confusion in her gaze, having no idea what he was talking about. He stretched out a finger and tilted her chin up.

"They always had somebody to love them. They always had someone to love back. I never did. It seemed like, while they were in this loving and warm cocoon, I was out in the cold. Maybe since I had no family life to speak of, the SEALs became my family. But I always felt unloved. Felt I had no one to love me back."

He took a deep breath and whispered against her hair.

"Until you."

---

D ENTON HAMILTON STARED at his email in disbelief.

He'd heard so much about Hathaway House from Brock and Cole that Denton had been living in a fantasy world, hoping a miracle would happen and he'd have a chance to join his friends at the same center.

But the costs … they were horrific.

He'd applied anyway. Made his case, knowing they took on a certain number of pro bono cases, and had hoped and waited.

He pulled out his cell phone and called Brock. It rang several times, then went to voice mail. He tried Cole.

"Denton, what's up?"

The curiosity in his friend's voice was justified. They'd been on the phone only a few minutes earlier. "I got in," Denton croaked, his voice clogging up. He cleared his throat several times, then repeated, "I got into Hathaway House. They have a bed for me." His voice rose at the end as the words in front of him finally settled in. "I'm coming there, Cole. I'll be there next week. We'll be together again."

"Holy crap, are you serious? That's the best news I've heard in a long time," Cole said warmly. "Wait until you see this place. You'll love it." He paused, then added in a teasing voice, "And you'll love the women."

"Nah, I'm not coming there for that. Besides, just because you and Brock found the perfect ladies for your lives, that doesn't mean Cupid is smiling in my direction. No, I'm happy to know I'm coming to Hathaway House and getting my best chance at regaining my strength and my health."

"Maybe so, but in this place, miracles do happen. I got mine. I know there is one here just for you."

This concludes Books 1–3 of Hathaway House.
Read about Hathaway House, Books 4–6

*Welcome to Hathaway House, a heartwarming military romance series from USA TODAY best-selling author Dale Mayer. Here you'll meet a whole new group of friends, along with a few favorite characters from Heroes for Hire. Instead of action, you'll find emotion. Instead of suspense, you'll find healing. Instead of romance, ... oh, wait. ... There is romance—of course!*

**Welcome to Hathaway House. Rehab Center. Safe Haven. Second chance at life and love.**

### Aaron

Navy SEAL Denton Hamilton has checked himself into Hathaway House, hoping for a fraction of the results his friends have gotten at the rehab center. Now missing a rib, muscles and a portion of his stomach, as well as suffering from PTSD, Denton would be happy to have his physical self healed. He's not so sure he'll ever get his mental health back, and finding a woman who'll have him now—as his friends have been lucky enough to do—is out of the question. Who would be willing to love a man like him?

Administrative Assistant Hannah Forsythe helps Dani run Hathaway House. A loner at heart, she's drawn to Denton's struggle and dismayed at his belief that no one could ever love him. But when an ill-advised observation she makes has unexpected consequences for Denton's recovery, Hannah's only choice is to separate herself from him to help him progress without her.

As time passes, Hannah wonders if her choice has cost her everything she's ever wanted or whether Denton can work through his feelings to give them both their happy ending at Hathaway House.

## Elliot

Former Navy SEAL Elliot Carver came to Hathaway House to get help with the lingering repercussions of a mission gone bad. His body is dealing with the physical trauma of a spinal cord injury, while his mind is caught in a loop of painful memories that he can't sideline, and both won't let him heal the way he'd like.

Former ER Nurse Sicily Lawrence has just made her way out of a difficult relationship, and the quietness of the night shift at Hathaway House gives her peace of mind. The last thing she needs is to get involved in another volatile union. But she has seen injuries like Elliot's before, and she knows that a certain type of therapy can help. One Elliot isn't interested in trying.

Now, for Elliot's sake, Sicily must push him toward the progress he needs, even it means losing him. And, with time and luck, maybe they can cross the hurdle and find each other at Hathaway House.

## Finn

Navy SEAL Finn MacGregor arrives at Hathaway House not only with half of one leg but with a stoma, one that necessitates the use of a colostomy bag. While it's nice to once again see his old friend Dani Hathaway and her father, the Major, it's tough to feel like the least sexy man on the face of the earth. Especially after he meets the pretty nurse in charge of his care …

Fiona Smithers has seen practically everything when it comes to the human body, and Finn's physical problems don't faze her. Emotionally she's wary though. Once before, one of her patients had confused the gratitude he felt for her as love. … That scenario left Fiona devastated to know her friendliness had been misunderstood. Whether deemed love or friendliness, those emotions directly effected that patient's initial healing and then his setbacks of body as well as of heart and of mind, making her more determined not to run the same risks again.

Yet, this time, she may not be able to help herself. She wants Finn in her life on a permanent basis, but, after seeing his obsession with her in his artwork, is that even possible?

Books 4–6 are available now!

To find out more visit Dale Mayer's website.

https://geni.us/DMHH4-6Universal

# Author's Note

Thank you for reading Hathaway House, Books 1–3! If you enjoyed the books, please take a moment and leave a short review.

Dear reader,

I love to hear from readers, and you can contact me at my website: www.dalemayer.com or at my Facebook author page. To be informed of new releases and special offers, sign up for my newsletter or follow me on BookBub. And if you are interested in joining Dale Mayer's Reader Group, here is the Facebook sign up page. http://geni.us/DaleMayerFBGroup

Cheers,
Dale Mayer

# About the Author

Dale Mayer is a *USA Today* best-selling author, best known for her SEALs military romances, her Psychic Visions series, and her Lovely Lethal Garden cozy series. Her contemporary romances are raw and full of passion and emotion (Broken But … Mending, Hathaway House series). Her thrillers will keep you guessing (Kate Morgan, By Death series), and her romantic comedies will keep you giggling (*It's a Dog's Life*, a stand-alone novella; and the Broken Protocols series, starring Charming Marvin, the cat).

Dale honors the stories that come to her—and some of them are crazy, break all the rules and cross multiple genres!

To go with her fiction, she also writes nonfiction in many different fields, with books available on résumé writing, companion gardening, and the US mortgage system. All her books are available in print and ebook format.

## Connect with Dale Mayer Online

*Dale's Website – www.dalemayer.com*

*Twitter – @DaleMayer*

*Facebook Page – geni.us/DaleMayerFBFanPage*

*Facebook Group – geni.us/DaleMayerFBGroup*

*BookBub – geni.us/DaleMayerBookbub*

*Instagram – geni.us/DaleMayerInstagram*

*Goodreads – geni.us/DaleMayerGoodreads*

*Newsletter – geni.us/DaleNews*

# Also by Dale Mayer

## Published Adult Books:

**Hathaway House**
Aaron, Book 1
Brock, Book 2
Cole, Book 3
Denton, Book 4
Elliot, Book 5
Finn, Book 6
Gregory, Book 7
Heath, Book 8
Iain, Book 9
Jaden, Book 10
Keith, Book 11
Lance, Book 12
Melissa, Book 13
Nash, Book 14
Hathaway House, Books 1–3
Hathaway House, Books 4–6
Hathaway House, Books 7–9

**The K9 Files**
Ethan, Book 1
Pierce, Book 2
Zane, Book 3
Blaze, Book 4
Lucas, Book 5

Parker, Book 6
Carter, Book 7
Weston, Book 8
Greyson, Book 9
Rowan, Book 10
Caleb, Book 11

## Lovely Lethal Gardens

Arsenic in the Azaleas, Book 1
Bones in the Begonias, Book 2
Corpse in the Carnations, Book 3
Daggers in the Dahlias, Book 4
Evidence in the Echinacea, Book 5
Footprints in the Ferns, Book 6
Gun in the Gardenias, Book 7
Handcuffs in the Heather, Book 8
Ice Pick in the Ivy, Book 9
Jewels in the Juniper, Book 10
Killer in the Kiwis, Book 11
Lovely Lethal Gardens, Books 1–2
Lovely Lethal Gardens, Books 3–4
Lovely Lethal Gardens, Books 5–6

## Psychic Vision Series

Tuesday's Child
Hide 'n Go Seek
Maddy's Floor
Garden of Sorrow
Knock Knock…
Rare Find
Eyes to the Soul
Now You See Her
Shattered

Into the Abyss
Seeds of Malice
Eye of the Falcon
Itsy-Bitsy Spider
Unmasked
Deep Beneath
From the Ashes
Stroke of Death
Ice Maiden
Psychic Visions Books 1–3
Psychic Visions Books 4–6
Psychic Visions Books 7–9

## By Death Series
Touched by Death
Haunted by Death
Chilled by Death
By Death Books 1–3

## Broken Protocols – Romantic Comedy Series
Cat's Meow
Cat's Pajamas
Cat's Cradle
Cat's Claus
Broken Protocols 1-4

## Broken and... Mending
Skin
Scars
Scales (of Justice)
Broken but... Mending 1-3

## Glory

Genesis
Tori
Celeste
Glory Trilogy

## Biker Blues

Morgan: Biker Blues, Volume 1
Cash: Biker Blues, Volume 2

## SEALs of Honor

Mason: SEALs of Honor, Book 1
Hawk: SEALs of Honor, Book 2
Dane: SEALs of Honor, Book 3
Swede: SEALs of Honor, Book 4
Shadow: SEALs of Honor, Book 5
Cooper: SEALs of Honor, Book 6
Markus: SEALs of Honor, Book 7
Evan: SEALs of Honor, Book 8
Mason's Wish: SEALs of Honor, Book 9
Chase: SEALs of Honor, Book 10
Brett: SEALs of Honor, Book 11
Devlin: SEALs of Honor, Book 12
Easton: SEALs of Honor, Book 13
Ryder: SEALs of Honor, Book 14
Macklin: SEALs of Honor, Book 15
Corey: SEALs of Honor, Book 16
Warrick: SEALs of Honor, Book 17
Tanner: SEALs of Honor, Book 18
Jackson: SEALs of Honor, Book 19
Kanen: SEALs of Honor, Book 20
Nelson: SEALs of Honor, Book 21
Taylor: SEALs of Honor, Book 22

Colton: SEALs of Honor, Book 23
Troy: SEALs of Honor, Book 24
Axel: SEALs of Honor, Book 25
SEALs of Honor, Books 1–3
SEALs of Honor, Books 4–6
SEALs of Honor, Books 7–10
SEALs of Honor, Books 11–13
SEALs of Honor, Books 14–16
SEALs of Honor, Books 17–19
SEALs of Honor, Books 20–22

## Heroes for Hire

Levi's Legend: Heroes for Hire, Book 1
Stone's Surrender: Heroes for Hire, Book 2
Merk's Mistake: Heroes for Hire, Book 3
Rhodes's Reward: Heroes for Hire, Book 4
Flynn's Firecracker: Heroes for Hire, Book 5
Logan's Light: Heroes for Hire, Book 6
Harrison's Heart: Heroes for Hire, Book 7
Saul's Sweetheart: Heroes for Hire, Book 8
Dakota's Delight: Heroes for Hire, Book 9
Michael's Mercy (Part of Sleeper SEAL Series)
Tyson's Treasure: Heroes for Hire, Book 10
Jace's Jewel: Heroes for Hire, Book 11
Rory's Rose: Heroes for Hire, Book 12
Brandon's Bliss: Heroes for Hire, Book 13
Liam's Lily: Heroes for Hire, Book 14
North's Nikki: Heroes for Hire, Book 15
Anders's Angel: Heroes for Hire, Book 16
Reyes's Raina: Heroes for Hire, Book 17
Dezi's Diamond: Heroes for Hire, Book 18
Vince's Vixen: Heroes for Hire, Book 19

Ice's Icing: Heroes for Hire, Book 20
Johan's Joy: Heroes for Hire, Book 21
Galen's Gemma: Heroes for Hire, Book 22
Zack's Zest: Heroes for Hire, Book 23
Heroes for Hire, Books 1–3
Heroes for Hire, Books 4–6
Heroes for Hire, Books 7–9
Heroes for Hire, Books 10–12
Heroes for Hire, Books 13–15

## SEALs of Steel

Badger: SEALs of Steel, Book 1
Erick: SEALs of Steel, Book 2
Cade: SEALs of Steel, Book 3
Talon: SEALs of Steel, Book 4
Laszlo: SEALs of Steel, Book 5
Geir: SEALs of Steel, Book 6
Jager: SEALs of Steel, Book 7
The Final Reveal: SEALs of Steel, Book 8
SEALs of Steel, Books 1–4
SEALs of Steel, Books 5–8
SEALs of Steel, Books 1–8

## The Mavericks

Kerrick, Book 1
Griffin, Book 2
Jax, Book 3
Beau, Book 4
Asher, Book 5
Ryker, Book 6
Miles, Book 7
Nico, Book 8
Keane, Book 9

Lennox, Book 10
Gavin, Book 11
Shane, Book 12

**Bullard's Battle Series**
Ryland's Reach, Book 1
Cain's Cross, Book 2
Eton's Escape, Book 3
Garret's Gambit, Book 4
Kano's Keep, Book 5
Fallon's Flaw, Book 6
Quinn's Quest, Book 7
Bullard's Beauty, Book 8

**Collections**
Dare to Be You…
Dare to Love…
Dare to be Strong…
RomanceX3

**Standalone Novellas**
It's a Dog's Life
Riana's Revenge
Second Chances

# Published Young Adult Books:

**Family Blood Ties Series**
Vampire in Denial
Vampire in Distress
Vampire in Design
Vampire in Deceit
Vampire in Defiance

Vampire in Conflict
Vampire in Chaos
Vampire in Crisis
Vampire in Control
Vampire in Charge
Family Blood Ties Set 1–3
Family Blood Ties Set 1–5
Family Blood Ties Set 4–6
Family Blood Ties Set 7–9
Sian's Solution, A Family Blood Ties Series Prequel
    Novelette

## Design series
Dangerous Designs
Deadly Designs
Darkest Designs
Design Series Trilogy

## Standalone
In Cassie's Corner
Gem Stone (a Gemma Stone Mystery)
Time Thieves

# Published Non-Fiction Books:

## Career Essentials
Career Essentials: The Résumé
Career Essentials: The Cover Letter
Career Essentials: The Interview
Career Essentials: 3 in 1